Praise for the novels of Joey W. Hill

"Sweet yet erotic . . . Will linger in your heart long after the story is over."
—*Sensual Romance Reviews*

"Reading this book was a physical experience because it pushes through every other plane until you feel it in your marrow."
—Shelby Reed, coauthor of *Love a Younger Man*

"The perfect blend of suspense and romance."
—*The Road to Romance*

"A beautifully told story of true love, magic, and strength . . . A wondrous tale . . . A must-read."
—*Romance Junkies*

"A passionate, poignant tale . . . The sex was emotional and charged with meaning . . . Yet another must-read story from the ever-talented Joey Hill."
—*Just Erotic Romance Reviews*

"This is not only a keeper but one you will want to run out and tell your friends about."
—*Fallen Angel Reviews*

"All the right touches of emotion, sex, and a wonderful plot that you would usually find in a much longer tale."
—*Romance Reviews Today*

"[Hill] stands out in a genre known for its out-of-the-ordinary love play."
—*The Romance Studio*

"Darkly rich erotica at its finest."
—*Two Lips Reviews*

"Dark and richly romantic . . . a feast for your libido and your most lasci
—*Romantic Times*

"Warning
—*Affaire de Coeur*

A
Witch's
Beauty

Joey W. Hill

BERKLEY SENSATION, NEW YORK

THE BERKLEY PUBLISHING GROUP
Published by the Penguin Group
Penguin Group (USA) Inc.
375 Hudson Street, New York, New York 10014, USA
Penguin Group (Canada), 90 Eglinton Avenue East, Suite 700, Toronto, Ontario M4P 2Y3, Canada
(a division of Pearson Penguin Canada Inc.)
Penguin Books Ltd., 80 Strand, London WC2R 0RL, England
Penguin Group Ireland, 25 St. Stephen's Green, Dublin 2, Ireland (a division of Penguin Books Ltd.)
Penguin Group (Australia), 250 Camberwell Road, Camberwell, Victoria 3124, Australia
(a division of Pearson Australia Group Pty. Ltd.)
Penguin Books India Pvt. Ltd., 11 Community Centre, Panchsheel Park, New Delhi—110 017, India
Penguin Group (NZ), 67 Apollo Drive, Rosedale, North Shore 0632, New Zealand
(a division of Pearson New Zealand Ltd.)
Penguin Books (South Africa) (Pty.) Ltd., 24 Sturdee Avenue, Rosebank, Johannesburg 2196,
South Africa

Penguin Books Ltd., Registered Offices: 80 Strand, London WC2R 0RL, England

This book is an original publication of The Berkley Publishing Group.

Copyright © 2009 by Joey W. Hill.
Cover art by Don Sipley.
Cover design by George Long.
Cover hand lettering by Ron Zinn.
Interior text design by Tiffany Estreicher.

PRINTING HISTORY
Berkley Sensation trade paperback edition / January 2009

Berkley Sensation trade paperback ISBN: 978-0-425-22567-7

An application to register this book for cataloging has been submitted to the Library of Congress.

PRINTED IN THE UNITED STATES OF AMERICA

10 9 8 7 6 5 4 3 2 1

Acknowledgments

While every book I write comes with implicit and fervent thanks to the many folks who make the book far better—family, critique partners, editors, agent, etc., I have a specific thanks for the mermaid-angel books.

My sincere gratitude to Janine, my childhood friend, now a wonderful, adventurous woman who jumps from planes, cave dives and generously offers her help (despite her own incredible schedule) to a frazzled author on a tight deadline. Without her, Mina and Anna's underwater world would have felt far more "land-based" and would have had some gross errors. Her assistance in both the mermaid-angel books has been invaluable. As always, any remaining errors are entirely mine.

One

"SHE doesn't need protection," Marcellus pronounced. Despite the fact most angels only had solid black eyes, no hint of white or colored iris, there was no mistaking the murderous intent in the captain's narrowed gaze. "She needs a cage. Manacles. A gag."

Affront accompanied every ripple of muscle and sinew as he stretched out what should have been two impressive wings. Marcellus's feathers were a glossy green so dark as to be almost black, except for an iridescent shimmer of color, caught by the beams of sunlight filtering in through the Citadel's arched open windows. One wing still displayed the plumage. The other was now leathery black and vestigial. On closer inspection, it was obvious it had been transformed into a bat's wing.

David had halted respectfully at the doorway to the main hall, but at Jonah's glance, he took a step in. He was smart enough not to interrupt an audience between the Prime Legion Commander and one of his upper-echelon captains. But the wing was flapping back and forth in an uncontrolled manner, as if it had a mind of its own and was trying to free itself from Marcellus's back by flagellation.

"At least she changed it to a fruit bat's wing," David ventured.

"That's the largest bat species in the world. The hog-nosed bat is only about three centimeters long."

From Jonah's searing look, David suspected the commander knew he wasn't trying to be helpful. If truth be known, he was hoping to instigate.

Marcellus, however, ignored him. "Raphael said he would fix it *when* he stopped laughing. Which meant I should come back after the next cycle of the moon."

Jonah's lips twitched. "Raphael does tend to view life more comically than most."

"Well, perhaps that's because he hasn't had to stand over the bodies of the four angels that have been killed in this pointless effort so far. Unfortunately what she did to them was beyond his healing skills."

"You can't blame her for that," David protested.

"David." Jonah sent him a more than searing look this time. "You're early, which I expect was deliberate. So if you don't stop speaking without leave, I'll send you to the training field until I'm ready for you."

Marcellus leveled a hard glance at the young lieutenant to reinforce the message, then shifted it back to the commander. "Let them have her. It's no more than she deserves. She's one of them anyway, isn't she? She's not of the Goddess's creation; that's for certain."

The amusement flickering through Jonah's gaze had died away at Marcellus's reference to the four they'd lost. Now there was a trace of steel there his angels all knew, well enough that Marcellus appeared to recall himself.

"Ah, by the bloody maze of Hades, Jonah. I don't mean any disrespect, but none of us believe she came to your mate's aid three moons ago to save you. The witch is bound by curse to protect the descendants of Arianne. If it weren't for that, she'd have turned on Anna, too."

David held his tongue with effort, but couldn't stop his fingers from closing into fists at his sides. From Jonah's sharp glance, he knew he'd caught it, and he tried to make himself relax. It was hard, for Marcellus hadn't run out of steam yet.

"There's never been a Dark Spawn who survived past five years old that didn't turn into a full Dark One in the end." The vestigial wing slapped against his shoulder as if underscoring his point. "If the Dark Ones had to take some of ours, I wish to Goddess they'd taken her down with them. Then we'd be done with this."

At his commander's silence, Marcellus sighed. "I serve you, Jonah. You know that. But this is almost too much. I speak only the truth of it."

Jonah studied him a long moment. Then he inclined his head. "Go see to your wing. I'm sure Raphael will restore it now. Tell him I have need of you for other duties in the morning, and that will hasten him."

David managed to stand without further expression as Marcellus bowed and took his leave. On the way out, the captain cast an almost pitying look toward him. The way one would look at the village idiot, David reflected. Still, he managed to wait until Marcellus had awkwardly winged off into the blue and white sky before he spoke. "So we just let them have her, like he said?"

"David, do me a favor. Shut up for a minute." Jonah sat down on the sill of a large open window and eased his silver white wings out to stretch them fully in the early morning air. As the breeze fluttered through the tips of his primary feathers, he closed his eyes.

Outside the window, a rainbow stretched over a green valley, diving behind a silver ribbon of river. The silver and ivory spires of the Citadel, piercing the seven layers of Heaven, were a gathering place specifically for the warrior class that fought the enemies of the Lady. Right now, they were in Third Heaven, Machanon, which overlooked the Garden of Eden. To plan battle strategy with his captains and lieutenants, Jonah would typically go down to Shamain, the layer of Heaven closest to Earth. The Machanon level of the Citadel was an oasis of sorts, a place for the angels who regularly had to fight the Dark Ones to take their ease. To remember, in such a serene setting, what they fought for.

Of course, like today, less tranquil business often came here to find Jonah. It was one of many reasons David did not envy the commander his position. He regretted adding to that burden, but he was sure of his duty. He could not shirk it, particularly in this matter.

For the moment, however, he went to a squat, traced the etchings on the floor tile with a finger. The design displayed a circular formation of angels, fighting the various shapes that evil had taken over many millions of years. Three symbols marked the outer boundaries of the circle. Courage. Loyalty. Commitment. The *Semper Fi* of the Dark Legion.

"What's your attachment to the witch, fledgling?"

David lifted his head to look at his commander. "I'm not sure I understand the question."

"I'm fairly certain you do. I assigned this responsibility to Marcellus's battalion, making it clear you were not to be involved in it. Yet over the past three months, he tells me you've badgered her security detail for frequent reports, and shadowed them when your other duties allow. Why do you champion her, David, when no one but you and I will?"

David straightened, feeling uncomfortable under the shrewd gaze of a born angel well over a millennium in age. Whereas he'd come from a human soul and was only thirty years old. Barely a child to most of this company, but enough of a fighter that he'd been made a lieutenant of one of Jonah's frontline platoons. Over time, that had become a source of quiet, fierce pride to him. But that desire wasn't what had brought him here in the beginning.

Regardless of skills, most angels had to undergo myriad trainings before getting their first assignments. Learn about being Watchers and Messengers, or participate in the heavenly choirs. But from the moment he'd crossed the Veil, David had needed something to fight. What he'd wanted was the oblivion of eternal dust, not an afterlife.

He often suspected that was why he'd been placed under Jonah's wing. The angel had not only trained him to fight. He'd broken David down, torn him open to let the rage and bitterness bleed out, built him up when despair would have taken him. Taken care of him until he could take care of himself. He'd given him a good-against-evil struggle with clear lines.

So he loved Jonah. He couldn't think of him as a father—too many horrible memories attendant to that—but he could think of him as an older brother. A friend, and a leader he respected more than any other.

A few months ago, he'd had the honor of rescuing Jonah from an army of Dark Ones. Or rather, David helped Anna and Mina rescue him. Because of the things he'd seen the witch do, he sure as hell wasn't going to let Marcellus talk Jonah into abandoning her.

"It *isn't* the curse. That's not why she helped you," he insisted. "When I first found her, and thought she was involved in your disappearance, I hurt her to get information." He didn't like the memory, that struggle on the sand, his daggers punching into her flesh to pin her to the ground, her cries of pain, but he faced it now. "It didn't matter. She wouldn't give you up."

Of course, Mina was contrary enough to hold her tongue just because someone wanted her to talk. It wouldn't matter if the subject was the secrets of Heaven or the color of the sky on a clear day.

Angels could share thoughts, but he didn't need to expend the effort in this case. Jonah's arch look told David the commander had likely had the same thought.

Jonah didn't give in to spontaneous bursts of humor, but David had seen more moments like that since he'd taken a mate. Anna, a mermaid of royal blood, a daughter of Arianne. A young mermaid to whom laughter and joy were as easy as breathing. She believed in Mina, too. Which bolstered David's argument considerably. He wasn't too proud to take advantage of it.

David pointed to the floor. "From what I've seen, Mina has all of these qualities. Courage, loyalty and a tremendous amount of commitment."

"We just don't know to what. Or whom." Jonah studied the ceiling, which, true to the tastes of the wholly male population that frequented these halls, depicted a lush and sensual scene of young women bathing. "She doesn't seem to want our protection, any more than my angels want to protect her."

"Yet four have died because of the necessity of providing her protection against attacks she couldn't have handled herself."

"Well, according to her conversation with my mate, she could have. They simply 'got in the way.'" His expression darkening, Jonah turned so his feet were propped against the opposite side of the window frame and one wing was curved under his body.

"Where is she now?" David ventured.

"We don't know. Which is why I called you. You're the only one with a blood link to her."

"Oh." At David's expression, Jonah's brow rose.

"Why did you think I called you?"

A muscle flexed in David's jaw. "Let me protect her, Jonah. Before you say that I'm too inexperienced, hear me out at least."

Jonah inclined his head. "You're always welcome to speak freely, David. You know that. Before I say no."

David's eyes narrowed. "A whole detail is an easier target to find than one angel and one—"

"Dark Spawn."

"Girl."

Jonah shot him a look as David lifted his chin. "She doesn't deserve what Marcellus said about her."

"David, you're still close enough to your human life to think that morality is always relative, shades of gray. This Legion has fought Dark Ones since before the skies were created. Not a one of my angels, and that includes me, has *ever* met a Dark Spawn worth saving. They're either wholly evil, the true children of their sires, or so physically deformed they don't survive. She is Dark Spawn, their child. Daughter of a mermaid, for certain, but that mermaid was a seawitch, from a line of seawitches who were known to embrace the Darkness far more often than the Light.

And her personality does nothing to convince us she's different," he added dryly.

"Everyone in this Legion has a preconceived notion of Dark Spawn, no room for the possibility of a rare exception—"

"Because there's never been one."

"That's why they're called exceptions," David argued. "I'm not saying there's no darkness to her. But no one, not even Marcellus, can deny there's something different about her. Maybe she *can* protect herself and just needs someone to watch her back. But if they do take her, they'll have to go through me. Worst case, you'll only have lost one of many lieutenants, rather than more members of your higher-ranking platoons."

"You're not listening. Typical young idiot." Jonah shook his head as David opened his mouth again. "I don't like her, David. But I love you well; you know this. You're baiting me, and I'm likely to bash your head in for it."

David's lips twisted. "You and Luc are always threatening me with bodily harm, and neither of you ever follows through."

"Would you like us to?"

"No." David put up both hands in surrender, allowing a small smile. "Training under you is punishment enough. But, Jonah, let me do this. I've felt a connection to her from the beginning. I think it should be me. Anna senses it, too; you know it."

Jonah rolled his eyes, an odd effect for the solid dark orbs, then pushed off the window to stand again. "She's been badgering me for a week about it. Though her methods are far more persuasive."

David pressed on. "We've been protecting Mina without trying to understand her. That's the key to keeping her safe. Anna said even she hasn't been able to get very close to Mina. And she knows more about her than anyone. She's given me everything she thinks may help me."

"So that's why you've been spending so much time with her. I was beginning to wonder if my young lieutenant had a crush on my mate."

That brought David up short. His gaze strayed to the bracelet, a thin braided strip of Anna's golden brown hair, Jonah had worn since the Canyon Battle. "Jonah, I wouldn't . . . couldn't . . . I mean, Anna is beautiful and truly I love her. But not . . . I mean, I don't *love* her . . ."

Jonah's lips quirked and he waved a hand. Goddess, the boy was young. On Earth, he might have been married by now, a father, but up here his age made him practically less than an embryo to the others.

He'd grown to physical manhood in the skies, though, and brought a rage so strong from his human life Jonah had at first wondered why the Lady had made him an angel, rather than simply reincarnating him into another soul to lance those boils in the earthly realms.

Then, underneath all that, he'd found the shock of a serene and steady soul, a levelheadedness far beyond David's years. He was more than a capable fighter. Using his wits at all times, no matter how thick the fighting got, he came up with ways to defeat greater numbers in hand-to-hand that had earned him the respect of the captains and extra duty to teach his techniques. No one could match his artistry when fighting with two daggers. Jonah had let him stop carrying a sword into battle some time ago when he realized the longer weapon was merely a hindrance to the young angel.

When the lieutenant of his platoon fell, David took over the command, brought them through a fight where they were outnumbered three to one. He'd served as acting lieutenant while Jonah looked for a replacement, but several battles after that, the commander realized he'd already found him.

However, it was in battle that he still saw remnants of what David had brought with him to the gates of Heaven. He preferred to be close to his enemy when he took him out, though Jonah suspected David wasn't seeing a Dark One when he plunged his knife in for the killing blow. Despite how far David had come, a darkness still lingered in him. It no longer ruled him, but it had not yet been resolved. That was what most concerned him about

David's desire to take guard detail over a witch who might be ruled by darkness entirely.

But Anna had drawn his attention to other attributes David could bring to the protection duty, which had little to do with his intelligence and fighting skills. When Anna had teased him about David's handsome face and body, he'd retorted that he didn't believe her prickly Dark Spawn friend even noticed such things.

"Oh, she notices," Anna had said, the twinkle in her blue violet eyes replaced by something more serious. "She definitely noticed David. That's why it should be him."

"The boy has little experience with women," he had replied. "She will drive him to insanity."

"If that's the problem, I'd be happy to educate him further, my lord. Purely to help him serve you better." She'd dived beneath the ocean waves then, laughing and evading his grasp, though he knew they could both look forward to the ways he would exact retribution later.

There was no denying David was a striking man. All angels were, but human-born angels, unlike born angels, retained the human characteristics of the eye, complete with iris. David's eyes were a rich brown, and his hair was a pleasing complement of brown and chestnut streaks that fell to his shoulders. He had a tensile strength to him that Jonah could evaluate with a commander's eye. The lad wasn't overly bulky, but his shoulders had a good breadth for the knife work he did. The fine length of arms and legs were well integrated with smooth, toned muscle.

He'd always liked the character in his lieutenant's face, even in the beginning when he was little more than a train wreck in the vessel of a fourteen-year-old's soul. Sharp-bladed nose, well-cut chin and jawline, high brow. Then there was his most impressive trait—his silence. David was serious, quiet, which made his sudden fierceness in the thick of battle so at odds with his contemplative nature and the flickers of humor that could ease the occasional tensions among the angels.

When David finally investigated other heavenly skills, it was found he was a deft musician, with impressive skills in magic wielding through the playing of instruments and singing. But he'd been clear that his preference was staying on the front line, fighting the Dark Ones until a higher purpose appealed to him. Jonah was glad to have him there, though at times he had an equal desire to send him into the safer climate of composing music. He'd become very fond of him.

"If this witch gets you killed, I will not think well of her."

"You don't think well of her now."

"True," Jonah admitted. He sighed. David's thinking on the matter was sound, even if there were things that made Jonah uncomfortable about it. He was running out of options, pure and simple. And he reluctantly admitted that David's reticence on so many things made his outspoken support of the witch even more significant.

"If I agree to your request, I need to be sure you can accept my terms."

David straightened. "I accept."

"Young idiot," Jonah repeated irritably. "Listen first. As much as I love Anna, there's a larger reason we're expending resources on protecting the witch. Over the Canyon, we saw evidence that the powers she can command are formidable. From the energy I felt when the Dark Ones had me, I believe she's only tapped into a tenth of her capabilities."

David's attention sharpened. "She was hiding her full range of power?"

"Anna said her mother died when she was seven years old and she's been on her own ever since. She may lack training, confidence. A goal." Jonah gave him a pointed look. "So far her goal appears to be survival. Much more might be possible if she has a greater aim."

"And that worries you as much as it gives you a reason to protect her."

"It worries me *more* than it gives me that reason to protect her," Jonah warned. "Anna insists Mina's heart is good. Much as I don't wish to admit it, you're right. Your connection with her might provide us valuable insight on whether she is an ally, an enemy or"—he held up a hand at David's expression—"could be used by our enemies."

David's eyes flashed. "So I could be the doorway to her death warrant."

"If she grasps that power and turns it to an evil purpose, she'll be the one who opened that door. You'll simply be the messenger."

David went back to a squat on the tiles and stared at the design. "Nothing's ever easy here, is it? Never like the storybooks, where you can just ride in, swinging your sword, save the day and the girl."

"No. You know that as well as any of us." Though Jonah regretted saying it, particularly when he saw David's head bow, the pain that crossed his face. Moving across the room, he laid a hand on the young man's shoulder, offering simple comfort for the unintentional prick at an old but nearly fatal wound. "Can you accept the task?"

"If we leave her alone, she might focus only on surviving and never grasp any potential, good or bad. Neutral."

"When it comes to power, there is no neutral. If the Dark Ones take her, they *will* force the decision."

"So we watch over her until she decides. If she makes the wrong decision, we kill her." David rose, facing his commander. "I guess I thought there was another reason we were protecting her."

"I've told you the reason this Legion must protect her. We serve the Goddess." Jonah's tone was sharp, all commander again, and David automatically shifted to respectful attention. "I've no problem with your desire to protect her for her own value. But if I order you onto this detail, it will be because I'm certain you can focus. Beyond the swinging of your sword."

David had the grace to flush and take a step back. "That's not—"

"It is some of it. There's no shame in wanting a female, and certainly not in wanting to protect her. Unlike Marcellus, I don't wish any harm upon the girl, though I wish she was a problem we didn't have." Jonah's expression hardened. "But no matter the personal feelings any of us have—you, me, Marcellus or Anna—it doesn't change the fact she has the power to be a strong ally for the Dark Ones. If she can become our ally instead, she'll be a lot safer. That I can promise you."

The Prime Legion Commander pinned David with his dark, direct gaze that could see through any lie, rationalization or half-truth. "Will you be able to stay clear enough to make the right decision? Can you accept the responsibility that comes with her protection? For you to get the answer you want, I need the answer *I* want."

———

JONAH had over a thousand years of wisdom on his shoulders. On many things, he was unambiguous as a sword point, but expressions like "the right decision" could have multiple levels, David knew. Like one of those flaky biscuits he'd liked to split open and eat, layer by layer, when he was a mortal child.

Ah, Goddess, over sixteen years and he could still smell the things. Well, in truth, he kept the memory fresh by sometimes hovering over one of the fast-food restaurants that made them in the early dark hours of dawn. Angels didn't eat human food because they couldn't taste it, but oh, the smell . . . It hurt and pleasured at once.

When he was six years old, he remembered reading *The Littlest Angel*, the tale of the young angel who longed to be a human boy. Had Mina ever wished for the life of a normal mermaid child? What did mermaid children do that was the equivalent of human children's wish to wade in a creek or play ball?

He didn't miss it, really. Not the way that poignant little angel had. The last eight years of his human life had been a taste of Hell that eradicated much of the pleasure of the first six. But being the youngest of the Dark Legion and a made angel, he sometimes longed for the familiar, something that was a true part both of who he'd been and who he was now. Something to tie those two things together and fill the emptiness that still existed in the lingering part of his human soul.

Maybe what drew him to the seawitch was his belief that Mina faced a similar struggle. He was tired of hearing she wasn't worth saving. That disastrous first time he'd met her, he'd tried to heal her after his attack, and she'd scathingly refused his aid. But there'd been such a stunned look in her eyes, as if no one had ever offered her such a kindness, a look that only grew more confused when he told her she could call on him if she needed aid.

Call me if harm threatens you . . .

On the other hand, he suspected she'd never take him up on it, even if the Dark Ones captured her and promised her a thousand years of torture.

"An eternity of hugging and having to share her feelings with someone," Anna had remarked. "*That* would be Hell to Mina."

Despite Anna's wit, he knew she worried about Mina. She'd been able to give him *her* sense of Mina, but little that was solid and concrete about or from Mina herself. So whether David liked it or not, Jonah's pessimistic predictions couldn't be discounted.

Until his meeting with the Prime Commander, David hadn't realized leaving Mina to her own devices was no longer an option. Ironically, by revealing her power during Jonah's rescue, she'd identified herself as a strong weapon—for whichever side could use her.

David had no question that the service of the Goddess was for the greater good. Free will was vital as well. But now Mina had only two choices. Fight for the angels, or fight for the Dark Ones, and if she chose the latter, they'd take her out the same way they would any Dark One. She could be dead or cooperative.

No one would call Jonah a warm and fuzzy angel. He knew his enemy and wasn't going to risk Mina being used by them. He not only had a universe to protect, but also a mate pregnant with their first child. And the ferocity he could wield to protect them was formidable.

But he was fair. So David just had to make sure that Mina was given a good chance. Tightening his jaw, he focused on what he did know of her. She was a shapeshifter, capable of human and dragon form, as well as a somewhat aberrant mermaid, with two long and deft dark tentacles in place of a tail. She'd demonstrated shielding capabilities that repelled the archery attack of a Dark One army for an amazing duration, though that and Jonah's blade would have cost the witch her life had it not been for Anna's sacrifice on her behalf.

Her spell-casting abilities were impressive, for she'd proven herself a capable fighter when he tried to corner her. She'd combined magic with physical strategy in a manner that nearly kicked his ass. Marcellus's wing had been just a whimsical taste of what she could do.

"Potions," Anna had added, on one of his visits. "She does potions for the merpeople. Love spells, sleeping, good fortune, all the usual things. I'm not sure why she does them, but maybe it amuses her, or what passes for amusement to Mina."

"Like pulling the wings off flies," Jonah had murmured, earning a sharp look from his mermaid.

If she had to be executed, would David volunteer to do it, no matter how much it would tear him apart? Was it better to be murdered by the one who'd hoped to save you, rather than by someone who considered your existence a mistake?

Stop it. He couldn't keep vacillating between the worst possible outcome, which he saw far too clearly, and the best one, which was murky at best. *This is not a thinking matter.*

When he saw her, he'd know the best way to handle it.

Two

MINA stared at the stolen dagger. The blade was nine inches long with a grooved grip. Pure silver with a stream of gold following the spiral pattern. A symbolism easy to decipher, the metals representing the Lord and Lady, the fiery gold of the sun's light forever connected to the ascending path of the silver moonlight. Steel lay beneath the overlay. A handsome exterior, a formidable core.

When she'd wrapped her hand around it, her fingers barely overlapped, a reminder of how much larger David's hands were. It also made her think of other parts of his anatomy in an embarrassingly obvious way. But still, she couldn't help gripping it and having such thoughts, once a week or so. Maybe more frequently. Sometimes the day got away from her and she couldn't remember how long she'd been thinking on one topic versus another, or how long it had been since she'd visited that same thought. One of the hazards of spending so much time alone, a hazard she'd accepted. The passage of time didn't bother her anymore.

Letting go of the grip, she ran a light fingertip down the edge of the spiral, following its smooth course to the pommel. Then against the grain, feeling the bump of the ridges up to the guard, a crescent curve of steel.

He wasn't the tallest or broadest angel she'd seen, but he had an earnest intensity, a denseness of personality, so to speak. It resonated, made her vibrate in a disturbing way. He was so young. A child, really, compared to the others. He knew nothing. And yet he wasn't innocent. She liked that he didn't have the solid-colored eyes of the other angels, that his eyes retained the chocolate brown coloring of his mortality, reminding her he'd been human once. It suggested he might know what it was to truly fight darkness.

Could that be why he'd tried to heal the wounds he'd inflicted when they first met, all those months ago? Wounds made with daggers like this one. She'd only let him heal one before she got away. Studying the two sleek black tentacles that extended below her hips like a human woman's slim legs, but were more powerful and much more versatile, she touched the scar his dagger had left on the right one.

Returning her attention to the weapon, she moved from the grip to the blade, slipping off the medial ridge to one of the edges. Razor sharp, a lethal tip. Once he'd freed her, she'd managed to hide it in her cloak and take it with her. The darkness of her nature made her dwell on that moment, look past the agonizing pain and fear to the way he'd thrust that dagger into her flesh, held her pinned . . .

Closing her eyes, she drew her hand down the edge, a long, slow glide where the nerves shuddered and her body shivered, caught between longing and pain as the blood flowed across the steel, some of it drifting away in a cloud in the water, but most clinging to her skin, a unique adhesive trait that she possessed.

Evil wasn't comprehensible to good. She knew that. Knew Anna considered herself Mina's friend, never realizing that there were so many times Mina had found the younger mermaid's proximity so difficult she had to drive her away. Visions would fill her head of wrapping golden brown silken hair around her fist, taking a knife like this, drawing it across the milk white throat . . . If Jonah knew how often Mina had fought that particular vision down, he would have already killed her.

Opening her eyes at a burning sensation, she saw she was

squeezing the hilt again. She concentrated, making her blood follow the spiral path to the guard, but the exercise didn't steady her
churning mind. It was an effort to let go and press the cut palm
to her forehead, seeking the balance from the energy center there.
As she sank back into the nest she'd made herself in the crevice of
coral reef, the dark tendrils of her cloak settled with her, like a
spider drawing its legs in to wait for prey.

She was in the place most of the merfolk called the Graveyard, and avoided. When she'd discovered it years ago, the vestiges of the child she was at that point had given it the name the
Forgotten Realm. The ghosts that floated through here caused
her no harm, even though some were angry. Lost. Vengeful. Others were confused. While sometimes her presence soothed, mostly
she suspected they thought she was one of them.

She called this part the castle. Jagged and tall protrusions of
coral had brought the ghosts here, wrecking their ships. Whether
a decade ago or centuries, vessels that had once known the sun
were now forever covered in sand and silt, laid to rest in the dark
green murky waters. A table shelf of rock above, populated like
these reefs with thick growths of tube sponges and sea fans, concealed the preserved timeline of seafaring history from human
instruments.

She'd tried on the metal helmets on the decaying Viking long-
ship, a *drakkar*. The shields, half-buried in the sand nearby, had
come loose when the ropes holding them to the ship's sides had
rotted away. She'd sat upon a cannon on the lower deck of a Brit-
ish ship of the line, staring at the Realm through an open hatch,
reducing it to a limited square of reality. From moments like that,
she'd learned that breaking things down into small components
made it easier to figure out how they worked. Complex spells
were only steps, individual ingredients, put together with one
unwavering focus.

A movement in the water snapped her mind to the present.
Just a barracuda, gliding through. She wasn't worried about anything that came from the sea. She could pass through a forest of
man-o'-war tentacles without a single sting, make a pack of

sharks veer off course to avoid her. They knew better. It was the angels she dreaded seeing, not the Dark Ones they were so worried about. Her kin. Her lip curled.

When she'd died, Mina's mother, like her mother before her, had transferred all her knowledge and memories to Mina's mind, a way that the seawitches carried and built upon the magic of the matriarch before them. The first time she'd slept after her mother's death, she'd experienced the nightmare of her own conception. The Dark One's rape, which had plunged the seawitch's mind into an abyss of desolation. She'd confronted an unending darkness that brought no peace, only nightmare after faceless nightmare. Striking out through the darkness, screaming with pain and fear as her body was invaded, Mina's mother had known no one would help, no one would come. The world went on, apathetic. It was no wonder her mother had always had difficulty looking at her. Mina didn't blame her.

She had that Dark One's blood, that very endless darkness, within her. Instead of shunning her entirely, however, her mother had taught Mina how to fight it. Staring into the face of what Hell was supposed to be, Mina's mother had become convinced clinging to life and its meager offerings as long as possible and not allowing anyone or anything to dictate how that life should be lived were the point. The greatest kindness she'd offered Mina had not been love, but harshness, teaching Mina in seven short years the tools to control the bloodlust within her.

The evil would never leave her, but it couldn't have her, either. That was that.

As blood gathered beneath her palm, still pressed against her forehead, it dispersed down her face to touch her lips. The metallic taste mixed with the salt water made her wonder what David's blood would taste like. His firm, muscular flesh. His body. Her own tightened, caught between hunger and fear. Why was he in her head so much?

When she floated out of the crevice again, restless, she saw him standing on a trawler, not more than a hundred feet from her.

Blinking, she wondered if she'd gotten light-headed from

blood loss and he was some kind of illusion. Or perhaps a Dark One had tapped into her mind and was trying to draw her out. He'd seen her, despite her ability to blend with the coral formations, the shadows of deep water, which had little light to illuminate a dark-cloaked creature that seemed just another element in a floating, wavering landscape of sea fans, human shipwrecks and craggy coral. Unlike her mermaid brethren, she could see at the much deeper levels of ocean darkness. But so could angels.

As he came toward her, she knew he wasn't a Dark One. Even a Dark One couldn't pull off the way angels moved through water. A relaxed flow of movement, unimpeded by the density of the water. Her thoughts dipped from baseline evil into a sensual well of wickedness.

She didn't want to dwell on his body, but of course with him moving toward her, it was impossible not to. Angels, much like sea creatures, had little use for modesty. Therefore, the angels of the Dark Legion wore only a half tunic, essentially a short, belted battle kilt, and their weaponry. Mina couldn't think of any female that would object. They were all finely made. With a twinkle in her eye, Anna had noted, *several times*, that it was proof the Deity in charge of their creation had to be female.

She focused on his weapons harness, a crisscross of straps across his chest that held his daggers in front, as well as some concealed beneath his wings in back. Her fingers tightened on the grip of the dagger under her cloak's concealing folds. But that was a mistake, for it reminded her of the nights, maybe just one or two, when she'd run the dagger over her body, feeling the wicked edge of the blade leave thin lines across her skin. Taking it down, down, so the pommel and those metal grooves beneath it teased her sex. She'd wanted to push it all the way in, but had been held back by her own uncertainty and a longing so great it had frightened her. So she'd shoved it in, defying her own fear.

She'd writhed around the thickness of it, her muscles milking those wonderful ridges, unable to stop the undulation of her hips as her body built higher and higher. Moving toward something she couldn't imagine, even as she couldn't stop imagining his hands holding her, pinning her, the weight of his body over her as he prepared to drive an entirely different type of dagger into her.

The tip had slashed her thighs on both sides from her movements, a pattern reflecting the needy gyrations of her lower body. She'd envisioned tumbling in his wings, tangled in her cloak, a chaotic yin and yang with no balance to it.

Returning to the present, she noted how the water molded the kilt against him in his forward progress such that she saw hints of the male sex organs beneath the fabric, a curve, a shadow. Then there was the ripple along his waistline, the diagonal muscles flowing down beneath the belted tunic, which stopped at midthigh. Just below a tight, firm ass. His thighs and calves showed the same battle-conditioned strength as his upper torso. But while he had the well-muscled arms, the defined chest, the striated abdomen, he was slim. His shoulders were pleasingly formed but not broad as a mountain, either. Maybe just the right breadth for letting a female lean on him, pillow a cheek close to his heart.

There it was again, that tug at something within her whenever she looked at him, as if she'd been enveloped by a warm current of water, interrupting the usual cold. Hades, she'd been infected by Anna's newly mated romantic drivel.

He was still a fledgling in the Legion's ranks, so his wings were ivory, with shades of pale brown in the primary feathers. Until he was fifty, they wouldn't know what his matured pattern and feather color would be.

His face, like his body, was lean, nothing wasted, etched perfection. She saw the bone structure, the fair line of the forehead, severe shape of cheekbones, resolute chin, firmly held lips. Brown hair to his shoulders, streaked with chestnut.

But it was those eyes that could rivet. She suspected whoever had created him had crafted his whole face specifically as a frame for those warm, syrupy brown eyes. Anna had described syrup to her, the way sunlight coming through a window could catch the flow as it poured out of the bottle onto things called pancakes. The sun would make it sparkle with pleasing hues, from amber gold to a vibrant, warm earth tone. Colors of peace, rest.

For twenty-nine years, Mina had survived in a world that wanted her dead. She knew how to read intent, purpose, from miles away. She knew almost everything about the nature of mermaids, humans, the variety of sea creatures. Everything she did was about survival or the accumulation of knowledge, one supporting the other. She'd salvaged books from these very wrecks and others to learn even more. It was one of the many talents her mother had taught her, restoring and protecting paper words beneath the weight of the water, handling the pages delicately so as not to tear them, creating a magic filter in a piece of glass and passing it over text to translate it, no matter the language. As a result, she'd been able to teach herself to read several of those languages without the filter.

Hades, come to that, even the angels weren't that difficult to read, though it didn't make them any less of a threat. Anna . . . Yes, she did understand Anna, though she didn't necessarily understand her own reaction to the mermaid who foolishly refused to consider Mina anything but a friend. Anna still stubbornly sought her out about once a week to impose a visit upon her, if Mina couldn't evade her.

But she couldn't read David. She couldn't fathom everything going on in those deep brown eyes. Maybe that was why he fascinated her to the point of utter stupidity.

She had three modes of existence. Run, kill, or defend herself in whatever manner was necessary. She just wasn't sure she knew how to defend herself against David, but of course she found herself too proud to run from him. An odd reaction for her, a witch who'd never let pride take the upper hand when it came to her survival.

There was always the other mode. Her hand tightened on the dagger as he got closer. He didn't know she had it. If he got close enough, she could do it.

Even as she had that thought, she vainly reached to pull it back. She knew better than to open that gate. The bloodlust roared up. It poured into her, heated her skin, tightened in her chest like her closed fist. One movement that he wouldn't expect, and that dagger could sink into his heart. He was a fledgling; it was his own weapon and the angel's heart was the key organ. She might not kill him, but she'd make him vulnerable enough that she could follow it up with a killing blow. Or she could take his heart, make him do her bidding. She had the power to do it . . .

No. The world around her started to reel. The roar in her head became that high-pitched shrieking, the call of the flock. Her lips trembled open, eager to emit the piercing call in response, take her place among them, find their kinship. Her fingers were elongating into sharp talons, starting to overlap the grip of the dagger. The skin stretched tight over her face, her bones in danger of splitting through the thin layer and showing her true nature.

Back up, back up. Her long tentacles used their sensitive feelers to take her swiftly back over the coral until she was in her concealed nest. Knowing he'd already pinpointed her location, she hoped it would buy her time to either strike or flee. Or make his blood run over her hands.

No. That wasn't what she wanted. She wanted to taste his flesh on her tongue, dig her nails into his back, feel his body on hers. Closing her eyes, she fought for control.

"Mina." David was saying her name in a calm voice. Steady. No fear, but no aggression or anger, either. Firm. In control. "What happened to your face?"

Angels had no language barriers. They were understood by, and could understand, any creature, in any language, and so the smooth, deep texture of his voice resounded in her head, uninhibited by their fluid environment.

Her free hand flew up to her face, terrified a transformation had occurred, but then she found he was talking about the blood. Her water-resistant blood remained smeared on her skin unless forcibly rubbed off. She did that now, scraping at it.

"Nothing," she rasped. "It's not from my face. It's fine."

"Give me my dagger, Mina."

She opened her eyes then. He stood before the stand of sharp coral spikes that represented a barrier, but which only separated them by two paces. She'd apparently lifted the dagger out from the concealment of her cloak as she retreated from him and now held it up in a defensive posture as she scrubbed at her face.

Still calm. He wasn't making any movement to protect himself. He didn't believe he was in any danger, the fool.

She came over the coral with the speed of a barracuda, going in under his guard, angling up toward the sensitive abdomen. Though in hindsight she wondered why she went for the blow she knew would inflict pain, not death.

But she'd been wrong about his intelligence. When she lunged, propelled by the greedy need within her to spill blood, to hear a cry of pain, he turned in the same moment so she missed her target entirely and he caught her coming forward.

She could have fought, but instead she froze. Her wrist was held in one of his hands; the other was around her waist. He'd caught her up to him, though he knew her tentacles could be whip-fast. She'd pulled his legs out from under him before.

But how did he know that holding her like this, where she could feel the solid heat of his body against every cold, aching line of hers, would make her want to coil the two six-foot-long appendages around him in an entirely different way? Yes, like a human woman's legs, only with the power and length to wrap around him twice, hold him no matter how violently their coupling sent them thrashing and spinning through the water?

She breathed hard through her gills, her heart pounding, as crimson fought with something else, something white-hot and just as fierce. "You left the dagger. I found it. It's mine."

He studied her. "I just found you. Does the same logic apply?"

The question disrupted her bloodlust. She normally did something similar, employing simple mind games to take it offtrack, give her a grip on herself again. But his holding her caused a reaction close to that violent need but different, such that she was having a hard time knowing what she wanted, let alone answering his question.

"Mina," he repeated. "Give me the dagger."

Her fingers loosened and he removed it, keeping his gaze on

her face. Laying the dagger in a crevice, he recaptured her wrist and stretched out her arm, pulling back the cloak so the pale flesh was revealed, as well as the palm she'd just cut.

Before the Canyon Battle, David had been the only one since Neptune's healers who'd seen her fully, who knew she was a macabre harlequin, one half of her body a landscape of scar tissue and craters formed by missing flesh. Two fingers gone, the remnants of a breast only. The other side was as perfect as the cruel laughter of Venus, with no scars to display. Or rather, there had been none the last time he'd seen it.

Now his gaze coursed up her arm, one limb of that revolting perfection, and took in the multiple thin lines, healed places where she'd marked herself over time, all the way down to her cut palm.

He cocked his head, his gaze darkening. Reaching down, still holding her about the waist, he brushed the cloak back to see her side, the indentation of waist, the curve of the one breast. Mina wanted to thrust away at this unexpected and gallingly intimate examination of her person, but somehow couldn't as his fingers traced that curve, the tiny jabs and long crescent scar she'd made one night, imagining the dagger's tip was his finger, even as the pain tingled through her nerve endings.

His attention lifted back to her face. At the same time, he picked up his dagger again, his fingers wrapping around the ridged hilt in a way that made the needy flesh of her sex thicken, her breath come short.

"This is my dagger. Mine. Only I may wield it. You understand? You may keep it, but if you want me to use it, on you, like this"—his gaze flicked to her arm and then back to her face—"you need to ask. All right?"

She stared at him in stunned silence. Surely he didn't . . . but yes, he did. She couldn't answer except for the jerky nod, the whisper that slipped through her lips.

"Please . . . use it."

Her attention latched onto his firm lips, the way they pressed together as he lifted her arm higher, making the cloak fall back so her side was exposed again. Positioning the tip of the knife, he drew it down, bisecting five of the old scars on her arm, creating a shallow line from which blood welled up and began to work its way down to the underside of her arm, like serpents merging together for a common destination.

She'd stopped breathing. Vaguely, she was aware her body leaned into his, and that his sex had become hard as a rock against her thigh. But still, there was no wildness to him, no unpredictable violence. In fact, everything he'd done was quiet, powerful, controlled. For the first time in her life, she felt caught in someone else's spell where she wasn't afraid. Not exactly. She was just feeling.

David bent, the hand with the dagger coming around so he could grasp her hair; the long raven thickness of it softly billowed in the current. The hilt of the weapon pressed against her nape. Her hair had been mostly unaffected on her scarred side. There was one streak of bare skull that arced back from her temple, revealing four or five inches of flesh, the ruined shell of the one ear, but her hair was so thick that she could draw it up to cover it, if she so chose. She liked the feel of his hands in it, too much.

Pressing his lips to the cut he'd made, he licked it, taking away the blood. Maybe he was putting his mouth on her to soothe, to cleanse, but the movement of his lips on her skin, the firm, suckling pressure, the way his fingers held her wrist in a sure, unshakable grip, the hard power of his body, the pressure of his cock against her leg, made it impossible for her to react in a tranquil manner.

Wrapping her arm around the breadth of his back, she dug her nails in. When his own arm tightened around her, she sank her teeth into his chest, the muscular part of his pectoral above a tight brown nipple. Curling her fingers into the diagonal strap of his weapons harness gave her better leverage and she bit harder. The accelerating drum of his heart called to her.

She half expected him to thrust her off him, but instead the strength of his arms increased, giving her permission to indulge her need to taste him, feel the purity of his blood in her mouth.

That ethereal blue angel's blood was tinged with the metallic flavor of the human he used to be, so it didn't scald her mouth, at least not past the point of bearing. As she savored them both, she realized she was shamelessly rubbing her body against him as she succored herself on that taste. She was acting no better than a beast. Beauty and the beast . . .

She lifted her head then, her body stilling. David turned his head, meeting her eye to eye. There was a fierceness there, a delicious danger, and she wondered if his warrior instinct had been roused by her in an unexpected way.

But she thought of what he must be seeing. Half-scarred face, fangs now exposed, revealing her heritage, and she was sure her one red eye was flaming with barely restrained violence. His blood, on her mouth.

She couldn't tell what he was thinking. Pity? Revulsion? He should have thrust her away in disgust by now, for she was emanating the Dark Ones' aura. Why wasn't he? Why was he even here?

"You're here to replace Marcellus." It should have been obvious. Curling her lips back in a snarl, she shoved away from him, retreating several lengths. "Jonah decided, because we worked together before, that you might have a chance of managing me where all the others have failed."

There was just a flicker in his eyes, but it was enough. "I asked to come."

"Really? Did you beg? 'Please, pretty please, let me protect the Dark Spawn.' I've told all of them. I'm telling you. I don't want you here. Go away."

To her mortification, he brought the dagger close to his nose and inhaled. Though surrounded by water, she knew that didn't hamper his senses in the least. All angels were keen trackers.

The fire in his eyes made her lower belly clutch, particularly when he took an experimental taste, a bare brush of his tongue done with the thoughtful expression of a hunter testing the musk his prey had left behind. "Your scent has lingered, Mina. A peculiar phenomenon underwater. I don't think you mind so much that I'm here. But whether you do or not, I'm staying."

He sheathed it, gave her a formidable look she wouldn't have expected from him, except she'd seen him in battle before. "The Dark Ones want you. To torment, to use. Jonah won't permit that, for his own reasons. I won't permit that, either, for a different reason. Whatever it takes, I'll protect you."

"You realize if you're killed, I'll feel nothing?" She assumed an impassive expression, shutting him out, shutting it all out. "When the other four angels died, I felt nothing. Nothing at all. Their death cries were just an annoyance, a disruption."

He moved closer to her, this time using his wings to bring him up the ten feet or so she'd drifted away. It was an effort not to move back, particularly when he hovered, his wings blanketing her, giving her an odd sense of being surrounded.

"You feel, Mina. In fact, you feel so much you keep finding ways to let some of it out so it doesn't drive you mad." Lifting her hand, he studied the scars again. "I'm sticking. And if I die"—a slight smile touched his firm lips, a ghost of reaction before it was gone—"I'll demand that you shed at least one tear, even if you have to pinch yourself really hard and pretend that it's for me."

If only he hadn't been human. It made him different in the way he dealt with her, harder for her to resist. For one thing, his presence didn't set off the maddening roar in her blood the way prolonged exposure to the other angels did. She even suspected the headache brewing behind her eyes was due more to his persistence than her blood's typical reaction to those born in the realms of the heavenly host.

"How did you die?"

Something flickered in the depths of his brown eyes. "Suicide, when I was fourteen."

That startled her, but she pushed past it. "So you're carrying your self-destructive tendencies into the afterlife?"

A wry smile appeared on his face. "I guess I opened myself up for that one. I thought Anna told you."

"I have no reason to speak to Anna about you," she said cuttingly. Though Anna had certainly talked enough about him, even when Mina put her hands over her ears and started imitating the mating calls of whales to get her to shut up. "And I like my solitude. You'll be in my way."

"Being dead or tortured at the hands of Dark Ones is preferable to enduring company?"

"Infinitely."

David's lips twitched, but he shifted forward, making her that much more aware of his proximity. She was floating at an almost forty-five degree angle now, nearly horizontal, with him looming over her. "Well, I don't prefer it. I won't be a nuisance to you, Mina. I don't require conversation. Angels spend a great deal of their time in meditation. I can find you food, and I'm willing to help you with whatever daily tasks you perform. Whatever it is that seawitches do."

She backed away. "I don't want your help, and if you insist, I'll just disappear and you'll have to find me again."

"You won't shake me, Mina. We share blood, remember?" Before she could get too far, he reached out, grasped her arm, the heat of his palm closing over her marble-cold flesh. "Get used to me being here."

She shook her head, denying that, but there didn't seem to be anything she could do at the moment. She needed space to gather her thoughts. "I have a potion to prepare, and you said you'd be useful," she said shortly. "Do you know anything about plants? Sea plants?"

"Yes."

She rattled off the names of several she knew would take him a while to locate and gather in the proper manner. The sea lily she mentioned only opened at one time of day, and it had to be plucked at that time. As she explained that, she added, "I need a handful of each of those."

Of course, he was an angel. He could be back in a blink of time, even if he went to a different ocean in another time zone to pick them. Maybe he wouldn't be clever enough to think of that, though. Even as she had the thought, her mind scoffed at her.

"When you come back," she said tersely, "I'll be here. You can sense me, as you said, so there's no need to seek me out. I'll come out when I'm ready. That should satisfy your self-imposed guard duty."

"I appreciate you promising that you'll stay here."

"I didn't—"

As he reached out this time, she reached up at the same moment, her arm blocking his wrist, but he simply stretched out his fingers, grazed them across her cheek. "Do they hurt? The scars?"

She'd been braced for "How did it happen?" Though of course everyone knew how it had happened. Or figured they knew, through a thousand different interpretations. She'd even overheard one version that said the evil of the Dark Ones' blood was eating its way outward over time and eventually would consume her mermaid features. That story was as good as any other.

David had asked a question no one ever had, not even the reluctant healers Neptune had assigned to treat her, to atone for the error that led to her scarring. An error most felt had been the right course of action, even if done for the wrong reason.

"Do your bones ache when it's cold, Mina?" That soft, persuasive voice was tormenting her in a different way. "I bet they do, and yet you made your home over the cold waters of the Abyss. Is that why you don't go on land? Because even with legs, it hurts to walk? And the sun reminds you of your scars, so you stay in dark places?" The tips of his fingers kept sliding along her face, her nose, the bow of her lips, while her forearm, now trembling, stayed up against his wrist, as if that could hold back his devastating assault. "When your muscles cramp, do you have to rub them yourself? Do you ever get a full night's rest, or have a day without pain?"

"Stop it." She backed away from his touch. "And stop touching me."

"I like touching you. And I want to protect you, Mina. You'd best get used to both of those things." He turned away before she could say anything to that astoundingly arrogant declaration. "I'll go get your plants. If you need me, I'm only a thought away. You know how to call me."

Glancing back over his shoulder, the tenderness became a measured glance. "Don't hesitate to do so, or I'll be extremely pissed off."

Mina managed to keep an indifferent, unimpressed stance until he was gone from her sight, his wings aiding him in a gliding flight through the water. Only then did she think to draw in an unsteady breath.

He might be young, but there was no denying he'd acquired the irritating tendency all angels had to think they could order everyone around. She shoved aside the fact that his measured look had made a shiver run through parts of her that were not supposed to be affected by him in any way at all.

It was going to take more than a bat wing to get rid of this latest emissary. But she had to figure out something. Not only was he more of a danger to her than the Dark Ones, he threatened the tenuous thread of control that protected him from *her*.

Three

WHEN David returned, he didn't find her in the same spot. While she'd implied he should wait until she emerged, he reasoned that she might want the plants, as well as the food he'd brought for her.

David tracked her to the looming shadow of a freighter, the largest of the edifices in this odd place she preferred. He couldn't argue with it as a strategic location. It would be difficult for an enemy to get a clear bead on her here, and if she knew the terrain as well as she seemed to, she could employ it as an effective maze to slow a pursuit.

As he stroked toward a gaping hole in the pilothouse, he turned in a graceful spiral with his wings coiled around him. He was surprised to see the skeleton of a captain still at the helm, one hand locked to it. His other hand floated free. After this amount of time, scavengers should have left nothing to keep the bones together, but here they were, waving gently in David's wake in serene, eerie movement, as if dancing in time to unheard music, a slow sway to some torch song melody.

He drifted past. However, as he descended through what had once been four stories of offices for the freighter, he found there were other skeletons. Three of them playing cards, hats still in place, one of them wearing gloves with the fingers open to show the bony clutch of the digits on the cards he held. David reached out to touch them and the cards dispersed, fluttering through the water, then they came back together in his hands, exactly the same way. Only now the skull tilted the other way, the chin jutting out at David as if in challenge.

"Holy Goddess," he murmured. Not a ghost. An enchantment.

He swam even more slowly now, finding skeletons at mess, in their bunks holding magazines, taking showers, doing laundry, running diagnostics on a ship long inert. All silently posed and yet moving in that rhythmic motion that was soothing, as if something were rocking them, babes in their mothers' arms.

If Mina was doing this as an idle pastime, assembling, preserving and animating a shipload of what appeared to be well over fifty crewmen, then she might be more tapped into her full powers than Jonah had realized. When David reached the belly of the ship, he was sure of it.

First off, there was no water. The hold was as dry as if he were sitting on land. Second, the cargo apparently had been horses. Over a hundred of them. All that was left, as with the crew, were their skeletons. Skeletons that were circling the hold area as if in a paddock, but in planned, geometric circles. Like a concentric dial, there was an inner circle trotting in counterclockwise rotations and an outer circle trotting clockwise, hooves just above the metal bilge so there was no sound to their movements. His dark-haired witch squatted in the center of the circle.

Mina had shifted to her human form, her feet bare, and was bent over, studying a pattern of shells she'd laid out before her on a flat tablet formed out of a cinderblock base and what might have been an oil drum lid. There was a foal, or rather a skeleton of one, that kept dropping its head—it was impossible to tell the sex—while she absently pushed the intruding nose away when it tried to disrupt the shells. There also had been a cat on the ship, because its skeleton was sitting on the opposite edge, staring down at the shells as intently as Mina was.

She still wore the cloak, but she'd pushed back the cowl. The side facing him was the unscarred side, and with her raven hair tumbling over one shoulder, her beauty managed to make the horses just . . . disappear. It was unearthly, how breathtaking that unscarred side was. The sooty dark lashes, the precise, delicate features. He could see the concentration, the wide range of thoughts going on behind the blue eye. Seeing this half of her face, without the other to detract from it, he wondered what she would look like if she smiled, and realized in the same unsteady breath that it would tear a man's heart right out of his chest.

The outer circle changed gait at the sight of him, wheeling at one time, same as the one inside, a perfect dressage maneuver that hid her for several seconds. When he could see past them again, she was gone. A very effective alert system.

Patiently, he waited for her to ascertain who had set off the alarm and reappear. Sure enough, he felt her pass behind him several moments later and then step out of the shadows to his left.

"Why did you come find me? I told you to wait."

He turned. She'd pulled up the cowl and now all he saw was the terrible scarring that at first glance would make someone think he was talking to a much older woman. Since the first time he'd met her, she'd always preferred to reveal the damaged part of her, not the perfect side. Of course that also was the side with the crimson eye. So much like the ones that burned in the skulls of the Dark Ones, that at her sudden appearance, he had to make a mental effort not to react as he would to his sworn enemy.

"I wanted to see what you were doing." He handed over the plants. The horses had stopped, frozen like a picture taken of them standing idly in a field. No heads were down, though, as if they knew there was no grazing to be found in this metal ground. "You removed the water in here."

"It's easier to mix potions and prepare spells that way," she explained impatiently.

"The horses are a brilliant protection plan." He ignored her curt tone. "But what purpose do the cat and foal serve?"

"I despise you. Do you understand that?"

"You don't despise me. I bother you. That's different. Do the cat and foal serve a purpose?"

"No," she said flatly. "Can you go somewhere else, where I don't have to see you?"

"No," he said, mimicking her tone.

A muscle in her jaw twitched. "I don't want you this close."

"How close?" Cocking his head, he took a step forward, spreading his wings a few degrees for balance. "This close?"

It put about a foot between them, making her tilt her head back. She didn't want to talk about anything at all. Didn't want him around. So she said. But either he was too thickheaded to believe it, or his intuition was telling him a different truth. He was hedging his bets on the latter.

"You're flirting with me."

"Giving it a try. I didn't get much practice as a human. How am I doing?"

Mina closed her mouth into a thin line. "I don't like to be teased." She moved around him, back through the horses, weaving her way to the center of her enchanted circle.

"Mina, I wasn't making fun of you." When he stepped forward and the horses closed ranks, he set his jaw and went over, a light movement that landed him squarely in front of her.

"Then why would you do it? It serves no purpose."

"Like the foal and the cat?" At her obvious discomfiture, he shifted the subject, nodding to the plants still clutched in her hands. "Did I get the right ones?"

"Yes," she said, grudgingly. "You have a decent eye. I'll mix these and then pack them for my cave. I have someone picking them up."

"At your cave?" David shifted his attention to his first priority. "I don't think that's wise."

"You chose to provide me protection," she snapped. "I didn't ask for it; I don't want it. If you don't wish to accompany me, it means nothing to me."

The seawitch who just wanted to be left alone. Pushing away his guilt, David sent a mental message to several of his platoon who'd been willing to lend reconnaissance support to the protection detail, asking them to run surveillance on her cave area to ensure he and Mina weren't walking into a trap. It didn't mean one couldn't be sprung after they got there, though. He didn't like it, but he preferred it to destroying the fragile trust he might be building with her by forcing a physical confrontation over her movements to and from her home.

Putting out a hand, he followed the nose bone of a tall stallion, feeling the residual energy. "It's no wonder the Dark Ones keep finding you. Maybe you should tone it down a little."

"They don't frighten me. If that overgrown bat hadn't gotten in my way, I could have taken care of the last attack. If nothing else, I could move with stealth. With an angel entourage, you might as well put a neon sign over my head that screams 'something worth protecting.' "

"Neon sign? How do you know about those?"

"I'm not ignorant of the land ways," she said shortly.

His brow furrowed. Anna had felt fairly certain Mina rarely, if ever, went on land. "Well, perhaps we're learning," he said at last. "This time Jonah did send just me, one lowly lieutenant."

Giving him a deprecating look, she produced a clean square of cloth from a closed container and spread it out on the oil drum lid, clearing the shells away. Then she drew a cutting knife from the folds of her cloak and began severing the plants into pieces with disconcerting precision, barely looking at them. "Jonah cares for you like a son. You probably had to nag him for days. He'll wear a hole in the Citadel, pacing and worrying about you."

"I'm sure he has a couple other things to keep his mind occupied. Mina, why don't *you* think you're worth protecting?"

The knife stilled and she looked up at him. "My opinion is irrelevant. The only reason the angels want to protect me is because of the power I could wield on their behalf."

"That's not why I'm here."

"I know that." She surprised him with the quiet response and began cutting again. "That's the only reason I haven't turned you into a bat as well."

David bit back a smile. Taking a seat on an oil drum near her, he watched her work and idly stroke the foal's nose when it became animated again. The horses started to move, as if a carousel had started up around them.

Was it excess energy? Did she have so much she had to occupy it? Or was it to create a world safe for her to inhabit, creatures to keep her company?

Mulling on that, he watched her cut. Swift, sure slices, making the plants the lengths she desired, then mixing them in a kettle she had next to her now at her makeshift table. He suspected the kettle and cloth might be relics of this ship or ones like it. Most merpeople were creative scavengers, having enough interest in their human cousins to gather what they left behind in the sea, whether by carelessness or mishap. Glancing into the kettle, he saw she'd already had some ingredients gathered, and apparently had been waiting for one of his contributions, the white sea lily.

"What's the potion for?"

"It's a love potion." She gave him a dismissive glance.

"You don't strike me as the romantic type."

She sighed. "It doesn't work like that. The merman drinks the potion, believing it will make the object of his desire fall in love with him. In reality, it neutralizes his sexual urges, taking that out of the equation. Now the potion drinker will only act on his true emotions, thinking sensibly and calmly, and proceed that way. He has a better chance of winning his target's affections, if there's any chance at all. If he doesn't, it won't matter as much anyway. Until the potion wears off."

"That seems to take something out of it."

She gave him a disparaging look. "Easy for you to say. Angels have no need of potions. They can just command anyone to love them."

David raised his brows. "That's news to me. Unless Jonah hasn't told me something."

She rolled her eyes. "Have you looked at yourselves? Your aura pounds out a fall-at-my-feet vibration that could knock any female down at fifty paces."

"Oh, really?" His lips curved.

She narrowed her eyes. "Any *idiot* female. That's why this type of potion is one I make only for males. Women's infatuations tend to be driven more by emotion than lust. Their potion is different."

"Either way," he reasoned, "to really fall in love with someone takes time. Getting to know them. Getting past the hormones . . ." At her ironic look, he grimaced. "All right, so your potion makes sense, in a way. But it still takes some of the joy out of it. It's part of the mix . . . the ingredients of love itself, if you will. Even if an angel could use otherworldly power to overwhelm someone, command her affections, he'd miss out on the excitement and uncertainty of falling in love. Physical attraction is part of that."

"For some people, that's just a torment, particularly if the other person doesn't reciprocate. It makes them do insane, ridiculous things that might put themselves or others at risk."

"You're far more conservative than I expected you to be." Cocking his head, he reached out to examine a plant with an interesting seedpod, and got his hand smacked by the flat blade of the knife.

"Don't touch," she snapped.

Knuckles stinging, David nevertheless kept his hand where it was, raised his gaze to lock with hers. "Would you like to try that again?"

Though her lips pressed together, she waited until he removed his hand at his own pace, and then she scraped up the plant, tossed it in. "I'm charging it with intent as I'm preparing it. Your energy could unbalance that intent."

"Wouldn't it have been more courteous to tell me that before assaulting me?"

"Wouldn't it have been more courteous for you to ask before putting your fingers where they don't belong?"

"You practice this," he decided. "Being disagreeable." Unfortunately, it didn't stop her words from planting a provocative double entendre in his mind.

"There's no need to practice or exercise it if I'm left alone," she said.

David settled back. "So I guess you don't want the snack I brought you." At her indifferent look, he rummaged through the waterproof sack he'd put at his feet and withdrew the orange and several foil-wrapped chocolates.

He looked up to find her staring at the food. "You didn't get those in the ocean."

"No." He held up the orange. "Do you know what this is?"

"It looks like a fruit. Anna described the land food sometimes. She never brought me anything. I never asked," she added quickly, but her attention stayed on the objects. "No one's ever brought me anything. From there."

"This is an orange. You're right; it's a fruit." When he offered it, she shook her head, circled around the table and gestured to him to put it down. Curious, he did, and watched her kneel, pushing a loose lock of her still-damp long hair behind one ear to lean forward and take a long sniff. Apparently some of the chocolate he'd put down next to it managed to filter into the aroma, for she adjusted her attention to it, then back to the orange. Carefully, she lifted the fruit in both palms, feeling the weight.

"You peel it to eat it," he explained. "Would you like me . . . ?" She extended it. "Show me."

Removing the top, he peeled some skin off the sides. When she reached out again, he handed it back, and she duplicated his actions. Only she sat down on the floor, her legs folded beneath her. His brow furrowed as he noted that she apparently had problems with the hip on her scarred side. While the one hand had only three fingers, she used those to steady the fruit on the low table as she peeled with the other.

He didn't speak, though, not wanting anything to break the spell. In a mere blink the bitter-tongued witch was a young woman eyeing an orange for the first time. With an unexpected flush to her cheeks and a brightness to her eyes. When she flicked a furtive glance at him, David made sure to be intrigued with the movement of the cat, the fluid swish of the bony segments of tail.

He couldn't help but notice, however, the way the change made the difference between the two halves of Mina's face less marked to him, as if she'd opened something inside herself, something far more fascinating than what was on the outside.

Macabre. Freakish. Abrasive. Those were just some of the distasteful words he'd heard other angels use to describe her. But, with one orange, he'd found a fissure through which he was getting a rare glimpse of something else.

So for the next five minutes, he remained still and silent as she removed the peel, sniffed each piece. When she had it all removed, she began to lift the whole sphere toward her mouth.

"Hold on . . . here." David reached forward. She was reluctant to relinquish it, as if she thought he might take it away, so instead of doing that, he put his hands over hers, guided her thumbs into the center and helped her split it open, trying not to think about how much that succulent channel was like the moist petals of a woman's sex.

Goddess, he wasn't a teenager. He'd had women before. He didn't know why being around her made him think about sex so much.

He withdrew his touch, albeit reluctantly. As she began to break off the individual slices, she laid them out in a precise fan pattern. On one piece, the outer skin had torn, and she touched the glistening teardrops layered beneath. Picking it up, she sniffed and gave him a glance.

"There's no hope of getting you to share that, is there?" he teased.

She put it down again. "I'll eat it later."

"You said you were hungry. Here." Lifting a slice, he took a bite to show her how to eat it, and then, rather than handing it back, he did what he wanted. He extended it toward her mouth.

Mina stared at him. David tried to keep his expression casual, even as he fiercely willed her to part her lips and let him place it on her tongue, demonstrate the potential for trust, acknowledge the inexplicable connection he'd felt since he'd met her. If she refused, he would release the slice, but for now he waited, made the offer.

She grazed his fingers with her mouth, such that she took a quick, jerky bite and managed to spray them both.

"Yeah, they do that." Unruffled, David extended another slice. "No point in cleaning up until you're done."

THERE were fruits in the ocean that smelled of the sea, tasted of its salt. But this was of the earth, exploding with sunlight, as if the sphere were plucked straight from the sky. And the taste. *Oh, gods*. The piece in her mouth was something she wanted to savor, so that she spent quite a while chewing that small bite, now that she'd gotten past her wariness at its unfamiliarity, his motives. She wasn't sure what the shiny blue squares were, but if they were anything like this, it was no wonder Anna spoke so well of the wide variety of things to eat in the human world. She'd been intensely fascinated by such stories, but, as she'd said, she'd never asked Anna to bring her anything. David had done it, without being asked.

The warmth of the fruit reached into the cold in her bones that hadn't left her since she was nine years old. She'd learned physical discomfort was an ally against her worst enemy, the dark urges she'd fought down so often. Now they couldn't get an upper hand except in her dreams. Or when she was unbalanced, out of her element, as she was with David.

But tasting his fruit, feeling his proximity, stimulated urges that had a different feeling from those that connected to her nightmares and the whisper of the Dark Ones. However, anything that suggested a loss of control wasn't to be trusted. Even so, she couldn't stop herself from tasting the tips of his fingers when she took the slice from them. As he stretched out on a hip and elbow beside her on the floor, the short kilt he wore casually inched up his thigh, revealing the inner line of muscle. The smooth ridges across his stomach tightened.

The urge to spray all of that with juice and lick it off had to be a dark compulsion. Didn't it?

When she finished chewing, he had the next slice in his hand. Instead of reaching for it, she shifted her glance to his face, then away. Such a brief moment that it might have escaped notice, but it didn't. The expression that flared in his eyes was enough to give her the courage—or foolishness—to wait and see what he would do.

He broke that second slice in half by biting it. Fed her those two pieces his lips had touched, leading with the side he'd bitten. It made her own lips vibrate more than could be explained by the tartness of the fruit.

He was focused on her face, making her realize the cowl of her cloak had fallen back. She rarely exposed her full face to another, but she realized he wasn't looking at *it*. He didn't latch on to the scarred half with macabre fascination, or obsess over the Venus side, as she spitefully called it. He was looking at *her*.

This was dangerous. He was creating confusion in her, changing things so she couldn't anticipate her reaction. And yet, when he dipped a fingertip to her chin to catch a stream of juice and take it back up to her lips, she parted them enough to let him spread the collected juice on her bottom lip. Then she pressed them together, trying not to look at the hand too obviously, too greedily, as he took it away. No, *greed* wasn't the word. *Need* was.

It seemed that after each slice, her body was drawing tighter and tighter, like a boat anchored in a rising gale, the pressure building to the point the rope would snap.

He'd stopped, his fingers touching her cheek, a light stroke, his eyes the warm brown that could reach inside her and melt things that were far too cold, things that needed to stay cold.

The cat collapsed into a pile of bone, clattering to the metal floor of the wrecked freighter in a racket amplified by her own fear. She started up, backing away. Concentration error. She certainly couldn't afford any of those. That was it. He was wrecking her concentration.

"I'm . . . you need to go somewhere else now. I need to finish this potion."

He rose, and her pulse leaped high in her throat at the loose, graceful way he moved, with a still intent as focused as the charging of her potion.

"Why are you afraid of me touching you?"

"I'm not. It doesn't mean anything. I can't . . . You need . . . Stop there. I'm not . . ."

She stopped, unable to find any coherent words. Her throat was seizing up. She coughed, mistakenly trying to breathe out of gills that weren't there. The horses began collapsing one by one, then in increasing groups, like puppets with severed strings, toppling back into piles of bone. The deafening clatter resounded within her head and had her spinning, seeking an escape.

When he caught her arm, before she could react in defense or violence, he pulled her close and put his hands over her ears. He also wrapped his wings around her, creating a comforting buffer with his solid body. Thankfully he was still human enough that the proximity of his wings wasn't too much. It didn't hurt. But one day soon, when he matured and was no longer a fledgling, she wouldn't be able to bear his touch, its disruption, its lack of balance. Good and evil had to be equally balanced. It was important, the first priority.

When she sank down, overcome with the weight of despair, he followed her. As he went to one knee, she somehow found herself on her back, gazing up at him, holding on to his upper arms with clenched hands. The night sky she'd formed for herself on the ceiling was dissipating, going with the same spell as the horses. Glancing up, he noticed it for the first time, the mist of the clouds and the sparkle of the stars she'd created. The moon drifted away like an errant balloon, getting smaller and smaller until it popped against the side of the freighter wall and left only ugly gray metal, a crisscrossing of beams.

"How did you know about the noise?" she managed.

"You had the horses running, but without touching the floor. You prefer the deeper, quieter places of the ocean. The louder it got, the more panicked you looked. I put it together."

Still keeping one hand on her, he reached into the waterproof sack from which he'd drawn the orange and came out with a square of paper cloth. "Those oranges were juicy," he said calmly, as if nothing were amiss. "Good thing I nabbed these napkins, too."

"You stole these things?"

"Somewhat." He looked charmingly abashed. "It was just a small handful from a wedding reception. I didn't think they'd mind."

Wetting the napkin with his own mouth, he wiped it along her lips, removing some of the stickiness. However, the way his eyes followed his motion made her lips part, a noise coming from her throat.

"Would you like me to use my mouth to remove the juice?" he asked, low. "Tell me yes, Mina."

"No." She shook her head. "I don't want you to do that."

"I think you're afraid to kiss me," he said. His warm brown eyes were serious, discomfiting her. Easing himself back to a reclining position beside her, he turned on his hip, a slow shift. As she watched him come closer, her fingers tightened on her stomach. He propped himself up on an elbow, leaned over her, his chestnut and brown hair falling over his shoulder so it was so . . . touchable. She needed to move. *Now.*

"You think I'd fall for a childish ploy like that?" she rasped.

"No playing, Mina." He was getting closer.

"Shouldn't you be afraid to kiss *me*?" She got the words out of a throat gone thick, as if she'd put a paralysis spell on her own voice.

He nodded. "I'm afraid you won't like it."

"I won't."

He kept coming, anyway, as her pulse leaped hard and high, lodging itself where her swallowing reflex was. It didn't matter. Her mouth had gone dry.

When his lips first brushed hers, she couldn't help it. She jerked. Her hands closed again, but nothing could stop the shudders from sweeping out from that movement as if it had been a rock thrown with force into a tide pool. Her heart felt like that thrown stone, sailing through the air, a quick, astonishing drop, the explosion of reaction around it.

And all he'd done was let that first bare touch happen. He held still, his mouth light upon hers, his gaze studying her face.

Then he slid his hand into her hair, just beneath her ear, a sweep along her neck, a caress of the scarred boundary of her jaw. When his hand coursed over the roughness, he didn't act as if he was feeling ruined flesh. Nor did she feel it, for the nerve endings were electrified beneath, her body wanting to move, gravitate up toward that touch. She couldn't possibly, but if she moved her chin, maybe he wouldn't notice how it brought their lips that much closer together, increased the pressure.

"Touch me, Mina," he murmured. "Please."

"I don't know how."

His eyes didn't shift from hers as he found one of her hands, brought it up to his chest, let her fingers curl of their own volition into his skin.

"Learn."

Four

H IS words not only brought a rush of response, but the return of water to the hold. She was at least able to choke it down to a simple rematerialization, rather than a tidal wave rush from the outside. The piles of bones floated off the metal floor, separating to drift in their own patterns now.

Had she ever been so overwhelmed? Panic drowned in sheer need for something she hadn't even realized she wanted so much. The practical side of her mind, which usually dominated most of her thinking, pointed out that she was sexually mature yet inexperienced. Since she'd never been seduced, let alone by an angel, this could of course result in an aroused response. But not the waking of a hunger so intense she could only be swept along by it when he issued that one-word command.

Flattening her palm on his chest, she felt the heat of him even through the water. Most angels didn't have body hair, and so what she found was hard, sleek muscle that flowed under her touch like a powerful animal. She supposed that was what he was, which quickened her blood even further. He slid his other arm beneath her to lift her into the demand of his body. No uncertainty, no hesitating. He was reading her desires, responding to them as if she were speaking them aloud. When his fingers stroked the small of her back, caressing the top of a buttock, she strained into him. Limbs loosened to his touch, even as need made her throat tight, leaving her unable to speak a word when he reclaimed her lips. And claim was the right word, for hers parted in mindless surrender.

His tongue found hers, tasted, tangled. Taking his time, he left nothing unexplored, even tracing the scar furrows on the roof of her mouth and the moist insides of her cheeks. Rather than causing him to withdraw, those discoveries just made him slow his pace, stroke her even more languorously with his clever tongue.

His lips were so firm that she put her hand up to wondrously feel the way they fit over hers. The thin film of wet heat just inside made her fingers slip, tease the corner of his mouth. Turning his head, he captured one digit and drew it in deep. Then he was holding her wrist, just below her pulse so he could bite her palm, jolting her body like the electric shock of an eel, but far more welcome.

With the water's return, she'd automatically shifted back to her mermaid form and had one tentacle curved over his back now, holding them bound together, even as they drifted like the bones. A sensual, aimless floating. His wings spread above like the shadows of clouds. She cried out when the hard length of him pressed between the tentacles, where her sex rested, just like a human, another thing the mermaids found so odd and different about her. But she found her differences wondrous now, for she used the hypersensitive feelers on the ends of the tentacles to explore every inch of his skin. Managing to wrap them around him, she still had enough left over to rest the tip in the feathers of one wing, soft as the mother's kiss she'd never had.

Even when she tightened her hold in her passion, he showed no fear. In fact, he even dropped his hand from her face to slide his palm along the black serpentine length of one, following it over his hip, learning the way of her, her unique anatomy. The smooth, firm texture of a sea creature in her element. When he explored beneath, finding the feelers, their joining point with her flesh, he detonated sensitive nerve centers so that she gasped and constricted farther around him.

"Easy, baby," he said quietly, against her mouth, soothing. "You can't harm me, but I don't want you too wound up."

Baby. An endearment, one that human males used, according to her books, reminding her that he was probably as much mortal in his mind as he was angel. She didn't mind that. It soothed, comforted even. Though she couldn't believe her nerves quivered at him calling her *baby*, it made her believe he wanted to give her a name that belonged to this type of intimacy only, so it couldn't be mistaken for anything less.

Taking her other tentacle up the inside of his ankle, she felt the shape of his foot, the fine line of calf, the backs of his knees, the muscled thighs, and then, as he shifted, the curve of tight, perfect buttocks. The vulnerable small of the back, where so many organs could be crushed, punctured . . . Swallowing, she began to turn her face away, her fingers clutching at his shoulders in ironic contrast, sending them spinning in an uneven circle and causing the nearest sets of floating bones to imitate the chaotic spiral. She couldn't do this. She couldn't control her reaction, stop the images from pouring in, and she didn't want them to ruin it.

"No, don't leave me yet. We'll stop in just a second. Let me just have this one . . . sweet . . . taste." His lips passed under her ear, finding the tiny dolphin bauble she hung from the lobe of her unscarred ear, usually well hidden by her hair. He teased it, then pressed his mouth against the side of her throat, sending things inside of her ricocheting. His other hand linked with her fingers, stretching out her arm and pressing it down, letting her feel his weight resting half across her, as he took them in a stomach-swirling descent to the bottom of the ship. That angel ability to adjust his gravity as he desired, even in the water, so that he was protective and dangerous, in all the right ways.

She could see their blurred, distorted reflection in the metal side of the ship as she turned her head. A strange, fantastical creature of white wings and sinuous black legs, pale flesh, black and brown hair, all of it emitting a soft glow because of his wings. It looked real, perfect, all twined together like that. The reality of it twisted inside her, painful and sharp. It was a lie.

He lifted his head then, reluctantly, his mouth moist from hers. "All right?" he asked.

"Why are you stopping?" she demanded. "Seducing me is okay, but fucking's not? Jonah's rules?"

He traced her lips. His sudden silence made her words feel like garbage flung from the back of a careless human's boat. When his gaze lifted, met hers, the annoyance was all too obvious in the hard flint of his eyes.

She'd faced all manner of anger in her life. Most of it she'd never allowed this close when she could help it, because it was likely to take a physical form. But she didn't feel that from David. In fact, she suspected if his temper toward her *did* take a physical form, she might welcome the way he chose to express it. Some part of her *wanted* to know how deeply rage could plumb inside him, if his usual quiet tranquility hid a fury that might consume him, as hers often did her.

"Let me go," she whispered, despite her betraying thoughts. Or probably because of them.

"I won't let that viper tongue of yours push me away, Mina. But be careful. I may just say to hell with being a gentleman." He brought his face close to hers until she couldn't pull away any farther. "Fucking you would be easy. Easy as sliding into a hot spring."

Mina gasped, crying out as he unerringly found her with two fingers, sinking into wetness as her tentacles contracted on him farther, her hands clutching as fierce satisfaction and frustration warred in his face.

"But what I want is your trust. I'll have that first, so what we do after *won't* be easy." His eyes flickered with ominous intent. "And it will be far more than fucking."

"Fine, I trust you now," she managed. "Can we get on with whatever you want to call it?"

Surprise disrupted his irritated look. His startled snort was close to a chuckle. The sound of it eased her heart, even as it did nothing for the pounding demand of what was happening inside her. When he withdrew his fingers, it made her squeeze as if he were still there, particularly as he tasted his fingers.

"Fortunately, I know you're an opportunistic liar." Putting his hands to her waist, he drew her up with a flexing of his arms, a careless sweep of his wings that sent water out in elegant swirls around them. He held her there for a second, studying her. "But I'm not. You can count on that, Mina. Even if Jonah *had* suggested I seduce you to gain compliance, I wouldn't have agreed to it, not as a strategy. Whatever I feel, I feel honestly. Besides which"—a wry look crossed his face—"he would have sent someone else for that. I don't have that much experience in seducing women."

He turned away as she blinked at his broad back, her body still vibrating. "So we need to go deliver this potion, then?" he asked.

She couldn't do this. She really couldn't. And in that moment, she threw the detonation spell at his back.

———

"WHY won't you understand?" She held pressure on the wound. As she checked his pupils, she noted with relief the burned area on his side was healing on its own. His head had rammed the metal wall, but apparently his skull was as hard as he'd demonstrated it to be with his unwise persistence.

"I don't want to hurt you. I just want to be left alone. Have to be left alone."

When he began to wake at last, she was smart enough to back off. She floated all the way across the ship's hold so she was well clear when he started up, his hand already on one dagger grip. As David felt the wound and obviously oriented himself, he shot her a narrow glance. "It will heal on its own, you know."

"Yes. But the water-resistant oil I smeared on it will help the pain until it disappears."

"Why do you care?"

"I don't." It was a ludicrous thing to say, but she stuck with it. "If I'd left you unconscious, unprotected down here, something bad could've happened to you. Then Jonah would send hunters after me. All I want is for you to be gone. Leave me be."

"Throw your worst at me, Mina." David drew himself upright, hovering, and took out two of the daggers.

"What?" She stared at him.

"You heard me. You think you can kill me? Try it."

"I've never tried to kill any of you." As she pushed down the fear his words evoked, it pushed back, becoming something far more disturbing than fear. "I could have killed you while you were unconscious, couldn't I? I just want you to leave me alone. I can't be around you."

"I just want to help."

"*Then leave me alone.*" The scream tore out of her before she could stop it. Her head exploded with pain, a berserker's violence surging through her. An absence of pain lay on the other side of death and killing. When blood was on her skin, the taste of it in her mouth, the screams of others would drown out the screams in her own head. It might take a thousand lives to do it, but somewhere at the end, when death reigned, there would be nothing to feel.

David stood frozen, watching as the scars shifted. Something lived beneath her flesh, struggling to get out. Her eyes snapped toward him, both red now. As her lips drew back grotesquely, she revealed fangs as long as his fingers, a mouthful of them, the skin of her face drawing tight, outlining her skull even as her arms elongated, became more skeletal, fingers now talons.

Dark One. He was looking at a Dark One, struggling to get out of her body. No, to take her body over.

Shrieking, that high-pitched shrieking he knew too well. His hands tightened on his weapons. He knew how to destroy a Dark One this size hand-to-hand, could cut its throat in a heartbeat.

The writhing creature dropped swiftly to the hold floor, apparently possessing a gravity far heavier than water could bear. Convulsing, it fought with an unseen assailant. Amazed, he watched it roll back and forth, clawing at itself, water churning around it. Words spat from its mouth, like the musical language of the merpeople, reminiscent of dolphin and whale speech, but guttural, as if its throat were being strangled. He made out the chant of containment, which galvanized a raw shriek of rage, answered by another shriek from the same throat, defiant, equally as furious. Two entities in the same skin, vying for control.

Both seemed to know they had to get the upper hand quickly, for the battle was swift, brutal and merciless. Then it was just Mina rocking in the turbulent current, holding to the metal floor. Her gills were working hard, but she was struggling to get herself upright. Her hair had come loose from its tie and was drifting in a swirl around her face, giving him brief glimpses of the scarred and unscarred sides, an ironic montage of what he'd just witnessed.

Throughout those tense few moments, he'd struggled with himself as well. When it came to fighting Dark Ones, pausing to question or think was a dead angel waiting to happen. He was prepared to kill. Trained to do it.

It must have shown on his face, for when he moved forward, her gaze lifted, focused on the daggers he'd drawn.

"If you kill me, kill me as I am. Don't kill me as one of them." Her voice was hoarse, but she managed to float upright, though she was unsteady even against the current inside the ship. "I'm Mina, daughter of the seawitch Inanna, descended from five generations of seawitches of Neptune's realm. If I die, I die as that, not as the filth that raped my mother."

As her stiff lips moved, one eye went from red back to blue, while the other remained crimson. David forced himself to take a breath, his violent reaction settling into a backseat. Deliberately sheathing the daggers, he started toward her. She had courage, for she didn't move, just tilted up her chin as he drifted closer. Her hair continued to float around her features, giving him a steadying desire to gather it. He could remember how it had felt, blooming with the fullness of water, passing over his fingers. That moment was separate from what he'd just seen. Just as that beast was separate from her.

"I'm not going to kill you, Mina," he said at last. "However, if you ever do something like that detonation spell again, I'll do something far worse."

"What?" Her brow drew down when he leaned in. He noticed she couldn't keep her attention off of his mouth, making him want to do all sorts of absurd things to her with it. Absurd, since she'd just tried her best to maim him, and demonstrated that there was more Dark One in her than any other angel would tolerate. But she could have left him, and she didn't. She'd treated his wound, watched over him and waited for him to wake. He didn't think it was because she feared the retribution of the Dark Legion, as she'd said.

This was Mina, with the perpetual frown line between her brows and a suspicious, wary look he found a challenge to replace with other expressions, like the faint flicker of panic as he got closer to her face, her lips. A lock of her hair floated over his cheek, caressed his shoulder, and her eyes followed it as if she wished it could be her fingers. Or maybe that was just his wish.

"I will put you over my knee and spank you."

Her gaze snapped up to him, shock coursing over her features. "You're . . . not teasing me."

"No." He was satisfied to see he'd come up with a threat that had caught her off guard, but captured her attention. He was tempted to do it right now. "So don't forget. Now, you said we needed to deliver a potion. Tell me about that."

Five

"THIS is going to be a bad idea," David commented as they set out from the Graveyard some time later. Mina carried her potion in a carefully prepared packet she had strapped beneath her cloak.

"You're welcome to stay here and preen," she pointed out. "I can handle a Dark One attack."

He shot her a look. The irritability and disdain were back in full measure, as if the trembling and uncertain female with soft lips and eager body had never existed.

"Preening? If your opinion of angels gets any higher, I might blush."

"If you don't blush from wearing that excuse for clothing, I doubt any flattery from me will cause it."

"I was going to go for the ghoulish cloak look, but apparently there was a run on them. This was all they had at the mall."

When she narrowed her gaze at him, he noted she understood what a mall was. She'd taken in stride several of his comments that would have baffled his fellow angels. Somehow, she had a fairly good grasp of what occurred on land, and it didn't all come from Anna.

"So if you're such an accomplished one-woman Dark One

Destroyer"—he changed direction—"why haven't you asked Jonah to sign you up for the Dark Legion?"

"I don't look good in red." She glanced at the battle skirt. "And I'm afraid of heights." Turning away, she swam through a defile between two ships that would take them out of the Graveyard. "Most of your fights are in the sky, you know."

"Afraid of . . ." Feeling a sixth sense prickling at his neck, David turned. He caught a movement at the porthole of the freighter. Blinking, he realized it was the skeletal cat. It disappeared at his regard.

"Did you forget to turn something off?"

"*Hmm?* Oh." Following his glance, she appeared to take a moment to focus, then turned back toward their exit.

"You're afraid of heights," he repeated. "You can shapeshift into a dragon. You flew over a canyon, did aerial maneuvers to escape a Dark One archery attack."

"*Hmm.*" She didn't pause, continuing to swim forward at a fairly swift pace, her gaze moving around them. It told him she was used to relying on herself to anticipate a threat. He was mildly gratified to see she wasn't including him in that surveillance, though, trusting him to guard her right flank. "So?"

"So I don't understand."

A school of fish parted as if cut by a scythe to let her pass through their ranks. "Let me know when you do. I'll wait for your comprehension with bated breath."

"I'm beginning to understand why Marcellus wanted a gag," he muttered darkly.

As they moved into a more open area, David fell back and went up, wanting to survey a wider scope of their surroundings, see more attack points.

She flicked a sidelong glance at him as he changed position but said nothing. The others had probably employed similar tactics. She seemed unconcerned with his movements, but dropped lower, so she became nothing more than a mundane sea creature making her way along the seafloor, brushing close to reefs when they were provided, minimizing her open exposure. The cloak spread out so at first glance, with tentacles curling and uncurling behind in graceful propulsion, she could be mistaken for a squid of some type, a creature without numerous enemies moving casually over the surface populated by myriad corals, sponges, sea fans and darting fish, in a silent, mostly blue green world.

Except he saw something entirely different down there. The rippling silk of the hair, the brief glimpse of slim arms, almost lost against the sandy portions of the seafloor. He remembered their strength around him, the desperate grip of the one undamaged hand, the press of the three fingers on the other. The odd, rough feel of the stumps where fingers no longer were, but pressing down even more fervently, as if making up for their deficit.

He'd unbalanced her, in more than one way, and maybe himself as well. He'd known that intuition would guide him, but he hadn't expected how innate it would be to employ the strategy of sexually dominating her, such that he wasn't sure whether or not it was a natural compulsion she seemed to provoke in him. But in the brief flash of vulnerability she'd shown as a result, he'd *known* it was the difficult but only sure road of winning her trust. If she didn't kill him first, or compel him to strangle her.

She stopped, her cloak waving around her, and settled to the ocean floor. David stilled, scouting the terrain and her position to see a group of merpeople skirting a line of the reef. Coming from a passageway that led down to Neptune's lower realm, if he recalled the layout of this area correctly.

It was a mixed group. Mermaids and mermen, perhaps a family and some extra friends thrown into the mix. Possibly a foraging party, or swimming as a group to go sun on the rocks. The males had an outer flanking position, for though there were only a few predators of merpeople, they were formidable ones. Killer whales, bands of sharks.

The formation reminded him that merpeople were a very patriarchal society, where women were not expected to be warriors. Mina was an apparent exception, with her lethal fighting skills.

He'd expected her to move after confirming it was her own people, but she remained motionless as they passed overhead, until they were well along their way. Then she rose from the bottom, a slow shift, like a sea creature in truth, nothing that would catch the eye, and continued on her way, sliding around the side of a coral bed and starting her swim across the more open area.

"Begone! Go!"

The combination of musical notes and shrill cries that signified the merpeople language resonated to him. Another group had been emerging from the passageway from Neptune's realm. Mina increased her speed, but something was hampering her. She was favoring her left side. As he dove, the position of the reef shifted so he could see a cut on her forehead. The wildly spinning disks of a cluster of sharp oyster shells floating toward the bottom helped him put it together.

"Dark Spawn! Begone from here. Filth! Seawitch."

He dropped into the space before her just as another projectile torpedoed her way. Merpeople used a modified form of underwater slingshot and crossbow to give them the propulsion to launch underwater missiles at foes. Fury spurted through him as he caught the sandstone, jagged with embedded shells, in one hand.

"*Angel.*" The group of merwomen shrieked at the sight of him and about-faced, diving behind the reefs. The two mermen with them backpedaled and then followed, creating a strong wake with the frantic propulsion of their tails. Merpeople, like most nonhumans, treated angels with fear and awe. In this case, David was glad for it, because he felt like bringing a storm of wrath down on them they wouldn't soon forget.

Releasing the stone with disgust, he turned to find his seawitch still in motion. Having crossed the passageway, she was now moving more swiftly on her way. When he caught up with her and tried to see how she was injured, she jerked away.

"Why did you do that?" she demanded.

"They were attacking you."

"They were throwing things at me. They always do that. All you did was draw attention to me. An angel, no less. That makes it worse."

"Maybe they'll be less likely to do it if they think someone is protecting you."

She came to such a sudden halt she swayed in the aborted flow of water. Eyes as sharp as his daggers leveled on him. "For the last time, I don't *need* your protection. I held off an archery attack of Dark Ones at the Canyon Battle to reclaim Jonah. I threw a detonation at you that knocked you unconscious. You think I couldn't annihilate a group of ignorant, superstitious merpeople? I can conjure fire spells that would—" As she cut herself off, obviously struggling with her frustration, he raised a brow.

"Make half my platoon look like naked chickens?"

Her attention snapped back to him. David arched his brow higher, waiting.

"You don't understand."

"I do. People suck." Coming closer despite her warning expression, he took a look at what was luckily a superficial cut. Her gaze narrowed, became more menacing. However, as he'd endured withering looks from not only Jonah but Lucifer, the overpowering Lord of the Hades Underworld, it would take more than a look to shake him.

"Where did the other one hit you?" He dropped his attention to where she was still clutching her side.

"They didn't hit me. It's a muscle cramp. It happens sometimes."

"Let me help."

"No," she snapped. Closing her eyes, Mina shook her head. "I can't have you disrupting my life like this."

"We want to keep you safe."

"I've never been safe a day in my life, David." Gritting her teeth, Mina moved back from him again. "Neptune tried to have me killed when I was nine years old. When he decided he *might* have made a mistake, he ordered his healers to help me as best they could. I felt their revulsion in every touch. If they'd had the courage to defy him, they'd have blocked off my gills and made it look like I died of my injuries. I know that, because they told me so.

"And you don't want *me* safe," she added. "You want my power safe."

Mina pressed on before he could deny it, aware that the shrillness in her voice was increasing, but unable to stop herself. "No one will use my power but me. If anyone tries to make me use it for their benefit, I will destroy myself in the process. Not for some greater good, but just to deny them the pleasure of taking what they were never offered. If I can convince you of that, will you leave me be? I don't want you, don't need you, any of you. To me, you're all the same side. You're—"

It clamped down on her, shoving her into a howling vortex of darkness. She clawed at the sides of it, but the sinking despair told her she'd lost the fight again. Rage. She knew better than to get this worked up. Twice in one day now. Or was it three? She couldn't have him around. Oh, gods, *why* couldn't she make him understand?

Maybe because if he did, he would try to kill her and be done with it, and for reasons she didn't comprehend, she still clung to the idea of life. She shot off through the water, hoping David, if he wouldn't leave her, at least wouldn't be stupid and try to slow her down this time.

She used the pain from the muscle cramp, pushing herself to the limits of her speed, stroking and pumping wildly with her tentacles, twisting her body so that it screamed in agony. Going faster and faster until her heart was laboring, gills flared wide along her neck. The pain became living fire in her side, a wall of flame between her and the red minotaur of rage that wanted to leapfrog over it, reduce that group of smug, useless merpeople to chunks of torn-apart meat. A meal that would summon an army of sharks while she perched on a nearby rock, glorying in the cloud of blood, opening her mouth to taste the remnants of it, of their laughter, as she laughed last. She'd catch the women's long, beautiful hair on her arms, weave herself a cloak out of it. Maybe she'd even take the delicate necklace of shells she'd seen one of the mergirls wearing. Probably given to her by an adoring father or friend. A sister or mother. Maybe she'd made it herself, with slim, dainty fingers that had never known a single twinge, let alone the clawing agony in joints that screamed for relief that would never come.

By the time she reached the entrance to her cave, she was shaking so hard she had to slow down or risk bumping into the jagged collar of stinging fire coral around it. Diving into its welcoming darkness, she pushed herself to keep moving, far into its depths. This was her place where no one else dared enter, warded to maintain that sense of apprehension in those that approached. Nothing could enter, except one annoying angel.

When she could go no farther, she spiraled down to a large, uneven stalagmite of rock that split the floor of this part of the cavern. She clung to it, letting it press into her aching side, waiting for the spasms to pass. It would take time, for the muscles had worked themselves into a fine knot. But more alarming to her was that the visions were continuing, spinning through her mind like a whirlpool, building in power, not lessening. As her now taloned fingers dug into the rock, she imagined them gouging into flesh, gleefully taking it off in ribbons, leaving a bare skull, empty sockets.

She rocked against the stone, moaning, and then with a snarl, she jammed the middle finger of the three-fingered hand against the unyielding stone, breaking the bone.

The pain was blinding, driving darkness from her vision with a glaring whiteness that threatened unconsciousness. She pressed her forehead against the rock, which even through the water smelled of the dank things that lived in a cave like this, like her. Is that what David smelled when he touched her damp flesh? Mold and stagnant, trapped water. And she was supposed to believe he was attracted to her, like she was some type of idiot?

No one would use her. *No one.* Not even the dark blood inside her.

Then she felt his hands. The bloodlust in her roared in fury. Trying to twist, she snapped at him, taking a swipe. When he caught her wrist, she cried out, her lower body rolling upward, the tentacles wrapping around the rock to protect her side.

"*Ssh* . . ." Gingerly, he guided her arm back around his neck, as if she didn't have six-inch claws capable of ripping his head right off.

Since she'd expected him to yank her off the rock, demand some response from her, it was confusing to realize he wasn't doing either of those things. Instead, his touch ran down her hair. The other hand sought her broken-fingered one. She tucked it against her, evading him.

"No healing." She gasped it. "No."

She could tell it bothered him, that he was set to overrule her, and she knew at this moment he easily could. But then he surprised her again. He nodded, his jaw pressed against the side of her head, and took his hand lower, to her side, where he found the knotted muscle and began to explore it.

"Can't heal it. Don't," she repeated.

"I won't," he promised. "I'm just going to rub it, make it feel better. Just relax."

"This is all your fault," she said. "I wouldn't have cared about their stupid shell necklaces or who gave them to them if it wasn't for your oranges and chocolate and stupid attempt to protect me."

"I know," he said, though she was sure he had no idea what she was babbling on about, sounding even to her own ears like an irritable, immature teenager.

He'd known what she meant about the healing, however. They'd gone down that road before. He'd given her his blood to heal her that very first time and as a side effect, he could track her anywhere. She couldn't escape him.

But that deed was done. What made her fear his healing touch was what else had happened. He'd not only managed to heal one of the fresh wounds, his energy had spilled over and begun to heal the scars on her face, something no angel should be able to do.

But apparently he had some practical skills, for his fingers had found the snarled muscles along her scarred side and were kneading them, applying pressure where needed, alternating between the fingers and heel of his hand. With his other hand, he was massaging her undamaged one, using pressure points there to ease what was going on in her side. More importantly, it was helping to calm her mind.

She made herself focus inward, use the unexpected assistance to drive back the darkness once more, find that equilibrium point. As the pain slowly began to recede, taking the whirling darkness with it, she became hyperaware of his body pressed behind her, holding her between his chest and the rock, another steadying influence. Water moved around them, buoying them and providing an additional familiar constant.

Her fingers were her fingers again, the bite of her nails no longer capable of deep gouges, though when he guided her hand back over her own shoulder to rest on his, she could feel the torn skin she'd caused in her internal struggle. It would heal, of course. She likely wouldn't even be able to see the wound on him by the time she turned, but she knew he experienced pain like any other creature. Yet he hadn't even flinched when she'd done it.

"Easy," he said softly, but when he tried to continue to massage the individual finger joints of the hand by his neck, she twined her fingers with his to make him stop. That, too, he seemed to anticipate. He simply let their interlaced grip rest there while he turned his full attention to the kneading of her side. When his probing became easy, full strokes, she couldn't stifle the relieved sigh that settled her body in the curve of his.

His hand drifted to her hip. With his mouth on the crown of her head, her hair would be moving in the water's grip, strands brushing against his jaw and cheek again. It made her uninjured hand itch to do the same, just as it had earlier. She closed her eyes. This was an impossible situation.

"Can I help you splint that finger?" he murmured.

Six

MINA raised her head from his shoulder and faced his expression. Their bodies were tangled together against the rocks like seaweed in a Gulf Stream current, and his expression was concerned. Maybe even angry with her, but in a way that made something lurch in her chest, tighten her lower abdomen, despite the throbbing in her finger. Gods, it hurt.

They were in the portion of her cave system that had her stores, so she directed him to where the proper supplies would be. When she laid her hand with some trepidation on the rock, he surprised her once again by setting the finger capably, needing little guidance. His hands were gentle, firm, unhurried, but he didn't rush as someone would who was nervous about causing additional pain, or go too slowly, which would prolong it. She wanted to ask him how he knew about mortal, nonmagic healing practices, but she couldn't afford to show curiosity.

Plus, the pain was overwhelming enough to make breathing difficult, let alone speech. Her gills were fluttering when he was done, her vision gray at the edges. It took effort to stave off the faint, and she realized he was holding her upper arms, steadying her.

"Seawitch?"

The voice filtered down from the cave mouth. David stiffened, but Mina shook her head. Shook herself. "It's the merman who requested the potion."

"You can't do this right now."

"I can." Loosening her grip on the rock at last, she got away from him with a slithering move and drew her cowl back over her head. Gerard's voice helped her remember herself. Push back her pain, clear her mind, get back on track. After all, she'd had situations where she'd had to recover far more quickly, with far more serious injuries.

The pain would ebb. The important thing was the hold of the darkness had been broken again, and she had to make it clear she'd have been perfectly capable of handling the situation herself. So glancing at David's all-too-knowing gaze, his taut mouth, which looked on the verge of issuing another high-handed order, she said, in a reasonably steady tone, "This won't take long. Stay here. Else you're going to destroy my reputation entirely."

"Your reputation?" David bit back his overwhelming urge to order her to stay right where she was. She was pale, paler than he'd expect even a merperson living out of sight of the sun to be, and there was still a tremor to her limbs. He forced himself to focus on her barbed comment, since he could tell she was desperate for him to do so. "What does that mean?"

"If I have an angel guardian, what does that look like? That I'm not only interesting, but approachable. An angel would never approach anything wholly evil except to kill her," Mina pointed out. "So if they see you, it will start speculation. And part of why they get the potions from me is because they think I draw from dark forces, which they feel lends the potion greater potency."

"So those who come for your potions are seeking evil?"

"No. Those who come for my potions have that perverse mortal desire to feel they've dared to grasp at darkness, when in fact they've only brushed it without the danger of actually realizing what it is." Her red eye glinted.

"So my goodness and purity is bad for business?"

"Exactly. Another reason you shouldn't have interfered earlier with the merpeople. Stay," she repeated in a sharp tone, as if to a mongrel dog she expected to disobey. "Gerard is nineteen years old, weighs less than I do and would soil himself if I looked at him sideways. I think I can manage."

She swam off, leaving David staring after her. One moment she was berating him for defending her honor. The next she was gasping, leaning against his body, reluctantly accepting his help to manage her pain. Now she was treating him as a mere annoyance, and an easily managed one at that. Grimly, he remembered the scrambling panic of the merpeople earlier at just the sight of him, but after getting a glimpse of what Mina appeared to be fighting within her, he was beginning to understand why she had little fear of the angels.

Typical Fate. Jonah had a millennium of experience with the nature of all beings, including females, and he got Anna. A gentle, mild-mannered spirit of golden light and air. David was thirty, and drawn to a female who would make a wounded, constipated badger look appealing. He could tell himself he was punishing himself for past sins, but he didn't think anyone was that masochistic. Even a reformed suicide.

He didn't often make jokes about that time in his life, but he realized he was enjoying the challenge of Mina. Maybe Marcellus *was* right, and he was an idiot.

With his heightened senses, and the fact sound traveled faster through water than through air, he could hear her, as she'd said. The stammering merman did sound barely out of puberty, utterly terrified and thrilled with his own bravado, daring to meet with the mysterious seawitch. Those who had never truly been in the grip of darkness *were* the only ones foolish enough to want to brush against it, and Mina was certainly not the first to take advantage of that.

She was taking time to explain to him how the potion should be taken for maximum effectiveness. She didn't describe its mechanics the way she had to David. She simply noted that Gerard would get the results the Higher Powers desired.

Satisfied with her safety for the moment, David glanced around, realizing he hadn't been this far into her cave before.

The last time he'd been here, he'd been intent on capturing her for information, which hadn't allowed time for impressions on her interior decorating choices.

The key is understanding her . . .

Sea glass. He moved into a cavern where seaweed and scavenged fishing line had been used to string all manner of glass pieces. The water currents moved them together, as the wind would if he was in a garden. Underwater, there was a sound, more muted, but still pleasing to the ears.

Sinister movements along the wall behind the chimes turned out to be additional cloaks pieced together with scraps of salvaged fabric. Pushing the fabric of one aside, he discovered a necklace, perhaps rescued from a sunken ship. A silver collar embedded with emeralds and diamonds, like an Indian princess's wedding dowry piece.

Money and treasure had no value to merpeople, but like most sea life, they were attracted to shiny things. A light smile touched his lips, even as he suspected there was more to this than an interesting light catcher, worth a fortune in the human world.

"But what if the Higher Powers don't let it happen? I'll just lose my mind if she doesn't fall in love with me."

"One could argue you've already lost your mind," Mina said dryly. "But the point, Gerard, is what is meant to be. Take the potion, see where it leads, but understand—"

"What if I give you more? I know where there's plenty more of these plants you wanted than what I brought."

"It doesn't have to do with that." There was a snap to her voice that David was sure would whip Gerard's tail between his legs, figuratively speaking, so fast it would slam into his balls. Remind him he was bickering with a witch.

When he'd arrived in the cave and touched her, wrapped hard against the rock, there'd been a powerful energy rushing in her veins, so close to the surface of her skin it felt as if it might spear through the flesh to free itself.

As David glided with the currents into the next cavern, he discovered a statue garden. Various figureheads from old ships: lions, mermaids, goblins. A statue of Venus held the artful curl of her hair across her groin area as she stood on her seashell. Next to her was Artemis with her bow and hounds. The eye of Osiris, from the planking of a ship, was propped in a crevice.

Turning, he faced a statue of a lovely woman, probably just a concrete form intended to be part of an estate's garden. A sapphire blue dress sparkling with intricate beadwork had been fitted over her sculpted body. The sleeves, long and flowing, moved in the water, making her into a riveting ghost. The statue wore a long black wig, a dark choker of onyx at her throat. Narrowing his eyes, he drew closer. When he examined the face, he realized it was a mermaid's hair, assembled into a wig with the help of a tightly woven mat of sea material, reinforced with some type of enchantment to preserve it, along with the dress and jewelry.

Thinking on that, he moved back into the cavern that held her stores. Hundreds of bottles, likely collected by her ancestors as well as herself, had ingredients that ranged from recognizable and relatively fresh vegetation and oils to things that appeared to be parts of previously living creatures. The farther he moved along this wall, the more menacing the ingredients became, until he knew he was seeing the unborn young of various species, human body parts and more. Then there were the tools of her trade. Cutting tools, pincers, pestles.

The muscles in his shoulders tightened as he found a host of items he knew. Things he'd seen in wretched, hellish places where he and other angels had been sent to fight dark magic.

Grateful to enter what appeared to be the final cavern, he discovered a vast wealth of spellbooks and magical texts dating back centuries. If she knew them, her command of her craft was impressive, perhaps the level of the Thrones in the Heavens. Like the dress, they were carefully maintained in an enchanted stasis.

As he turned his gaze from them, he discovered why Mina had such a familiar grasp of human society. She had their books. A library of literary classics, paperbacks, hardbacks, coffee table books. Apparently everything that survived wrecks, or what she could get her clientele to bring her in trade.

She'd never asked Anna to bring her anything. Never showed an inordinate interest in the human world. Yet Anna had remembered Mina rarely interrupted her or drove her off when she spoke of the land world.

His mind moved over all of it, thinking. He wanted to reject what lay behind him, those disturbing corners of her stores, the magical texts that delved into unthinkable areas. Cleanse the dark magic out of the place with a fire that would overwhelm the water and her protection spells. But it would also take her books, the chimes, the statues. Spellbooks and grimoires that reflected generations of magical study.

Perhaps the potions maintained her tenuous acceptance by the mermaid community. They threw rocks at her and drove her to their outskirts, but used her for her knowledge. And she tolerated it, because that way she could call someplace home.

The key is to understand her . . .

Probing, he determined that her protection spells went mainly into disguise, not deterrence, which would leave a more noticeable energy signature. To any nonangelic life-form who disregarded the pervading uneasiness about entering the cave, an illusion spell would make the caverns appear empty.

Many mortal magics didn't affect angels. Unfortunately and unexpectedly, some of her spells did, and therefore, it would be wise to cast a standing Inert spell over himself to give him a supernatural bulletproof vest of sorts. However, he did want to make a serious attempt at the trust issue, and that had to go two ways.

Village idiot. He could almost hear Marcellus scoffing at him. Jonah as well.

The stalagmites told him this cave, like much of this area of the ocean, had once been above ground. As he considered the layout of the five caverns, he realized they were in a circular arrangement, the tunnel entrance leading into the stores area first. The five caverns were formed around a wide column of solid rock. Each cavern was triangular in shape. Visualizing it in his mind, he realized it was a pentagram. The sign of the Lord and

Lady, a symbol of power that, like all symbols of power, could be used for good or evil. But which held sway over Mina?

The common wisdom was that no creature was perfectly balanced. That the struggle between good and evil went on throughout every life, and the best that could be done was to try to stay on the light side of the line. But in these caverns, even in Mina herself, he sensed a strange battle not toward either side, but to straddle the middle exactly. To create her own axis around which everything else turned.

Musing, he ran his fingers along the spines of the books on the wall, coming to a halt on a cheerful pale yellow binding. Withdrawing it, he found he'd discovered a children's picture book. *The Littlest Angel*. There were few coincidences in life, he knew. As he noted a gap on this portion of the shelf and ran his fingers along it, he discovered something even more remarkable. An angel's personal weaponry had a strong connection to its owner, carrying some of the angel's aura. One of the reasons it had struck him so hard in the gut—and other lower extremities—when he'd taken the dagger and determined the sensual use to which Mina had put it.

So now as he ran his fingers over that shelf, he realized this was where she'd laid his dagger, kept it. It made him think again about those self-inflicted thin lines, the way it had aroused her when he'd licked the blood away from her flesh. As a surge of the same desire shuddered through him like a minor quake, he wondered if, angel or not, he was little different from Gerard when it came to Mina. Willing to brush close to the darkness for the thrill of being near her. But not because of her darkness. Because of what lay beneath it all—a fascinating mix of both light and dark.

Remembering his early teens, how he'd played fantasy role-playing games, he'd been most intrigued by the "morally neutral" characters that were supposed to make their decisions based on logic, opportunity and survival only, not conscience. He wondered if the Goddess had been training him for this, even then.

Opening the book, he discovered one of his feathers pressed

in the pages. She had to have found it after their fight that day of their first meeting.

Replacing the book, he let the waters turn him, floated as he took it all in, the dichotomy of items, the different insights they offered about the same witch. Woman. He'd never gotten out of the habit of referring to humanoid life-forms such as angels and mermaids as men and women. Even knowing it was one of the quirks that amused his fellow angels, he liked thinking of Mina that way. Woman. But as he passed the spellbooks and drifted back into the cavern with the dark-magic items, he couldn't ignore the other images he'd seen of her. Dark One. Seawitch.

He also couldn't ignore something else. The central column of solid rock around which the caverns were arranged was *not* solid. As he brushed his hand along it, power vibrated beneath his palm. A warding here, extremely powerful versus the lighter touch of the other cavern protections. But when he concentrated on it, impressed by the complexity, the command of knowledge demonstrated by the magic wielder who had cast it, it slowly unwound itself, as most magics would at an angel's touch, to reveal a narrow doorway. The waft of energy that came from within reminded him of a door creaking inward on its hinges in one of the old horror movies, beckoning the teenager into the cellar.

Though the water had shaped and smoothed the edges, this doorway had not been created as long ago as the whole cave system had. Moving into the narrow opening, he kept his fingers along the wall line. While he could see in the dark, this was a pitch-black. Taking another step, he suppressed the urge to jump back when the blackness closed around him in reality, as if fingers had curved over his shoulders, pulling him forward.

He could no longer hear Mina's voice, patiently going over things with Gerard. Earlier, he'd been impressed with her patience with the boy, her desire to have him use the potion correctly. Despite her studied indifference, her claimed intention of doing the potions only for what they might bring her, she had an integrity. He'd seen it in her. If he was in a cave that had been shared by her ancestors, he reasoned many of these items might not be hers. The lore, the knowledge, had been shared, and she would preserve it. But she'd enhanced it, learned from it, used it. Perhaps exceeded it.

He could be rationalizing the hell out of things, not wanting to accept that the woman to whom he was so attracted could in fact be as dark as Marcellus and the other angels feared. He was still missing too many pieces.

Even so, there was an alarm going off in him and gaining strength, telling him he didn't want to know what was ahead. But he'd promised to protect her. To do that, he had to understand whom or what he was protecting.

But was he forging ahead as an angel dedicated to a mission, or as the male who needed the key to her, needed it *now*, for he'd touched his mouth to hers and found himself hungry for more? Felt her body rise to his, seen the confusion in her eyes. Both of them. The crimson eye of the Dark One and the blue eye of the woman.

That thought slammed out of his mind as he was hit by a wave of pure Dark One energy. Bile rose in his throat, his fingers closing on his daggers. But oddly, he didn't sense Dark Ones ahead. Taking a deep breath, he made the final step and passed through a wall of water into a small, bone-dry chamber, where the water beading on his body evaporated before it hit the ground. Drawing back like a curtain, the darkness was dispelled by the dim light cast by bloodred stones embedded into the rock wall. The stones' glow came from what appeared to be a high-level binding charm carved into their surfaces. They were arranged in an arc pattern, as if over a doorway, though he only saw an unbroken line of rock wall beneath them. The vibration of energy was so strong he had to strain to step toward that wall, using the propulsion of his wings, such as was possible in the cramped space.

The warning hum in his head was becoming painful, the pressure of a migraine, something angels didn't get. He needed to get out of here. But first he had to feel what was behind there. What was locked in this room. Clenching his teeth, his muscles bunched, he lifted one arm and brushed the rock beneath the binding stones with his wet fingertips.

When he first became an angel, he'd experienced gales, hit wind pockets that sent him somersaulting. Still clinging to his mortal, earthbound memories, he'd panicked, then realized it was like riding a wave in to shore, as he had as a boy at the beach. He'd learned to laugh at the buffeting, the wild spin of it, and recover from it unscathed.

There was nothing of the Goddess's creation to this. What struck him was beyond the comprehensible power of ocean or wind, slamming him into a maelstrom of chaos and all its terrifying despair. There was no beginning or end. He was tumbling, flat on his back, being crushed under its weight, a weight that didn't promise darkness. Only terror, hopelessness without an end.

He knew that Hell, Lucifer's Hades, was about redemption, justice, payment. Not the Hell of eternal damnation and torment he'd learned about as a mortal. But now he knew that place wasn't a myth. It was here, hidden in the tiny chamber of a sea-witch's cave.

Seven

NIGHTMARISH images assailed him from all sides, slashed at him, laughed at his fear, turned an apathetic eye to his existence.

We are your future. She will deliver you to us soon, angel. Your wings do not exonerate you for your sins. Your failures.

"David."

His name. Someone heard him after all. But he couldn't reach out. The maelstrom shrieked. It grasped at his vitals, repulsive as a rapist's touch. Death was a gift they wouldn't offer, not until every ounce of pain had been milked from him, until his throat bled from screaming and nothing was left of his soul to rescue.

When a chanting cut through the shriek, a wave of fury roared over him like fire, burning his flesh but cleansing it, too. Freeing it from the Dark Ones' touch, so that he embraced the pain, crying out in relief. The physical drove away the emotional, and the emotional was a far worse torment. As both faded, there was water again, the darkness of the short tunnel, and then a sense of a wider area. Floating.

"David." Urgently now, a hand on his face. Cooling. Stroking.

The burns were receding, for of course they would. He could heal. He was an angel, and most all physical wounds could be healed. But he still couldn't move on his own, as if a pike had been driven through his chest, below the layers of physical matter, to the wound that mattered the most, the one that would never heal. Evil had ripped away the illusion that it could be ignored and managed.

"You angels think nothing can harm you. Just because you can untangle a warding doesn't mean you *should*. I bet you didn't even think to protect yourself. Arrogant idiot."

Mina. It was her irritable, familiar voice, but there was fear under it as well. Was it fear for him, or because of what he'd seen? "David. Open your eyes."

There was a tinge of desperation behind the demand. He was distressing her. It helped orient him, bring him back to a world where there was some semblance of civility, order. Those things could be illusions as well.

He'd fought so hard to believe he could forget, thinking that the higher he piled Dark One bodies, the faster he flew, the farther it would be from him. In the end he'd discovered the only way to handle the memories was to stay still enough to accept their presence. Meditation. Gods, he'd never expected that meditation would be the hardest thing for him to learn, but there it was. It was easier to kill than to face what the stillness inside of him held.

His nightmares had been waiting for him there, and he'd had to get through them, to learn that there *was* meaning and purpose, despite his firsthand knowledge of evil beyond the comprehension and endurance of any living being.

But he'd done it. He'd figured it out, in a way that had no words, and that understanding was here now. He forced back the fear and gripped her slim fingers, which were gripping his back. Maybe for the same reason. Need. Connection. That magic, even when elusive, which existed inside every heart. It would be there until there were no hearts left to beat, because that was the simple truth of existence. It had to be. He couldn't afford to believe otherwise.

David opened his eyes. Her face was over him, an ironic map of the fight between good and evil, the way it had been mapped over his heart, leaving it a scarred battlefield like hers. Maybe they were the mirror of each other, after all.

She closed her eyes briefly, as if she was dealing with some great emotion, before her lids sprang back open, her mouth going to a thin, firm line. *Here it comes*, he thought. The unexpected surge of humor was a gift straight from the Lady, he was sure, providing a beam of warmth, which shattered the hold of the lingering despair.

"What, in all the names of Hades, were you thinking? I told you to stay, not go roaming about and searching through my personal things."

"You . . ." He cleared his throat of whatever ash it seemed had burned there. They were back in her library. She'd apparently formed an airbell to lay him on a dry ledge of rock. When he struggled to one elbow, he'd intended the gesture to be an attempt to retain some authority over the situation, but since she had to help steady him, it lost some of its impact. "You have a rift to the Dark Ones' world."

His chest felt as if the cavern had collapsed and the debris was sitting on it, but once he made it to that elbow, he got from there to an upright position, tested his wings. The world reeled, and he would have toppled again, except she braced herself against his shoulder, his wing dropping limply over her like a cloak. When he swiveled his head drunkenly to make sure the other one was there, he had to look down, for it was wilted onto the rock as well.

"Let me get something to help." She made sure he was all right to sit up, staying within watchful eyesight of him as she moved out of the airbell, swam into the adjacent cavern and began to rummage through her stores. "Sit still a moment. And it's not a rift. It's a doorway."

"What?" He'd thought his wits were returning, but her remarkable statement made him rethink that.

Mina turned from the wall, the vial of restorative clutched in her hand, and surveyed him. He was still paler than the white on his wings, and his skin was blackened in places. If he hadn't somehow managed to call out, if she hadn't sensed the energy shift . . . Gerard had just taken his leave; otherwise, she might not have paid attention in time. She didn't want to think about what she would have found if she came a couple minutes later. A creature of an angel's purity standing in that chamber, let alone touching the doorway, as he'd started to do, barely a fingertip brush . . .

She returned to the small airbell she'd manufactured. He'd been choking when she dragged him out, so she'd assumed air would help. Gliding in between his knees, her lower body still in the sea's embrace, she brought the glass to his lips. "Drink this. It will help bring back your energy."

"I don't want—"

"Damn it, do it."

His gaze snapped to her. While she knew he was hardly the type to meekly obey orders, maybe he'd caught the embarrassing catch in her voice. He still had enough pride to take it from her hand, but his was trembling. Reaching out, she steadied it with both of hers as he tipped the bottle and took the mixture in three grimacing swallows.

If he'd been there much longer, the long and graceful fingers gripping the bottle would have been stripped of flesh.

"Mina?"

She'd closed her eyes again and realized she was squeezing those fingers tightly. "I was so stupid to leave you alone," she said low, vicious. "You don't belong here. This is why you shouldn't be doing this. You can't understand my life. You can't protect me."

He freed a hand to touch her face. It seemed light, tentative, which of course could have been because he was still recovering, but she wondered if it was because he wasn't as sure of her as he'd been before.

Months ago, she hadn't wanted him to see her dragon form. Now he'd seen a far worse side. Fine. She shouldn't care. Maybe it would revolt him and he'd turn away. Leave her be. Best that way.

"I know I don't understand you," he said. "That's what I was trying to do by looking at your home."

She stared into his brown eyes, which were getting back that steady, intent look. She wanted to pound on him. She wanted to wrap her arms around him and feel his heart beat against her chest, know the strength of his limbs around her, inhale the fresh, warm smell of him. And that deep, dark part of her wanted to rip at his wounded skin, have him fight her until he overwhelmed her, took her to oblivion.

"I don't want you to understand me." Why did he make her blurt out these things that were going to lead to further conversations she didn't want to have?

"Why?"

See? She couldn't explain that. For the answer was the same as everything with her. A paradox. He was an angel, and the angels were her enemies. But for inexplicable reasons, she didn't want to see this particular angel become repulsed by her, even though there was nothing else he could be. Shamefully, she'd prefer his tentative acceptance of her pathetic façade than his rejection of the truth, and she knew the despairing futility of that.

She shook her head. His hand slid up her arm, over the curve of her shoulder to the side of her face, his thumb finding the line of her throat. Trying to tip her face to an angle where he could see her eyes.

"Mina, tell me what that place is."

"It's a doorway, as I said. My mother created it. Opened it by accident when she was studying the Dark Ones' powers. She got it sealed again, but not before one got through."

"That was how you—"

She nodded, quick, cutting off his words.

"Why haven't you destroyed it? Do you need help? It must be destroyed. You know that."

"No." Her head came up in alarm. "You can't destroy it." She pushed away from him now, retreating into the familiar cold grip of the sea, in order to position herself between the defile and him. "It's mine. Mine to decide to destroy or keep."

Like hell. David could almost hear Jonah's voice. The water was rising around him now, a deliberate action to weaken his position and strengthen hers, he was sure. He let himself slide back into it as the airbell disappeared. As he moved, she tensed.

"Will you try to kill me over it?" he demanded. "Seal your Fate, so there are no choices left to be made?"

When something flickered in her eyes, he blinked, startled. "That's the key to it, isn't it?"

She moved back farther, so she was now directly in front of the defile.

"Mina, please don't."

"It calls to me. If I go through, you can't follow me there."

David made himself stop. That glint was rising in her eyes. Bloodlust eager to take over, force this into a fatal confrontation. "Mina." He spoke softly, and saw it bank somewhat. "Will you tell me something? What kind of day have you had?"

He couldn't see her blue eye at all now. That part of her face was shadowed in the cowl of her cloak she'd pulled back up and tied. It was just the crimson and scars, and with the emanations behind her, it was too easy to imagine he was facing a Dark One, such that his fingers again rested on the grip of one dagger, even as he moved forward. Tension thrummed off her, amplified by his own, by that ready battle stance. If one of them struck, it would be over.

She was a formidable fighter when she considered herself cornered. While he couldn't deny the spear of admiration, it came with fear—for her. No matter how formidable she was, he could defeat her if he fought her as he would fight an enemy, and they both knew it.

"See?" she said softly. "Even you feel it. All I have to do is turn it up, just a little, and I look more and more like your enemy. Until you wouldn't hesitate to strike me down."

"Is that what you want?"

Did she want the fight? The death? The end of fighting? He'd been in that state of mind for a few years. She'd been there all her life. With that startling realization came the thought that, while he might be physically more powerful, she might have him out-matched in other ways. The outcome, who would win or lose, wasn't as certain as he'd first thought, but David knew one thing. One of them would die, and the ramifications of that might take them both down.

"Answer my question. What was today like? Answer it, for both of us." He forced himself to focus. He'd instinctively slipped one of the daggers half out of its scabbard. Sliding it back home in its sheath, he made himself let go of it one finger at a time. Lowered his arm to his side, though everything in him screamed at the folly. Well, it wouldn't be the first time today. His survival and gut instincts were two different animals, and with Mina he was following the latter, probably more than was wise.

"Mina, I don't want us to do this. Please answer me."

Her eye was the color of fresh blood; her scarred skin stretched too tightly over her skull. She looked like a creature of death and destruction, no trace left of the mermaid who'd eaten slices of an orange from his fingertips.

But something flickered in her face. "Confusing," she said at last. Her tentacles twitched, a quick spasm, where they'd fastened her against the rock wall to give her a good propulsion point. "Hateful. I wanted to kill those mermaids. Thought how easy it would be. Remembered kissing you."

"Well, I'm glad you chose the latter." He dared to get closer. "Did you like the orange? We didn't even get to the chocolate."

"I kept it." She made as if to search for it, then stopped, casting a glance at him.

"We can't stand at a stalemate forever," he observed.

"No. One of us has to strike, or back down."

"I will never back down from you, Mina. You don't want me to do that." And to prove it, he moved forward again. If he reached out, he could touch the floating edge of her cloak. "There is another option. Why don't we call a truce and talk about this instead? I promise I won't try to seal the doorway until we've discussed it. If that's what I decide I must do, I'll give you time to get in a position to defend it. Then we can do our best to kill each other. Sound civilized enough?"

"Like gunfighters. Ten paces and all that." She studied him a long moment. "All right. Promise me."

"I did. If I say it, it's a promise."

"Most of your kind don't consider a promise to me worth anything."

David didn't like the implication of that, but that wasn't his problem at the moment. "A promise is a reflection on the one giving the promise, not the one accepting it. If I make a promise, I keep it."

"No matter to whom—or what—it's made." The red lights in her eyes flickered, disconcertingly, as if the monster behind them was assessing his answer.

"I'm making a promise to you." He closed that last space, touched her chin with his fingers. She pressed her lips together.

"Will you remove your daggers?"

"No, I won't lay aside the best weapons I have to protect you. Plus, you just threatened to kill me, and you haven't promised me anything."

"You don't trust me. You think I'm a liar." When her slim jaw flexed, he saw a glimpse of the unscarred part of her face.

"I know you're a liar," he said gently. "But I'm learning when to trust you. Where's the chocolate?"

She lowered her gaze in quick, mistrustful darts, then allowed herself a more thorough search of her robe when David kept his stance relaxed. "So, there've been angels who guarded you, that acted like those mermaids?"

She lifted a shoulder. "It wasn't Marcellus. He and his two pretended like they were guarding something inanimate, so they wouldn't have to talk to me. That suited me fine, except when they tried to order me about.

"Before that, a couple of them passed the time by speculating on names to call me, throwing pebbles and other trash to disturb whatever I was doing. They were bored, and of course they considered guarding me a waste of time." She freed one of the blue foil squares and stared at it, holding it loosely closed in her hand so it wouldn't float away in the water. "On that at least, we were in complete agreement."

"Is that why you turned Marcellus's wing into a bat's?"

"He was pompous, overbearing and he bored *me*." When she looked up this time, he was relieved to see the red hue that had flared in her blue eye was toned down, all but gone. "I figured if I goaded him enough, he would try to kill me. I could prove I could handle myself against him and wouldn't need any of you. He didn't try, though he looked angry enough to do so."

"Marcellus is honorable. Plus, he never would have defied Jonah that way."

"You answer to each other. You look at the world differently when you answer to no one." She took one square to her mouth. Made a face. "This is metal."

"A wrapper. A covering like the orange," he agreed. "Only man-made, and easier to remove." When he started to help her, she shrank back, did it herself despite some obvious trouble freeing the wet, closely wrapped foil from the candy. He had to command himself to patience. Rolling the foil in a ball, she tucked it back into the recesses of her cloak.

"Who were the two who threw things at you?"

"It doesn't matter. They're two of the four who died. They might not have died, but they didn't trust me behind them. They divided their attention."

"They were probably just making sure a Dark One didn't come up beneath you, or from overhead."

"No. They felt like what they were fighting was no different from what they were guarding." Raising the now naked square to her mouth, she bit. Blinked. Took another bite, slower this time. Then she appeared to roll it around in her mouth until it melted. "Wow," she said, matter-of-factly, David would have smiled, except her previous comment didn't make him want to smile at all.

"They shouldn't have picked on you like that, Mina. But they took their assignment seriously. They died for you."

"No. Angels fight Dark Ones. I was irrelevant, except that I was the unknown variable that split their attention and got them killed. *Sshh*. Don't talk during this." Rummaging for the other three pieces, she backed up to a rock and anchored herself with her tentacles to continue her consumption.

She had moved to the right of the defile. Her body language might not be as defensive, but she still didn't trust him enough to let him between her and her portal.

David waited, trying not to let the distracting vibrations coming down that tunnel cloud his thinking. Much as he didn't want to admit it, she was right. Because of the purity of their blood, angels were compelled to eradicate Dark Ones, unable to tolerate their unnatural presence.

Mina had enough of her mother in her that she didn't send that meter immediately into the point of no return, but enough of her sire that most angels were ready to write her off. Just now, when she'd stood before that corridor, her cloak floating around her, her eyes flat, purposeful, he'd seen what it was they all saw in her. In fact, if he'd been Jonah or Marcellus, he'd have seen enough to seal her Fate.

But there was more to her. It was impossible for him not to see it as she curled up on the rock, savoring chocolate as human females had since the cocoa bean was discovered.

She was alone. No expectations about her life except what she herself or circumstances of survival imposed. Friends, family, a larger purpose—those were the factors that gave a life a path, an arrow, when choices arose. What if a life had no compass? What did one become if there was nothing and no one guiding her, except the insidious whisper of a doorway?

She insisted on keeping it open, but she continued to resist. Could she want to keep it open, at least partly, for that specific reason? Perhaps the only true meaning to Mina's life was saying no to that which most wanted her to say yes. For if she said yes, the tide of evil would take her, swallow her, and that would be the end of any sense of individual existence she'd ever had.

She was holding the last bite in her hand, and abruptly she looked up at him. "Did you want it?"

"Yes. But no." He couldn't smile. She wasn't generous. Did she force herself to offer that last bite, the one she would want most of all, because she viewed any temptation as an enemy?

At her curious expression, he summoned a shrug. "Angels don't eat, not in this sense. We consume a bread, what the human texts call *manna*. It comes from the Lady and nourishes us. Nothing else has taste for us, though older angels have some ability to experience it. But I used to like chocolate."

"Like. Not love." She put the last piece away, an obvious effort, and leveled that penetrating stare on him. "What was your favorite food?"

"I was fourteen. Just about anything that moved. Pizza was good. Chocolate chip cookies right out of the oven, those were the best." He stopped there. "I didn't have wings, though. Or really cool daggers."

When she cocked her head, he raised a brow. "What?"

"The way you said that. You sounded . . . like a fourteen-year-old. You meant to do that."

He gave a half smile. "I thought it might amuse you."

"Or yourself, so it wouldn't make you sad. Did you want to be an angel?"

"It's not like that. I am an angel." Pushing aside her intuition, which stirred up shadows too close to what the doorway had violated him to find, he searched for an explanation. "It doesn't really matter what you were at another time. It's there, just waiting. The first time I opened my eyes, felt the wings, felt it inside me, I knew. There were other things I had to work through, but I never had to work through that."

She shifted her tentacles on the rock, adjusting her hold there. "That's what I wonder about the doorway," she said, glancing at the dark opening. "If stepping through it would be like that.

This feeling, all of a sudden, of being exactly what I was supposed to be."

"No." David glided closer, slowly. He didn't want to spook her, but she was too close to that damn door. He wanted to be within pouncing distance.

She tilted her head, met his gaze. "Every day I don't give in to it is another day that I have chosen my own path," she said, confirming part of his theory. "But each day, it gets harder. Everyone wants me to be evil, so they don't have to deal with me anymore." Her expression became more resolute. "You can't take this door from me."

"So that when it gets to be too much, it will be easier for you to join them?"

"So that when the angels or the merpeople or whoever decides my existence will no longer be tolerated, I have another option." She lifted her chin. "It's been here, every day of my life. And every day I deny it. Even though it promises me a place where I'll be accepted. That's a lie," she murmured, before he could say it. "But it's a manageable option. And it's a nice lie—probably one of the nicest I've ever been told."

She studied him with that odd look she had, as if staring at things far beyond him. "When I was an infant, my mother had to keep me near it. Though it's sealed so they can't come through, I had to have the energy, or I would start screaming, try to hurt myself. It balanced the Dark One part of me until I got older and was able to do it myself. So, in essence"—she gestured—"you're sitting in my nursery. My mother made the first set of sea glass chimes for me, that blue and brown one. I made the others, hanging them in her chamber until she died of the illness the Dark Ones gave her, some type of wasting disease that eventually claimed her when I was seven."

"It doesn't mean you belong there, Mina."

She considered him, lingering on his wings. "What if you had opened your eyes, felt that sense of utter rightness about being an angel, but then you told yourself that wasn't what was written in the stars, or even if it was, you were going to defy it? Every day, even as it called to you until you thought you'd go mad."

"It's different."

"Is it? Then why can't I bear the touch of anything too good, David?" Crossing her arms, she floated away from the rock so they were almost eye to eye. "Why can't I bear anything but darkness and shadows? Why was I nursed on a doorway to chaos and evil I refuse to close? Why shouldn't I step through that doorway? What's stopping me? Why can't I just accept that I'm evil, the way you accept you're an angel, and let the world keep turning the way it's meant to turn?"

"Because I won't let you." David closed the gap between them now. She didn't stop him this time, just kept her eyes fastened on his as he pushed her cowl off her skull, revealing both sides of her, the frame of silk hair for it all. As he did it, he managed to move them farther away from the defile, easing some of the tension in his chest. He'd sensed the rising storm in her eyes, her voice, so he was surprised she didn't resist, but the energy running over her skin was not the energy of the Dark Ones. It was the witch. He could tell the difference and felt a fierce triumph in the knowledge. When his fingers closed on her, she swallowed, but didn't break his gaze.

"I forbid it," he said, low. "It *is* different, Mina. I've had the blood of Dark Ones on my blade, seen what's in their eyes, what drives them. Pure madness and evil. Whether some insane god or goddess created them, cruelly creating a race with no soul, no hope, no ability to laugh or love, it doesn't matter. You don't belong with them."

"I don't love anyone. I don't laugh. I don't hope for anything, and you're the only one who imagines I might have a soul." She lifted her hands, closed them over his wrists. "And no one forbids me to do anything."

"Want to bet? We've gone through this once. Don't keep testing me. You're a good fighter. But I'm faster, stronger, and I can stop you."

He should have anticipated it, but he'd been anticipating her retort with words, not action. Her ability to use magic without any verbal or energy warning was phenomenal, for the propulsion spell knocked him back and put her an unexpected length ahead of him before he spun to go after her.

He refused to think of what would happen if she reached that debilitating chamber. He didn't have to. He'd follow her through the portal itself, damn it all, where he was sure he'd die in some Dark One world. With her standing over him, that dispassionate look on her face that could tear his heart to shreds even faster than the crushing weight of all that evil.

Thanks to angels' faster-than-light speed, he reached the tunnel entrance first, hitting the outside with his shoulder hard enough to crack rock. As he snagged her cloak, she turned on him with a snarl and a swing of the pipe he recognized too well from their first encounter. In addition to the Inert spell he was too proud to execute, he needed to keep her naked all the time. She apparently carried the whole world under that hideous garment.

Knocking the pipe from her hand with a sweep of his arm, he followed up with a yank that twisted her around. Ducking under him, she forced him to release her or break her arm. When he got a new grip on her, he followed her in the spin, jamming both of them up against the sharp rock beside the tunnel entrance. She cried out, but managed to latch on to an outcropping of rock on either side of the opening as if she could shove herself into the corridor by the strength of her upper body alone.

Enough of this. Locking an arm around her waist, David yanked her back against him, both his wings stretched out to either side to hold them in stasis. For all she was skin and bones, she had a round, tight little backside that slammed into his groin and turned his thoughts decidedly elsewhere as she struggled.

Though angels were pretty carnal, they had unflappable concentration during a fight, which told him his reaction was part of the fight, the weapon he needed to win it.

No one forbids me to do anything.

If he was going to influence her, she expected him to prove he could do it. But he was going to do it with something other than violence, something that proved he could overpower her without pain and fear.

He activated the Inert spell at last, so when she tried to break his grip with magic, it bounced off him harmlessly. Then she went for a fierce hand-to-hand struggle, but she couldn't turn around. Wrapping her tentacles around his legs, she attempted to yank him away from her, but he'd fixed himself to this point in space, forming an immovable wall of air and water at his back. She wouldn't let go of the two sides of the entrance, still trying to pull herself forward. Her hands were not that strong. He could have ripped her away from it, but he didn't want her injuring her broken finger further. So he made the decision to stay where they were, the dull, sinister vibrations humming in front, even as her body stayed flush against him, her heart pounding frantically, a trapped moth.

"Let go," she snarled. Whipping her tentacles from his legs, she thrust them forward, using her more powerful appendages to try to pull herself out of his grip so she could go to that chamber where she'd feed off energy that would whisper to her that she belonged to them. She was theirs.

The nicest lie I've ever heard . . . To hell with that.

Holding her fast about the waist, David shifted his weight, so she could feel his cock, which had gotten conveniently erect from her squirming. She froze, even as her undamaged fingers curled a little farther into the rock. Her head tilted, capturing him in the corner of her blue eye.

"Got your attention?" he muttered. At the same time, he used the other hand to trace the curve of her undamaged breast, tease himself with the weight of it.

"You belong to *me*," he said quietly in her ear, following his gut. He knew he might be going down the wrong path, because this was more than what his instinct was telling him to say. It was what he wanted to say himself, crazy as it sounded, primarily because it didn't sound crazy at all. "You're mine, not theirs. And if we have to fight about that every day for the next thousand years, I'm ready to do it. Especially if it gets me hot and hard like this."

Putting his lips closer to her ear so that he could taste the tender skin beneath, he felt her nipple harden against his palm, making his cock respond with increased insistence against her ass. "Are you ready to fight the way I can fight, sweet witch?"

Her fingers convulsed on the rock. He expected it to crumble as a hard shiver ran through her body. "You have different methods from"—she sucked in a breath as he used his fingers—"Marcellus."

"Sure as hell hope so." Because she wouldn't let go of the rock, it was easy to untie and pull the cloak free, with an abrupt, decisive jerk that left nothing but her bare skin pressed back against his chest.

Pushing her hair forward on her neck, he studied the almost perfectly straight dividing line that left a minefield on one side, pure, creamy silk on the other. He put his lips on that demarcation at the top of her spine, the nape of her neck.

It was that delicate, vulnerable point that gentled his touch.

"If I wasn't so determined to have you right now," he murmured, "I'd find you a beach, where the sun is so warm on the sand it would banish any cold in your bones. I'd lay you on it, just like this, spread you open to take me inside you."

She shuddered again. He could transport her to such a place in a blink, but the first time he took her needed to be here, on this threshold. He had to win this battle, in order to win the others that would inevitably come.

Her left tentacle slowly let go of the tunnel lip, came back and wound around his leg, all the way to his upper thigh. The tip, the soft, brushlike feelers, caressed the base of his testicles beneath the battle kilt, making him suppress a growl of response with effort. She could still set off another wrestling match, but her shift of focus seemed genuine. A tentative victory. He set himself to making it decisive, in more ways than one.

He was bruised, aching, and had never been harder in his life.

Putting his hands over hers on the rock, he closed them over her wrists. A controlled, downward glide using his wings and the sensual weight of the water molded him against her back in a slow friction until he could caress her spinal column with his lips. He kept going, all the way down to the small of her back. Then back up, his legs tangled with her tentacles so his cock found the open channel between them. With one tentacle anchored around his leg and the other wrapped around a spear of rock, she was spread, ironically vulnerable. Trembling. Her fingers straightened, releasing the rock at last, her signal of surrender both inflaming him and giving his heart a hard lurch. When his mouth reached her nape, the broad head of his cock was stretching her tender mouth below.

"Mina." He laid his jaw against her temple now. One hand released her to follow the bones of her rib cage and the jut of her hips, a disconcerting thinness. Then up again to her breast, the aroused nipple. She jerked against him when he pinched it between his knuckles, feeling a dark satisfaction as it made her undulate against him again, even though the press of her buttocks broke his control.

As he moved to caress the other side in the same way, the scarred side, she stiffened. He didn't hesitate, though, that tension becoming something else as he ran his fingers over the uneven flesh where the other breast would have been. She was still trembling. Harder than before, even.

"That's arousing, too, isn't it?" He whispered it. "As if the nerve endings that would have made the breast swell and lift into my hand, the nipple harden, just as the other one did, are still there. Are you wet for me, Mina? Is it just the ocean's fluid between those serpent legs, or is it your honey?"

She made a noise that he couldn't understand, not phonetically at least. Moving down the front of her body, over scar tissue, the few patches of soft, unblemished skin and the marked curve of her pubic mound, he found the lips of her sex. He slid over their satiny surface, where they were stretched by just the head of his cock. Like all mermaids, she had no body hair. "It's difficult to tell in the water, isn't it? I think I'll just have to feel inside, see if you're ready for me."

She arched against him with a harsh gasp that provoked something equally fierce in him, particularly when the other tentacle curled up his free leg, keeping him cinched in close behind her. He sensed she wasn't binding him to her as much as she was clinging, seeking an anchor. She didn't realize an anchor could drag you down and drown you in bliss. He wanted to show her that.

Ah, Goddess. Wet and warm as honey in truth when he worked his finger with careful tenderness between the wall of her sweet cunt and the insistent reminder of his cock poised at the opening. He wanted to bury his cock in it, feel the tight passage. When he traced the sleek tentacle, so like a woman's thigh, he kept his thumb resting on her clit so that she was shuddering as he began to ease into her from behind. He moved slowly, wanting to savor every single millimeter. The way she was making soft cries in her throat, how her tentacles constricted around him thigh to calf so that he felt the pain—it all made him harder. He tightened his buttocks, pushing deeper, looking for the heart of her.

Cupping her unmarked breast briefly, he kept his other hand moving up toward her throat, in a slow, inexorable movement that she followed with her body, arching up and begging for touch. Quelling the surge of violent lust it created, he kept going until he brushed his fingers along her throat to the tiny movement of her gills, trying to process her air as he did his best to make her gasp for it.

She was so tight below. Very tight. Virginally tight. From her body's inexperienced struggle between tension and desire, he realized suddenly he was the first. The only.

Then he was in, all the way to the hilt, his balls pressed up against the lips of her sex, her body shuddering. All his. He hadn't known what compelled him to say it before, but now he knew, for it was simple truth.

She *was* his. This complex being, torn between the forces of evil and the confusion of her own soul, was his.

Eight

MINA couldn't have sorted out her own thoughts if she'd tried. Poised in the tunnel entrance, she'd been pulled toward the Dark Ones' energy while David held her fast from behind, his cock deep inside her, filling her. Riding the two points, she'd discovered the closest thing to ecstasy she'd ever felt, both parts of her balanced perfectly, if only for that second. No fight to be had, no fear of too much goodness, too much evil. She was between the overpowering call of one, the irresistible demand of the other.

This act *was* the balancing act, the one that put them in sync, that took the mind out of the equation. She'd been afraid it would hurt, and it had, a little, but she knew pain could also provide pleasure. Her body wanted something, wanted to move against him to get it.

Beyond the need for balance, for the first time in her life, something empty in her seemed as if it was being given an offering to appease it. Something that wouldn't be a cruel trick or make the craving grow in an uncontrolled direction. This wasn't being out of control. This was giving him all of her wildness, trusting him to control it, channel it.

It was an odd jumble of thoughts as she sat on the fulcrum between the bloodlust of the Dark Ones and possession by an angel. When he put his mouth to her throat again, she let her head fall back against his shoulder, increased her hold on his long, muscular legs, teased the base of his taut buttocks, enjoyed every delectable inch of him against the back of her body. She liked what she felt beneath the delicate sensor system of her tentacles, his buttocks clenching and releasing in a slow, sensual rhythm that made her want to see it, maybe sink her teeth into that delectable haunch. And gods, the ridged head pushing in, the thick length of him dragging out . . .

"More," she gasped.

His wings cast a shadow forward as he granted her wish, body slowly descending, moving down, stroking her channel, then surging back in, wrenching a guttural sound from her throat.

"Like that, did you?" His voice was a wicked thought in her ear. "And this?"

He did it again. Then again. She started to move in rhythm with him, anticipating, arching, pushing forward, their bodies coming together and then apart, but only enough to increase the driving pressure of coming back in again. His fingers were back on her mound, sweeping against the furled bud of flesh over the wet opening, and she bucked against lightning bolts of sensation as he created magic in her body, holding her tighter.

"I can't . . ."

"You can. I've got you." His voice was firm, implacable.

"I'll lose myself."

"No. Goddess, no. Here." His hand found her breast, her chest, pressing against the scar tissue, the remnants of fear and pain now aroused by that warm, firm palm through which she could hear her heartbeat. "Right here, Mina. You're right here, in this moment, as real as you've ever been." His voice took on a husky undertone that was thrilling and frightening at once, for she'd never known an angel could bring such a sinful touch of sensation, more powerful than the call of any Dark One's power. "And I'm not giving you a choice."

His fingers took possession of her clit then. Where before he'd employed a teasing stroke, it was an inexorable manipulation now, a firm pinch under his hand as he rolled it, made it spasm as he combined it with the sudden hard, hot surge of his body into her, pounding, moving.

"Oh . . ." Mina didn't call upon any deity in moments of great emotion or pain. As far as she knew, none had ever claimed her as part of their flesh, one to whom wishes could be pleaded. So now she simply called out the one name that *had* responded. "David."

"Here. I'm here." His voice broke. His loss of control was another unexpected flood of pleasure that made her intuitively increase the grip of her tentacles, drive herself even deeper on him, relishing the raw, new sensitivity, wishing she could hold him inside forever, and then she wouldn't think at all. As her lips parted and she cried out, long and hard, one continuous flow of sound, the sensation was like that. Flowing light, a spell of never-ending fireworks that shattered around her, flashed through the water, made the Dark Ones' energy recede, made the water churn around them like the beginnings of a whirlpool as his wings spread out wide, holding their balance. His deep groan matched her cry and she jerked upon him wildly, milking every last essence of him. His seed, a part of him, inside of her. Her flesh quivered at that connection as much as at the cock filling her. It steadied her, possessed her in a way she'd never associated with the coupling act. But then, she'd never gotten intimate with an angel before. With anyone.

When she could think again, he was leaning against her, his arm wrapped tightly around her front, breath hard in her ear as his wings came forward, caressed her fingers on the rock. "Let go," he murmured.

Reluctantly, she loosened her grip. The wings moved back then forward, like watching an eagle in slow motion, graceful and powerful, taking them away from the doorway, turning them in a slow swirl. Turning her in his arms. They drifted down to a rock ledge and he lowered her to her back on it, keeping his arm around her so her skin was not scraped or abraded by the lack of smooth surface, even as he used his command of the elements to hold them there. Nevertheless, her hair drifted up in the flow of the water to brush across his chest, tangle with the secondary feathers. He was over her now, his body lightly upon her, such that she wished for the absence of the water, or that she had the courage to ask him to let her feel his full weight upon her. Instead, her hips arched up, seeking him. It seemed miraculous and natural for him to slide back in, even in his now semierect state. Biting her lip as his chest brushed her bare skin, she watched him adjust himself more deeply as he held her onto the rock, pinning and penetrating her in a way that should have felt like a trap, but didn't.

Darkness was moving restlessly within her, telling her this wouldn't last much longer. She hadn't expected it to, but she was amazed at the brief moment she had been given. Soon there would be an overpowering need to withdraw, to take time to analyze this closely, and what it meant.

Particularly when it compelled her to do odd things like reach up and touch his face, the clean line of bone, the soft but firm lips that made her hurt just to look at them, even as she was unable to pull her gaze away.

"Why did you do this?" she whispered. "Not for Jonah."

"No." Though his eyes stayed serious, the hint of a smile appeared there. "Definitely not for Jonah. I need you to trust me. You've submitted to me, enough to trust me for this moment. Trust me for the next moment. And maybe just the next one."

She swallowed. David saw her process his words, saw some of the wariness and that shield of thorns returning to her expression. He didn't want them to, but he knew she needed a short retreat. Perhaps he'd moved too soon, but wanting her had been too overwhelming. Seeing her poised in that door, where she might step through and become one of the Dark Ones on his blade, his battle instinct had surged up, telling him he would not tolerate that outcome. He'd grasped at physical arousal as the weapon to fight the battle, but that battle had become something far more than physical. In truth, it had shaken him enough to feel a need for a short respite as well.

"I wasn't really planning to go through," she said. "You just made me angry, ordering me about like that."

That was a lie and truth rolled together, he knew. Defiance may have motivated her, but he was learning the darkness in her could be goaded to take the reins. He also knew he needed to figure out the key to that, because while setting it off was all too easy, reining it back in was not.

If he could be sure this method would work every time, of course he'd gladly employ it as a technique. He suppressed a smile at the thought, knowing his prickly witch would likely not appreciate that observation. Then again, maybe she would. Now her attention was moving down his body, and she pushed at him, getting him to lift up. She constricted her tentacles, however, telling him she didn't want him to withdraw. It amused and aroused him at once when he realized her intent was to study with academic interest the way their bodies looked joined together.

"Mina—" Then the darkness swept through him.

Mina only had time for a startled flutter of water through her gills, the equivalent of a gasp, before he had her up and behind him, backed up to the wall, the water swirling around them at the speed of his movements. The dagger blades flashed as he twirled them dexterously out into the palms which had held her a blink before.

Her scent was on his fingers, she thought, her mind still clouded by their coupling. Even as blood splashed over those lethal blades, it would be there, beneath it all.

"Is there any other exit from this cave you can take?" His voice was sharp, as if he'd repeated himself.

"Yes. Down that tunnel there." She nodded at the wall between the library and storage chamber. "It's spelled to hide a narrow tunnel. It descends about a league and then comes out in the lower level of the Abyss. We'll use it if we need it."

"*We're* not using it. Go ahead of me. I'll catch up."

She pressed her lips together. "It will be a tight fit for your wings. I wouldn't want you to get your feathers mussed, if we can help it."

"Mina." He shot her a warning glance. "Go down that tunnel, now. I'm ordering you to leave."

Stepping from behind his shoulder, she took a stance beside him and recovered her cloak. As she settled it back over her shoulders, the ends fluttered down to shadow her body once again while she worked the front ties. "This is my home. They have no right to be here." Her gaze turned toward the mouth of the cavern, where both of their unique senses were tuned to detect the threat coming. "And we're out of time to argue."

The Dark Ones had approached the entrance tunnel cautiously, but once they'd come into it, their progress became much swifter. She could feel their proximity, gauge it exactly, as could David.

He gave her one last snarl and then surged forward through the water as if it didn't exist, meeting the Dark Ones at the cavern opening rather than giving them a chance to get through and have a wider area for maneuvering room. There were three of them, but they obviously hadn't expected to find him here.

Mina cursed at his maneuver, which put him squarely between her and the invaders, denying her a clear path for spell work. *Fine, then. Noble idiot.*

Recovering her pipe and one of the knives she used for cutting work, she floated, watching for an opening. One thing she could do now, however. She sent a blast of energy through the water, creating a violent swell, a crushing wave of surf. While it smacked into the tunnel opening, disorienting their foes, David was unaffected, riding it as if he'd spent his life in the California waves. She knew what that looked like, for she'd drawn close enough to beaches to watch surfers, nothing but the top part of her head visible.

This was not the Dark Ones' favorite element, whereas angels were comfortably in command of all of them. So he took first blood, slicing the blade hard and deep across one opponent's chest cavity, following through with a straight punch into the throat. The Dark One fell back, its shrieks throttled with its own blood.

Those shrieks resonated inside of her, making her flinch, but she shoved it aside, focused on David. Gods, but he was a graceful fighter, purely savage and intent, and she couldn't help but think of how he'd held her against the door the same way. Sliding into her, piercing her as cleanly as that blade.

But she couldn't afford to get distracted. He wasn't used to fighting Dark Ones in water, was used to their blood splashing to earth, not floating out in malevolent clouds. Just like touching their skin, prolonged contact with their blood could drag down the speed of his movements, eat at his flesh. The flash of red flame shimmered through the water, illuminating the combat as she incinerated the insidious fluid before it could reach him.

A clear note, resounding like a bell tone, came from David's throat. Mina saw him draw a new blade. As he threw it after the backpedaling Dark One, it shot straight through the water as if fired from a mermaid's slingshot, only much faster. While he didn't look to see if it reached its target, Mina did. The knife lodged in the Dark One's throat and—she blinked, not sure if she'd seen what she'd just witnessed—went all the way through, tearing open the flesh and permanently disabling the creature before the weapon came out the other side, flipped, and spiraled through the water back to its owner in a shower of sparks.

David caught the knife as he ducked under the second one's assault, dealing the third a sharp smack with a powerful wing as he jabbed upward with another blade. Piercing the tough muscle of the Dark One's abdomen, he ripped the blade back out before his flesh could be defiled by the poisoned blood or skin. He'd apparently noticed her assistance, for he concentrated on the hand-to-hand work. His attention didn't even flicker as she illuminated the water around him to dispose of the toxic fluid. Reminded of how Marcellus's men didn't trust her at their backs, Mina felt a lurch in her chest at David's implicit trust.

The Dark One dove at him again and he rolled back, the water sending streams of bubbles off his pumping wings like strings of gleaming pearls. David kicked upward, went over the head of his foe and followed through with a cut across the spine that handicapped it for the key moment. Charging the blade, he shoved it back in, incinerating the body and sending it tumbling, a ball of fire despite the water, back out the tunnel the way it came.

At a hiss, David whirled to face his remaining opponent. Or so he'd thought. An additional Dark One came out of the tunnel as well, Hades curse it. Hopefully, it was the last. He knew the injured creature would be even more deadly and mindless in its bloodlust, but the new one was eager. It shot forward with a shrill scream and then was forced to choke on it as a black tentacle whipped around its throat and yanked it back and down, below David's line of sight.

The injured one leaped forward in his place, but David was already in motion, ramming with his full body. His fear for Mina took away anything but the need to finish this. Jamming his blade in almost to his wrist, he intoned the proper note. Angel fire seared over his skin as the black blood took on life, trying to claw at him and seek entry. Then the Dark One screamed, a banshee shriek into his face, and exploded at close range, so that David ducked his head, closing his eyes as the fire encapsulated him and then fell away.

Spinning, he found Mina and the remaining Dark One circling each other below, the water churning like Charybdis. His witch had blood on her face, but the Dark One was panting, its fangs visible. It was saying something to her, but David didn't catch the malevolent words before Mina struck again.

It was a paralysis spell, and the effort of holding it on the Dark One apparently cost her, because her face went rigid with the strain. However, she floated forward, one foot, two feet, while it tried to get away. Its shrieks intensified the closer she came.

David's first instinct was to drop and finish the creature before she got anywhere near it, but he experienced a peculiar immobility himself, watching her face. She showed no fear. None. Though his own natural revulsion to their evil was great, he preferred his kills clean, quick, with minimal suffering. So in a way it seemed almost pitiable, how the creature screamed and struggled while she moved toward it, steady, no hurry. The inexorable purpose mapped on her face was so clear he could almost hear her saying it.

You are about to die, and it means nothing to me.

Stopping before it, she stared into its eyes. No words, just that stare, as it hissed and made its shrill whimpers. Then she placed her hand on its forehead and spoke two sharp words.

The flash blinded him, but the smell of burning flesh reached his nostrils, one last, horrendous shriek reverberating in his ears. When he could see again, the water was swirling with ash and Mina was sitting on the rock, her hands folded into her cloak, tentacles wrapped around the stone, looking like a disconcerting cross between the statue of Buddha and the many-limbed Kali. Her hair floated down around her shoulders, shifting like graceful sea fronds as she looked up at him.

David dropped down until he was in front of the rock. She studied him in the same dispassionate way she'd just dispatched the Dark One, but if he still felt the reverberations of the sudden battle thrumming through his nerves, he suspected she did, too.

"All right?"

She blinked. "As beautiful as ever."

David ignored the caustic tone. "What did it say to you, right before you killed it?"

"The usual name-calling."

"You're lying."

"Yes, I am." While her face quickly shifted back to dispassion, he saw the weariness.

"You're tired."

"I'll manage." She looked around the cavern, the remnants of Dark One ash still floating about like lost plankton. He noticed none of it approached her protected books, veering off as if directed away by current.

"I'm sorry your home was invaded like this."

"I hate this place. I've always hated it. But all the answers about who I have to be are here. It protects and destroys me at once. Does that make sense?"

While he wasn't sure of her motive in sharing such a remarkable insight, David settled down next to her and considered their surroundings. Though they should get moving, he couldn't do it yet, watching her pale face, her bicolored eyes staring at the items representing her life. He also admitted he needed a mental breath to deal with how effectively she'd just handled herself. "Yeah. I understand that. It's part of who you are, and you have to accept that to be more. But in some ways, it also tries its best to make you less."

Mina turned her head then, looking at him. He thought he saw surprise that he understood. Giving her a sidelong glance, he offered her what he couldn't deny she'd earned. "You fight well. I knew that from the first time we met, but you can hold your own against Dark Ones. I apologize for doubting your skill."

"So you'll go now?"

He wished he could tell if there was regret in the flat tone, and then chided himself for acting like a lovesick teenager. "No. I said you can hold your own. You couldn't have taken all four of them." When she started to open her mouth, he turned, just put his over hers to silence whatever sharp thing was going to come out of it next. He wasn't surprised when she bit him, but he put a hand on the back of her neck, held her firmly to deepen the kiss, letting her taste the blood she drew, even as he teased her so that one hand fastened itself to the strap of the weapons harness across his chest, her fingers caressing his skin.

It brought back all the things they'd been doing just before the Dark Ones arrived, but it didn't dispel the upper concern in his mind. When he drew back, he had a cut lip. The blue and red mix of his blood, a small stream of it, wafted away in the water, seeming to distract her, but he flexed his hand on her neck. "You couldn't have held your own against all four of them. Admit it."

Mina shifted her grip, and had the dagger out and beneath his throat. "What do you thi—"

He knocked it from her hand in a movement so swift, Mina didn't see it, but he still captured the blade in its flip through the water, bringing it back so the tip was pressed to the left of her sternum. A tiny prick, one that drew blood.

He was apparently tired of her forgetting what he was. He *was* different with his human mannerisms, disarming in many ways. But it was an abrupt, oddly thrilling reminder that, just like any angel, he would only suffer so much defiance.

Staring into her face, the brown eyes dark as battle lust, he closed his fingers on the cloak's neckline. While he pulled it a mere inch to the side, the way he did it, as if daring her to stop him, felt like he'd ripped it away, baring the scarred area entirely. Bending his head so his chestnut hair wafted across her face, teasing her flesh, her throat and gills, he put his lips to those areas and tasted her. Rivulets of sensation shot through the other thin lines she'd inflicted on herself from his weapon.

She was glad for the reminder, for gods, she couldn't deny she hungered for this side of him. It was simple, violent, overwhelming her mind and will. The strength of the angel with the balancing darkness of the human—that made it all right to want him, for now. But even as she had the thought, she thought of the orange and chocolates and knew there was a larger part she was denying herself, a part she feared. For if she came too close, her Dark Blood would jealously destroy the carefully crafted part of herself that wasn't total darkness, sear that away and prove that darkness was her true soul.

But he was dangerous to her on other levels as well. Since she'd dedicated herself to study most of her life, she knew the puzzle of him was intriguing to her. As a human he'd dealt with something so hopeless he'd taken his life over it. Yet there was something so strong about him the Goddess had recognized his potential and made him an angel. He was light and dark, his power possessing a flip side, a vulnerability that would draw her ever closer as he used his own darkness to bind them together this way. Whether he realized it or not, it could give her the key to destroying him.

Pushing that away, she touched his hair as the thick strands drifted in the water and wound around her fingers. His lips at her breast went from hunger to worship, moving over to the mound of cratered flesh to kiss and tease her there when she laid her chin against his temple. Letting some of her weariness have her, she gave herself a quiet, stirring moment to just feel his movements, marvel at how it translated into her body's response.

"I don't know if I could have taken all four of them, any more than you know if you could have," she said at last, watching the way his wings held his balance to let him lave her body, the feather tips trembling in the water's movement, glowing white with the tips of light brown.

David lifted his head. "Mina, we surprised them. They didn't expect us to be here, and they were moving with purpose. They were headed for this chamber. That's the access to your portal."

"They don't know of it. This cave is warded."

"Those wards discourage earthly creatures from venturing in here. They're a disguise, not a weapon, right?"

She lifted a shoulder, refusing to answer, but he continued. "What if the Dark Ones *can* feel that portal if they get close enough? They've been trying to pin you down since the Canyon Battle. It's possible they did some reconnaissance on this cave and found it. These four might have been a contingent sent to try and use it as an escape route from the angels."

"I may have benign wards on the cave, but those are complicated protections over the portal itself. You just unraveled them because you're an angel, and the only magics that work on you are non-earth-based."

"Oh." He considered her. "So that's what it is. The spells you've used to blast me, they're using your Dark One blood?"

"Yes. But your Inert spell neutralizes even them. For now." Mina shot him a withering glance, which he returned with a challenging one of his own.

"But is it possible the Dark Ones could unravel those complex protections?"

"They have some high-level magic users," she admitted grudgingly. "But I would know if they'd done it, if anyone had passed through."

"So no one has. Yet. It needs to be shut down, Mina. Destroyed."

"No."

Sighing, David reached out and pried open the hand she'd balled into a fist. "At least, I need to let Jonah know about it."

"And once he finds out, he'll order you to destroy it, and you will." She moved back from him, her tentacles unfurling. "Don't be a coward about it. If you're going to just destroy it, try it, and let's be done with the fight. Don't put me off with an evasion about going to Jonah."

His jaw firmed, those brown eyes now snapping with temper. "Damn it, I'm trying to make you understand without using force. Mina, we can't—"

"This is my life, who I am. You can't just turn that upside down and change everything. What about free will? Aren't you all so devoted to that concept? Yet you'll just—"

"I'm not taking away your choices—"

"Just something that helps me make them, every day."

"Find something else that helps you. I can help you. Anna can help you."

She scoffed, sneering at him with an unattractive curl of her lip. "You say you want to understand me, but you don't. You just want to make me into something you can comprehend." She pointed toward the doorway with the three-fingered hand. "That's a part of who I am. Like your wings."

"And the items of dark magic down here. What are they?"

"Years of dedicated study and experimentation by me, my mother, and her mother, and so on." She shrugged. "I use what will work. Dark magic is a danger for humans who are taking steps too far from the light. I'm already part of the darkness, so it's rather pointless for the magic to try to corrupt me."

David frowned, but bit back his automatic protest. He *was* dealing with a creature with a different relationship to evil, and before he went with his instinctive desire to try to dissuade her, he would think it through.

"If I destroy the door, what will you do?"

"Fight you as the enemy you are."

He stared at her for a long moment. Her upturned face, thinly held lips. The intriguing map of depressions on her face, both the beautiful and destructive sides. The light flutter of her gills at her neck, as if she was holding her breath, stilling herself.

"Even after my body was in yours, my mouth on you, you would see me as an enemy," he said quietly. "You would fight me to the death."

"As you would kill me if I proved myself a Dark One in truth. I won't betray who I am for ten minutes of fleeting pleasure."

MINA saw the flicker of hurt. Maybe she would have missed it, for he was good at not showing his feelings, but she'd spent her life studying and paying attention to the details. Setting her jaw, she willed herself not to react to that, though gods, it was getting difficult. His human qualities could disturb her more than the angel ones.

"You don't know me," she said, the silence grating on her nerves. "You don't get inside of who I am just through my cu—"

"Don't." The word was sharp enough to stop her. Suddenly he was close enough for his hand to clamp on one wrist. "Don't do that."

"Let go of me, then."

David surprised her by complying, though she felt the loss of his touch. The water's coolness was settling into her bones, and the spell with the Dark One had taken strength from her. Magic in this world was barely a passing thought to her, but working against Dark Ones was draining, because there was a resistance to it, as if it tore pieces of herself away as she fought them. It was why preventing the archery attack on Anna had nearly killed her.

"All right," he said at last. "Here's what we're going to do. You make sure your wards are in place. I'm going to ask three of my platoon to guard the entrance to your cave. I'll tell them that I'm expecting Dark Ones to try and scope it periodically for your presence. I'll tell them not to go beyond the first cavern, where you met with Gerard."

"What if they don't listen?"

"They follow my direction."

"So they're better at that than you?"

"Don't push it," he warned. "In exchange, I want you to do something for me."

"Why should I?" she demanded.

"Christ, you're a pain in the ass," he said with an exasperated sigh. "Because all I have to do is communicate with Jonah, and that doorway is gone."

"So you're blackmailing me."

"I'm trying to negotiate a temporary solution we can both accept." He crossed his arms, hovered in front of her, giving her a raised brow.

"What is it you want me to do in return?"

"Wear pink, put ribbons in your hair and kiss puppies."

"I look horrid in pink, and I have no sense of humor," she said without missing a beat. "I've never met a puppy. What do you really want?"

David found he wanted to touch her then, but he didn't. Because she was right about what would happen if he told Jonah. He needed time for her to trust him, and the hourglass on that would run out if he followed that course.

"I want you to go to the Citadel with me."

Nine

HE anticipated she'd say no. Absolutely no, and by the way—hell, no. But he got her wary acceptance of an interim step. After they took care of dispatching the Dark One remains properly and posted the guard from his platoon, he would take her to the surface, though their agreed-upon destination was a tiny strip of sand under a night sky. A sandbar that existed when the ocean tide was lower. It was where they'd had their volatile first meeting.

So he'd sent the message about guarding her home to his three most trusted soldiers, via the mental communication angels used. They were only minutes away from the cave when he and Mina departed. While it still bothered him, he didn't feel he was sending his men in blind, for he'd communicated the strong possibility of Dark One attack on the cave holdings to keep them vigilant.

But not telling Jonah about an engineered doorway to the Dark Ones' world, hidden beneath the ocean's surface, was a different matter. He could delay on that only a day or two at most, and even that made him uneasy as hell. Hopefully he'd make adequate progress toward winning her trust by then, such that she'd react more calmly to the idea of telling the Prime Legion Commander. Maybe they'd even figure out an alternative to destroying the door. Though he doubted it, for his own gut said it needed to be done.

Well, he was an angel. He was professionally required to believe in miracles. And he hoped the Citadel would provide answers. He'd told her he needed to make a face-to-face report to his battalion captain, a daily requirement, and he refused to leave her unguarded. The latter was true.

Yeah. Lying. That's a great way to build trust.

It wasn't lying. He was putting off telling her the truth for the exact same reason he was delaying his report to Jonah. A strategy to gain more of her trust.

He winced, his mind invaded by a fleeting memory of his mother. *"David, I know you're only seven, but I'm going to teach you another word for a lie. Rationalization."* Her hands on his shoulders. *Soft, loving. Motherly.*

"David?"

They'd been swimming toward their destination. Or rather, she'd been swimming, and he'd been moving in the way angels traveled through water. He'd curtailed his speed for her, because of course the seawitch hadn't been willing to let him help her. Now she'd been dropping back. Reluctance, he'd assumed, so he'd kept a steady pace to keep urging her along, holding her in his peripheral vision. Now he turned to see her hovering. Well, sinking. The contours of the seafloor were rising like hills under a watery sky, signaling that they were drawing close to the spit of land.

"I want to stop a moment."

He pushed aside his own thoughts, not without relief, for they were going places he didn't want to visit. As he gave her a more thorough appraisal, he realized with shame her slowing pace wasn't due to orneriness.

She was capable, yes. A hell of a fighter. But while her magical skills were uncharted, her physical body had limitations, though she did a damn good job of covering them. She was just too damn proud to tell him what he could now see—she was worn-out.

"Here." Sliding an arm around her waist before she could attempt to slither away, he guided her hands to his neck. "Hang on and I'll take us the rest of the way. What do you say to a short flight?"

"I think I'm against it."

The first smile he'd had in the past couple of hours twitched at his mouth. He had to admit he was a little frayed at the edges himself. Up to his ass in Dark Ones, then an ethical dilemma that could impact his integrity with his Legion Commander, followed by a flashback to his mother. All that after he'd had one of the most powerful experiences he'd ever had with a female. Which she'd crossly told him meant nothing more than a ten-minute release of tension and bodily fluids. It had been a busy day.

He knew it meant more than that to Mina. It was part of her enigma, how she kept him at arm's length and yet he could feel a desperate need emanating from her to do just the opposite, an unstable and unseen force.

Focus on the primary objective, be ready for the unexpected and everything else would work out. It was a soldier's strategy he'd lived and followed, from the first moment Jonah put a weapon in his hand and pointed him toward a battlefield. He used it now. Protecting her was the most important thing. Caring for her. He viewed the two as one and the same, in a way her other guards hadn't. Guardian, not just guard.

Her arms tightened around him as his pace picked up, since he was no longer modulating it to hers. But he didn't go too fast as he ascended to the surface. While that was partly for her peace of mind, he rather enjoyed the lazy sensation of his wings moving like those of a bird, the wing strokes steady, gradual, using the water currents to adjust his upward movement. "The statue in your cave. With the dress and the wig. Will you tell me what that is?"

Mina turned her unsettling gaze to him. "It was the dress the seawitch Ceruleah wore when she visited Arianne on land, the day the prince said he would marry another. You're familiar with the tale?"

"Probably a couple different versions of it. I read it when I was human, but Anna told me the fairy tale wasn't accurate to the true story. Like it didn't mention that Arianne was turned to stone by the witch initially."

Mina nodded. "Arianne knew as soon as the prince wed she would die and become foam on the sea, just as my ancestor had promised. But then Ceruleah donned the beautiful sapphire dress and came to her at the palace." Mina dropped her head back, inadvertently laying it on his shoulder so she could study the changing patterns of the light above the water as they drew closer to the surface. David felt the ends of her hair whisper across his bare back. "She walked into the palace unimpeded, for no one had ever seen a woman so beautiful. She even crossed the path of the prince. When he could not take his eyes from her, she toyed with the idea of changing the direction of his heart to inflict more cruelty on Arianne, but that was not her purpose.

"Ceruleah brought Arianne an enchanted knife and told her if she would slay the prince with it, she would break the curse and allow Arianne to live her full three hundred years, like all mermaids. Arianne refused her. For as much as the prince had hurt her, repaid her sacrifice and devotion with pain, she loved him still. The witch was enraged. She told Arianne that love was an illusion and turned her to stone, so she would have neither the release of death nor the hope of an immortal soul. Just the interminable agony of staring at the palace, watching the prince live out his life with his princess and their children, generation after generation.

"Eventually, of course, Neptune forced my ancestor to release Arianne from the stone, though the statue remains."

As Mina spoke, David remembered the feel of the filmy material, the hair floating over his fingertips as Mina's was now. "Why did the witch despise Arianne so much?"

"Arianne had everyone's love." Mina shrugged. "She was a kindhearted princess, beautiful as well. Neptune's favorite. Yet for all the love she had, she wanted more—the prince's heart. Such greed offended my ancestor, who didn't have love—just envied beauty and feared power."

She looked toward David with her unsettling red eye and scars. "Can you imagine being given something everyone loathes you for having? They're willing to take it, borrow from it, reap the benefits, but they hate you for having it, wondering why they weren't the special one. But the ironic thing is, it was no different for Ceruleah. She hated Arianne because she hadn't been given what the princess had. It's a never-ending cycle. I understand why in the end they felt a connection to each other, even though it has always been a destructive one."

"Until you and Anna."

"Anna broke free of it, through luck and an angel's love." Her grip shifted to his nape after that remarkably matter-of-fact statement. The increasing light and lessening pressure indicated they were getting close to the surface.

David paused a moment, not wanting to break the thread yet, sensing he was getting close to something important. "So you don't share your ancestor's view, that love is an illusion?"

"If your beauty and power shine so brightly that no one can see through it, the love *is* an illusion. Because if love is offered, it's only offered to the beauty and power, never to the woman behind it. A sham of whatever true love is."

"But true love can see through anything."

Mina made a derisive face, a disturbing effect with the scarring. "Like any weapon, it's only as strong as the wielder. And no one was strong enough to prove otherwise to Ceruleah."

"The hair—"

"My mother's," she said shortly.

"Hmm." He resumed his ascent, thinking about the dress, the witch who wore it. Thinking about Mina painstakingly weaving her mother's hair into a wig so she could reach out and touch it. Having lost her at such a young age, had Mina ever pressed her face into the strands, imagining her mother leaning over her, letting her hair cover her daughter's face? His mother had done that. He remembered it from when he was perhaps four, or five, still in a small child's bed.

Jesus. Not going there. Fortunately, Mina's fingers, pressing urgently into the cords of muscle at the juncture between his neck and shoulder, distracted him.

"Go slow this time," she said. There was a tremor to her voice he could tell she tried to mask. His brow winged up.

"You really are afraid of heights. How can you have the ability to shapeshift to a dragon and—"

"Welcome to the irony of my life," she said stonily.

While he tried to keep to a steady, nonalarming pace, he did have to increase his speed to make a smoother transition from water to air. As he did, he realized she'd made her own transition. What was twined around his body now was a pair of slim legs. When he'd first taken her to the spit of land, he'd done it so quickly there was no time to switch to human form before he speared her tentacles. Then, after she was freed, unable to shift to legs because of the wounds, she'd had to drag herself down to the water. Maybe she was remembering that, wanting to be able to stand on her feet on the land and not be hampered, or forced to crawl before him as she had then.

"I'm sorry about that day," he said.

She rotated her head toward him, her movements jerky. The way someone moved who was trying to deal with being nervous by appearing calm, the result being a slightly more animated form of rigor mortis.

"Sshh . . . " He rubbed her back, his other arm tightening on her waist. "You're fine. I've got you."

"You dropped me that day," she reminded him.

"Yes, I did. But you'll remember I caught you before you hit the ground. In my defense, you were still fighting me, not a smart idea when someone's got you five hundred feet or so in the air."

"The island's over there," she said, worriedly.

"I know. I want to do something else first. Hey." He eased a hand under her hair to cup her cheek, force her to look away from the land. "It's all right. I'm not going to drop you, I swear. If I did, I could catch you."

"Unless you got a cramp or something, and couldn't go as

fast. Or maybe a stray missile shoots you out of the sky. Or a flock of birds gets between you and me."

"You are giving this way too much thought."

"We're still going higher. Why are we going higher? I want down."

"Can you let me try one thing first?"

Mina only had two alternatives. Stare directly into his face, confronting those vibrant and intent brown eyes, or look elsewhere, which would emphasize that they were not in the nice, solid net of her ocean.

"Aren't I a little exposed to Dark Ones here? Aren't you shirking your duty?"

"Mina."

"Fine. Do whatever it is and be done with it."

"Do you ever float on your back in the water and look up at the stars and moon?"

"Every once in a while. A long while."

"Okay, then. I need you to let go of me. I'll hold you, I promise. I just want to shift us."

Mina looked at him in alarm, her legs and arms automatically clamping, irrespective of the fact she had one injured hand.

"It's all right." He pried one hand off and brought it to his mouth, nuzzling her palm with his lips, stroking his thumb over it. "Trust me for just this moment. Just this one moment, remember?"

"I don't think I can let go."

"Okay. Let's do this, then." He shifted the daggers he wore from the front sheaths to the back, securing her with one arm throughout. Holding himself in the air during the process was effortless, and he was hoping she was noticing that, to help her confidence. Then he altered the angle of his wings so he was leaning back, back, taking her with him as he went to a horizontal position, floating. Instead of hanging in his arms, feeling like her life depended on how tightly she could cling, now she was lying on top of his body, her one arm still around his neck, the other still in his grasp, her fingers grazing his jaw. Her body was stretched full against his, breast to chest, hips nestled in the cradle of his, one leg still twined around him, only now her foot dangled over the bracing strength of his calf.

"How are you doing that? Birds can't do that."

"I'm not a bird. For angels, flying isn't entirely about aerodynamics."

Of course. Mina steadied herself with that thought, with any damn thing she could grasp. Angels weren't necessarily explained by the laws of science, any more than certain things about her were.

"Angels achieve lift not just based on their wings, but on their own powers," he explained further, as if reading her mind. "But the wings are vital to that lift. Controlling direction, hovering, things like that. And the repository of that lift magic is in the wings, which means if they're cut off, we don't have access to that power. Or if they're injured, it limits us. Now," he said, his tone lowering as he looked into her face, his lips so close, "turn over on your back. I've got you. Don't worry. Feel me under you. I'm not going anywhere."

"Why are you doing this?"

"You ask that a lot. Hasn't anyone ever just wanted to do something to make you happy?"

"If that was the case, you'd take me down to the land. Or back to the ocean."

"Mina." When he let go of her hand, he quelled her instant alarm by smoothing a thumb over her lips, slowly enough that he made them part and traced the wetness just within. Grudgingly, she found that was also an effective distraction.

"No," she said. "They haven't."

His eyes darkened. "Then let me be the first to do that as well."

Reminding her that he knew he'd been the first male inside her body. She could tell that knowledge pleased him deeply, in a way that made her swallow.

"Turn over for me," he urged. "No leap of faith. Just a turn."

Her limbs were quivering so much she couldn't stop them, but she made herself turn. It would be necessary to let go of him as she executed the maneuver, but she should have known he would make it easier. As she rocked to her side and thought she couldn't let go, not with all this sky around her, his hand closed on her upper arm, steadying her. Her fingers released, the cool air touching the nervous perspiration on her palms, and then he helped ease her to her back. Her bare feet pressed against his calves, her toes curled on his shin bones. When he wrapped his arm over her chest, she hooked her hands into reassuring hard sinew, taking care with her splinted finger. He overlaid her crossed arms with his other one, fitting his fingers in the available spaces between those of her uninjured hand. Her head was on his shoulder, temple rolling inward and braced against his jaw, which moved as he murmured to her.

"Now, imagine you're in the water, and you're floating, watching the moon and stars, the occasional comet. The lights of an airplane. Shooting stars. The breeze on your face. And the ocean is just rocking you to sleep. The wind is singing to you, touching your face . . ."

He was moving the same way, a slight, gentle rock. Only instead of floating in the ocean, where inattention could result in a slap of water in her face, it was like sailing across the sea in a small boat.

She knew they were far up in the night sky. Her stomach was a ball of tension, but he had caught her that day; she couldn't deny that. He would catch her if she fell. He'd promised, after all. She could say that promises meant nothing, based on their earlier discussion, but in all honesty, no one had ever promised her anything.

This was his element. His body rested as easily in the grip of the wind as if he lay in a mother's arms.

"What would the wind sing to me?" she ventured.

He began to hum. Mina had already seen how he employed music magic in his fighting, and Anna had told her he could play any instrument. She'd also said that while he had a passable voice, his true gift was in his fingers. Mina certainly couldn't argue with the latter, but she found herself entranced as he switched to words.

He sang a poignant ballad about a boy's soft pledge to never be a burden to his girl. Instead, he would make sweet love to her, creating a quiet, dark world where there was just the embrace, the promise. And when he sang a chord about how pretty his girl was, his pretty, pretty, pretty girl, his arms tightened around her further, his fingers tangling in her hair, lips brushing her temple.

With each chorus she relaxed a little more, though she kept her hands firmly on his arm. His body was solid and strong, their respective hollows and curves fitting well. The breeze moved through his still wings, which had slowly adjusted downward and curved up such that she could lift a damp palm and rest it on the edge of one—if she was that brave—like on the lip of a boat. With the wings positioned like that, she could only see up, not down. The wind made a soft whisper of sound behind his voice.

She wouldn't have believed it, but it was as if she were under the comforting weight of a blanket. She was charmed into a dreamlike lassitude. His voice was against her ear, the vibration of it in his chest, while his arms held her, warm, strong. With her hips nestled into the cradle of his, the sensual enticement of his cock fitted between her buttocks under the silken kilt, the strap of his belt pressed against her back. His wings were still wet from the ocean, droplets shimmering off the tips, making them look jeweled in the moonlight, bringing her the faint fragrance of salt and enhancing the sense that they were in the sea.

"What is that?" she asked sleepily.

"It's an old rock ballad. Rolling Stones. Pretty, pretty, pretty girl," he crooned, his lips pulling in a smile against her temple.

"You're still so human. You know that?"

"I'm here with you now. That's all there is."

Raising her five-fingered hand, his own came between the digits, splitting them open to run along the spaces in between. It made her think of him lying between her legs so she couldn't close herself off from him. He was doing the same thing here, in an inexorable manner that turned apprehension into an unsettled yearning.

Gently, he stretched her arm out to her side and up. Coaxing her to release her hold on his arm across her chest, he moved past her breast, over the aching nipple and the phantom one to lay his forearm across her stomach. His hand molded to her bare hip bone beneath her cloak, while her fingertips brushed his elbow.

She'd hardly steadied herself from that sensation before he had her other hand lying in the cup of the upper arch of his wing, her knuckles resting in soft feathers. He stroked her wrist with his thumb, while keeping it lightly manacled, a sense of support as well as a quiet command to remain there. Trusting him to hold her without her having to hold on to him.

"Oh," she breathed, as a thrum of sensations tingled and ran down the tender underside of her arm and through her chest, doing a liquid, warm slide to her belly, lying beneath his other arm.

"Look at the stars," he reminded her, a whisper against her ear.

Stars and a moon, so bright and heavy in its lopsided crescent state, like that feeling low in her stomach. When his hand on her hip moved, her nervous hand followed. His fingertips grazed her thigh, the sensation jolting her. For all that her cloak had always provided her a versatile disguise, she was learning it did little to prevent a determined angel from accessing her lower body.

When he traced the crease between thigh and sex, her legs trembled.

"Open for me, Mina," he said. Quiet. Not to be denied. "Spread your legs so they're over my calves. Feel the air on your skin."

"I don't want to fall."

His arm immediately returned to her waist, his other fingers tightening on the wrist he had resting in his wing's concave shape. "Do you think I'd let you fall? Look up. See the stars in the sky. Feel the air moving over us, a body beneath you. There's no fear of falling. I've got you."

She could definitely feel his body, one quite hard part of him. When at last she moved, which necessarily meant her buttocks clenched, he contracted against her. Curious, she shifted again, felt him push back from the shift into a single, dragging stroke.

"*Now*, Mina. Spread your legs for me."

Why that commanding tone could compel her in moments like this, when so often his authority tempted her to turn him into plankton, she didn't know. But gods, it did.

As she tentatively shifted one leg, he slid down her thigh to grip her just above the knee. He pulled it over his leg, easy and steady, so the ball of her foot brushed the outside of his calf.

"Now the other. That's a good girl." It rubbed her against his turgid cock further and she registered his stifled moan. Hundreds of feet in the air or not, she was getting a strong desire to keep rubbing, to see if she could make him groan like that again.

But he had his own plans. As he shifted, tilting, her heart stuttered up, making her clutch his arm again.

"*Sshh* . . ." he whispered. "You're okay. Can you put your arms up, around my neck? Trust me to hold on to you?"

Inching her uninjured hand up first because it was closest, she found the side of his throat, the line of his jaw. His arm low on her belly shifted carefully beneath the hold of her three-fingered hand. He had a marvelously strong forearm. Roped with muscle from his knife skill, she assumed, and she let the thought of that tangible strength bolster her. He was here, solid, real. He wouldn't let her fall. She couldn't believe in anything for long, but he'd said if she could, just for a moment . . .

He helped, guiding the other hand into that harrowing arc over her head. Her upper body lifted as if seeking his touch. His fingers whispered over the broken finger.

"I wish you'd let me heal at least that."

When she shook her head, he sighed, pressing a kiss to her temple, putting her hands around his neck.

The sky was vast, a jeweled dome around them, everything for her to fear far below. She'd never seen so many stars, and realized they must have ascended above the cloud cover, for her breath was short, as if the oxygen was thin. At least that was what she told herself. The immensity of it all was overpowering, and yet somehow reassuring.

As her fingers twined in his hair, warm at the nape of his neck, the cushion of wings brushed her wrist bones. His hands were under her cloak, stroking her skin, learning her.

His total attention absorbed her. She'd had adversaries, or those who'd mistrusted her—which was everyone, except the foolish Anna—who watched her every move. She had to gauge their every reaction as well, being just as wary. This was so different from that. Her body was resting fully in the cradle of his, and her focus was on what those clever fingers would do next. She didn't have to think, be defensive . . .

Just for this moment . . .

As he was discovering her response to each unique touch, so was she, for no one had touched her like this before.

His fingers moving up her thighs curled something in her stomach, and even in her chest, making her shudder, making her thighs tremble and the flesh between them swell. The rush of air over the sensitive and still deliciously sore opening told her those lips were wet, needing again.

His other hand slid down her rib cage, tracing the bones there, then explored her hip bone, across to her navel, a tender outline, a gentle probe.

"You're not ticklish."

"No. I don't . . . What's ticklish?"

She felt that smile again. "You answered the question, sweet witch."

"You didn't."

"I'm not telling you, because you'll figure out a way to use it against me." He moved up under her breast, his knuckle sliding along it as she gasped, for his lower fingers pressed over her clitoris and then down, seeking that wet heat.

A star shot across the sky, ending its life as others burned with fierce brilliance, not conserving their light or worried about their end. And why would they, when they could have that final blaze of glory across a deep, dark sky? Where did shooting stars go?

He was tracing the lips of her sex, and as her legs tightened, his muscles did the same, shifting her wider, driving her backside down more intimately against his cock.

"Be still, baby. Let me bring you pleasure. I want to hear you cry out."

She couldn't breathe. How could she possibly scream?

He cupped her breast in his palm, those sensitive pads of his fingers caressing the nipple so it hardened further. Without her volition, her body tried to shift, press into the contact, and he shifted with her automatically, keeping them level, though taking them into a curved turn where she saw a creamy expanse of clouds beneath them.

"Oh," she said faintly, but fear couldn't find a foothold when his fingers eased into her sex and his thumb began a slow massage of that incredibly sensitive oblong flesh just above the wet opening. He had increased his grip on her breast as he made the turn, and now he held the weight solidly in his hand, his thumb rasping over the nipple, his skin the perfect coarse texture to provide friction to the softer flesh.

"David."

"You have the most perfect ass," he mouthed in her ear, his cock pressing insistently against her such that she couldn't help but flex the muscles against him, for what he was doing with his fingers was making it impossible for her not to move. She gave in to the desire now, lifting up, rotating, trying to squeeze on him as she rubbed herself against him. The cloak worked up so now her bare body was stroking against him through the thin stuff of the half tunic. The cold metal of his belt pressed into her lower back, adding a sharp edge to her need.

"Goddess." His breath left him in another groan that gave her a primal surge of delight. Then he moved across her sternum, forearm high on her breast, enough pressure just above her nipple to make her ache, strain for touch, as he caressed the flesh where another might have been. Her flesh quickened beneath his magical touch. She'd been so surprised to have the aching desire to be touched there, caressed. But had he yet discovered a place where she *didn't?*

"*Oh.*" That building sensation again.

"You're getting close." His voice was harsh, almost guttural. "I want you to tell me when you think you're close, Mina. I want you to ask me before you go over. Let me prolong your pleasure."

Ask him . . . as in permission? Or was it a way to enhance this, as he said? Perhaps, for the idea of having to wait until he gave the word for it was daring, thrilling. She wouldn't mind feeling like this for eternity, mindlessly writhing on an angel's body up high in the firmament, his hands all over her, her arms linked around his neck, her legs spread open at his insistence.

The bar of steel in her back—not his belt—was a delicious pain, and said her compliance might be driving him as crazy as his dominance was driving her. She wasn't giving up anything; it was just temporary. Why did it feel so incredible, though? Dangerously . . . eternal.

"Oh . . ." A sharper cry tore from her throat this time as he changed his rhythm, worked her mons insistently, three fingers moving inside as well, the other hand clasping her chest. "I'm . . . David . . ."

"Are you close?"

"Yeesss." A long syllable, her body shuddering.

"Ask me, Mina. Make me harder; drive me fucking insane."

The words, dark and primal, so much of the flesh and things mortal, temporary, pushed her past question or rational thought.

"Please . . . let me go . . ."

"I'll let you come, sweet witch. I won't ever let you go. Come for me. Let me hear you."

She had a second to think—*but we're not joined; he can't get any release from this*—but then those wonderful, ruthless fingers shoved her over that edge and she was free-falling in a marvelous way. He made it more wondrous then, increasing the speed of their flight, soaring higher as she bucked against his body, her nails digging into his neck, her legs locked rigid around his legs as she spun through the air. He let her see the clouds and the sky, feel the glory of flying without the fear, and her scream became a cry of amazement as the stars and moon spun around her. It reminded her of her glass chimes moved by the water, dancing and singing around her.

His warm, solid body stayed along every inch of the back of hers, never altering, never making her feel abandoned or apprehensive. His powerful wings sent air currents over her face like the crashing delight of the surf. At last, at the most magnificent spasm, she had to close her eyes and let it shudder hard through her, bringing heat to parts that had always been cold, driving away pain with this rush of bittersweet, carnal pleasure.

When she could draw a steady breath again, her body was still jerking, small aftershocks that had her fingers and legs vibrating against her wishes. His hand left her with gratifying reluctance, but only to slide up her belly, so he could join the other hand in caressing the area of her breasts. Then he came out of the neckline of her cloak to find her hair. Twining it in his fingers, he tugged until she tilted her head and let out a soft, decidedly unlike-her whimper as he kissed her throat, teased her with a nip of teeth. Her lips needed the wet heat of his mouth. She needed too much.

As her body was settling, other things were surging up. The exhilarating flight through the air was about to turn and send her plummeting wildly to earth, spiraling back down into the blackness of her soul.

Please don't, she begged. *Let me have this . . .* Though she knew better than to entreat it. It was an enemy, and enemies mocked mercy.

"It's too much," she managed. "Gods, it's too much. I can't . . . I have to get down.

"David." It was an urgent cry. Since he'd turned the weaponry to lie along his back and hip for her comfort, she could feel the muscular expanse of stomach and chest beneath her, but now her fingers dug hard into his hip near the grip of the one weapon she could almost reach. Her clumsy seeking rucked up the edge of the short kilt so she found his bare thigh, the lower curve of buttock beneath her grasping fingers.

"It hurts, David." It was growing, a pain that seemed to be affecting her heart. Oddly, it hurt more than anything she'd ever felt, but a part of her wanted it to go on. She couldn't bear it. "Use it . . . please."

He'd told her she had to ask, and she mindlessly followed that compulsion now, just as she'd sought his permission to give herself release. There was no time or desire to make a token show of independence. Survival of this passing wave was more important. It was like the ferocity of the Dark Blood, the insidious call of it, but different as well.

As if he stood inside her mind and knew exactly what she needed, he pulled the blade. In a stomach-dropping move, he swiftly brought them upright so she faced the division of terra from firmament in a panoramic view, the stars and moon a cold glitter over thickly layered storm waves of clouds through which she could see the earth below. Still there, still turning. Waiting.

The blade slid across her lower abdomen, just above the pubic mound, making her shudder, clench at the sensual, possessive implication. But as she felt the blood slip down her thighs, join her own fluids, a powerful release on the scale of the climax rocked through her, balancing the worst of the overwhelming feeling, easing out of her with the life fluid. When she put her hand over the sharp blade, she wanted to grip it, cut deeply into her fingers. Even though just that bare contact caused a cut. His hand was inevitably there, taking hers, even as his arm locked strongly around her.

"No," he said, with finality. "Only by my hand, Mina. Remember. *Ssshhh.* Deep breath. Be easy. You'll be fine."

And she was. He'd done it at just the right moment, and everything was okay. Except now the weariness she'd experienced just before their flight crashed down on her, the adrenaline sliding away. She was tired and weak, with an abruptness that suggested he'd somehow suspended time for her, so she could experience this first.

"All right?" he asked quietly.

She groped for a meaningful response. "You're still—"

"Don't worry about me. The pleasure was in watching you. Feeling you. Goddess." He passed a hand over her hair, discomfiting her with that tender gesture more than he had with anything thus far, then pressed another soft kiss to her temple, her hair. Her lips trembled open, still wanting. She swallowed, made them press together again.

"I've exhausted you," he said. "Let's get you on the ground."

The descent was somewhat of a hazy blur, but then they reached that sandspit where their first meeting had occurred, a far more volatile but perhaps less powerful encounter than what had just happened in the sky.

"Tide," she said muzzily.

"Won't be up for a few hours. Sleep, baby. I'll watch over you."

"Sing that song again."

As he adjusted one wing beneath her and laid her down, David saw her eyes had already fallen closed. Though he knew she slept almost immediately, he hummed the Stones song, the one that spoke to him still, with its rough yearning. He used tones and vibrations to enhance his weaponry skills, a practical magic. But every mother who'd hummed a baby to sleep, or a man his lover, as he was doing now, knew music possessed magic just by being. One of the few true unifiers. Like love.

He drew a deep breath at that thought, let it out. How long had it been since he'd been needed? Meaning that he had something unique to give to one being, who might look to him specifically for it. How much longer had it been since he believed he had the ability to offer such a thing?

I won't fail you, Mina. Cradling her in his arms and wing, he traced the scars along her face as she slept, still with a frown on her face. "Even if it destroys me this time. I won't fail again."

She muttered with endearing crankiness and curled up on her

side to sleep, spooning back against him, gathering his arm into her body, holding it close. It tightened his heart, which confirmed the remarkable things he was thinking. Though he imagined her reaction to them would be nothing short of horror.

He watched over her for quite a while, the wind moving his feathers as he thought it all through. Then a smile curled his mouth. Extricating himself carefully, he rose and began to work.

Ten

MINA woke to see David at the water's edge, apparently enjoying the feel of the water rushing over his bare calves. Shifting to an upright position on the sand, she noticed she had some of his feathers sticking to her salt-spray-damp skin. Twisting, she discovered her sleep had been so deep, he'd been able to create her a shallow nest in the sand and line it with an extraordinary amount of his feathers to pillow her body, though his wings appeared as thickly layered as before she'd fallen into slumber.

Bringing her attention back to him, her heart caught in her throat unexpectedly. The rising sun was behind him, his wings spread to feel the full effect of that breeze, his hair fluttering back, teasing the bare skin of his broad shoulders. Gods, he was too beautiful. Angels were a source of fear and awe to all creatures who knew about them. But here was one who'd watched over her sleep with a quiet, oddly soothing presence. Sung to her. Kneaded her cramps, set her broken finger.

An angel who'd also taken her body and let her touch him. Who wanted her to touch *him*, though he'd given her a mind-shattering release and taken none for himself. The hard length of him was as vividly imprinted on her mind as it had been against her buttocks before he brought them down to the soft sand.

As he turned from the water, registering that she was conscious, her gaze coursed down the fine length of his body, clothed so briefly by that short half tunic. The weapons harness only accentuated the musculature of his back, the tempting lines of his waist and thigh.

She knew about basic anatomy and physical urges. Knew that many species of humanoid males woke from sleep in a naturally aroused state. She hadn't known it could happen to females, but as she stared at him, she knew what she wanted to do. Something that made saliva gather in her mouth and that inexplicable hunger stir in her belly.

She'd seen merwomen do it to mermen in the shadowy corners of reefs where they thought they were unobserved. She'd been intrigued by it but had not understood the compulsion, until now. Until David.

When he started up the sand toward her, she shifted onto her knees, watching his powerful grace. When he reached for her hands to help her up, she moved inside his grasp to lay her palms on his thighs. Far up his thighs.

David's jaw tightened in a manner that made her want to take a bite out of him, and her fingers curled in, gathering the hem of his tunic, her thumbs scraping his inner thigh, feeling the heat of him, even as she leaned forward and tasted the salt on his skin, just below the edge of the fabric.

"Mina."

Heat flared to life in his eyes as the near-violent reaction at his groin just above her head drew her gaze. She was darkly thrilled to discover it. When she breathed on him through the fabric, he caught her wrist in one hand, her hair in the other.

He wanted. Hungered for her. For her mouth. That could be simple lust, a man drawn by any female's stimulation. She had no experience and plenty of cynicism to relegate it to that. But she saw the struggle in his gaze between what he wanted and what he thought he could or should demand from her.

"Let me," she whispered, straining against his hold.

He closed his eyes, as if it was easier to speak without seeing her on her knees, her mouth so close to his eager cock. "I can't let you do this. I don't deserve this."

"What?" she asked. "This?"

Opening her mouth, she licked him, one firm, lingering stroke from the root to the head, even though she had to do it through the cloth.

"Holy Mother," he muttered. He caught both of her wrists then. "Mina, I need you to understand. You know that you don't . . . You don't owe me. No matter what you feel, or don't feel for me, I'll protect you. You understand?"

She hadn't asked for his damn protection, so why on earth would he feel she was paying for it in such a misguided way? Why couldn't she just want for the sake of wanting? Maybe he was trying to provoke her to anger, to drive her back. Maybe he thought that was the honorable thing to do. But the temptation at her lips, so close, the intriguing vibration of his powerful body as he restrained himself, meant that she was going to shatter his honor without remorse.

"I didn't ask for your protection," she said, resting her chin on his legs, rubbing her cheek over his groin, brushing his cock with her lips, taking a quick nip, liking the taste. "Don't need it. I think you're afraid."

Looking up into his eyes, she saw a deep shadow, something with the power to consume him, so much like her own it almost startled her. And yet her fingers inched higher. Intrigued, she held that dark gaze, pushing against his restraint. His grip was weakening. An all-powerful angel giving way before her insistence.

"I want to do this," she said. "I want you in my mouth. I didn't think about why, David. I just saw you standing there, and I could taste you, feel you, smell you. Don't deny me."

David swallowed as she leaned against his hold, her kittenish breath teasing his cock so that it was straining like a raging pit bull, wanting to take her down and devour her.

He ordered his brain to engage in something like coherent words rather than animal noises of approval. Jesus, he was a grown man, an angel. He had control with women, knew it was especially important with an inexperienced female. But then there was this position, her serving him on her knees. It shamed him that it could tear something loose in him like this. Something that made him want to grip her hair again, drive her down on him.

Easing his hold on her wrists, he muttered another oath. Mina nuzzled up the skirt, and his cock was there, free, hard, so erect the fabric bunched between his pubic area and the upright angle of it. She had to rise higher on her knees to reach the tip, and she did now, opening her mouth to envelope the ridged head.

Oh, gods. It was life itself, pulsing in her mouth. All the heat of the world, the rush of blood.

After having David stroking inside her, it wasn't hard to figure out that the same rhythm and heat might be the key to the pleasure of it. When his hand seized her hair, far less tentative now, an animallike noise coming from his lips, she went mindless with her victory. Sliding down on him, she took him as deep as she could, gripping the base. Squeezing, she explored the heavy weight of his testicles, the smooth flesh inside his hard thighs, the tender, protected skin at odds with the straining, bunched muscle.

Being here on her knees, tasting him, response gathered between her legs once more. A reaction that intensified when his hands took possession of her movements, came around to guide her in her grip upon him, showing her the way to best please him.

Gratitude wasn't causing her renewed wetness. It was that craving to be under his control again, serving his pleasure. Oh, gods, what *was* this? It was a compulsion spell without the spell, and her own body was roaring her capitulation. She knew so much about every dark corner of herself, it was a shock to find this whole area of intertwined light and dark unexplored.

The joining part of his testicles led to the tight crease of his buttocks, for he was deliciously clenched as he thrust harder into her mouth, stretching it. Like the cut of his knife, she gloried in the feel of it—discomfort mixed with pleasure.

She was whimpering in the back of her throat, she realized. Her eyes closed, tearing. His bare foot was next to her knee, the toes digging into the sand beneath it. Her lower back and hips were cramping, but she didn't care; she needed this first, needed to feel it.

But, suddenly, in a move too swift for her to counter or follow, he'd pulled her away and laid her down on the sand, putting himself between her legs. She had time for one swift, indrawn breath before his hands gripped her thighs, pulling them high on his hips so he could ram into her to the hilt, splitting her apart with his size and violence.

She cried out at the glory of it. He was a savage animal, his face intent, fierce, dangerous. When she reared up and bit him, he pinned her back to the ground with one hand on her throat, grasping her buttock in bruising fingers as he pumped into her, once, twice, three times. His seed flooded her, hot, scalding; she arched and moaned, shuddering with it. Not a climax, but a deep, gut-quivering sensation that went to the soul of who she was. He'd somehow found his way there, was inside her. Not breaking her apart, but taking ownership of her, from the inside out.

She wanted to find her cynicism, tell herself that she'd never had sex before, so this could be the hormonal tricks of the body, masquerading as magic. But she knew enough about magic to recognize it when it occurred, and she also knew all magic carried a price. Some types required high sacrifices from the soul of the giver. Those magics could dismantle the soul, and she'd no doubt this had the power to do that.

She also knew she'd gladly pay that price again and again, until there were no pieces of her soul left that didn't rest firmly in his grasp. So she'd obviously lost her mind. Her perspective. This apparently was what physical intimacy did to people.

He'd shifted and now lay beside her, scooting her with an amusingly male, short *umph* into the cradle of his body. As she rested her head on his arm, felt him getting his breath back and his hand on her hair, stroking, she looked absently toward the shoreline to make certain their island wasn't about to disappear under the rising tide, because surely she'd slept several hours.

He'd built a sandcastle. Complete with turrets embellished with pieces of straw and shells, even sea glass and shaped aluminum that had washed ashore with the tide cycle. As she propped herself on her elbows, she realized the low walls had been built in a large circle all the way around her, guarding her in a simple, charming way. Absorbed by her lust when she woke, she'd completely missed it. Rising to her feet, her heart thudding dully in her ears, her gaze strayed past the wall to clumps of slick brown sea vegetation he'd used to form words and shapes, outlining them with tiny shells.

He stood just behind her now, his wings at half-mast, shadowing them both. "I know it seems silly," he said as her silence drew out. "But I thought, neither of us really got to be teenagers. Why shouldn't we have the chance to express love the way kids do? Passionate, kind of silly. Kind of perfect."

When she continued to stare, his hands came down on her shoulders. She couldn't make her body move, could only stand there woodenly as he spoke. "You don't have to say anything. I don't expect anything from you, and it doesn't have to be anything complicated. I just wanted you to know."

I love Mina. That was what the words spelled. She'd taught herself enough about languages without the enchanted glass to know that. And the word *love* was depicted with a heart shape. She'd seen scratchings on rocks and shells, tossed into the ocean by romantic humans like wishes, so she knew that as well.

"Don't do this. You don't know me, David."

"Most people don't know much about someone when they fall in love." He was speaking carefully now, picking up on the tension mounting around her, she was sure. "And sometimes finding out can make that love end. But angels are different. We know—regardless of what we do or don't know about the object of our love—when we're in love."

He made her turn even though she didn't want to, the serious brown eyes, the sweet, sensual mouth tearing into her soul. "You love darkness, David," she accused. "An angel isn't supposed to love darkness. This is wrong." *So wrong.*

"I love you," he responded.

"We've barely met."

"I don't need time to understand this." She heard a hint of impatience in his tone, though she could sense his effort to keep his voice even. "I felt the bond with you the first time we met, months ago. And when I hold you, I don't feel any emptiness. I can't remember the last time I felt that way."

She'd never felt that way. Except when he'd held her. "So"— she broke from that intense eye contact, ostensibly to look back at the etching in the sand, but really to give her the courage to inject the necessary sarcasm into her voice—"I'm your first love."

"Yes." His voice was firm. Determined. "And my last. Angels only fall in love once, Mina. Most wait centuries for it. So I'm lucky."

Shock had her head whipping up, meeting his gaze again. "You're wrong. About all of it. There's no way this could—"

"I'm not wrong."

"You . . . I can't give you . . ." Breaking away, she backpedaled on unsteady feet, her body far more used to the movement of the ocean, and ended up stumbling into the sandcastle wall. She would have landed ignominiously on her backside, but of course he caught her. She flailed, struggling, and got away in another shower of sand, sending shells and straw pennants scattering. "See? I've ruined it. You're just making me confused, and I can't . . . David, I can't be anyone's eternal love. Is it eternal? Does it last forever?" She was panic-stricken at the thought, as if she'd given him an incurable disease. If she believed any of this at all.

"If I was an immortal being, given only one chance to fall in love, I'd hope that would be the case."

"I can't give you what you need for that. You *are* wrong. You have to be. *Look* at me."

A slight smile touched his lips, increasing her distress. Despite the curiously innocent way he'd chosen to tell her, she knew he understood his own mind quite well. He was an angel, after all. In contrast, she was falling out of the sky, this time with no possible safety net.

"I am looking at you. I have from the very beginning, and I've never stopped. And you give me what I need, just by existing."

Stepping over the wall, he followed her movements as she re-treated toward the water, but then flashed forward to grab her hand before she could reach the tide line. "Mina, stop. Listen to me. *Look* at me."

"I don't want to. You can't make me."

It was ridiculous, but her normal belligerence was the only weapon she had against this. He unmasked the desperation be-hind it with nothing more than a simple touch along her cheek with his clever fingers. She closed her eyes, still refusing. He didn't understand. If she looked at him, she would break. She wished she *had* done something terrible to him the very first time he'd come to her in the Graveyard. Something that would have made him agree with Marcellus and never seek her out again. He'd be safe, beautiful. Perfect forever.

"I demand nothing, Mina. I promise. Except that you let me keep you safe." When she opened despairing eyes, he cocked his head, regarded her with a gaze that had the ability to rip her into four pieces, like a medieval torturer. "And while you can't say it back to me, not with your mouth, I know you will one day, if Fate is kind. For now, I'll say it for you. Show it to you. Prove it to you."

"Can you . . ." It was cruel, but she'd never balked at being heartless before. Though could she be heartless, if it felt like something lethal was being driven into her heart? "Could you please get rid of it? The castle and the words?"

He pressed his lips together, but other than that, and an un-comfortable pause, his expression stayed patient, his tone even. "I won't undo what I've done. But if you have a good spell for a stiff breeze?"

Pulling her hand away, she stood apart and swept her arm across that area with violent purpose, summoning the magic needed. And as it came at her bidding, she had to watch it, direct the magic, while simultaneously trying *not* to watch the isolated sphere of wind dismantle the sand walls and towers, scatter the shells, pieces of sea glass and words, until only the impression of his painstaking work remained. She tried not to notice how still he stood, the weight of his eyes upon her as her wind blew pieces of it around his ankles, ruffled the feathers along his arms and the hair across his forehead.

"I'm not going to the Citadel," she said decisively when she was done. "You can't make me do that, either."

Eleven

A T his look, Mina's brows drew down. "Fine. Perhaps you can, but I'll make it decidedly unpleasant."

"If you didn't, I'd think you'd been possessed by someone else."

Even as he made the wry comment, eliciting her scowl, David was drawing a mental deep breath. He'd known she'd probably react this way. Hadn't he told himself that about fifty times while he'd done it? Maybe he *was* as young and impulsive as the other angels said. But he didn't regret it. And he wasn't going to let her reaction deter him. So for now, he'd let it go and focus on the more immediate issue.

He tried a different tack. "I thought you said angels didn't scare you."

"They don't." Her chin jerked up. "I just don't care to spend any time in their company. Your company," she added cuttingly. "I'll wait here. Or I'll go back to the Graveyard, wait for you there."

He shook his head. While he might be an incurable romantic, when it came to protecting her, he was not impulsive in the least. Now was not the time to advise her of part two of his plan, which meant they wouldn't be returning to the sea for a while. "I want you where I can protect you. Indulge me in my delusion," he added, before she could launch her litany about not needing anyone's protection. "There might be more oranges and chocolate in it."

As he watched the words sink in, the uncontrolled panic and frustration that had suffused her face for the past several moments was abruptly supplanted by a reassuring surge of female fury. *Good.*

"Have I given you the impression that I'm a child or a pet, David? That I can be bribed with *treats*? I should have turned you into a mollusk," she muttered.

"No," he said, now stepping forward. "I didn't think that. But you've had to rely on yourself so long you may not recognize when you could use an extra hand. You fight well, but we surprised them, and there were only four. I'm *asking* you," he said firmly, "to go with me to the Citadel. I just have to give a report to my captain. Please don't make it into a fight."

"David." She shifted her gaze back to the ocean. "I can't go there."

"An hour," he broke in. "Go with me for an hour. That's all. We'll leave right after that. You don't have to talk to anyone." In fact, he thought it would be a good idea for her not to speak at all, but he wisely kept that observation to himself.

Moving another step forward, he snaked an arm around her waist and brought her to his chest, taking her lips in a frustrated kiss. She surprised him, for he expected her to fight him. Almost immediately, her mouth opened beneath his as if she'd been starving for it, and he recalled the hunger in her gaze at the end of their sky flight, the way her gaze had fixed on his lips. She liked kissing him. The thought didn't do anything to cool his sudden ardor, but he would take advantage of it, plundering her mouth, teasing her lips, even catching a lip to suckle it briefly, causing a low whimper in the back of her throat.

He knew he'd scared the hell out of her with his declaration, but he also wanted it clear he wasn't backing off. This was how he felt. He'd known it within that first month after meeting her, when he found it impossible to stop hounding Marcellus's men for information and updates about her well-being. Initially, he'd shared her own incredulity about it, but the bond was there, whether or not she was or would ever be capable of returning the feeling. He just hoped the Goddess wouldn't be that cruel, for he reacted to her like flame. And when she put her hands between them to thrust him back, she was satisfyingly breathless.

"David." She glowered at him anyway. "You can't seduce me every time you want to get your way."

"Well, I could, and then you could still say no afterward. That way we're both getting something out of it."

"I think my lack of integrity is rubbing off on you," she growled.

"Mina." He sobered, putting his hands on her hips. "I just need to know you're safe. I've let Jonah know we're coming. He'll make sure no one bothers you."

"Thirty minutes," she said at last.

"An hour is what we said at first."

"No more than. Thirty minutes would be better."

Even as she got a nod from him, the dread clogging her throat told Mina she was making a mistake. Not going at all was best. What was that expression? Out of the boiling water, into the fire. She'd wanted off this island so she could avoid the terrifying and absolutely ridiculous idea that an angel thought he was in love with her. But going to the Citadel to avoid further conversation about it might be taking things too far.

Damn it, she should hate this. She *did* hate this. He needed to be gone, far, far away. She didn't want anyone to expect more of her than she had to offer. She didn't want to want him, to be drugged and completely intoxicated by him. To forget the day would come when the truth would permeate his unusually mortal heart and mind, and he would realize she was something repulsive to his kind.

How had he done this to her? Gods, there was no secret to it. It was pathetic, really. No one in her life, with the exception of

Anna, had ever shown her lasting kindness, and she'd kept Anna at bay. David was overwhelming, with all the charisma and potency of an angel as well as the appealing darkness of a human mortal. So for the first time in her life, she had someone interested in her for herself, and she didn't know how to handle it. She'd just agreed to go to the *Citadel*, and she feared the only reason she'd said yes was for that tiny curl of warmth in her belly at the pleasure in his eyes. She was going to have to find a way to end this, once and for all.

He's an angel. She repeated it to herself, because she wasn't sure her heart and body were listening. It radiated from him. She'd know it by doing nothing more than looking into his dark eyes, feeling it through the touch of his hand, seeing it in the noble turn of his head, the magnificent spread of his wings. A young angel, to be sure, but an angel, no question. What had he said? That being an angel was something that "just was." Like her nature.

She had the strangest desire to talk to Anna about this, and wondered if she'd be at the Citadel.

What? Startled, she shut down that avenue with a resounding slam in her mind. *See?* She was actively wanting to see her. Be friendly. *Gods*.

"I'm not being carried," she said, backing away from him. "I'll fly."

David stopped in the process of sliding his arms around her to lift her. "What? I thought you said—"

"I did. But I'm flying myself. Or I don't go."

A muscle flexed in his jaw, that appealing indication of annoyance or temper that only intrigued her, made her want to trace her tongue over it . . .

Focus, damn it.

"It's a long flight," he pointed out.

"Good thing I'm well rested, then."

———

HE could have made it much faster at his usual pace, but David was surprised at how swiftly she could move through the clouds, the dragon's scales glittering with the sun's light, her large serpentine eyes blinking as she adjusted to his course changes smoothly.

They went to Shamain, of course, the level of Heaven closest to the Earth. To his amusement, when she got there she insisted on maintaining the dragon form. She perched on a gray stone spire, wreathed with ivy blooming with white flowers. Grasping the steeplelike structure in long talons, she hunched there like a misplaced vulture.

Jonah was reading on the open balcony to the bailey below. As she settled fifty feet above him, he tilted his head to eye her, while she glared back balefully.

"And a good day to you, too." He nodded to her, then glanced over at David as he landed next to him on the mosaic tile ironically depicting St. George's fight with the dragon. "So much for an inconspicuous approach."

"It was the only way she'd come, short of dragging her kicking and screaming. Sure you don't mind?"

"I'm just glad you called ahead, so to speak. Some of the more eager of our ranks would have used her for archery practice."

A rumble from above drew Jonah's dark gaze.

"From what I've seen of their aim," she rasped, "they likely need the practice."

"Hurry," Jonah advised David. "My patience has limits."

David nodded, but found himself uneasy about leaving her. She was unsettled, a certain urgency to her that he could attribute to her dislike of angels, though that didn't feel like all of it. But she'd refused to say anything further on their flight here.

"Feeling a little overprotective?" Jonah's shrewd gaze was on him.

David shrugged uncomfortably. Glancing down at the book Jonah was reading, he saw the commander was reviewing a text on the spiritual history of the Australian Aborigines. *She likes books. And her eyesight is very good, if the book is turned in the right direction. That might help keep her occupied.*

Jonah gave him a curious look. Shifted casually in accordance with David's wishes. *She doesn't know what you're really doing here, does she?*

David shook his head. "I'll be back soon."

"A male lying to a female is already in trouble," Jonah observed, though David thought he saw a glint of humor in his commander's gaze. Before he could respond to that, the older angel waved a hand. "Gabriel is bringing the Resurrection Trumpet here to readjust the latest tonal spells on it, so I'll be here anyhow."

David recalled the Trumpet protections had to be modified before every new moon, since its magic was organic, ever changing. "Do you need my help?"

"No, I've got the Master of Music meeting him here. You know Gabriel. He just prefers to do the adjustment at the Citadel, where more angels congregate. Ezekial's battalion is meditating in the bailey, and he'll use them to raise the light energy, for a smooth transition."

David nodded. "I'll be right back," he repeated.

Jonah raised a brow. *If you think there's someone more capable of watching over her . . . ?*

David had the grace to flush. But when he started to take off, Jonah stayed him with a gesture and a sigh. *Anna had a thought about where you might take Mina after this . . .*

When he projected the location into David's mind, the younger angel's brows raised and he met his commander's gaze. "Are you certain—"

It might give her a temporary place of safety. As well as resolve the issue of how to take care of her human needs, if you're determined to keep her land-based for a while. Think it over. But go now and we will discuss it later. Your witch is getting restless and she's marking up the stone.

David gave his commander a look of thanks that Jonah returned with an inscrutable nod before David ascended the necessary elevation to hover at Mina's side.

"Jonah will be just below if you need anything," he said. "And I'll return shortly."

She fluttered her lashes at him, a very disconcerting effect when she bared teeth that were half a foot long. "I'll count the minutes."

Well, at least she and Jonah had that in common. Feeling that sense of uneasiness again, he placed a hand on her broad, scaled shoulder, even knowing he might be risking a stump for Raphael to repair. "Thank you for coming with me. It eases my heart to know you're safe here."

"I'm not safe here, David." She kept up a darting surveillance of her surroundings, her talons rasping along the stone as she shifted, the ivy rustling. The movement resulted in several crushed flowers, and the fragrance wafted up. When she sneezed, David glided back at the short flash of fire, a puff of smoke.

"Mina, what—"

"An hour," she interrupted. "The hourglass is running. You promised. If you're not back, I leave."

He gave her a warning look, but took off. He had to do what he'd come to do. The longer he took, the more she'd begin mulling on why he was here. And she was too clever to accept his thin explanation for long.

———

THE Full Submission angels were usually found at Araboth, the Seventh Heaven. Raphael was his first stop. Since he had duties other than that as a healer, including guarding the Tree of Life and overseeing Raquia, the Second Heaven, David knew he was fortunate to find him. He was in one of the gardens, stretched out beneath a tree heavy in bloom with blue flowers and hung with smooth white fruits that reminded David of the texture of Mina's unmarked skin. Pale with just a touch of pink, silky enough to tempt touch.

Raphael had his fingers crossed over his chest and appeared to be sleeping or meditating, his spill of golden hair spread out on the grass, glittering among the blades. At David's approach, he opened his eyes and turned his head, his dark eyes narrowing on either side of the sharp-bladed nose, the firm, unsmiling lips.

"Why, it's our young lieutenant. Since you're on your feet, I assume it's not a grievous injury." His gaze lingered on the scratches Mina had left at David's neck. David tried not to squirm as Raphael rose, passed behind him and let his fingers linger over the marks, bringing not only a touch of healing power, but laughter.

"I think you've been wrestling with a badger, Lieutenant."

Unlike the warrior class, Raphael wore a full midthigh tunic and rich red velvet cloak over it that brushed David's calf as he passed, bringing his unique aroma as well. Raphael's healing power was so much a part of him it emanated out, comforting the heart as well as the body. David took a deep breath of it now, not too proud to let it ease some of the tensions he'd been carrying. Raphael completed his circle around him, a clockwise motion, offering a spiraling sense of well-being.

"You never trouble me needlessly, youngling. It is something I appreciate."

"Even so, I offer an apology for disturbing you."

Raphael shrugged and returned to the tree, his back against the trunk. "It's been quiet. No battles to be fought, a rare thing these days. Only a worried Prime Legion Commander, who had me check his pregnant mermaid wife for any abnormalities. I pronounced her still pregnant." His eyes twinkled. "The only abnormality she is experiencing is a commander who, serving a Goddess, should realize that females have been managing this process quite capably since the beginning of time."

"Well, there is a history there," David pointed out.

Anna had been born under the curse of the daughters of Arianne, which took their lives before they reached their twenty-first year, soon after bearing their firstborn. Anna was twenty-one now, and it was hoped the events of the Canyon Battle would exonerate her from the curse's touch. Jonah had wanted to wait until she was twenty-two to have the child, to perhaps foil the potential of any lingering effect, but Anna hadn't, for exactly the same reason. If she died, she wanted Jonah to have someone to live for and protect.

"I know. I tease him only out of kindness. I would not chastise him for his worry and love. Or remind him that the danger to the mother is not in the pregnancy itself, but the aftermath." Raphael's eyes shadowed. "But we all hope the events of the past months have broken the curse. I suspect it is so, but the Lady sees fit that we make decisions based on love and faith. At least decisions of the heart and soul."

At David's pensive look, he raised an elegant golden brow. "So what is it you seek of me?"

"You healed Mina. After the Canyon Battle."

"Anna did most of it. I did minor things only. Neither I nor my healers can heal the wounds of a Dark One."

"She's not a Dark One."

"I meant no offense," Raphael said mildly. "We are fortunate she has enough merperson in her that I was able to restore her energy and heal her recent injuries. But old wounds . . . they integrate too closely with the Dark One blood she carries. You understand?"

"Yes." David cleared his throat beneath the angel's sharpened gaze. "When you try to heal someone, you told me you can feel what they feel. What their body feels." When Raphael inclined his head, he continued. "I'm trying to understand what she feels, every day, based on the injuries she has. Can you tell me that?"

"Why don't you ask her? She seems the type to talk your ear off, given the chance. Or is that *chew* your ear off?"

"I am charged to protect her," David persisted. "If she has physical limitations, I need to know."

"I'd heard that you'd become her sole protector. At first I assumed you'd drawn the short straw. Then I found out you volunteered. Your fixation with the witch may be unhealthy, David." Raphael's gaze gleamed, but there was a trace of seriousness there. "I may need to give you a tonic."

"That's not the question I asked," David snapped.

Silence. *Gods, what was he doing?* David dropped to one knee without thought, bowing his head. "My lord, my apologies.

I cannot . . ." He squeezed his eyes shut. "It has been a difficult day. I feel an anxiety I can't seem to shake, being here. And I never feel anxious here. I never have, not from the very first."

"I know. Rise." Raphael touched his shoulder, but David remained on the one knee.

"I think I better stay this way another moment. It helps me to remember who I am."

"That may be about to change. And that may be part of it." When David lifted his head, surprised, Raphael nodded. "There you are. Tell me what causes you to speak this way to me, Lieutenant."

"I mean you no disrespect, my lord. But I gave an oath to protect her, and that's what I'll do."

"I don't think Jonah is going to hold you to it, if you—"

"I didn't make the oath to Jonah."

Raphael studied him for a long moment. "Do you truly know what you're doing?"

David gave him a tight smile. "Proceeding on love and faith, I think."

"Clever. And honest. You are ever honest, youngling."

David rose now, paced around the tree. "No one seems to think it's wise for me to protect her. And it's the first time since I've been here that—"

"You have not been in perfect accord with your angel brethren," Raphael finished. "I suspect you are quite sick of hearing this, but you are very young by our standards, David. One day, I will tell you about the first fight that Uriel had with Lucifer. What a fireworks show that was. Or how Jonah took my spear and pinned my foot to a root of the Tree of Life. A tomato plant sprouted through my foot, twined up the spear and put on several quite healthy, heavy fruits, in less than a blink. I gave him boils in return."

David started. "What?"

"Oh, no. You get no more than that." Raphael chuckled. "Some information must be earned by time and great sacrifice. Needless to say, change is a constant, Lieutenant, even in the

Heavens. And positive change often comes through conflict. So, be silent and think on that, while I tell you what you need to know."

Raphael closed his eyes then. And stayed that way. David waited as the moments passed. As remarkable as the golden angel's revelations were, it was difficult to focus on that instead of the passage of time. He had one more stop after this, with the Powers. Perhaps he could hurry them along more easily than he could Raphael. One didn't prod a Seraphim, a Full Submission angel, one of the highest echelon who were in close, constant contact with the Lady's mind.

"Frequent muscle spasms, cramps and joint pain." Raphael spoke at last, and David let out a relieved breath before he could stop himself. The healer gave him an arch look, but continued. "As would be expected for such extensive injuries. It is my suspicion that the Dark One blood hampers the healing on the wounds that should have occurred years ago. Phantom pain from the missing fingers and flesh on the one side of her torso still exists. She's susceptible to painful external skin infections, as well as mouth ulcers, the result of deep cuts from a shell, I think. She's an able apothecary. She treats herself.

"She carries the physical problems equally between merperson and human forms, though the damage relocates accordingly. Shifting is probably quite painful for her, but from what I could tell when treating her, she is excellent at mastering her reaction to pain, at astoundingly high levels. There would be little visible evidence of her disfigurement in the dragon form," he added, "for the damage would be beneath the scales, with the exception of the three talons she has on the one front leg."

He leaned back against the tree. "The joint pain is the effect not only of those injuries, but of environment. I think she chooses the colder water, using the pain and discomfort for some purpose of her own. All in all, she'd do far better in a warm, dry climate, and there's no reason she couldn't live in one."

At David's questioning look, Raphael nodded. "She's not dependent on her merperson form the way Jonah's mate is. Mina is a true shapeshifter. She can assume any of her shapes—human, Dark One, dragon or mercreature—and maintain them as long as she wishes. There's no apparent effort to it for her."

"So she has no primary form?"

"Not as I can tell. It's intriguing and unusual, to say the least. Of course, she doesn't leave her Dark One blood behind, no matter her form." He gave David a level look. "So her true face may be that of a Dark One. The other forms just give her a foothold in our world. As you know, Dark Ones can't live here. They can fight and reconnoiter, but after a certain amount of time, they must go back into the rifts to their own world. Even though she's never lived in a Dark One world, as far as we know, that craving is strong in her. But the desire is precariously balanced by other parts of her."

"When I first met her," David ventured, "I was able to heal one of her older scars, but she wouldn't let me do anything else for her. If it's beyond your skill, if angels can't heal old scars that are integrated with Dark One blood, how did I do that?"

Raphael's brows drew together. Another long silence, such that David almost regretted asking. Then the angel spoke.

"That is incredibly interesting, and unfortunately, I have no sure answer. There have been cases, when there was an unusual bond between beings, where equally unusual healings occurred." Raphael stared into space thoughtfully. "She is an anomaly, a creature created out of many different creatures. A Franken-stein's monster, if you will."

He gave a faint smile. "One of my favorite books inspired by our Muses. Imagine that monster, implanted with a murderer's heart and a wise man's brain, while the soul remains a question mark between the two. All I know for certain is that she is an enigma, David. That is what I can tell you."

David nodded. Executed a short bow. "I don't wish to leave in haste, but I promised Jonah I would be back shortly, and I must visit Zebul as well. Thank you for your time, my lord. I am grate-ful, as always."

"Lieutenant?" Raphael held him with a hand on his shoulder,

but instead of comfort, this time the touch and his dark eyes held a piercing warning. "Her way is not set. Walking inside her soul was like walking the abandoned, fallow fields of Hell, where battles have been fought over and over. There is only carnage, and no clear winner. Be cautious."

Twelve

NEXT stop.

Every soul had a Memory Keeper, who cataloged and maintained all the memories of that soul and archived them, for recall later when the soul reincarnated, or reached the final resting place as an enlightened being. Memory Keepers were typically Powers. When he made his inquiry at the Hall of Souls, David was surprised to find that Pericles was Mina's Memory Keeper.

Pericles consistently served as a Memory Keeper for souls that might have a significant impact on whatever world they inhabited. Considering Mina was the only Dark Spawn known who hadn't surrendered to the blood within her, it made some sense.

He found Pericles in Zebul, the Sixth Heaven, immersed in discussion with several Thrones about the wisdom of having ever given Michelangelo a brush. The Sixth Heaven was dedicated to study, and he was sure the text Jonah was reading had been borrowed from here. The iridescent, cylindrical Thrones hovered in the mist of a fountain, their many eyes turning toward David as he approached. Pericles sat on the fountain wall, wearing a long, sleeveless robe and sandals, making David feel he'd stepped through a time portal. But then, Pericles had been born during the time of the ancient Greeks.

"May I have a moment of your time, Memory Keeper?" David bowed, giving indication of the nature of his business with the title. Pericles glanced toward David from under a thick fall of raven black hair held off his forehead with a simple gold circlet.

While the Thrones drifted away, David felt their warm touch in his mind, though they did not speak. He returned it, offering a simple blessing and thanks for their well-being and courtesy.

As he explained what he wanted, Pericles's wings, a pale blue with silver tips, gleamed as he adjusted them. He lifted, stretched, and then folded them over his back, giving the same impression as a parent folding his arms to reinforce the cool, probing stare he leveled upon David.

"I understand the request. But a Memory Keeper does not typically spill the memories of one of his souls into the mind of an infant lieutenant."

David bit back his impatience. He suspected attorney-client privilege might have been divinely inspired.

"I'm charged to protect her, and think if I know more of her background . . . experience her worst memory directly, I'll be able to better anticipate her. She's not easy to guard."

"My understanding is that's an understatement," the Memory Keeper said dryly. "You comprehend what her worst memory is?"

"I do."

"Your intent is pure," Pericles said at last. "If ill-advised. Very well, then. Sit here, on the wall a few feet away from me."

David complied, watching as Pericles rummaged in his robes, reminding him of Mina, and came forth with a small fabric pouch. Loosening the strings, he reached in and withdrew one seed. Where a moment before there had been nothing on the fountain wall between them, now there was an elegant clay cup. Picking up an urn that appeared next to it, Pericles poured. The dark liquid, with an aroma reminiscent of green tea, churned into the cup, becoming moist earth that covered the seed. Kicking off his sandals, the Memory Keeper curled his toes in the green grass around the fountain, leaning back on his arms in a waiting posture. On his leanly muscled arms were tattoos of ancient script, praises to the Artemis form of the Goddess.

"You know, many up here think you are simply young and foolish. That you will realize the best thing in the end is to kill the witch."

David studied the earth in the cup, which appeared to be sifting itself. "Jonah isn't hampered by inexperience, and he hasn't come to that conclusion yet. But since everyone feels the need to remind me of my youth, maybe I should have 'young and foolish' tattooed across my chest."

"Hmm." Pericles pursed his lips. "Wasn't there a dwarf in that Disney movie? Dopey? That one word covered it, and will save you extra lettering."

David snorted. "That it will. I thank you for your suggestion."

"I am sure." Pericles gave him a smile and glanced down at the cup as well. "The memories I carry can be amusing. Unfortunately, this is not one of them. This is not done lightly, Lieutenant. While all memories are scripted, once I've given you a memory, it will fade from my mind. But I will not miss this particular one."

"I'm sworn to protect her, no matter what type of protection she needs."

"Somehow, I believe your interpretation of her protection is a bit beyond the scope of what Jonah envisioned."

"Yet you've never spoken in favor of her death." David recalled the meeting several months before, when all those involved with the seawitch had been called together for discussion. "You said you preferred less biased minds to make the decision."

"That is because I honestly do not know what is the best course for the witch."

The earth tumbled in the cup and a stem poked through. As David watched, it extended and spread, took on needles. The bonsai grew swiftly, taking the shape of a small dragon, with one small, spherical white fruit where the eye might have been.

Pericles plucked it, extended it to David. "The memory is in the fruit. You need to anchor yourself. Stay aware of who you

are. That's very important. A mind is often disoriented after experiencing a strong memory not its own. It can permanently
change you."

David thought of Raphael's words. "If I feared change, Pericles, it would do me little good, for it is the only inevitable thing
in the universe. A promise."

"And a curse," the Power observed dourly. "I will watch over
you." He motioned downward and David, respecting his wisdom, slid to the ground, using the fountain wall as a brace to his
back. He brought the fruit to his lips.

"You do not hesitate," Pericles observed. "Definitely a sign of
foolishness. Most would meditate a bit before experiencing a
memory this strong."

"I don't have that kind of time. Is it entirely necessary?"

"No, but it will be far more unpleasant. You will have more
difficulty remembering you are in her memory, not your own reality."

HE didn't remember the taste, or even the texture. In the time it
took to take the bite, all that was swept away.

Like most, he'd heard a secondhand account of what had happened to Mina when she was nine, but there was a vast difference
between knowing what had happened and experiencing it. As the
memory thrust into his mind like the growth of the bonsai, the
heavy silence of the water closed in.

His arms were bound. No. A child's were. A nine-year-old
child. For a blink, a sliver of his mind struggled to remain separate, clinging to the fading words of a distant Power. But as the
emotions flooded him, the first wave of what he was about to see
and feel her endure, David knew he couldn't do it. He let the
memory rip away who he was, so that he became his seawitch.

Chain pulled her arms back at an excruciating angle. Her
wrists were bound tightly to her tentacles with pronged restraints
that sunk into her serpentine appendages so the cuffs would not
slip. If they dropped her, she would sink and roll like an unbalanced jellyfish, her vulnerable stomach ripped open by contact

with the coral reefs of the Abyss, and predators would close in to feed on the tender young flesh.

As they took her down deeper into the Abyss, she began to beg. To plead.

It was pointless. She knew that. Her mother had taught her not to seek compassion from anyone, even from her. But though she was ashamed, the fear broke her. When she screamed too loudly, one of the mermen jammed an oyster shell into her mouth. Gods, it cut into her tongue and the roof of her mouth, blood clotting inside and on her lips grotesquely, refusing to let go of her skin. Her cries intensified—she couldn't help it—but they were garbled, which seemed to satisfy the merman.

Don't leave me here . . .

She'd been alone all her short life, but this was different. Being abandoned, helpless and bound, was so different from just being alone.

Four manacles of varying lengths hung from an iron ring embedded in the reef. She sensed the magic hovering over the restraints as well as the ghostly impressions of terrified merpeople, sentenced for crimes warranting death, who'd died and had their bodies picked apart here.

When they put her in the four manacles, the magic clamped down on her. The manacles were spelled to hold the flesh painfully tight, adjusting as necessary so that even a captive whose appendages were being decimated by scavengers couldn't escape. A clever conjuring by Neptune's own wizards, the bindings also prohibited the use of magic by the captive, including shifting. With her mobility limited by the manacles, she couldn't completely control the direction she floated, and almost immediately drifted up against the stinging bed of fire coral clustered around the iron ring. She cried out, tried to push away, but the mermen shoved her back against it, using the wall of the Abyss to hold her still so they could finish their task, ignoring her struggles.

They blindfolded her with a strip of metal that pressed more short, sharp prongs into her skin at angles on either side of her nose, above her ears, at the back of her skull, holding it in place.

It didn't matter to them, to any of them, that she hadn't done what they thought.

She'd stood in the shadows of the birthing room, watching the baby emerge from the mother's womb. Feeling the shape of the curse, Mina had known what that new daughter of Arianne, the princess Anna, would face. She would have the worst curse of all. Nothing but pure air and water would be able to touch her skin without causing her great pain. Any living being who touched her would be turned to chaotic, evil purpose. Princess Anna would be better off dead. But Mina could fix it. Her first understanding of irony. She could change for another what she could not change for herself.

Then, unexpectedly, the new baby's mother had let go of the carved pillars of stone that countless generations of royal women had clasped as they bore their children. She'd floated over, despite the admonitions of her retainers to stay and be cosseted, to watch the midwife place the new babe in the birth net.

"I'm sorry . . . I can't bear to see you suffer, but I do not have the courage to take you with me."

She'd somehow gotten the knife that cut the umbilical cord and in one motion, too shocking and quick to stop, she had cut her own throat. The blood had swirled away toward Mina while the midwife and attendants cried out, abandoned the secured babe to cluster around the mother's floating, dying body.

She should have done nothing. She had every reason to hate that baby, but she'd drawn close to the enclosed bassinet and looked down as two small hands reached for her.

She had known for over a month what the specific curse would be, because she'd stepped into the world of dark visions and sinister magic to summon the knowledge to her. In her hate and anger, she'd thought of using the cure she found as a bargaining chip with Neptune. Just as her ancestor had once stood toe-to-toe with the sea king and defied him. Only this time she wouldn't lose.

But in the end, one child had stood over the bassinet of another, looked into violet eyes and a pale face, and acted for reasons that had nothing to do with any of that.

Opening her mouth, Mina had summoned the mother's swirling blood to her—there'd been so much of it—and taken it in like a bird carrying food to its young. Removing the infant from the spherical birthing net, she'd sealed her lips over the babe's, and forced the blood down the tender new throat. She'd cut her own lip with sharp teeth to make sure her seawitch blood mingled with it.

"Least you deserve for trying to kill the princess," one of the mermen spat at her irritably, as if her cries and pain were something she should be ashamed of. "Should have executed your whole line long ago, before you were ever born."

They left her there, pulling against those chains and begging them to come back, the blindfold putting her in total darkness.

The sea was very efficient, full of those with radar for the dead and dying, and of course every creature in the ocean knew that being immobilized and exposed was the worst of Fates. The area quickly became full of the opportunistic scavengers.

Eventually, she swore if she got free, she'd spend her life dining on every crawling, slithering one of them. But at first she screamed in horror, cried, shook them off, again and again, until she battled exhaustion as hard as she fought them. When she tired, crabs and shrimp attached to her skin, pinching, scraping in their horribly slow, methodical way. Eels slithered up around her legs, taking more aggressive bites. Jellyfish bumped into her, leaving welts, their poison bringing more agony.

If she'd been mortal, possessing the soul of a mermaid only or any other creature made by the Goddess, she would have succumbed. But she refused. The Dark Blood in her, as well as the life she'd lived for her first nine years, told her there was no kindly Goddess Mother waiting to welcome her. Death at best might simply be oblivion, but she had too much rage and hate to give in to that.

In between her war with the sea creatures, she tried every spell. Most ricocheted off the spell-block on the manacles and burned her skin. Her only bulwark against despair was that they occasionally struck her mundane attackers. But she wouldn't give up, and she finally found one the wizards hadn't considered. She was able to shift half of her upper body and both tentacles with their manacles into the Abyss wall, embedding herself there like a fossil to protect at least that much of her. Unfortunately, that left the rest of her protected only by her wits, one arm and her teeth.

But she learned. She'd overcome the excruciating pain caused by working at the oyster shell with her tongue and movements of her jaw, and gotten the shell out. Since she could almost reach her mouth with her one hand, to eat she captured her scavenger attackers, crushed or tore the life out of them with the aid of her often bleeding and infected mouth. She fought others off as they charged back in for an additional meal. Sometimes there were so many she couldn't protect her face and body from all of them, and of course when she passed out from pain and exhaustion, they could feast until she roused and beat them off again.

Her body became a map of the failures, as well as the successes. While they tried to eat their way around the prongs of the mask, get beneath it to her eye, they were never successful. Ironically, the barbaric cruelty of the merpeople saved her eye.

When they came to get her, her sentence rescinded because they'd discovered she'd actually saved the babe a life of torment, she had no idea that over twenty-six days had passed. Later she learned they'd waited a full day after the decision before dispatching someone to go after her, because no one expected her to be alive. However, with no apologies, but visibly shaken by her appearance and the fact she was alive, the same pair of mermen unchained and brought her back to Neptune's realm. To the ambivalent and sometimes malevolent attentions of the healers.

Before she left Neptune's realm, never to return, she only asked for one thing. She asked to see Anna. She'd peered at the baby in her crib, a sphere woven of enchanted willow for protection. Anna floated about, chortling and staring about her with those wide violet eyes. The hovering nurse had strongly opposed the witch's request, not only for fear of the witch herself, but saying her appearance would give the babe nightmares. She'd had to swallow her words as Anna floated to the edge and reached through the diamond-shaped holes of the willow toward Mina's destroyed face.

There'd been a few things already in the sphere. Toys. A sparkling medallion from Neptune. Mina reached in, tied the tiny set of chimes she'd made out of softened glass to a bar, and departed, leaving the baby's tiny hand still reaching for her. She hadn't allowed Anna to touch her. Then, and only then, did Anna begin to cry.

DAVID surfaced. For a moment he blinked, unsure of where he was. Then he bolted upright from the ground, his hands going to his face, his arms, his legs. The sensation of touching them and finding them whole shuddered through him like an electric shock.

"Easy, boy." Pericles was there with a hand on his shoulder, steadying him, pressing him back against the stone wall. "Easy."

"Jesus." David bent forward, putting his head down, taking deep breaths. He was soaked in sweat, his hands trembling, and he had the unusual but not forgotten sensation of nausea.

"I told you to stay separate."

"No." David shook his head, shook it hard, pressing the heels of his hands against his eyes as if that would help dispel the horror. Pericles was right. He wished *he* could forget that, but he never could. *Oh, Mina.* "I had to do it as her."

"But why? Why was that necessary?" Pericles squatted next to him and took David's hands from his eyes. He squeezed the younger angel's wrists, a reassurance, a reminder of his current reality. The Thrones had drawn close again, hovering, their eyes seeing, knowing. When David shook his head, unable to answer, they did, in quiet, humming tones that vibrated through his and Pericles's minds.

Because watching something terrible happen to someone you care about is a far greater torment than going through it yourself. No matter what that torment is.

David drew a shaky breath. He wanted to hunt down everyone who'd hurt her, from Neptune to that nurse. Make them suffer in a way that made Lucifer's Hades look like a theme park. Christ.

"No wonder you said nothing against her," he said, when he could trust himself to speak. He stared into the Memory Keeper's enigmatic dark eyes. "She's been through enough."

"That was just the beginning, I'm afraid. Perhaps the worst, physically, but many other things have occurred in her life to enforce the lessons of those twenty-six days. Of the first nine years of her life, really."

"The way they treat her, no wonder she's always alone."

"And sometimes not as alone as a female would wish to be."

David's eyes narrowed. "What does that mean?"

"I shared the memory you requested. You understand the most important root—"

Pericles's voice cut off abruptly. Though weak and unsteady still, David had propelled himself off the ground, launched by the trigger of those words. He stood over the angel, gripping his tunic. "What do you mean?"

Pericles did not appear concerned about David's anger. In fact, there was compassion in his eyes. "I will not let you experience another of her memories. One has been enough to overtax your system. But"—he removed David's hand, squeezed his fingers in silent reproof—"I will tell it to you. There were those, when she was just an adolescent, who dared to corner her, take advantage of her prettier features, perversely fascinated by her harlequin nature. She learned to fight them, to put an end to it, and they regretted their foolishness. At least one young merman disappeared, his fellows claiming he was attacked and killed by a whale, because they would not own up to the truth. He tried to force her to his will before she let her darkness take over and dispatched him. He exploded. Literally."

David backed off, tried to steady himself, gain his bearings while assimilating that knowledge with the vibrating horror of what he'd just experienced through Mina's memories.

"There are many things I do not understand, Lieutenant. Not

only does her blood give her every reason to capitulate to evil, everything in her life has pushed her toward it. I suspect whatever tether holds her from that is tenuous. We can pity her, but the ultimate mercy may be in destroying her, as something that never should have been born, the way we treat most Dark Spawn.

"Was her survival a matter of savagery or nobility? You've been in battle. You know at times there is a close overlap between the two. In that memory, you saw there are times there is no separation between them. Do not mistake her Dark One blood as an illness for her to overcome. It is a vital part of who she is, such that she cannot bear too great a threat to it."

David frowned, forcing himself to focus. That uneasiness was back, as if Pericles's words had tripped a switch. "What do you mean?"

"I mean she is the very embodiment of yin and yang. Split between darkness and light, she cannot move toward light without a proportionate response from the darkness. It will not tolerate being abandoned, and of course it would like to take over completely. So she draws in precise amounts from the light to keep it in check. Just as she was half in rock, half in water in the Abyss, so she stands, precariously balanced between two forces. She herself is the greatest potion she's ever concocted."

"So that explains why she stays away from others? Too much light, too little dark . . ." David's pulse was increasing again, his heart pounding up toward his throat. "She uses the pain to help her."

Pericles nodded. "I have told you far more than I intended. But it is important that you do not let your desire to help her blind you to what may be the ultimate truth. That when her will snaps, others will pay with their lives. Perhaps many others. It is what Jonah fears."

David rubbed his forehead, paced in an agitated circle.

"I didn't speak in her defense, young David," Pericles continued. "I only did not speak against her. She bears blood in her that embraces hatred and death, feeds on fear and pain for nourishment as well as pleasure. She cannot bear the proximity of too much white light. It drives her as mad as cornering does a rabid animal."

Oh, holy Christ. That's it.

As the truth echoed through him, he glanced at the sunlight and swore in a way that Zebul's hallowed hall had never heard. He was way past the hour he'd promised her. Nearly two, in fact.

Almost at the moment he registered that, Jonah's urgent call exploded into his mind.

Thirteen

Even before he left Zebul, Jonah's sharp call came to David again, spurring his speed so that he somersaulted a pair of fiery phoenixes drifting through the library area. As he shot down through the levels of Heaven, heading for Shamain, he received more snippets from Jonah's mind. She'd lost patience with the wait, had tried to leave. Became more and more agitated as Jonah tried to reason with her, then as other angels got involved, her reaction had detonated unexpectedly.

They'd not yet harmed her, but that effort was wearing thin.

Don't make her feel cornered, Jonah.

I believe that opportunity has already passed.

The revelations of the last hour had warned him, but even so, the change in the dragon grasping the stone point of Shamain's tallest spire above the keep was startling. The sapphire blue and silver scales were now the ruby brightness of blood, both snake-like eyes a savage match, fangs bared as she roared and shot hot flame in a wide arc around her. Angels leaped easily out of reach, but they had her well surrounded above and below. Many had arrows notched and swords at the ready, prepared to move in.

He'd achieved what he sought here, but the cost might be the exact opposite of what he intended. David cursed himself. Her reluctance, her obsessive insistence on the time limitation, had

been warnings, and he hadn't heeded them. She didn't trust easily. He should have paid more attention to what she hadn't said
to him, rather than preemptively celebrating what she had.

Pericles was right. He'd been assuming it was a sickness, a
disease that wasn't truly part of her. Before his eyes was Jonah's
worst-case scenario coming true. The Dark One blood was overpowering everything else. It had surged up, hot and feral, unbalanced by prolonged exposure to light energy surroundings that
couldn't be stronger if he'd thrown Mina into the Lady's lap.
Great Goddess, Ezekial's whole battalion had been here, meditating to raise white light for the Trumpet.

Making it worse now was the physical threat posed by the angels. Trained to go into battle mode at the first hint of a Dark One,
their senses would have already been on edge with her there.

Now only Jonah's word was holding them back, and the commander had his own sword at the ready.

Perhaps he should be thankful it was her dragon form, for the
animal part of her seemed to have claimed most of her rational
thinking. Though he knew she could cast spells in this form, he'd
seen her do it when she was fully cognizant, the essence of the
seawitch still blinking at him out of the serpentine eyes. He saw
very little of Mina in this enraged creature's expression.

David arrived at Jonah's side as the latest flame blast seared
between two flanks of angels. They parted, then re-formed ranks
again, driving her back against the spire as she tried to stretch
out her wings, launch herself. Mina opened her jaws and howled,
a chilling, Dark One shriek magnified into a raw scream of rage
and warning.

"Nice of you to show up."

"I found what I needed. Just let her go."

"*What?*" Jonah glanced at him. "Let her go to wreak havoc
on everything in her path? She's turned, David."

"No, she hasn't." *I won't let her.* "If I get her away from here,
she'll be all right. But the longer she stays, the worse she'll get. I
didn't know. That's one of the things I found out. It's my fault.
Let me fix it."

"She could have told you that. She didn't. I'll send a squadron with you."

"No. She can't perceive any threat. Just me. I know what I'm doing."

"And what will that change?" Jonah's head whipped up at a shout, but the dragon was just repositioning, the angels adjusting accordingly.

"She can control this better. She'll be—"

"She'll still have the blood and the power," Jonah snapped. "The two things occupying the same space, something way too damn thin in between them. She's mortal, David, invested with more power than a mortal can have, and the stronger it gets, the more fiercely that dark side of her is going to want to take control of it. It's time to end this."

"Duck." The other angels shouted it out, and David and Jonah cut under the swath of fire the dragon spat out. It covered over a hundred yards of space. As it died back, the stone resisting the flame, her predatory gaze was darting about, calculating. An escape. David could tell she was trying to escape. Mina was in there, fighting the darkness still, trying to escape before it unleashed.

"Feel her power, David? She's got enough of her own brain to tell her not to move, but in a moment, it will go in one of two directions. Toward the dragon, which means she'll attack indiscriminately, focused on rage, or she'll get back in touch with the witch part of herself and start retaliating with spells. And they won't be harmless bat wings. The time for this is over," Jonah repeated. "We did the best we could on her behalf. Your bringing her here was likely one of the best ways to bring it to a head."

"*No.* I brought her here as a mistake. To help her." Knowing he was no match for Jonah, let alone a full battalion, David nevertheless shifted in front of his commander, meeting his gaze head-on, putting everything he had into it. "You can't kill her because of my mistake."

"Watch out."

The warning fired through the air like an arrow behind them. David focused, creating the shield over himself as her fire raced over and through him, engulfing him before the spray dissipated with another shriek of rage from the beast.

"Holy Mother," Jonah muttered, and David spun, following his gaze in time to see her large, spiked tail sweep through the air, narrowly missing another handful of those circling around her. Her claws crumbled the Citadel rock as she shifted to get a better angle. David wondered if he was the only one who heard the desperation behind the shrieks. She *was* in there, hanging on to the reins by a thread. He had to get her out of here.

Please don't make this decision here and now. Jonah, the last thing I would ever wish to do in this universe or any other is defy you. By the holy Goddess, I am asking for your trust on this, based on everything I am to you. Give me more time. Don't do this, not when it's because of something I did.

Though quite aware of Jonah's feelings toward him, David had never used that privilege as leverage. Perhaps it was a measure of how close he knew Jonah was to giving the order to take her life that he did it now. Was he prepared to fight them if they tried to harm her? Gods, he didn't want to find out, for he was fairly certain he knew the answer.

Please, Jonah. You all are my family. Don't make me choose. I have to protect her.

She is not your sister, David. Do you understand that?

David froze. Despite the barely leashed chaos around them, everything disappeared for a blink except the angel in front of him, who knew more than any what those words might mean. "I know that," he said out loud. He kept his tone carefully measured, even though he himself could hear the vibrations in it that spoke of terrible, dark things.

"I'm not sure you do. You can't save what was born by blood to be evil, David. No Dark One—"

"*She's not a Dark One.*" Only when it was echoing through the keep did David realize he'd thundered it as if a storm had erupted inside of him. The dragon yowled.

Jonah's expression had gone blank. He had lost. Gods, he knew he had lost, but David wouldn't stop. He couldn't.

"She has fought it. Despite everything, *she has fought it*. Fought it alone. There has to be a purpose and reason for that. She's fought them, the way we fight them. Only she never gets to leave the battlefield, because her blood *is* the battlefield." *Her insides are like a fallow field* . . . "She's a soldier, like any of us. Just like you, or Marcellus, or any of my platoon. I will *not* abandon her."

"Even if it comes to a choice of her or us." Jonah said it flatly, his gaze assessing his lieutenant. Assessing whether an angel he'd trusted was someone whose judgment had become suspect. David couldn't dispute Jonah's concern, but it struck him hard.

"It's not that choice." He managed, with Herculean effort, to keep his voice steady now. "It's about right and wrong. Please don't make it about that. What if you had to make a choice between Anna's well-being and this?"

"Goddess," Jonah swore. Leaping faster than David could follow or defend, he plowed into the younger angel. David landed hard against the keep side, caving in stone, Jonah's hand fisted in his tunic. The angels cried out above as the dragon tried to leave the spire, wings slashing through the air, spitting fire.

"*Mina.*"

"Be still, Lieutenant. They won't harm her. Yet."

He couldn't move, Jonah's arm like a solid wall of rock pressed against his chest. Held there immobile, David knew his commander had made his point effectively. He could swat David aside like a fly. Take Mina's life with a word. But he hadn't yet.

"You are not going to compare *that* to Anna."

"Yes. I am." David said it through gritted teeth. "Jonah, I'm begging you."

The commander stared at him, his expression unfathomable, battle-ready. David held that terrifying gaze, his body at respectful attention as much as possible, or so he thought. When Jonah's attention dropped, David realized he'd put his hands on the grips of two of the daggers. He made himself release them, put his hands to his sides as Jonah watched, considered. When he raised his attention to David's face again, David wondered if he'd lost, no matter what Jonah's decision was.

"Save your strength for getting her out of here," Jonah said curtly, releasing him. "We'll be talking about this again. If she hurts anyone, David—including you—it's over."

David took to the air almost before Jonah finished the statement, not wanting to give the dragon another chance to change the commander's mind. And he couldn't spare the emotional energy to think about what he himself might have destroyed here.

"Here." David shouted it. "Mina. Here. I'm here."

As the angels started to back off, presumably upon Jonah's mental command, David shot up, coming in beneath the dragon's maw, narrowly missing the swipe of talons. The tail dealt him a blow in the shoulder that sent him spinning, but a rush of adrenaline took over as he envisioned Jonah taking that as a sign to attack. It galvanized him and he surged up in the sky, headed away from the Citadel.

Mina, follow me. Please, Goddess, don't let them kill you. He fired his next thought toward his commander. *I've got this. Please, Jonah. Let me do this.*

The dragon exploded off the turret, and David's heart stopped as he realized a handful of arrows had already been released. Then they veered up sharply, clattering back down to the stone floor of the keep when Jonah swept his hand before him, sending out an arc of power. David heard an inventive curse in his head, followed by a sharp command.

Watch out.

David spun and twisted left so sharply he thought he heard his spine crack as the dragon's claws swept down upon him, more swiftly than he'd anticipated. He slid between the front talons, which ripped a healthy piece of flesh from his shoulder as he followed the line of her belly, causing her to make an awkward somersault to reach him. It, as well as the smell of blood, served the intended purpose of enraging her further and sending her in renewed pursuit after him.

David.

I'll be fine. David grunted as he executed another narrow miss just over her head. Flame seared through the wounded shoulder. *Will . . . report later. Thanks . . .*

Jonah sighed, pinched the bridge of his nose as the angels who had engaged made landings at various points on the keep. He noted Raphael had joined them, was standing at his shoulder.

"That boy is going to give me gray hairs," he informed the healer.

Raphael offered a smile that, as usual, comforted, but there was uncertainty in his own expression, which didn't comfort in the least. "No cure for that, I'm afraid."

"I should have killed her."

"You couldn't do it. You love him too well, perhaps."

Jonah shifted his attention to the other angel. At Raphael's knowing look, he swore again. "You helped me with him when he first came here. What will it do to his soul if I have to kill her, which everything suggests is the way this will end? She can't control it in herself except under certain restricted conditions, and you just felt her power. We were lucky she was more animal than witch just then or she might have brought the Citadel down around us."

He turned back to watch, grudgingly admiring when David made an elegant turn, still an evasive maneuver. It was clear he was going to keep goading her to chase him until she ran out of energy and perhaps became manageable again. For now, short of another careless move, he should be fine, for his speed far surpassed hers.

"If it has to be done, make sure he's the one that does it." Raphael said it quietly. "He's not that boy anymore, Jonah. He's a young man, for certain. And he's in love, for the first time in his life. Being an angel, I expect that means the last time as well."

At Jonah's stunned expression, Raphael inclined his head. "The one thing a healer recognizes is love, because there is no greater healing agent in the universe. If it must be done, it is likely to shatter him either way, but that way he will know it has been done with mercy."

———————

DAVID feared the conversations he'd left in the wake of their swift departure, but there was nothing he could do about that now. One focus. At this moment, that was exhausting Mina. He went up, down, and when she appeared to be giving up the chase, he'd get close enough to rake her scales with a dagger or taunt her by flying just beneath her nose. Once, he was able to yank a scale from her sensitive underbelly. She was impressively quick, enough to get in a couple swipes that raked off some more skin, divested him of a few handfuls of feathers. In the harrowingly close maneuvers, he knew he risked the potential of being knocked unconscious and having himself eaten like a bucketful of chicken. Since he was immortal, he wasn't sure how he would be digested until she got to the crucial heart organ that *could* end his life, but he imagined it wouldn't be pleasant.

Thank Goddess, she was tiring. Once he fell into a rhythm of keeping her moving and chasing him, he'd worked on their destination. So now, as he maneuvered her closer and closer to the surface, they were over the Nevada desert, the long stretch of barren area Jonah and Anna had traversed on foot months before. It was unpopulated enough that an aerial display by an angel and a dragon might go largely unnoted in the fading afternoon light.

He'd explored the area during sweeps for Dark One activity after the Canyon Battle and found himself curiously drawn to the strange land. It had hidden pocket canyons with streams and lush greenery as well as long stretches of sand and scrub, populated by various unusual animal species and only a scattering of eccentric human inhabitants and infrequent structures.

There.

Nevada, like a handful of the western states, had ghost towns dating back to the 1800s. One in particular he'd explored was too far off the beaten path to be a preserved historic attraction. He knew, because it had become a favored haunt for him for meditation, a familiar touchstone to the Westerns he'd preferred as a teen. The only people who'd been here recently were a lone group of hikers who'd moved on after a day, and a film crew, who'd used it for about a week to gather stock footage.

As he landed on the ground on the main road through the town, he watched the dragon circle. At a certain point, she'd stopped trying to kill him and just followed. A hopeful sign that she was back in control. She hadn't spoken to him, though, and he hadn't pressed it, knowing her remaining energy was being put into flight.

Mina. All angels had the power to speak within the mortal mind, though he'd always found Mina's a very difficult mind to navigate. While the blood link helped, he still couldn't hear her thoughts unless she spoke to him directly. But he was hoping . . . *Mina, are you with me?*

The dragon came down on top of the building that had been the saloon, then made a quick but clumsy leap to the sandy main strip as the roof groaned alarmingly. They faced each other, about sixty feet between them. All they needed were six-shooters, he thought.

Her sides were heaving, mouth foam- and blood-flecked. However, in a surge of relief so fierce it seized his heart in a squeezing grip, he saw that the dragon's eyes were once again bicolored. One red. One blue.

"Mina, I'm so sorry. Please forgive me for not understanding."

The jaws pulled back in a bitter snarl that was disconcerting, but she didn't move.

How could you understand? You're an angel. You know nothing of my kind of darkness. The only ones that understand my true nature are those you revile. Those you will destroy, as you'll have to destroy me in the end.

"No."

You can't understand unless you are evil. Even in her thoughts, he could hear how tired she was. Soul sick. Stretching out her long neck, she laid her large head on the sand. Her body rolled to the side, like an animal hit by a car.

"You're *not* evil." He surged across the ground to her, heedless now of any potential danger, but even as he began to move, she was metamorphosing, diminishing. When she was done, her hair stuck to her face and bare body, slick with sweat. Her cloak was probably lying on the ground at the Citadel like some dark tarantula, the angels poking their blades at it to figure out what it was.

She was the human Mina again, lying crumpled in the dirt, so small and deceptively defenseless compared to the dragon form. Only at this moment, he suspected she *was* defenseless. Or rather, past caring.

He was wrong. When she registered his advance, by some miracle she struggled to her feet, swaying, and backed away from him. Her eyes were still wild, hands clenched for battle, even though she was staggering. She made a noise of protest. "No, don't touch me. I can't bear it."

He stopped, his heart in his throat. As she stumbled and fell, he wanted nothing more than to move forward, but he saw the flash in her mind, a rough concept she was still too disoriented to put into words. Even his muddled light was too much for her raw senses right now.

So he stopped, spread his hands to show her he understood and would come no farther. Taking a cross-legged position on the ground, he put his hands on his knees, though meditating was the last thing on his mind. Goddess, had he screwed up. Nearly gotten her killed by the only ones with any motive to protect her. The condition she was in was because of him.

But he'd been an angel long enough to know self-flagellation was pointless. It was done. Savagely, he told himself he'd gained invaluable knowledge she wouldn't have shared with him. He could use it to keep from making a mistake that *would* be fatal next time. Then he watched her, his heart breaking.

Letting her body sink to the ground again, she put her cheek to the dirt, lips clotting with sand she didn't bother to wipe away. She'd lain on her unmarked side, tucking it beneath her so he had an eerie impression of what she might have looked like embedded in the rock in the Abyss. She appeared to be struggling with something going on within her, and he couldn't think of how to help her.

Or could he? Slowly, he drew the dagger, studied the blade. Not going to her and pulling her into his lap, cosseting her, was against everything he was. Just like it was to give her an object that could cause her further pain.

You don't know me . . .

Knowing someone meant not denying the truth of who they were. Which dovetailed into the corollary of being what she needed him to be. He looked toward her, a disfigured woman coated in dirt, gasping like a horse down with a broken leg. Suffering.

Tossing the dagger with an oath, he embedded it in the dirt above where her hand curled and uncurled.

At first, he thought she hadn't seen it, for she didn't flinch. But then, her hand moved forward. An inch, then another as he waited, all muscles tense, fighting the overwhelming urge to take it back.

Only by your hand?

It was whispered in his head, a question. He clenched his teeth. She could bear the bite of the unforgiving steel, but not his freely offered touch? *Or with my permission. You have it.*

Evil is a choice, and only the one making it can unmake it. Jonah understands that in a way you don't. Her voice echoed in his head, distant, wandering, as if she spoke to herself, more than to him. *Good has to fight evil until that decision happens, to keep it from harming others.*

"Which is exactly what you do, Mina. You're not evil." He spoke it aloud this time.

Her fingers closed on the grip, rested there for a while. The sun continued to disappear, a day ending, like all others the Goddess had created. Wondrous, strange, normal. The sandstone strata of the rock hills that formed the backdrop of the town were pink and brown in the deepening twilight. He wondered if she'd passed out, for she'd bowed her head so he couldn't see her face. Maybe she had, for it was a long time before she stirred.

David?

I'm here.

He sensed her twinge of relief, like an ache in an old wound. Familiar. Then she raised her head, lifted the dagger and drove it into the open, loosely curled palm of her three-fingered hand. The one on which she'd broken the middle finger only hours before. Her dragon form had destroyed the splint.

Her scream echoed and bounced off of the silent buildings, the hills beyond, the long expanses of desert and scrub that reflected sound and yet swallowed it at once.

His own hand was clenched into a hard fist on his knee. She was destroying him. Was she right? What if he and the angels *were* making a difficult life even more so? For the past sixteen years, he'd vowed no cry of help that reached his ears would go unanswered, that he would never cause harm to an innocent.

Would his winged brethren scoff at him, because he thought of Mina as an innocent? *Savagery is not nobility . . .* She was both. The dichotomy as well as the synthesis.

She'd left her hand pinned, and now she *had* passed out. Cautious, he rose and went to her, taking slow steps to see if anything appeared to be repelled by his proximity.

When David squatted down at her side at last, he immediately shielded her face from the harsh glare of the sun with the angle of his wings. The blood on her hand, the slight twitch of her fingers, made him feel a fury he hadn't felt in so long. A fury he thought he'd vented time and again in the battlefield until he'd purged it for good.

Apparently not.

As he slid the blade free, he held her wrist to make it a steady motion. So thin, so fragile. And yet he vividly remembered the hot breath of the dragon singeing him several times, the way her mermaid tentacles yanked his feet from beneath him. How she'd nailed him with that pipe in the jaw the first time they'd met.

She's fought them. She's fought us. Everyone, even herself, all her life.

He was certain she couldn't bear him healing the wound, but he could take three heartbeats to go to the nearest place to lift some basic first-aid supplies without notice, hoping the cause would balance the pilfering.

"David." She opened her eyes as he squatted there, one hand still holding her wrist, bloodstained knife in the other.

"It's all right. I'm here." Though he didn't read anything in her face, her lack of response mocked the words. "Maybe I'm making things worse, Mina," he said. "But for whatever reason, I can't seem to stay away from you. I've got to believe there's a reason for that."

He'd expected her to agree, or argue, but instead she gazed pensively down the long stretch of street, the desert beyond it. "If they do decide I have to die," she said, "you need to do it. Okay?"

"We're not talking about this."

When her other hand clamped over his, the ferocity, the sudden, contorted intensity of her ravaged face, surprised him. "Promise me. You say I matter to you." She shook her head as he opened his mouth. "Don't say it. I don't believe in love, and it doesn't matter anyway. But I know you're honorable. Promise me, when it comes to that, you'll . . . You're the only one I want to do it. The only one it's possible that I'll *let* do it without fighting and costing lives. You'll care, and you'll do it when it has to be done."

He couldn't stop himself anymore. He slid an arm around her, moving her so she was cradled in his lap, her injured hand pressed to her breast, smearing it with blood.

"I will be with you at the end and the beginning," he promised. "Angels say that to our fallen comrades. Okay?"

She stared at him, and it broke his heart, her obvious struggle to accept his words as truth, as if no one had ever made her a promise. So he made himself say the hated words to remove all doubt from her gaze. He suspected it was the closest thing to a declaration of love she would accept from him.

"If Jonah orders your death, I'll be the one to do it."

Fourteen

SHE laid her head on his chest. He tightened his arms around her, moved beyond words at the simple gesture of acceptance.

Lifting her, he rose and began to move toward the saloon. "There's a clean place in there for you to rest," he explained. She moved her head in a silent nod.

The door to one of the small upstairs rooms had apparently gotten stuck when pulled closed on the last day of filming. When he worked with the swollen wood and rusty hinges, fixing it with carpentry skills he'd remembered better than he'd expected, he'd found a utility cot, two folding chairs and a small pile of costumes and accessories starting to gather some dust. He suspected the cleanup team that came in after the film crew hadn't been able to get the door open, either, and so assumed the room that lay beyond it hadn't been used.

Since the cot was clean and had sheets, he laid her down on it, adjusted the covers to make her feel less exposed by her nakedness and sat on the edge. She tilted her head to look around the room, her expression distant, probing. A bit wary. She was back to being his witch again.

"Bad things happened here. What is this place?"

"It's a ghost town. Nevada has a small handful of them still standing. Most were abandoned when the gold was gone and nineteenth-century settlers moved on. But this place . . . disease hit it. Killed a lot of the settlers, enough that the rest were forced to move on, posting signs warning others against coming into the town. Looters came anyway, died here of the same disease, which was justice, since they killed some of the sick people to get their families to turn over the few valuables they had left. It was a long time ago, but you can feel the spirits that have lingered."

His gaze shifted as the thin layer of dirt on the floorboards stirred, a small ripple of acknowledgment. They both watched it settle.

"That's why you brought me here."

"I thought it would help."

"It did. I felt the dark energy when I was balancing. It confused me at first. But you don't belong here. How do you know so much about this place?"

He lifted a shoulder. "I explored the area after the Canyon Battle. Searching for any Dark Ones that went to ground. I liked the desert, the quiet of it, the open space. And I liked this place."

David stared down at her. The power of Mina's memory still haunted him, on a variety of levels, prompting him to continue, to say more than he'd intended. "Sometimes . . . I'm an angel, but the human part of me is drawn, for lack of a better word, to the remains of human spirits who don't understand why things happen the way they do."

"So this is your Graveyard." Mina swept her gaze over the room again, then back to his face. He had broken his promise at the Citadel, but maybe he was learning from his mistakes. She'd felt his frustration and distress when he couldn't help her the way he wanted, out on the street. He'd surprised her when he got past that to determine what she needed, and respected those needs more than his own desires. Now his voice, the steady, thoughtful tones, were soothing the bumpy terrain of her still-roused psyche, even as she sensed he could use some reassurance himself, though for what she didn't know. His skirmish with her as a dragon certainly wasn't the most intense battle he'd ever experienced.

Regardless, it was moot, for reassurance wasn't something she knew how to offer.

"You didn't go to the Citadel to report to your captain, did you?"

"No. I needed to know more about you. To make sure I can protect you to the best of my ability."

She'd spent all her life guarding herself, hiding in the shadows, knowing that ignorance about her nature and capabilities was her best weapon in a world full of enemies. But for the first time, she had the hint that knowledge could be equally potent in the hand of an ally. From the way he looked at her, as well as how he'd dealt with her struggle in the street, she could tell he now understood about the darkness in her. Once he'd had a grasp on that knowledge, he'd saved her from his own folly, standing between her and a battalion of angels, his own Legion Commander. She'd never had an ally.

But that wasn't the only thing he'd learned. As he sat on the edge of her bed, so careful and still, she thought of the way he'd carried her up here. As if she were precious and fragile. There were shadows in his gaze as he looked at her, seeing something more than he'd seen before. As she looked more closely, she thought what was simmering beneath his calm façade wasn't distress. It was fury, barely banked. And not with her.

"And did what you find make me worth protecting?" she ventured. Though she didn't want to ask him the specifics, she was too fragile to deal with what that fury was. He already had the ability to make her feel things she'd never expected.

"You were that before I went there. I learned what I needed to learn. It just came at a much higher cost to you than it should have. I'm sorry."

"I don't understand you at all." Before he could respond to that with something she was sure would make him even more incomprehensible to her, she pressed on. "What did Jonah mean when he said I'm not your sister?"

David's features stilled. "He let you hear that. He didn't say it aloud."

"No."

"Son of a bitch." David rose, paced away. Since the skies didn't blacken and the building didn't crumble around them, Mina surmised that it was a general expletive, not specifically aimed at Jonah or his Maker. "This isn't about that."

"Are you sure?" she asked quietly.

His wing tips left trails in the dust on the scarred wood floors. She wondered if he would answer her, for the long moments before he did.

"You're right." David said at last, the two words barely audible. Then more strongly, "He's right, too. It *is* about her. It's about you as well. It's about anyone forced to accept a life so intolerable they view death with indifference." Turning to face her, he pinned her with that intense gaze that made her so uncomfortable, yet unable to look away.

"I didn't take a woman until I was twenty-seven."

That was a surprise, for she knew from Anna that angels, particularly the Legion, were very carnal, using sensual pleasure to help ground themselves.

"I couldn't bear the touch of a woman for a very long time," he continued, maintaining that rigid stance, as if he were making a report before his battalion captain. "The other angels . . . they regularly ground themselves after battle in a woman's body. I'd go when they went in groups. Kept thinking I'd join them, but I'd reach out and . . ." He shook his head, something rippling over his skin, a tremor, but it had the odd look of a specter, a goblin hunched over him as he shrugged his shoulders.

"You couldn't," she said softly. She wanted to reach out to him. Fortunately she was too weak and he was too far away. "Why?"

He sighed. "Because I'd start to touch her and two things would happen. One, I'd hear that damnable thumping in my head. Thud. Thud." He flinched and turned toward the window. With his head bowed, eyes troubled and focused on the floor, he reminded her of one of the art books she'd rescued, the poses that depicted the struggle of man against eternal truths. It bothered her, but he continued before she could grope for something to say.

"That was the sound my sister's bed made, hitting the wall as my father raped her at night. She knew I couldn't bear to hear her cries. I burst in one night, tried to pull him off her. He beat me up pretty badly. Broke my arm. After that, she'd bite down on the pillow, wouldn't make a sound, afraid I'd interfere. But we were twins. I could hear it in my head. I'd go in the next day when she wasn't there, when my father was gone, and see the bite marks in the pillow, the marks in the wall where the headboard hit."

She knew now what else he'd found out about her at the Citadel. And she understood his fury, even as she couldn't breathe. *It is about her. And it's about you . . .* The picture was coming into focus, an understanding of the darkness within him. He was giving her the fringe shadows, and though she knew it was dangerous, that it would only strengthen the illusion of a bond between them, Mina couldn't stop him. She wanted to know. Even more strangely, that compulsion to go to him was growing in her. She wished she was strong enough to do it, slide her arms around him, lay her cheek against that broad back, between the wings, offer comfort. Something she hadn't even known she had in her to offer.

"I'd see the other angels with women, and I knew what they were doing was clean, real, the way it should be. But I didn't protect her, and he hurt her, so when I touched a female, I was repulsed. Eaten up with guilt. I didn't save my sister, so the act held nothing but revulsion for me.

"It was that way for a long time," he said after another moment. "At one point, I stopped going with them. It was too awkward. I started using meditation to ground instead. That's why I've discovered places like this. They called me the Monk. Teased me, but not in a bad way. Angels . . . we know each other's minds, so they knew what was happening with me, maybe even better than I did. I know you've seen the worst side of them, but we share each other's thoughts. Just as close as reaching out your mind to one another, never alone."

He gave a half chuckle that had little humor in it. "What my heart and mind couldn't handle, my body was raging to do, so I had to meditate pretty hard to keep those hormones under control." He arched a brow in her direction. "You think *you* fight darkness? Try being a twenty-seven-year-old guy who's never even had a girlfriend, surrounded by a species that regularly uses intense and creative sex to ground itself."

"I can't think of a worse torment. So what changed?"

His quick, gratifying grin at her dry tone changed to a thoughtful thin line. "One afternoon, I'd found a quiet place by a pond. I've always preferred Earth locales for my meditation, rather than the Seven Heavens or the stars, other planets. A girl came while I was there, about my age. She didn't see me, so I thought, and she was going for a swim. Took off her clothes, one piece at a time. Slow. So slow it was like I was the fabric sliding off her skin. I could feel it. Feel her, even before I touched her." He stared out the window, obviously caught in the memory, but Mina didn't feel offended, for she heard many things in his tone. Awe. A man who'd faced salvation, just waiting for him to reach out and grasp it.

"She let down her hair. This beautiful, raven black hair."

David swallowed, remembering the way his loins had ached, so hard. It had almost brought him to his knees, torn between lust and despair, self-loathing, wonder. For one horrid moment, his pain was so great he almost wanted to break her neck for making him feel this way.

Right as he had that thought, she turned and looked at him. She had the softest, pinkest lips, wet, and they formed words.

"I don't know what she said. Don't know to this day, but it was an invitation, and my feet were moving. Even though I remember her features, in hindsight, there was nothing exceptional about the way she looked. Just a girl with a pretty face and kind eyes. So kind. The eyes were what were different. So still. Tranquil. She was gentle, innocent, but also . . . trusting. I swam with her and she played with me, got us splashing, carrying on." The cadence of his voice slowed, dropping oddly, catching her attention as much as the story itself. "And then just as suddenly she was in my arms, all wet and naked, and I couldn't stop myself. I was trying to outrun the demons, so I was rushing, but she whispered to slow down, take my time, take my pleasure, and nothing would chase me from her.

"She took me into her body, but more than that, she took me into her soul, and I got lost in her, all the parts of myself coming unglued so I could see them, all those terrible memories, floating away, separate from all the things I'd wanted to do but couldn't.

"And she forgave me. For my sister. I don't mean she spoke it. It was just there, and as I lay upon her body, and she clasped me with her legs, kissed my throat and chest with her lips, it was like everywhere she put her mouth tore open those wounds, let them bleed out. I cried."

When David averted his face briefly, embarrassed, Mina felt a bittersweet twist in her heart.

"I'd never thought about what the word *forgiveness* meant until then. Maybe I figured it was just a way to get out of a responsibility, but then I understood it. Forgiveness is something given by someone who sees all of you, every dark and light corner, who knows where you've been, where you'll walk, where you'll misstep again, sees it against what everyone else is or has done, and knows it's going to be okay. That things are the way they were meant to be, that everything has a reason, even those that can't be explained. That it's okay to just be, to take that precious moment of stillness and hold on to it, use it to give you the strength to fuel everything else."

When he turned his head now, Mina saw the glitter of tears in his eyes. "It was then I knew that lying with a woman was like every other powerful magic in the world. A force for good or evil, depending on your intent. And I was denying myself that magic, and how it could make me stronger, a better angel. A better man. One who would help people like my sister."

"What happened to the girl?"

"I slept, and when I woke, she was gone. I've never told anyone about it, not even Jonah." He paused, stared out the window, then shifted his gaze to her. "Maybe because the more I've thought about it, the more I believe the girl I was with that day was the Lady Herself, helping me heal."

He cleared his throat, came back to sit on the edge of her bed. "So again, I'm sorry."

Mina studied him. "Well," she said at last. "I'm glad I didn't know that the first time we . . . you know. It would have been a really hard act to follow."

David's startled reaction turned to the smile that had that still-unexpected ability to make her feel better about . . . well, everything. Reaching out, he curved a lock of her hair behind her ear. "That moment was a turning point for me. Just as being with you was another."

"Were their many after Her?"

"A few. Not like you."

"Males always say that. It just means it was different from the last one, as the next one will be different."

That elicited a chuckle, and the sound of it sent a shiver down her spine. Angels really did need to turn it down, she thought irritably. But she was unable to move as he twined that lock of hair around his fingers, wouldn't let her pull away, and the look in his eyes stilled her as the humor died away.

"There are some incredibly rare people in the world," he said. "It doesn't matter what they endure, what shitty cards they're dealt. Life knocks them down again and again, until anyone with a shred of compassion is saying, 'Don't get up again. For God's sake, just stay down.'"

When his expression shifted, Mina saw raw, exposed emotion. The simple core of who he was, evident in every tautly held plane of his face, the dark, intense fire of his eyes, the way his long fingers clenched into a fist on her hair, holding her still.

"But they keep getting up. And there's something in their eyes. It might be almost gone, hidden, dulled, but if you try to force them to cross that one line deep inside them, you'll find it. It's that thing that says, 'I have the fury and the will to destroy the whole world, and I will use whatever weapon I have to *end* you.'"

His gaze shifted back to her. "It's not the Dark Blood that let you live through what few could. It's that spark in you. You may use the blood, but the resilience is *you*."

She was fairly sure she was about to be consumed by the power of what she saw in his expression, resonating inside her breast, in the pounding of her heart. "How do you know that?"

"Because you looked at an infant mermaid and had pity for her, enough to risk yourself even as a child." Tracing her face from her temple until he reached the curve of her chin, he caressed her bottom lip with his thumb. His gaze softened, in a way that muddled her mind. "You turned Marcellus's wing into a bat's wing, because deep inside it amused you. Goddess, I want to be around long enough to see you smile."

He leaned over her then, bracing one arm at her opposite hip. It was a protective and relaxed pose that didn't disturb her. If anything, she felt comforted by that sheltering presence, though a quietly alert part of her was aware of the thin sheet between them, of his gaze lingering on her bare shoulder.

As he cupped the side of her head, it felt natural to lean into his touch, let his strength hold her as lassitude sank in. It seemed she was always falling asleep around him, and not just because of the exertion of being around him, both pleasurable and life threatening. With him, she slept in a way she hadn't ever slept. Whatever her conscious mind felt, her subconscious trusted him to watch over her, so that it succumbed easily, like now. Of a sudden, all she wanted was sleep. Sleep, with his touch upon her. This male angel who was turning out to be far more than she'd expected.

"When you talk," she observed drowsily, "the way you were speaking just now, about the Lady, your voice changed."

"How so?"

"The syllables, like they're drawn out, musical, but rolling . . . the *l*'s especially."

He looked surprised. She could tell he was thinking about it, hearing himself in his own mind. Then his expression became amused. "That is a Southern drawl, sweet witch," he said, exaggerating so she heard it clearly. "Took me a while before I stopped saying 'y'all.' First time I told my platoon to meet me 'rightchere' or said 'idinit,' I got the same blank look you have now, their translation skills notwithstanding."

"What?"

"Idinit. As in, 'idinit a wonderful day?' I don't do it as much now, but with Southern boys it always comes back to us, particularly when we get riled up."

The skin on either side of his eyes crinkled. Unlike him, she didn't care if she ever produced a smile, but she was beginning to wonder if there was anything as irresistible as David's. It stirred warmth in her it shouldn't, helping her to relax further.

Though her body felt heavy, devoid of energy, her arm seemed to float up of its own accord to his mouth to touch his lips, the sensual bottom curve, as his gaze intensified. Her simplest gestures seemed to arouse an emotional or physical response from him that mesmerized her. It gave her the unwise compulsion to keep making them.

He didn't touch her, though she could sense his desire to do so as she moved to his cheek, into the loose hair falling forward on his bare shoulder, and buried her fingers there, beneath that curtain.

"Jonah said human-made angels often retain characteristics like that," he continued conversationally, but his eyes remained locked on her face. The hand braced next to her hip was stroking it with his thumb. "Until they feel comfortable enough to let those things go. He says I'll likely lose it when I reach maturity at fifty, or when I can let go of my human roots without regret or worry. Whichever comes first."

When I mature at fifty. Why that should bother her, since living beyond the next few days seemed to provide an immediate challenge, she didn't know, but his hand on her head made her hurt anew. Though she didn't want him to stop touching her. And she didn't want to think anymore.

"Riiiiled . . ." she drawled, her eyes drifting closed. "I get riiiled. A lot."

David held his breath. He wished one of his powers was the ability to hold time still a moment, or at least rewind, for he was almost certain he'd seen the tiniest curve at one corner of her mouth.

He kept up that simple stroke along her face while her breathing evened out. He wished he could erase the tension in her features that didn't leave her, even in her dreams. But he nursed the fantasy that the slight smoothing of her brow as she succumbed to sleep might be due to his touch.

As much as he loved to arouse her, bury himself in her, there was something almost sacred about watching over her sleep, as if he were being given a gift she'd never thought she'd bestow on anyone.

If only she'd let him try to heal her scars. Not just the recent ones. Repair her left side, the damage in her mouth. Though fortunately, his kisses didn't seem to bother that. He just wanted to give her less pain.

She uses the pain for something.

He'd made a nearly fatal mistake earlier, assuming he had a complete picture when he didn't. He wouldn't do that again. Particularly when he'd watched her do it twice now, use extremes of pain to achieve that balance when it was almost past recall. However, what if *he* could give her the pain she needed? Those enticing, erotic rituals with the daggers, the shallow cuts along her skin. He'd found her response fascinating, despite himself.

She avoided stresses that could unbalance her. What if giving her lesser amounts of pain, in measured intervals, would allow her to handle rather than avoid those stresses, allowing her to do more? Wouldn't that be preferable to resorting to destructive extremes or chronic pain she exacerbated by living in cold climes?

That said, he knew his motives weren't entirely altruistic. There was no coincidence between his desire to take over that responsibility and the fact such a transition would make her dependent on him.

Time to turn his thoughts elsewhere, for the moment. Get those first-aid supplies, so he could care for her while she slept, minimizing her discomfort. Then do another quick trip out to find her some food and other things to make her feel more at ease here. Before they moved on to the place he hoped he'd convince her could be home for a while.

Fifteen

MINA surfaced slowly. As she usually did when she emerged from the landscape of her nightmares, she carefully evaluated her surroundings for several minutes before moving, not giving away that she was awake. It took an extra moment to recall where she was and why. She'd been part of the ocean for so long that even when she'd drifted off, David's hand upon her, she'd felt the rocking of her body, the rhythm still with her. Just as her missing parts of flesh still reminded her of their presence. Some things imprinted on the mind and didn't leave.

Since her dreams were never peaceful, what was uppermost in her mind as she roused was her flight from the Citadel. The mindless bloodlust that had taken over, that David had recklessly drawn upon him. She'd made a conscious choice in her losing battle with the Dark One blood, to let the bloodlust infuse the dragon rather than the witch part of her. She'd known which one was likely to cause less damage. Still, she remembered how he'd risked the clutch of her talons. If she'd caught him, she could have rent him in two and ended him.

Forcing her thoughts from that, she moved on to her second waking ritual, which was finding something mundane and even possibly pleasant to think about, in order to drive back the dark and bloody dreams that accompanied her sleep. She found something almost immediately.

Her hand had been cleaned and bandaged, the broken finger resplinted. Someone had also wiped her body down with soap and water, cleaned her hair, brushed it. Used to living in the water, it was odd to think of using it to clean oneself, but she'd been so sandy and sweaty in her human form. She felt better.

While she found it astounding that she'd slept through all of that, since she knew it was David's doing, the surprise was short-lived. She'd been exhausted, and for good or ill, she was beginning to have a tentative trust in him. Which of course was a mistake.

As she sat up, something slipped across her throat. Feeling a black silk cord there, she unhooked the choker after figuring out the magnetic clasp to discover a polished piece of turquoise, carved into the shape of a tiny angel.

Things were changing. Her life always had been a certain way. Now, in the course of barely two days, she'd been confronted with a flood of new experiences. She was on land, in an abandoned human town, in the middle of the desert. Except for the time she'd gone to the surface to help Anna, there were very few times she'd ventured more than a handful of feet from the water's edge, and only when absolutely necessary. The deep, dark depths of the ocean kept her as protected as any environment could, or at least she'd always thought so. But now, it was just her and David, in a place no one would expect them to be. It was warm and dry, and there was no one around to see her interest in the things that had always fascinated her when Anna spoke about them. She touched the brush that was still sitting on the folding chair. It was plastic and red, and some of her hair was in it.

As she moved around the room, her hand closed over the angel pendant, smoothing the polished stone with her fingers. Her life worked because she'd rigidly controlled her environment, her access to others who could possibly disrupt it. Now she was bemused to recognize her rhythmic gesture as a replacement for that, an automatic reassurance of the one thing that seemed stable, for the moment. David.

She'd read about soldiers returning home from war, exploring how the warrior felt, stepping off the screaming chaos of a battlefield into a sunny kitchen with warm coffee, a wife's smile and relaxed chatter about changing the wallpaper. Whatever that was.

When she'd trawled the surface for sun-dependent water plants and come upon merpeople, sunning on a temporary raft of floating driftwood they'd woven together, she'd thought of that. The way they laughed and talked, easily dozing while a couple of them kept a casual watch, knowing they had little to fear.

No one but David knew how she'd collected books from wrecks. While she handled her spellbooks and scrolls as the precious grimoires they were, she took equal care of the dog-eared paperback books, for in the lives and struggles of the humans she found more kinship. Yet she stayed hidden in the water, because that was where she was constantly reminded of what she was, and it felt safer. There was no one to watch her back; she had to depend completely on herself. So staying where she knew the terrain and environment had made the most sense.

Now she had someone who claimed to be willing to watch her back. And he'd made the decision to bring her on land, where she could not only see the things that had fascinated her, but be away from the world that knew everything about her, their tolerance always precariously dependent on how inconspicuous she made herself.

She'd read Arabic poetry, fairy tales, espionage, books designated as "horror" that were full of dark, all-too-familiar shadows from her dreams. Romances, populated with heroes who were confident and virile, heroines who were spirited but ready and willing to be swept off their feet with the right incentives.

As that thought took her mind in a different direction, she remembered that a couple of the books she'd salvaged were set in towns like this. *Westerns*, the spines called them. With a saloon—wasn't that what David had called this building?—and a long, dusty street on which gunfighters squared off. The general store sold peppermint candy and the air outside would have been punctuated by the sound of clopping hooves, a horse jingling the bit as he shook his head to rid himself of trail dust. His rider would tie him to the hitching post and push through the saloon's swinging doors, looking for a whiskey and a pretty girl.

In the specific book she'd read, the cowboy had removed his hat when he'd seen the saloon whore. Salome, who used to be Sally, a farmer's daughter before misfortune brought her to whoring and serving drinks, had been caught off guard by it. She'd grown a hard shell, hard as the hardest mollusk—which of course had been Mina's mental comparison, since the author's terse voice hadn't provided an analogy—but it was as if that gesture of automatic respect and kindness had targeted a weak area she hadn't even known she still had. For a brief flash, she'd felt like the girl she'd once been, what she could have been. And something more than what she was now.

In the corner, Mina found the basin of soapy water and damp cloth, carefully folded gauze pads and packets of wipes with a strong chemical smell she assumed had been for tending her wound. He'd respected her wishes and not used his healing power. However, the array of items suggested he was a very particular and adept thief, a scavenger himself. Perhaps it was her corrupting influence.

She went back to the brush. Salome had had a silver-backed brush with a porcelain handle, her prized possession from her mother. She'd used it on her hair while the cowboy watched in the close privacy of her room. He'd surprised her by sitting down behind her on the bed, taking it from her hand and brushing her hair himself. Closing her eyes, Mina recalled the passage, not questioning why she'd read it so often that she knew it by heart.

For once Salome didn't feel like a receptacle, a tool, but important for her own self. She knew it was dangerous, but there came a time a girl was ready to risk everything, just so she didn't have to feel the way she always felt. Even if it was for just a minute . . .

Mina raised her hand to her brushed hair. David had tied it

loosely into a long tail on her shoulder with another piece of silk cord. While she didn't sense him near, he'd left two feathers in a dusty cracked bottle, his way of saying he was within calling distance.

Fingering the brush, she lifted and pulled it through the tail of her hair, testing it. Loosened the cord and did it again, starting at the scalp. And she remembered, through the shadows. His hand, following the track of the brush while she slept, working out tangles, disturbing the black storm clouds of her dreams with stray bits of soft, silver moonlight.

Laying the brush down at last, she turned to the remaining folding chair, because what she'd noted on it when she made her first circuit around the room had called the Western novel to mind. Lifting the stiff yet silky fabric draped over the back, she recognized what she imagined a saloon girl's dress would look like.

Did books open portals? Were Salome and her cowboy here somewhere, or were her thoughts conjuring things? Perhaps she *had* died, struck out of the sky by Jonah and his angels, and this was her odd, drifting afterlife, caught in the dream world of a favored book. She couldn't complain, especially since she'd imagined a far worse afterlife. Examining the dress, she found it was velvet blue, the skirt split and trimmed in black feathers along the split and the off-the-shoulder neckline. Stockings and what must be garters. Elbow-length gloves.

Thinking, or maybe not really thinking, she awkwardly drew the glove on her nondisfigured hand. Tight, silken, hugging her fingers and wrist, sending a frisson of sensation coursing through the underside of her arm and down the side of her breast. Unexpectedly, it tightened the nipple, as if David were standing behind her, sliding up her rib cage, where she'd feel the heat of his touch even if she was wearing the thin garment of the dress. She picked up another lace piece, with rows of tiny holes and lace ties. Holding it against the dress, she figured it out. A corset.

Well, she *was* naked at the moment. And while she was certain David had probably gone in search of more conventional clothes for her, she considered the dress. Pulling it over her head, she faced with wary pleasure the task of figuring out how it should be worn.

———

DAVID knew he needed to seek Citadel counsel on how to supply Mina's needs without constant pilfering, but he'd wait until things had settled down there. The phrase "timing was everything" was more universal than he'd once realized.

Gauging her size, he'd found some things he knew would be comfortable for her and help her blend in. They also could be carried in the hiker's backpack he'd picked up.

He was a bit more problematic. While he could compel humans not to "see" his wings, at his age and level of experience it only worked in focused attention on one or two humans, not large groups. Of course, he wasn't planning to take her to a Major League Baseball game or shopping at Wal-Mart. Though he couldn't help but think how she'd react to either one of those things.

That was the least of his concerns, however. While she'd slept and he'd cared for her and shopped, he'd reviewed the events of the past couple days.

Yes, she was half Dark One, and therefore the darkness was an intrinsic part of her. Mina insisted that a balance between light and dark was necessary, and he no longer disagreed with her on that. But there were so many shades of gray she'd never attempted to maintain that balance. What if she *could* go to a baseball game? Plant a garden. Sleep unmolested. While he didn't know what went on in her dreams, he'd yet to see her rest in her sleep. It was obvious the place she went was a place no one would wish to go when sleeping.

He was attracted to the woman—Goddess, was he ever—but when he looked at her, he also still saw the child, never truly loved by the mother. Tortured by Neptune, surviving by sheer determination. Her reactions to certain things, like the chocolate and orange, even the way she needed his sexual dominance to give herself permission to feel pleasure, suggested that certain parts of her mind had never been able to develop beyond a child's fear or caution.

If he coaxed her out, made her believe she was no longer stuck in that wall of the Abyss, that she had more choices, would she trust him to help her find them?

Mina the witch was capable of taking care of herself physically. She'd been more than a little smug to win that acknowledgment from him. But on the other hand, she'd also held herself back all her life, concerned that the bloodlust would take her over. What would happen if she could let go of that fear? Test it in safe environments? How much further could her power reach? How much more control could she discover? Most importantly, what kind of life could she choose for herself?

Landing on the roof outside the room where he'd left her, he peered in the window. Alarm registered as he saw the room empty, the covers rumpled. Concentrating, he sensed her below, in the main saloon. Good. In addition to the clothes, he'd also brought her some food. He'd had to restrain himself from bringing her far too much, too much variety.

She's a Dark Spawn seawitch, David. She's not your girl-friend. I think you keep forgetting not only what she is, but what you are not.

He winced, recalling his commander's admonition. He had checked in with Jonah, as he'd promised. While one portion of his mind was occupied with his mental report, the other had been caught by the array of turquoise trinkets in an outdoor cart in San Diego, where he'd gone for the first-aid supplies, since it was easier to flash unnoticed through a large urban center. The desire to get her a token of his affection was a thought he definitely hadn't meant for Jonah to pick up as part of their conversation. He really needed to remember that an angel over a thousand years old had little trouble plumbing all corners of his mind once he opened the door to it.

While the Prime Legion Commander was still feeling under-standably out of sorts about how things had played out at the

Citadel, David knew there was uncomfortable truth to Jonah's words. Gods, if she knew how to laugh, Mina would probably laugh at his fantasy scenarios for the two of them, things not remotely connected to him being an angel or her being what she was. Just a man and a woman, together. Quiet, uncomplicated.

It wasn't that he railed against destiny. Being an angel, going into battle behind Jonah, knowing each blow he struck defended and strengthened the Lady, all that was good, was what he was meant to be. He knew that. He treasured the ability to connect to the angels. Soaring up over the clouds and watching the sun burst into glorious color each morning and evening had quickly gone from being one of the initial perks to a basic need.

But there were things he wanted to share with Mina as well. In fact, he could share that last one, if he could coax her past her fear of heights. He wanted to give her a home. Like a human male would. A place with a fence and an apple tree. Maybe a dog. Would Mina like a puppy? No, maybe a cat. A cat had enough balance of darkness and light. A puppy was way too far on the light energy side of the line, particularly the sunny golden retriever he'd initially pictured. She'd probably turn into a dragon and eat his fuzzy, little yellow body in one gulp.

His grimly amused thoughts were disrupted as he headed toward the street. He heard voices, piano music. Touching down in front of the saloon, he surveyed the area, all senses on alert, but detected no presence other than himself and Mina. With the exception of a few lizards, a desert turtle and, not too far away, a pair of coyotes who'd stopped to listen, ears pricked forward at the unusual noise of the piano.

When he peered over the saloon doors that were fairly new, replaced for the film crew's needs since the original ones had been long gone, he was reminded of the ship's hold, the display of skeletal horses running in circles as an alert system. He'd wondered then if they were more than that. What he was seeing now was the answer to his question.

In her salvaged books there'd been one or two Westerns,

probably a way for a freighter crewman to pass the time. It was a surprise to find Mina'd liked them enough to create the world of his teenaged imaginings now.

Since she lacked actual skeletal remains this time, the images were transparent, ghostlike. Fitting for a ghost town. He wouldn't be surprised if, scattered amid the illusion, the actual ghosts were participating.

He marveled at her recall of details, but then, he expected that a witch who had to recall the exact words and measurements for spell work and potions wouldn't ever skim a text, even a piece of fiction. Especially if she used it to create worlds like this to exercise her power. Or keep her company.

The men sitting at the tables wore the myriad outfits of gunslingers, riverboat gamblers and cattle punchers. Many of them smoked. The clink of whiskey glasses and poker chips was an undercurrent to the conversations. A handful of saloon girls with swiveling hips sashayed around them, their laughter punctuating the environment as they tossed feather-plumed heads, the tight ringlets of their hair grazing mostly exposed bosoms.

As an angel, he was capable of splicing reality from illusion. But when reality and fantasy blended together so seamlessly, he suspected he might be excused for having missed her on his first pass through the room. He didn't make the mistake for more than a blink, his gaze snapping back to the woman leaning against the piano on the stage.

Dark blue velvet snugly fitted over her hips, then split high on the thigh to reveal stocking-clad legs, a riveting lace garter with a tiny bow. The skirt's long slit was edged with black feathers, which grazed the top of a pair of laced boots. There was a waist cincher, a modified black lace corset that hugged her waist and fitted just beneath her bosom. Because the off-the-shoulder style was liberally edged with feathers, he got only a tempting hint of the elevated cleavage.

She had her body angled so all he saw was her unscarred side. When she turned, he saw she'd combined reality and fantasy upon herself as well. She was unscarred, the illusion perfect except for a slight wavering from the energy that a nonangel wouldn't have detected. She looked almost how she would have if Neptune had never made his unfortunate decree. Red, wet lips, thick black lashes over eyes so blue they likely had inspired the color of predawn light.

David knew Jonah's Anna was probably one of the most physically and spiritually beautiful women he'd ever seen, golden innocence and love just shining from her. But what he was looking at was Woman in all her dark mystery, everything that drew a man and enslaved him to her, just by the fact she breathed and stood before him.

Air brushed him, causing him to glance down at himself. To his surprise, he discovered his appearance had changed, at least to the eye. He was wearing the classic garb of a gunslinger. Black trousers over heeled boots, gun at his hip and the holster tied to his thigh. Duster coat, charcoal gray vest over a cotton shirt. And a black cowboy hat with braided trim. Bemused, he felt for his wings, found that they were there, shimmering into brief awareness as he touched them, but otherwise invisible. It was a magic the likes of which he'd never seen. Illusion with the weight of reality.

The lady had invited him into her game. While he was uncertain where this was headed, he knew everything with Mina could be a test, not just a way to pass the time. He was more than willing to play, though he surmised that might be the wrong word for it.

As a boy, like so many others, he'd mastered the John Wayne saunter that suggested confidence. Not to be confused with a cocky swagger. He used that learned saunter now to shoulder into the doors, just as he would have in his imaginings with his friends, only then he would have prepared for a violent shoot-out. Of course, he'd no doubt this could become just as intensely heated.

As he stepped in, his gaze locked on hers. He removed his hat, a courtesy to a lady, and nodded.

Her lips parted, a breath slipping out that stole his own. Something flickered in her gaze, and then she strolled to the edge of the stage as he navigated the tables, feeling the astounding weight of the gun on his hip. Suspecting it would fire real bullets, he thought it best to keep it out of her reach.

When she stopped at the edge of the stage, he was there to reach out a hand. Gloves on those slim fingers fitted her wrist and forearm up to the elbow and just beyond like a second skin. Though he could tell no difference between them with the enchantment, he noted she offered the undamaged right hand. Gratified, he also noted she still wore the angel pendant he'd left her, and there was a bouquet of black feathers with a sparkling comb pulling back her hair on one side.

"I'm in need of some assistance," she said. Her voice was low, throaty, something he knew wasn't affected. Something had stirred her. He wasn't sure if her own magic had stimulated her, or his willingness to step into it without a word to break the spell, but whatever it was, unless a herd of Dark Ones invaded, he wasn't going to do anything to screw it up.

"Anything the lady desires."

Mina wet her lips. He had no idea that his sculpted jaw and steady brown eyes, so serious and focused, went perfectly with the character she'd imagined, almost as if David had inspired it. She'd seen those eyes flash dangerously, become as hard as flint or gentle as a father's touch, the way a father's eyes and touch were supposed to be. A gunslinger would protect, killing if necessary, to bring women and children out of harm's way. There was nothing irreconcilable about the warrior's face he showed his enemies or the tender countenance seen by those he protected. Implacability versus infinite compassion. An angel and a man.

He'd taken off his hat, but now she touched the brim with a light finger where it rested on his chest. She leaned over as she did, so that his eyes couldn't help focusing on the elevated positioning of her breasts in the neckline, one an illusory match for the other. It didn't matter what was charm or reality. She could easily imagine the sensation of his fingers trailing in the cleft between them. Or his mouth.

Taking the hat from his hands, she guided it back to his head, and he helped, laying his fingers over hers to put it squarely there again. "You said something about assistance." He cleared his throat, charmingly. "How can I help you, ma'am?"

One thumb caught in the gun belt, the other in the waist pocket of the vest, but his fingers were tensely curled, as if he were doing it to keep from reaching out and touching her. Or rather, that's what she wanted to think.

"Can you help me off the stage?"

He nodded, freed his hands and put them to her waist. As she rested her fingers on the broad shoulders beneath his duster, she tried not to think how easy it would be to dispel the spell and feel bare flesh. Real flesh.

Lifting her, he brought her down to the floor. Close. So her body slid down his, inch by inch, his strength on blatant display as he drew it out and her fingers curved into his hard biceps, one leg itching to hook itself around the back of his thigh, feel the taut buttock slide along the inside of her thigh. Her breasts pushed against the vest, rising even higher, the bodice so low that it was possible to see the pink circle around one nipple. When she reached the ground, his hands were still on her hips, her body against his, so that she felt his reaction, hard and high against her corseted abdomen.

It took effort to recall her intention. She eased back, a little thrilled when his fingers didn't release her. Then, apparently remembering the role he was playing, his grip eased.

"It's hard to lace a corset by yourself. It's a little loose. Do you think you could tighten it for me?"

She turned so his breath was on her nape, the catch of it as the skirt, gathered in back, brushed his groin. "The more curves they can see, the better these boys tend to tip. Above and below." She drew out her words the way she'd heard him do it, that thing he called a Southern drawl, giving them a touch of honey as she imagined Salome would.

When his hands found the lacings, she shivered. Brushing the top of her buttocks with his knuckles, he began adjusting the ties. "I imagine that's true, ma'am, though I don't think you have anything to worry about on that score." He leaned in, his jaw touching her cheek, his mouth distractingly close. "Unless you got a man. I think he might have something to say about other men eyeing what's his."

He was *so* much better at that Southern drawl than she was. Her breath left her in a gasp, as much because of her reaction to the sexy cadence as the way he drew the laces tighter in one even jerk, making her feel the increase in constriction from above her pubic bone to the nipple area.

"How's that? Tight enough?"

Her response trickled down her thigh, dampening the top of her stocking. "Tighter," she said, in little more than a whisper.

He obliged, and when the jerk came this time, she let out a small moan, particularly when his hand came up under one now highly perched breast and grazed just the top with his finger. So close to the barely concealed nipple she arched, her buttocks pressing into his cock as he moved up to her throat, to the ribbon and cameo choker she wore, the tiny angel just below it. His fingers laid over it, collaring her as he held her back against him, rubbing his cock slow and sure against the seam of her buttocks through the dress. The piano shimmered, her control faltering, just like at the ship, as if David's ability to arouse her could disrupt the simplest magic.

"Are you wet for me, girl?" His voice, the husky, dangerous voice of a gunslinger, goaded her, daring her to continue to play.

When she nodded, he guided her hand. "Show me. Take me there. Let me feel your fingers dip into that honey. I've been in the desert a long time."

She thanked whatever deity or demon might be responsible that he was still close enough to his human roots to remember how to be this kind of man. The long split made it easy to do as he demanded, as did the fact there were no undergarments beneath except the garters. His hand stopped hers along the soaked edge of the stocking, caressing and learning that, before following the garter up, up until he found her, guided both of their fingers in together, her forefinger and his, sinking deep into her as she cried out, trembling with her passion.

Taking his hand away then, he turned her, his face suffused with a pure male lust that rocked through her before he lifted her, laid her back on the stage. But he didn't ruck up her skirts and drive into her as she expected. Or lay his body on hers. He spread her legs, his gaze intent upon her bare sex, holding her wide and vulnerable for him. Went still, making her self-conscious and almost incoherent with need at the same moment.

His gaze flicked up to her face, a brief but potent look. "As I said, I've been in the desert awhile. And I've a powerful thirst." Then he dropped to one knee and put his mouth directly on her.

She nearly came off the stage, but he held her down. Plunging his tongue in deep, he sucked on her, taking in her juices, savoring the taste of her with a muffled growl, flicking the lips with his firm tongue, stroking then plunging deep into her again.

Twisting and arching, too overcome with the sensation to give her body a controlled purpose or rhythm, she sought a purchase on the flat boards of the stage, digging her fingers into the wood. Her movements and the tight, restrictive hold of the corset freed the one breast, where the feathers teased and caressed it to an even harder point. David's hand clamped over it, squeezed hard and possessive as she cried out again. She was a symphony of discordant whimpers, moans and soft, entreating cries, sharper screams coming from her in bursts.

It was too much. Oh, gods, it felt so good. His mouth was divinely blessed or the greatest of sins. She wanted to taste it, taste herself.

"You . . . Want you." She was astounded she could form coherent words, actually make them come from her throat. It was even possible she'd simply thought it, said it to him in that direct way he could hear but she rarely used because of the intimacy it implied.

He rose over her, his brown eyes like the fires deep in the Earth's crust. It filled her with liquid heat, threatening to erupt. Gods, his mouth was glistening from her juices, what he'd taken from her, and as she watched, he passed the back of his hand over it like a man who'd just had a satisfying draught of whiskey.

As her ankle touched the holster, she let the laced boots, one part of her costume that was pure illusion, disappear so that she could run her toes over the grip of the gun. Finding the steel, the lethal metal, she slid her foot under the thin strap that held the holster to his hard thigh. He bent, his lips touching the inside of her leg again, high up, but when she reached for him, wanting to bring him down to her, he caught her wrist. Holding it away from him, he took his time, one tiny nibble at a time, down to her knee, then back up again.

"Now," she gasped. "I can't bear it. Please." Her fingers were curled, her arm pulling taut against his hold, wanting to know he could overpower her, that she couldn't stop him or influence him, except by begging.

"Do you love me, saloon girl?"

Sixteen

I F he'd said her name, perhaps it would have called her out of the fantasy enough to dampen the moment. But as if he understood what she was and wasn't capable of doing, he knew the right words. The safe ones.

He'd made a mistake at the Citadel, but there were mistakes that were perhaps meant to be. Because he now knew more about her than before, and the man was a damn quick study. Before long, he'd have maneuvered his way into the bottom of her soul, God help him in that dark place.

"You're tolerable."

He smiled against her flesh, a slow, sexy gesture, and then he bent to put his mouth on her again.

"Nooo . . ." She tried to fight him, but he forced himself between her legs and kept her wrists captured in one hand as he worked her flesh, taking her up so close, but not there. Holding her on a pinnacle with his clever, licking tongue, so that she started to gasp as if she'd been running for miles, running away from a pursuit that wouldn't be evaded. Her backside was sore from thumping down on the boards in jerking reaction to the rhythmic manipulation of his mouth.

"Yes," she gasped at last.

"Yes, what?" He lifted his head, his fingers tightening on her wrists. As he straightened above her she was so very conscious of how he manacled her that way, the manner in which he'd bound her tightly in the corset. The fact she was spread and vulnerable before him. She couldn't hold it anymore. The illusion dissipated, showing her the powerful spread of wings, the bare muscle of his chest and thighs, the glint of his daggers.

He didn't look like the gunslinger anymore, so what came out of her mouth would be to him. To David.

"I don't know what that is," she said, and her voice broke, defeating her. "I don't know what love feels like."

He nodded, and her flesh spasmed as his gaze descended, took a slow, leisurely appraisal of what he had revealed.

"Good girl," he murmured. "You didn't lie to me." Moving forward, he pressed his thigh against her mound, making her jerk.

"Rub yourself against me, Mina. Show me what you want."

She did it shamelessly, driven to insanity by the way he watched her with visible male pleasure as she thrust her hips up, again and again. The way his attention shifted to the quiver of her naked breast, the sharp thrusting point.

Finally, he laid his palm on her taut stomach, stilling her movements, quivering nerves beneath his hand. His touch dropped, his thumb settling just over her opening, that electric bundle of nerves, so close she could feel the heat. If he touched her, she would shatter, but he wasn't as kind and merciful as she'd thought.

"Who do you belong to, Mina?"

She couldn't breathe, everything held so tightly by him, within and without, even as those words threatened to crack her open.

"Who do you belong to, saloon girl?" he repeated. She was so close, but the panic was rising. It was going to be lost. She couldn't give him that—it wasn't in her—and despair was going to close in.

Then something shifted, and she was both terrified and swept away to see understanding dawn in his eyes. "Who do you *want* to belong to?"

"You." The single, trembling word erupted from her lips, commanded by a spell uttered in just the right way, which made the honest answer impossible to block.

"Then come, now, before my cock ever enters you, only on my command."

Did his thumb touch her, or was it just that single potent demand that struck her lower belly, electrifying the nerve endings deep in the womb where all forms of birth and life began? She surged up, a scream tearing out of her throat as he took hold of her hips and drove into her on the pinnacle of that mind-shattering release, pumping into her hard and fast, rocking her against the boards, mixing rough possession with delirious pleasure. She kept coming, driven up, each wave taking her up to a higher level as everything released, even things she didn't know were prisoners within her.

Quiet David. The qualities that had turned him into a lieutenant were so evident now. His command of the situation, his confidence, the ability to take control. A man would trust his direction. While a woman would surrender, knowing with one tip of his hat that her heart, soul and mind were safe with him.

She realized her fear was no longer of him, but of what she would do to him if he truly convinced her of that. Horrified, she felt a teardrop slide from the corner of her eye to pool in the curve of her ear.

The saloon was a quiet, empty room again, all furniture long gone except for one round table with a broken leg and the scarred impressions in the floorboards where the bar had once rested.

David couldn't take his eyes off her. She wasn't a saloon girl with siren red lips and a perfect face anymore. The dress she wore was ill-fitting at the top because of her lack of a breast on one side. The map of scars along half of her face, throat and one arm was a mockery against the beauty of the silk. None of that mattered.

Lifting her under her elbows, he brought her back to her feet and folded her in his arms, holding her against his heart, feeling the wetness of her mouth against his chest. Did she realize she'd let out a sob or two among her cries of pleasure? He pressed his hand against the side of her face, the heel of his hand high on her cheekbone to absorb the telltale dampness he knew she didn't want him to see.

A broken soul, not a dark one. There *was* a difference.

"It's okay," he murmured.

"We both know that's not true," she mumbled into his skin, her fingers curled into his arm. "You can hold me like this, and it will only feel good for so long. Eventually, what's inside of me will need to push you away, repelled by the very thing that brought me close in the first place."

"Then stay until it doesn't feel good, and let go. I'll be here when you can bear it, when you need it."

"It's not that simple. You *can't* make it that simple." Pushing away from him then, she yanked the fallen sleeve of the dress up, held it there as it tried to fall again. "I don't cry. This isn't me."

"You were the one who started this." David worked to keep his tone mild as he gestured around him. "Who are you trying to convince?"

"You appeared in the middle of it," she said hotly.

When he stepped forward, she backed into the stage. "Mina." He didn't reach forward like he'd done before, instigating one of those power struggles he knew she might use to either make him prove himself or push him away. He wasn't in the mood. It was the second time she'd taken an earth-shattering connection between them and tried to destroy its meaning. While he knew what she fought, and was willing to stick with her through eternity to overcome it, it didn't mean he'd lie down and accept the denial, let her roll over him with it.

"It's not that simple; you're right. Jesus, nothing with you is." At her narrow glance, he inclined his head, letting his annoyance slip a sardonic edge in his tone. "I get it. You're dangerous, or rather, you *think* you're a danger to others—"

She blinked at him. Twice, if he remembered correctly. By the third blink, he was airborne, as the saloon floor exploded beneath his feet, throwing him up and through the roof, the planks shattering, nails tearing his skin. The roar of the explosion deafened him to everything, including his cry as she was lost to his view, gone despite his fierce struggles to flip against the concussion and shoot back toward her.

He landed hard on the street and was assaulted by planking, raining down toward the ground like arrows, such that he sprang away and aloft to get out of the shower of debris, striking through it with fists and a twisting body.

"Mina," he shouted. The saloon was a ball of flame. A breath before he prepared to dive into it, she walked out.

Walked out of the flame in bare feet and that ill-fitting dress. The fire split before her like subjects before a monarch as she stepped into the street, no dirt or debris on her, not even a scorch mark that he could see.

He landed before her, trying to process that she was unhurt. Trying to suppress his reaction when he realized she'd done this purposely, a rather overly violent reaction to his mild irritation with her.

No, that was wrong. He struggled to look past himself and analyze the way she stood, stiff, rigid, staring at him with that chilling distance he'd confronted before. It hadn't been his words, but her tears. She wouldn't tolerate those from herself. It was herself she was punishing, denying *herself* the moment they'd been given, not him.

"I'm not something you can fix, David," she said. That flat, passionless voice he'd heard far too often settled back in place like the equally despised black cloak. "I'm part of chaos and Dark Magic. There's a great deal of difference in that. I dream of the Dark Ones every night, have been connected with them since I became self-aware. They've been trying to coax me back through that portal for nearly twenty-five years, and in the last few months it's gotten worse. Much worse. Eventually, Jonah, Marcellus and all of them will be right. I won't be able to hold them off any longer."

As she watched him process the disturbing revelation, she cocked her head. "What do you think your Legion would do if it knew that? You think if I have the capacity to shed tears or feel a woman's desire, if I have a moment of kindness or pity toward an infant, it will outweigh the hundreds—maybe thousands—of times I've thought of slitting Anna's throat, letting her blood flow over my hands, savoring the last gasps of her breath?"

The sudden venom from her, the graphic image she painted, sent him back a step before he could stop himself, and her eyes darkened. The lines at her mouth deepened, somehow making her look far older, as if he were face-to-face with the wicked witch of every fairy tale with a dark wood to traverse. "Don't ever patronize me," she said, low. "It's dangerous, and stupid."

David studied her face. Gave her an imperceptible but unfathomable nod. Then he moved.

The electrical charge slammed through her system, paralyzing Mina's mind for the key moment it took for him to put her on her back. His knee was uncomfortably high on her thigh, depressing the important human artery there so that her heart rate stuttered. He had his dagger point at the soft tissue under her throat. In one movement, he could drive the blade, charged with more of that angel fire that could kill Dark Ones, up into her brain.

"I get it," he said, his voice stern and ruthless. She noted, with a lick of terror, his eyes had gone entirely dark. Apparently even a human-born angel's eyes changed in combat. "I'm not innocent or simple. For sixteen years I've fought the kind that sired you. I know their capabilities. If I reversed this knife now"—in a blink he had the power-charged dagger in *her* hand, his curled around it, the point under *his* throat—"and I goaded the blood in you, just enough . . ."

Light energy invaded her body through that grip, spreading out from her throat, paralyzing her vocal cords, rushing toward her heart.

The Darkness roared up, reacting like a cornered wild predator. The redness rushed over her, and David was painted in the blood of it in her vision as the Dark One took over. Her fingers, now talons, swiped at his abdomen with a flash of lethal tips while she drove the dagger up with the other hand.

One push should have sent it into his brain, but he wasn't there anymore. Suddenly Mina was in the air, as if propelled by the same type of explosion she had just created. With no way to slow her fall, the electrical charge still rocketing through her, she flipped and flailed through the air, her joints popping, muscles straining. She would not scream. She refused to scream.

"Got you."

She hit David's chest with a jarring thud and found herself gripping his shoulders for dear life. He took them back to the ground, cradling her in his arms as if he hadn't just had a knife to her throat. When he reached the street, he lowered her feet to it, even as he held on to her waist with one hand, steadying her.

They faced each other. She was gasping, the darkness as well as the witch part of her swirling in confusion, uncertain which direction her compass was pointing. She'd kept her hands on his shoulders, sliding to his chest when he lowered her, and now she had her fingers hooked into the belt of his half tunic, clinging there between the metal buckle and the hard line of stomach muscle and hip bone. His pulse was pounding in his throat, but his eyes were level, his tone even as he finally spoke.

"Perhaps we both underestimate each other." As she blinked at his casual observation, he continued, his voice sharpening, "If you want me to prove every day that I can control you, protect you from harming others, I will. But hear me . . ." He lifted her chin then, and she couldn't stop the quiver of her body from his touch, any more than the sullen defiance of the beast within her. "It won't change how much I want you. Love you. I meant that. It won't affect the way I feel for you."

"The Darkness *is* me, as much as the other half. You can't love me if you understand that."

"Yes, I can. But I'm beginning to wonder if you understand it."

Her brow furrowed. "What do you mean?"

"I see a woman who conducts her life as if she's under siege by an invader. She's fought an admirable lifelong battle of deception and strategy to keep it from taking the ground she fights so hard to hold within herself, for herself. And in the process she's been deprived of any joy that life can give her. Which is why she's weakening, even as her powers grow stronger."

"No." She shook her head. "You don't—"

"What if I *do* understand? What if it's you who can't afford to think of it my way?"

Perplexed, she couldn't think of any reply to that, and he nodded, his brown eyes holding her gaze with that determined look she found hard to deny. "Fine, then. Can you afford to invite me onto that battlefield, let me fight at your back until I prove it to you?"

She bit her lip. "What if you die there?"

"I've already died once before. There are worse things."

The air seemed less charged, the daylight softening along with her resistance, such that she didn't move when he reached out and pushed back a lock of her hair. "It's not my way to prove something like this in such a violent way." His tone changed, became more gentle, as if he felt the shift within her as well. "But you've been testing me from the beginning, and it was time to show you that I won't ever let you hurt Anna, Mina. Or me. Or anyone you're afraid of hurting. Okay?" He bent his knees a little so he could look directly into her pensive face. "And I'll still hold you whenever you think you need it. Or as long as you can stand it."

Mina swallowed, looked at the carnage she'd created. "I wish I could trust you. Believe you."

"Trust comes with time. And it has to be earned."

"It's not a matter of that. I can't trust you, David. That part of me . . ."

"Once again, is it possible that you've confused the defenses you've built for yourself with the enemy outside of them?" He tipped her chin up again when she tried to look away. "It's just a leap of faith. That's something you'll have to decide for your-self.

"Now." He forced a lighter tone. "Good thing I left the food and clothes outside in the street. Are you interested at all in what I brought you for lunch?"

Seventeen

MIND-SHATTERING orgasm, a violent argument, a harrowing revelation, and now food. Mina would never be a dull companion.

"So if the Dark Ones have been in your dreams all these years, maintaining a connection and awareness of you, why do you think they're pursuing you more aggressively now?"

She shrugged. "I don't really know. I just know their interest has increased over the past couple of months. My assumption was it was the Canyon Battle. It revealed more of the powers I have. All Dark Spawn, while they survive, are connected to the Dark One world in their dreams. I was just one more, until I started keeping questionable company with angels."

"Can you see their world?"

"Can we eat before we talk about this? Some of us don't live on manna alone."

The way she was eyeing the food, he could tell she was hungry. And of course, living in a survival mode as she did, she would want to dispense with it first, before the next crisis confronted them. "Getting between you and the call of the Dark Ones I can do," he said lightly. "Getting between you and food—I'm not that brave."

She narrowed her eyes at him, but David said nothing further as he gave her the sandwich, his tongue tucked into his cheek.

First she dismantled it and studied all the separate pieces. Chopped almonds, lettuce, tomato, the soft golden spread of hummus, cucumbers, wheat bread. Then she reassembled them, nibbling a corner of the bread first, after smelling the fresh-baked aroma—several times. Potato chips startled her with their loud crunch, but she quickly got over that.

While she ate, David considered his approach. Before the disruption at the Citadel, the unexpected offer Jonah had made had two parts. One was that Anna was prepared to give Mina money to exist in the human world. The portion of Neptune's treasure Anna had at her fingertips would be enough to support one mermaid, plus one hundred witches, for five or six lifetimes. Part two was a little more complicated, but it was time to present it. While his witch was eating seemed the best time. While he loved to watch her eat, it also pained him. The initial caution followed by a ravenous hunger, the way she would pull it close and hover over it like a pack animal, expecting to have to fight others off for it. He suspected she wasn't even aware she did it.

"Did Anna ever tell you about the house she and Jonah stayed at when they were at the Schism?" He referenced the magical fault line in the Nevada desert, where Anna had taken Jonah to heal his soul.

"Briefly." Mina swallowed a mouthful of hummus and then followed David's gesture to pick up the bottle of water and wash down the spiced spread. "She said it belonged to a couple helping the shaman maintain the Schism's balance."

"Matt and Maggie. Yes. They returned to their home in another state recently, and left the care of the house and its use to Jonah and Anna. Jonah has suggested we go there, for now. If it will let us in."

"Why wouldn't it?"

"The Schism won't allow Dark Ones in, and the house is just inside the perimeter. It's not a white light zone," he added quickly at her furrowed brow, the worry it indicated. "But it's one of the magical principles."

After Jonah's stinging comment earlier, David had worried the offer might be rescinded, but the commander was still willing to proceed with it. Reassured, David had tentatively suggested that Mina could help Sam, the aging shaman and guardian of the Schism, maintain the Schism balance and protect it. An equitable exchange for a safe and protected place to be while she investigated her abilities with greater freedom.

Jonah had been dubious. First step, he advised, was seeing how she dealt with being on land for a prolonged period. Not to mention whether the Schism would even accept her.

Thinking on that as well as the volatile exchange they'd just had, the pleasurable and not so pleasurable, he couldn't deny that Jonah's advice to proceed with caution was worth heeding. No matter the disarming nature of her current appearance.

When he'd judged her size, which he thought grimly would be somewhere between junior and preadolescent, he'd gotten her a brown T-shirt with a desert scene on it, and a broomstick skirt that picked up the pink, rose, blue and brown desert colors. He hadn't been thinking much about them matching, but they'd been paired on the same rack. He'd also gotten her a pair of pale pink panties that she'd studied with interest before discarding the saloon-girl dress and wriggling into them with little modesty, a casual intimacy that had been . . . stirring. Because of the disfigurement and the fact she was small breasted, he hadn't bothered with a bra, but he was rethinking that as her nipple distracted him with its tempting protrusion against the cotton. It made him want to stroke her through the soft shirt.

He'd also gotten her a pink ball cap to guard her face from the sun. Apparently feeling vulnerable without her cloak, she'd pulled the bill low on her brow and arranged her hair so it fell mostly over the nonscarred side.

"Why do you do that?"

"What?" She glanced up, a potato chip ready to be put in her mouth.

"Cover the nonscarred side. Most people would do just the opposite."

She shrugged, interestingly unconcerned with the question. "The scars say I can take care of myself. Survive. The beauty is a trick of creation, the luck of chance. And luck is fickle. I have no use for it. Beauty also attracts attention," she added. "Deformity tends to make people want to avoid contact with you, and then they don't notice other details."

"Is that why you didn't want me to heal your scars?"

That startled her. Even as he watched her expression shutter, he knew she was going to lie to him.

"Yes," she said. She ate the chip then, closing her eyes, a nonverbal cue to discourage conversation until she finished.

He waited, but when she was done, he put a hand on hers. "There've been males who tried to take advantage of that beauty. That's a reason to hide it as well."

She tried to withdraw her hand. "They weren't successful. Which you know, if you know that much."

"I'm glad. I'm sorry you had to . . ."

As she studied him, her impassive expression gave way to curiosity. "What?"

"I'm just sorry." David gave a half shrug, unsure himself of what he'd been trying to say. "I understand a lot about the world I didn't know when I was human. About why people go through terrible things, the balance between good and evil, and how life is a journey and all that. Anna told me once she didn't regret anything she'd suffered, because every bit of it made her who she was. I look at you . . ." He gave her an appraising look, causing Mina's brow to furrow. But when she drew away, her body language defensive, he reached out again, only this time he waited patiently and with a pointed look until she relented, laid her hand in his again. The three-fingered one, so that his touch slid over the maimed stumps, gently handled the splint. "I look at you and see a powerful witch who's that way because she's a powerful soul. But at the same time, I want to go back and break into pieces anyone who thought he had the right to cause you a moment of fear, hurt you because he thought himself stronger and wanted something you might not be willing to give him."

The surge of fury he thought he'd managed to control since his visit to the Heavens came back then. He didn't want violence of that kind to flood out and over her. So instead, he did the next best thing. "Oh, hell. Just come here."

Mina emitted a surprised squawk as he tumbled her into his lap, gathered her in close and bent his head over hers, putting his lips in distracting proximity to her face. It almost made her forget he'd scattered her chips and the remains of her sandwich across the boards of the general store's shaded porch. "I want to protect you from everything," he said. "I can't separate the woman from the girl from the child from the witch. You're just going to have to deal with that."

She could feel it, in the hard tremor that ran through him. Whether he was in fact motivated by a mortal life where he hadn't been able to help someone he'd truly loved, such that she'd become a surrogate despite his denial, she still knew it was truth. He'd made it clear that he wasn't starry-eyed when it came to her potential for evil. While proving that he would kill her if he had to do it wouldn't be viewed by most females as a way to increase trust in a relationship, it had done it for her.

He seemed intent on demonstrating that he'd stand by her, through petty irritation and tedious guard duty, as well as the possibility of death, dismemberment and torment of kinds that couldn't be imagined.

"I'd offer you a chip, if you could taste it," she said. His quick smile warmed her.

"True generosity. Thank you." He angled his head to give her a considering look. "But I like the taste of you better than anything. Would you consider a kiss instead?"

It was the first time he'd ever asked, instead of taken, which made it harder for her. Regardless, she arched a brow at him, trying to appear as if she were casually considering it, even as his words reminded her vividly of what his mouth could do. Not just to her mouth, but to other parts of her body.

Reaching up so abruptly she almost hit his face with her knuckles, she recovered enough to slow herself down, feather her hand through his hair, drifting forward along the line of his face. He stayed still, letting her have the chance to take something for her own pleasure.

"I like the taste of you, too," she said. "So much, sometimes I don't know if I can stop myself from tearing into your skin. You frighten me, David, because you make control hard, and that's already very difficult for me."

"Maybe you should just trust me," he suggested. "You won't hurt me more than I can bear. And when I draw your passion to the bloodlust level, I'll hold you down, focus all that energy here."

She gasped as the hand she hadn't been watching found its way up her skirt, laid itself between her thighs, fingered her intimately so her legs loosened to him. "I'll make that passion rise," he continued, his voice thickening, "so violence becomes something else. We have angels in Heaven who write poetry, put it to song. They sing of how Creation is unstable, as unstable as destruction, though far more beautiful." He hummed what she imagined were those words, before he nuzzled her forehead. She closed her eyes, her fingers in his hair as he did remarkable things between her thighs.

His voice was a seduction like the wind, sifting through the sand on the street, carrying it along effortlessly. "If you channel your tremendous power into something else, it helps, right? The skeletons of horses, the phantoms of people long dead by violent or tragic means."

She mewled as his hand rocked against her, making her hips rise to his touch as his arm tightened around her back. "Create for me. Create magic while I get you wet and gasping. Let me see what your mind will do."

Her nails dug in, and his expression got more fierce and intent. "Use your claws if you must, kitten, but do magic. Make magic for me."

He'd doused the saloon fire, sent the smoke billowing away from them, so there were just the charred bones of the building now. The sun was almost gone, a moment or two away from plunging them into night, the air already hinting of the coolness coming. She was far more susceptible to cold, fairly unaffected by the heat of the desert. She'd been fighting Dark One fire for a long time, after all.

David picked up a chip, brought it to her lips just as he slid two more fingers deep into her. She chewed, swallowed, her glazed eyes on him, lips moist.

He leaned forward, licked salt off her lips. "Create for me, little witch."

Watching her get aroused was all-absorbing to him, but David made himself pay attention, so he noticed the first leap of fire. From the charred remains of the saloon, she'd found a lingering spark, and created an arch of flame that sprang from the embers, twisted like a confused snake on the sand, then steadied. As it turned toward them, it spread, then became the wide bloom of a fiery rose. Small spouts of flame bounced out of the crevices of the petals, scattered across the dusty main street and created smaller buds, each one different.

Other tongues of flame split off to become shiny and thin, gold red waving blades of grass, a meadow for the flowers that now dotted the debris, turning the saloon remains into a landscape.

Still, the fire spread, the street becoming a garden of flame blossoms, the heat of them preceding their approach. As David worked her clit, he felt it swell with blood, a rose of flesh instead of flame. Even with her legs open to him, her body straining, her eyes stayed locked with his, apparently her focal point for the magic she was spinning. Her nails had gouged into him at some point, and he could feel the stickiness of his own blood, knew it was on her fingers.

Goddess, he'd just had her, right before their fight. He couldn't get enough of her.

"Put one of the flowers in your hand." Uncurling her tense fingers from her side, he opened the palm. Her gaze flickered, and one of the blooms rose from the ground as if plucked, coming through the air in a graceful float, landing in her hand. Because it was her magic, he knew it wouldn't burn her flesh.

Letting go, he drew one of his daggers. He ran the tip lightly down the center of her palm, through the flame petals, creating a swirl of magic, a shower of sparks that fell upon them both but didn't disrupt the form of the enchantment. Her control was too refined for that. He wanted to disrupt it. His body tightened when she reacted to the erotic kiss of the pain with a parting of her lips.

Resheathing the weapon and taking her flame-engulfed, bleeding hand, he pressed it to his chest, just over his heart.

Mina gasped as his face contorted with what she knew had to be searing pain, shooting through his nerve endings, screaming their rejection of that Dark fire. But his grip became bruising, holding her there. His other hand amazingly kept moving, driving up her arousal. Helpless, she pumped herself against his fingers with the rhythm her body dictated, her gaze on that hand and his burning flesh.

"That's it," he rasped. "Work yourself against me. Come. Come now."

The harshly delivered command sent her over, pushing furiously against his friction. Feeling his flesh burning beneath her magic, and yet experiencing his command of her, his control of her release, was a moment of such perfect balance the only thing Mina wished for more was having him inside of her.

But this was what she would have. She cried out, the climax overtaking her, as his expression became triumphant. Now she was held in the cup of one of his wings as he pinned her there with a hand at the base of her throat, the other hand working her even more powerfully, increasing her sense of helplessness and the intensity of the energy at once. She completed the triad of connection, keeping her flame-engulfed hand flat against his chest.

When at last she stopped, chest heaving with deep, shuddering breaths, the fire flickered and slowly died away. Mina felt his fierce gaze on her as she slowly lifted her palm. He'd known about fire magic and his own anatomy, knowing what could scar an angel permanently if it wasn't treated. He'd let her mark him.

She didn't see the rose brand she'd expected, but a shadowy image of her handprint. Of course. This kind of magic took the form it felt was most appropriate. Not letting herself think about why she was doing it, she leaned forward, holding on to his hair and the side of his neck, and pressed her lips there.

"You can heal it," she said after a long, long moment while she felt him quiver with pain and something else. Something that made it hard for her to speak or even breathe.

"Yes. But I won't." When her gaze lifted to him, his eyes were so full of that indefinable thing, Mina swallowed. She shifted so she was straddling him, a scrambling, almost violent movement like an attack, his hands having time only to come around to cup her bottom as she reached beneath his kilt and found him. Shoving the fabric away, she forced herself down on his rock-hard length. Spreading the skirt over his legs, as if by concealing the joining point it made them one animal, inseparable, she let out a breathy moan. Her ultrasensitive, postclimax tissues contracted on him. When he seized her hips and drove her to the hilt, she cried out, but then went still as he held her there, his gaze fixed on hers, their two bodies quivering, vibrating together.

She couldn't think of what to say to him. Things had gotten so complex so quickly between them. Was she selfish—and foolish—enough to think she could claim an angel just because she was starting to think she wanted his company?

Then he started to move, and she let all that get swept away by the dark thrill of how he surged into her, his eyes still fired, mouth held firm. She plunged her hands into his wings, gripping handfuls of soft feathers. His arms cinched around her, so she was pressed against his body, that brand. As he began to come, her muscles contracted further, squeezing him inside where her feelings couldn't be seen. She closed her eyes.

"Thank you," she whispered.

For being willing to follow me into Hell. She knew she didn't have a pure enough soul to resist the temptation to let him do just that, if that was where she was headed. For the first time in her life, she wished she had more to offer.

But then, in an unexpected shift caused by the realization that the thing he'd called a cake donut was mashed beneath her knee, she thought maybe there was one thing she *could* give him, something he couldn't provide himself.

If she didn't get him killed before the opportunity presented itself.

Eighteen

D AVID told her they weren't far from the Schism. Since she
found herself dreading the confrontation, not knowing
whether or not it would permit her access to the safe house Jonah
had offered, Mina opted to walk the last few miles, despite the
nagging ache she knew it would cause in her hips.

She could feel the vibration of the fault line already, tendrils
of its energy reaching out. Anna had told her about the remarkable mirages she and Jonah had seen on the shimmering horizon
when they'd gotten this close, so she distracted herself by looking
for them.

For the most part, David chose to walk with her, though occasionally he went aloft to scout. She studied the vegetation,
tasted the leaves of a few plants, curious about their medicinal
properties. Examined the array of lizards, turtles, bugs and
snakes that populated their desert wilderness. It made sense the
Schism would be here. Power was rampant among the silent, ancient rock formations which had sealed in evidence of life
throughout the ages as the ocean receded from it. In her imaginings, she could see the whales swimming lazily by with schools of
fish. Only they were great, prehistoric creatures, with much longer teeth and bigger eyes. If she focused, she could expand their

size even further, take the distant rocks, put them underwater again, watch the baffled lizards float and swim, twist . . .

"Mina."

She tuned in to his voice to find herself in a shimmering heat current, a handful of panic-stricken lizards and snakes floating in it. One of the snakes had attached itself to her arm, considering her the most stable thing in the unexpected gravitational shift. Slowly, the other creatures drifted back to the ground, and the wavering illusion of water disappeared. David pried the snake off her arm and sent the offended reptile slithering off in a rapid sideways motion across the sand.

He gestured. "We're coming up on what looks like a highway. There's a roadside diner, about a mile that way." When he pointed, she made out the structure, the corners and lines too straight to be a contour of the Earth. "If you want, I can just fly you past it, or you can walk while I go over it, out of sight."

She studied it. "Something seems off about it. The energy is unusual."

"Yeah, but I don't think it's a threat. Jonah said things aren't always what they seem here. Real, but different. Like it might be something that does exist in the world, just not here."

Intrigued, she gave it a closer study, trying to determine the energy readings from it. It was a confusing mixture, though it seemed benign. "So you're saying this could be a diner from somewhere else, but the inhabitants don't realize they've been blinked into the Schism to serve a magical purpose?"

"Maybe. He didn't go into a lot of detail. He's still pissed off at me."

"I doubt that. He thinks you're making a terrible error in judgment. Because he's protective of you, the best thing he can do is get me somewhere that Dark Ones won't go. Then, assured of my safety, you can return to your platoon duties, where he hopes you'll go back to being sensible again."

David crossed his arms over his chest. "Really?"

"I suspect so." She went to a squat, considering the diner

still. "I'd prefer to walk toward the restaurant. I want to go in."

In the proximity of a magical fault line, she knew it was possible that, having thought of what she could offer to David as a gift, the solution had materialized in the form of this diner. She just wondered what price it would exact or what it was seeking.

"Do you agree with him?"

"What? Oh. Would it matter?" She gave him an absent glance, but her mind had shifted to something even more unsettling. "David, my power is humming here, and it's getting stronger, the closer we come to the Schism. It's like feeling the blood in my body moving along, only I can feel its heat, the rush and speed."

"Is that good or bad?"

She was gratified, though a little disconcerted, that he picked up on her concern so quickly.

"I don't know. Just different. I think I like it," she ventured cautiously. "But since I don't know *which* part of me likes it, that's not necessarily a good thing. And this is a *sentient* magical fault line, which can also be trouble, because they're typically more curious than moral."

"So we could be walking into a kid's science experiment, where he's throwing us in the mix just to see what will happen," he observed.

"It's usually best not to compare an entity of uncharted power to a careless child."

"Point well taken." His lips curved, communicating a sense of irony she chose to ignore. Still, he joined her in a second perusal of the diner, his eyes giving it a harder study. Finally, he glanced at her. "Okay, then. You go toward it; I'll go over it. If something goes wrong, we'll figure it out, okay?"

She wasn't used to hearing that word. *We*. She found she liked it, despite her best attempt to disregard it. So she nodded.

"I'll be close." Reaching out, he brushed his hand along her arm, caressed her hip. "I'll come to your aid. If I think it's the sensible thing to do," he added soberly.

"I *can* turn you into a lizard. And pick you up by your tail."

A quick grin and he was gone, leaving behind at least one feather. Did angels molt? She should ask. For now, she picked it up and tucked it into her hair.

It came upon her sooner than expected. It was startling to be this close to a real human establishment, whether magically transported or not. There were cars in the parking lot, just four or five, but they were the first she'd seen close up. Mina was cautious, but reminded herself that she was dressed like the people in the diner, so she shouldn't cause remark, particularly when she took further precautions. Since either side of her face could cause excessive attention, she spun an illusion over it, making it unremarkable.

Interestingly, the power of the Schism tugged at it, making it clear that it disagreed with her decision to mask herself. However, she'd been making her own decisions and surviving because of them too long to simply abdicate that because a nameless, formless energy wanted to throw its weight around. When she yanked back, it finally let go, though with an impression of sullen acquiescence. She grudgingly appeased it by leaving her hand unchanged.

Though the odors of cooked food coming from inside the restaurant were tempting, she lingered in the parking area to study the cars, peering into the windows. She wondered how it would feel to ride in one, particularly one with an open top where she wouldn't feel closed in as she went fast.

When she at last entered the glass front door, she jumped as a bell rang above her. She stopped, studied it, her hand gripping the door handle so hard her knuckles were white. David was nearby, she reminded herself. Using that to calm her nerves, she stepped inside to assimilate all the unexpected sights, movements and sounds around her.

A quiet murmur of noise. The clink of silverware, conversation, the scraping of chairs. It was like walking into one of her books, she realized. Just like the saloon. She would be one of the characters. But was she the main character here? What was the Schism's purpose?

"You can just take a seat, miss." This from a woman in an

apron and a yellow dress, who breezed by with a pot emitting one of the strongest, most pleasurable aromas.

Examining the room, Mina moved to a booth. There were fresh flowers on each table, desert-type blossoms mixed in artistically with some dried grasses.

Mina, are you all right?

Fine. Just looking. Where are you?

She was curious, because he suddenly felt so close, an unexpected reassurance.

On the roof. It's pitched, so I'm on the back side, facing the desert, not the highway. If you need me, all you have to do is call me in your mind.

He'd already told her that. Twice. She pressed her lips together. "Okay."

She'd spoken without thinking and the waitress was now there, handing her a menu. Or rather, laying it on the table after a quick hesitation, for Mina's three-fingered hand was closest to the table's end, with the splint on the one finger and the bandage wrapped around the palm.

"Okay what, honey? Oh, my goodness, what happened to your fingers?" The waitress shook her head before Mina could think of a response. "I'm sorry. You don't have to answer that. I'm as curious as a cat on her eighth life. Things are always just popping out of my mouth without me thinking about it. Of course, then again, people are going to stare, so I always think, 'Isn't it more natural just to ask?' Then you can answer or not, but it's all out in the open, on the table."

"True," Mina responded, fascinated with the flood of words. She didn't think anyone could speak that fast. And while the waitress was obviously worried she'd offended her, most beings who met her knew exactly how she'd lost the fingers, so it had rarely come up in conversation. She found the waitress's observation quite logical. "It's a little too difficult to explain."

"Fair enough." She beamed. "What can I get you to drink?"

"Some of that?" Mina gestured at the pot.

"Coffee. Sure thing." The waitress turned over an upside-down cup on a saucer in front of Mina and poured. "I'll give you a couple minutes with the menu. I'm just about to end my shift, so it's going to be Diane who takes your order. She's a sweet little thing, just like you."

Mina blinked. Nodded. Felt David's amusement.

Are you listening in?

In a way. My sense of hearing is very refined.

Eavesdropper.

Well, after the saloon, I realized you're full of surprises. I thought you might start flirting.

Do I strike you as the type of person who flirts? But she felt something ripple through her stomach at his velvet teasing. *Would you like me to practice? There's a man at the counter who looks very broad in the shoulders, broader than yours. He is wearing these blue, somewhat tight pants that make a very noticeable display of his—*

You're baiting me.

Am I? Or am I flirting with you? She felt his surprise, as well as some of her own. *Besides, why would I bait you?*

Because you enjoy it.

What would you do if I did flirt with one of them?

A hum of energy moved through her body, slow, like a thick liquid spread by his fingers over her vital organs. His palms were on her skin, his breath in her ear, the heat and weight of him bearing her down. So real, it seemed she could twine her arms and legs around him, feel the silk of his feathers through her fingers as she stroked him with her wet, heated muscles.

I would remind you of my touch, my mouth, until you couldn't think of another.

"Oh," she said faintly. Despite herself, she pressed her lips together, compressing the sense of his touch there, a pleasant combination with the coffee's rich aroma. *How did you do that? Is it the blood we share?*

Yes and no. I'm in you, Mina, as you're in me.

"Okay, have you decided what you want?"

Mina tuned in to the new waitress in front of her with effort. Diane was not much taller than herself, dark-haired and brown-eyed. Eyes red-rimmed from crying. From the uncomfortable shift of the girl's gaze, it was obvious she was hoping no one would point out the obvious and trigger a new flood.

Mina knew all about not wanting someone to push, and unlike a certain angel, she respected that. Plus, she was far more interested in the inanimate objects of the human world than the irritatingly complex animated ones. She wanted to examine napkins, utensils, the array of dishes before her. Study how people dressed, their jewelry, what they chose to eat. If she could figure out how to be invisible, she'd go from table to table, looking. Visit the kitchen and watch them prepare food.

I can snatch the toy from the baby in the elevated chair behind me and determine how it is making that incessant rattling noise.

Mina.

I didn't say I was going to.

"Ma'am?"

"I want chocolate chip cookies. A dozen of them. Warm, from the oven. Do you have those?"

"Sure." Diane nodded. "That's, like, one of our specialties. It will take just a few minutes to do a new batch. Anything else?"

"That's all." Mina didn't have any money, but eyeing the few bills that the man at the counter had just handed to the older woman behind it to pay for his meal, she could illusion a facsimile of them that would pass inspection until they left. While she didn't care for stealing any more than David did, she figured there was a reason she was here that was more important than the relative cost of a few cookies.

Though going from table to table wasn't feasible, she spent the wait gazing around her with interest. A couple of families. A pair of men in dust-covered clothing, both lean as whips but eating enormous amounts of food. In a corner booth, a trio of old men analyzed human politics, looking so comfortable they had to come here often. The brawny man she'd mentioned to David was drinking his coffee alone, but speaking on some type of phone.

She didn't see anything that suggested the Schism's reason for bringing them here. Perhaps the Schism *had* experienced a benign moment and was merely giving her the opportunity to provide David cookies. Her surroundings felt magic and threat free.

Still, she didn't relax entirely. Though she didn't particularly want to interact with people, she did pay attention to their mannerisms. If they were going to be among humans for a while, she needed to blend, a vital technique every sea creature knew was necessary for survival. All in all, their behavior didn't seem much different from that of average merpeople.

However, it *was* different to be an unremarkable part of that, not treated as a pariah. But she was disturbed by her own comfort with it. It had been the other way for too long. It would be too easy to embrace this, to forget to be wary.

Fortunately, as normal as her surroundings might seem, the Schism wasn't about to let her forget its presence. A shimmer when she looked out the window gave her the opportunity to see a school of sea horses swim by, followed by a whale who surged forward with a flick of his tail, despite the background of the desert landscape. Apparently the Schism had co-opted her imaginings and was amusing itself with them. No one in the diner seemed to see the creatures except the wide-eyed baby perched in the high chair in the next booth. She gurgled. Mina noticed she also seemed very preoccupied with looking toward the ceiling and waving her arms, as if she wanted whatever was up there to come down and see her. Hold her.

Yes, angels had that effect. One particular angel had that effect on Mina, not that she cared to admit it. She wanted to say that they'd only known each other several days, use that as a way to deny his love, but she knew as well as he did that it had been going on far longer than that between them. Since they'd first met, he hadn't been far. She'd sensed his presence even when other angels were guarding her. Knew from conversations she had over-heard between Marcellus's men that he'd talked to them often. And it had reassured her, when it shouldn't have.

I think the Schism has a sense of humor.

David spoke in her mind, indicating he, too, had seen the whale.

Or it could just be free-form chaos, she responded. *This place is a sketch pad, a workbook for outlining magics before imple-menting them elsewhere. Something's subconscious.*

Have any idea yet whether it's good or bad?

Either. It's a design board. But whatever runs it is territorial, and recognizes the wrong kind of chaos, if it doesn't permit Dark Ones.

So you must be the right kind, if you're this close to the main Schism and it's interacting with you.

I'm not sure this is about us.

"Here you are." Diane was back. She'd put two of the cookies on a plate, and the smell coming from them had several heads turning. Mina had to agree with their interest, but unfortunately, it seemed to have the opposite effect on her waitress. She was growing pale, her skin looking clammy. "If that's all . . ." Diane ripped the ticket from her pad and laid it down. "Here you go. I've put the rest in this bag to keep them warm and in case you want them to go. Excuse me."

Turning on her heel, she fled, her hand clapping over her mouth. As she retreated, her hip struck the baby's high chair. So intent on being sick, Diane didn't notice until she was past the chair and startled cries alerted her. As she spun, the baby's chair was going over. Mother and father both made a lunge for it. Missed.

The front door whipped inward and hit the concrete wall, the glass shattering in the metal frame. More cries erupted at the shocking noise, but Mina's gaze was frozen on the high chair, which made one last slight rock as it settled back in its upright position. Like everyone else, she'd seen nothing, but the baby was laughing and twisting her head this way and that. Looking for her guardian angel, Mina suspected. The child had a white and brown feather clamped possessively in a chubby fist.

A snowstorm of napkins was spinning off tables and floating toward the floor, the tinny noise of shattered glass pinging off the tiles of the entranceway.

Diane stood stock-still, staring at the baby.

"What the hell is the matter with you?" The father was up and shouting at the white-faced waitress, his fists clenched. "Why are you running when you have children sitting in the aisle like that?"

"I-I'm sorry," Diane stammered.

"Stupid idiot." He shook off his wife's hand as she tried to get him to sit back down, making soothing noises. The baby, sensing her parents' mood, began to look alarmed, scrunching up her face. "God help the kid who gets you for a mom."

Diane's stomach made an alarming noise. Tears flooding her face, she spun and ran again, crashing through the kitchen door.

Putting the two cookies in the bag with the others, Mina rose and went out the side door as the manager tried to placate the man. A pair of waitresses was examining the front door, speculating on whether or not it was a sudden gust of wind. The baby's screaming began in earnest, ironically spurred by the family's reaction to the aversion of tragedy rather than the actuality of it.

She circled to the back, but instead of finding David, she found Diane, retching into a trash can that was apparently the receptacle for kitchen leavings. The smell of the garbage was vile enough to have Mina's stomach heaving. The girl was not only vomiting, she was crying at the same time, so the result was pitiful, grunting animal noises of distress.

Mina approached as she saw David leave the roof, drift down and tuck his wings in tight behind his shoulders. An extremely quick, cursory glance would have him passing as human. A mostly naked, extraordinarily beautiful human in the middle of the blinding desert.

It didn't seem to be a major concern right now, however. Diane held the sides of the trash can, her arms trembling. David was nearly behind her, so Mina hung back. While she was surprised he was getting involved, comfort wasn't really her area, so she was happy to let David handle this.

He'd halted and was studying the girl's bent head, with eyes gone sharp and probing. Reaching out cautiously, he passed his hand just above her back, as if feeling for an aura, a magical signature of some kind.

Diane stiffened. When her head snapped up, she saw Mina first, but she dismissed her, spinning around to seek David.

He was already backing up. To decrease the sense of threat, Mina was sure, since being confronted by a man of his height and musculature, wearing nothing more than the unorthodox short battle kilt and brace of daggers, would likely be cause for alarm in Diane's world.

But she didn't seem to register any of that. Diane stared at him through tear-filled eyes, gracelessly wiping her hand over her mouth and running nose.

Seeing a cue for something she could do, Mina moved forward with a napkin she'd put in the bag with the cookies. She'd been tempted to put a handful of the myriad little packets on the table in the bag, but had resisted, with effort. "Here."

Diane pulled her gaze from David reluctantly, focused on the paper napkin. "Thank you."

As she took it, Mina managed to retrieve the lid of the can and replace it. At least there was no trash in the sea. Waste came from natural things or was utilized by them, so the only garbage came from what humans threw into the ocean. Even many of those things the sea could convert or use, like the sea glass, or, on a larger scale, turning downed ships into coral reefs.

"I'm sorry. I . . ." Diane's gaze filled with tears again, and her knees trembled. Mina saw a discarded fruit crate and shoved it under her as the woman crumpled. "I've got to sit down," she rasped, unnecessarily.

Mina shot a glance at David. The angel was still keeping his distance, and she couldn't read his expression. Was this some kind of angel thing, the silence before humans? Why had he made himself known, then? She wished he'd say something. He was certainly better at this than she was. Gods, a sponge was better at this.

Awkwardly, she patted the girl's shoulder. That's what Anna would do. Actually, Anna would have subsumed her into one of her soul-deep comfort hugs. Since even the thought of them terrified Mina, she didn't think her attempt to imitate one would work, since it seemed to require an effusion of the happy, fuzzy vibrations Anna had in ample supply.

Instead, she tried to think of Diane as she would one of the merpeople who came to her for potions. Why would she be crying? Nothing appeared to be wrong with her, other than a little indigestion. Teenage merpeople often acted this way, though. Usually due to some dramatic tragedy about unrequited love.

But this was the Schism. Magic was often irritating, dangerous and hard to understand, but there was always a purpose. And Mina's intuition was picking up more than hormonal histrionics.

"What's the problem? Why are you crying?" Direct was best, she decided, since she didn't have patience for any other approach and her companion had become mute.

David, what are you doing, damn it?

"Nothing. Just nothing. I'm sixteen years old. Almost seventeen." Diane said that with a gulping sob and managed a quick look at Mina, as if that statement might have some hope attached to it, but at Mina's blank look, she burst into tears again.

David.

She practically shouted it in her mind, and he continued to stand there like a statue. Mina was prepared to give him a fierce glare, anything to compel him to step in. Unfortunately, not only was his mind silent, he wouldn't look at her. Only at Diane.

Up until now, he'd always seemed so confident—he was an *angel*, damn it. She'd had the freedom to be the unpredictable and moody one.

That was the danger of depending on someone else's dependability, she reminded herself darkly. What was she doing out here in the desert, anyway? She should have stayed in the ocean where she knew her environment.

"I'm pregnant." It was said so softly, Mina almost lost it in her own wave of irritation, which she knew was just a desperate shellacking over the rising tide of her own panic.

Mina turned her attention back to the girl. "Of course you're pregnant. What does that . . . ?" She bit her lip, realizing that humans didn't have her ability to pick up changes in a woman's body the way a trained witch could. And in the same moment, she recalled the significance of a teenager pregnant in this particular type of human society.

"Oh, I guess you could tell. The getting sick and all." Diane wiped at her eyes again. "Isn't that something? I can't imagine it. I've got almost nobody. How am I going to take care of two babies? Twins. They're twins. My momma says I have to kill them or she'll throw me out. Says she's not going to raise my babies. I was doing real well in school. I made cheerleader this year, too. Nobody ever imagined white trash like me as a cheerleader, but my grades are good."

Human society ran on money. This girl's mother sounded like she'd administered a hard dose of reality.

Diane stood, but she was still shaky. Mina reached out. It wasn't a normal gesture for her, but she continued to try to imagine what Anna would do, even as she questioned whether that was what *she* should do. What did the Schism want? Maybe Mina's actions, or lack thereof, were completely irrelevant.

Diane turned, looked toward David again. When Mina followed her gaze, she drew in a breath. David's eyes were dark, the whites gone. Earlier she'd surmised that it was triggered by battle situations for human-born angels, and served a functional purpose, giving them increased sight scope. Perhaps it became permanent when they matured. But this wasn't about battle, was it? There was nothing in the sky, nothing near except one young waitress and the hushed breath of the Schism.

As Mina watched, his wings straightened and spread out to either side of him, an impressive mantle that made him appear otherworldly, unapproachable. Something to fear. The way most creatures felt toward angels, including her own merpeople.

Why was he trying to intimidate a young woman barely out of girlhood?

Diane took a step toward him as if she didn't see any of that. He, in contrast, took a step back. Ended up against the brick corner of the building.

"What did she call you?" Diane asked.

"David." His answer came slow, in a voice that was flat, remote.

"David." She repeated it.

"We're done here." He turned, and Mina realized he wasn't talking to her. To either of the women. He was looking around him, as if seeking some agent of the Schism to give him a free pass. "I won't do this."

"David." Mina snapped it. As he tensed his wings to fly, she felt the rumblings of energy beneath her feet, volcanic lava. He was defying something that wouldn't be defied. "She needs . . ." Gods, what did she need that they could give her? *Why* were they here?

Diane took another step toward him. "I know you," she said quietly. Though her hands still shook from the physical exertion of her upset stomach, her expression had gotten more serious, strangely more focused.

David went still. A muscle twitched in his jaw, his fists clenched. "Don't touch me."

The waitress came to a halt, but it had a strange quality to it, as if she were straining on the end of a tether toward him.

Since she'd met him, Mina had seen David in myriad situations. She knew he was a powerful fighter, lightning quick and strong. That he was musical and had a quietness to him, a core of tranquility that soothed and steadied anyone around him. She was even cultivating an appreciation for it, warily.

She'd gathered these and a multitude of other impressions about him over the past few months. Initially they'd been stored as possible defenses against him, ways to exploit weakness, but she'd admitted they'd also evolved into a regard for him, an understanding of what she could expect when dealing with him.

So to feel this unstable response pulsing off of him toward a young girl was unsettling. While Mina had no reason to interfere, she had a sense she might need to do so. She just didn't know whom she would be defending.

Diane stared at him. "I feel like I'm supposed to touch you."

Mina narrowed her eyes. Well, her thoughts about that were far less confusing, if unexpected. She had no claim on David, and angels had that magnetism—like vampires, she reflected sourly—that made every woman feel like they were "supposed to touch." It didn't make her think any less about breaking those slim fingers if they reached toward him.

David took a step sideways in reaction, and his heel hit a trash can, clanging and startling him.

Diane's expression became pensive. "And even weirder than that," she continued, the teenager returning to her voice, "is that while I know I want to touch you, there's something more important than that. I feel like everything about these babies hinges on your willingness to touch *me*."

"Nó," David said. "*No*." And his voice, like his expression, was terrible.

"Please." Diane's voice altered, became pleading. "I know you. In my heart, I know you."

As David refused to move toward her, her hand wavered in the air, abruptly dropped. The air became heavy, oppressive, whatever spell holding the three of them broken as the desert heat returned. Diane blinked, looked at Mina as if she'd forgotten David was there. "Maybe I should give them up for adoption," she said wearily. "Everyone says little white babies go to good homes, that they'd be loved and wanted, but, oh, God, I just don't know." She dropped to her knees abruptly, ignoring the crate. Covering her face with her hands, she began to sob again.

Mina studied the tableau before her. An unresponsive and vengeful angel, a child weeping in his implacable shadow, trying to make a woman's decision all by herself.

Vengeful. Where had that come from? But that was what was in his face. Something she'd never seen there before. A dangerous, frightening David. The threat of uncontrolled violence simmering, waiting to strike in any direction it chose.

Not the David she knew, who was fierce only when it came to protecting those he perceived in need of protection.

It was clear the Schism was demanding something. Or was it offering? Something David didn't want, wasn't prepared to want.

Reality and illusion. Mina shifted her gaze between the two of them. David, dead as a mortal at fourteen. He'd said he was thirty now. This girl, sixteen, pregnant with twins.

Mina stepped forward, realizing Diane might really be in danger.

But in that same moment, something altered in David's face. Slowly, so slowly, he dropped to one knee, then the other, and bent his head over the waitress, so that the hair falling over his forehead grazed her crown.

"Oh." Diane raised her face, made a soft sound. He kept his head down, averted so that he wasn't looking at her, but their bodies and faces were so close together. His shoulders tensed as she lifted her hand.

Considerable energy was gathering, sharpening Mina's senses. If a horde of Dark Ones were sweeping toward him, he wouldn't flinch, but he was trembling at the threat of one young woman's touch.

It was as if something were eating him from the inside, tearing through vital organs and muscles, ripping open veins and arteries so he'd bleed to death where no one could see. It was a horrible thing to witness, particularly when he was so still, becoming a shell of himself before her eyes.

It provoked something unexpected in her. A need to protect. She took another determined step forward, her demeanor far less friendly. "You will not harm him." She said it not only to Diane, but to the energy around her. "I won't permit it."

Instead of following through on that anticipated touch, Diane backed onto her heels and rose to her feet, carefully avoiding contact, but staying close, her hand hovering within inches of his tense shoulder.

The confusion and pain in the glance she sent toward Mina was reassuring, though her words weren't. "I'm not sure, but I think I already have."

She looked back down at David, who was still staring at a point in the ground as if she weren't there, though the quivering of his body said he was very much aware of her every move.

It's all right, David. I'm here. Never in her life would Mina have thought she'd be offering such a reassurance to an angel, but she was no longer intrigued by the Schism. It was pissing her off. Whatever this was, she wanted it to finish. Or back off.

"It wasn't your fault," Diane spoke softly. "Not any of it, you understand? It was mine. And if I could have done it over . . ." She stopped, swallowed. Her hand came to lie over her stomach. "I guess that may be what's happening, isn't it?" She blinked, swayed. "God, I'm not sure what I'm saying. But *please* touch me. If you don't, I don't know if I can do it. Please, I'm so sorry." Tears were coming again, falling. "Just let me know it's going to be okay."

The diamond drop fell, hit his shoulder. Then another. David's head bowed lower, and the fist he had braced against the ground tightened. Then he gave an almost imperceptible nod.

In a move that looked as if it cost him, his arms weighted like an old man's, he slid them around her waist and brought her close to him, laying his cheek over her abdomen and the promises that waited there.

"Oh." Diane's sobs broke through anew. She closed her arms carefully around his shoulders, as if he were made of a delicate, brittle glass. Mina couldn't argue with her assessment, for it seemed as if the air itself could crush him.

Now though, for the first time, Diane seemed to notice his wings. "Oh my. Oh. That's . . . unexpected." A tiny smile appeared on her bow-shaped mouth. "Actually, I'm wrong. I don't know why, but it's not unexpected at all."

Dropping her head over his then, she laid her cheek on his hair.

It was a long series of minutes, while Diane softly wept and David held her in that strange, stiff way. Then, in a quick, jerky movement, with none of his usual grace, he dragged her to her knees and wrapped his arms around her shoulders, a frantic move of need.

Tucking her head under his jaw, Diane kept crying. Her arms slid under his and she folded into him. Rocked him. As she did, her sobs lessened. She reached up and stroked his hair. Burying his face in the tender junction of her neck, David held her tighter, his fingers pressed so hard against her back it made depressions in the pale yellow uniform. His wings had lowered, sweeping the ground behind him, almost as if he'd forgotten he had them.

At length, Diane lifted her head. For a remarkable moment, David's face looked younger, and Diane's older. But there was a harsh anguish to his expression that was unbearable to see, and Mina saw Diane's heart break at the sight of it. The way only a mother's heart could break.

"Don't kill them," he said.

"I won't," Diane promised fiercely, and youthful indecision was gone. "I'll learn how to be a good mom. I'll take care of them." Hesitantly, she put her hand up to his face and he closed his eyes when she made contact. "I do feel I need to say I'm sorry to you. But at the same time, I think it was something so bad, saying I'm sorry is an insult. It can never cover it."

"No, it can't." David's eyes opened. "But it's all I need." Reaching between them now, taking a breath, he put a hand over her abdomen. "Give all the rest to them. You need to go inside now."

She nodded and rose. While he gave her his hand to help her to her feet, Mina could tell he was done, drained. Ready for some distance between them. Perhaps half a world. Pocketing her tissue, Diane took an uncertain step back. Looked at him once more. Wonderingly. "Good-bye," she said. "Thank you." Then she turned and went back to the kitchen door. As she grasped the handle, she gave Mina a puzzled look.

"This has been a really strange day, but I think it's going to be okay. I mean, I'm scared and all, but this is what's right for me. I'm going to have my babies. Have them and keep them."

"Okay," Mina said, at a loss. "Good luck."

Diane gave her a tentative smile, then something shifted in her gaze. Something Mina had seen when the waitress had put her arms around her angel and rocked him against her breast. The teenager vanished behind the face of the woman she would become. Had been.

"Take care of him," she said.

As Diane stepped back through the kitchen door, the restaurant faded away, likely returning to the actual time and place from which it had come.

Leaving Mina standing between a still-kneeling angel and a bag of warm, just-from-the-oven, chocolate chip cookies.

Nineteen

A T least the Schism had left the cookies. That made her feel a little better about the whole confusing thing, as well as the worried feeling inside, which she suspected was worry about him.

"David?" Walking over to him, she cautiously sat down cross-legged, her knee a few inches from his foot. He was still kneeling, his fist closed as if holding in Diane's touch, uncertain whether to squeeze it into nothing or imprint it forever into his skin. Reaching into the bag, Mina pulled out a cookie. Tapped on his white, strained knuckle. "Here."

His gaze shifted. Looked at the cookie, identified it, then lifted back to her face. "I can't taste it."

"Yes, you can." His eyes had returned to their normal brown. But he looked so drawn, she couldn't help herself. Putting a hand to his face, she ran her knuckles down his cheek, the gesture apparently surprising him as much as it did her, for it broke his focus on whatever inner struggle he was having.

Embarrassed, she dropped her touch and considered the natural, empty landscape again, the shimmer of energy that a few moments before had been explosive. Then she remembered what she was doing and turned her attention to the cookie in her hand.

As she murmured the proper charm over it, the cookie bubbled as if still in the oven, then became solid again. "See if I got it right."

With a curious look, David picked it up out of her palm, brought it to his nose, inhaled. It made his eyes close again. There was such a tiredness to his face, Mina didn't question her need to reach out again. This time she laid her hand over his free hand, braced on the ground. Just resting there, making contact.

"Goddess," he murmured, still not opening his eyes. "It's childhood, in a single smell. Why is it we never get away from it? From wanting the things we wanted as kids? Not the specifics. Not the bike with the chrome plating or the G.I. Joe. The sense of everything being the way it should be."

"Being safe. Loved. Never alone. Never going anywhere without the sense of someone watching out for you. Or standing beside you, holding your hand."

He opened his eyes. "How did you know that?"

"I've been providing potions for a long time. It's what they all want, in one form or another, even if they look for it the wrong way."

And even though she'd never had it, she'd recently wondered if it was something imprinted on the soul at birth and her knowledge of it had simply lain dormant, unused. Because in the past couple of days, it had surged up like an unleashed force of nature, overwhelming her senses as if to make up for lost time. It was there, every time he took her in his arms and she felt a hunger to get so close to him she'd tear him open to crawl inside.

He bit into the cookie without further hesitation. As he chewed, his face changed. "Oh, holy Goddess." He swallowed. "Are there more?"

It was such a relief to have him back, she didn't realize he'd frozen until she brought out the next cookie. "What?" She looked around quickly, seeking the threat.

"You smiled. You smiled at me."

"What—" But he'd caught her upper arms, lifting her onto her knees, and was kissing her. She couldn't form words when he did that, let alone thoughts. Not when his hand slid under her head, cupped the back of it, holding her to him in a way as effective as the most potent binding spell.

There was a desperation to his kiss, though, an urgency that made her wonder if he was going to take her right here on the sand. But there was something beyond sexual to it, something so strong, it was as if he was seeking to find her soul—or maybe his own—in that kiss. Maybe he had the urge to get so close he could crawl inside of her, too.

His breath had the flavor of the freshly baked cookies, making her understand instantly why it had been one of his favorite foods. She revised her opinion on sharing them with him. If he thought a few kisses were going to earn him the right to eat all the rest, before she had even had one, well . . .

When at last he reined himself in, she didn't know who was more shaken, though she noted the tremor in the hand he ran down her arm, strumming nerve endings there. His hand was sticky with the cookie, leaving a tiny brown streak from melted chocolate.

"I gave her the last napkin." She cleared her throat, pressing moist lips together. "So you'll just have to lick your fingers."

Lifting her arm, he put his lips over the spot on her skin instead, his tongue teasing it away, mouth caressing her as her breath left her. When he raised his head, he gave her a small smile of his own. "If you won't do it for me, I guess I'll manage. Did you say there were more of them?"

"I'll *share* some," she said, taking firm possession of the bag.

They walked together as he ate them, with her charming each one to ensure he could taste them. In the end, she only took two, discovering it was more important to her to help him establish some distance from that dark place in his mind. But she did have questions. She managed to walk a couple of miles with him in companionable silence before she asked the one uppermost in her mind.

"If Diane is . . . was, your mother, that means your mother died at the same time you did. Right?"

"I'm not that person anymore," he said curtly. "It doesn't matter."

After the wary peace of the past few minutes, the crisp response brought her up short. He'd actually used his *you will not defy me* angel voice, as if he thought that would shut her down. And after she had charmed cookies for him.

It took him several moments to notice she was no longer walking with him, and he turned and returned to her. "What is it?"

"That was a stupid, entirely human thing to say," she said. "I don't think you need any more cookies."

He raised a brow, looking startled. "It's—"

"You can be as high-handed with me as you want to be; that was just denial. A soul is comprised of every experience it's ever accumulated. She's a pregnant sixteen-year-old, but she's also the soul of a woman whose son killed himself at fourteen. And it seems as if that had to do with your sister. You couldn't stop it, but your mother ignored it, which is why Diane tried to take away your guilt."

He gave her a dark look, but when she stubbornly refused to move out of the shade of the Joshua tree where she'd planted herself, he let out an oath, paced away. Then circled back and glared at her.

"Do you know in many tribal societies the age of sexual maturity—twelve or thirteen—is the age of manhood or womanhood? Some scholars think that's why teenagers in industrialized nations are so troubled. Because they're denied their natural right to assume the mantle of adult responsibility at the age they should."

"Nice culture lesson. I don't have the whole story, do I?"

His gaze snapped back to her, and that muscle in his jaw flexed, giving her the answer. "It was a large part of it," he said at last.

"I can't go to a Memory Keeper and wrest the worst memory you have out of your head," she said, watching him stiffen in surprise. "I may not know everything about angels, but I know some things."

"I can see that." He sat down on a rock, gestured. Surprised, she came to sit at his side as he spread one wing behind her, providing her a comfortable backrest. "What's bothering me is the Schism's purpose for doing all this."

"We'll likely encounter the reason for it at another time. Magic, for all its capriciousness, can be deadly predictable that way."

"Deadly. Great choice of words," he said dryly.

She pressed her lips together. "You already know the nature of magic, the way it works. You're trying to avoid the issue."

"Maybe." He shrugged.

"You're going to get mad if I keep asking about this, aren't you?"

"You can ask me anything, Mina. Always." Even as the wing brushed her arm, a quick, reassuring caress, a corner of his mouth curved up. "And yes, I know that answer doesn't guarantee I won't get mad. But you have such a tactful and soothing way about you, I'm sure I can keep it down to a simmer."

She ignored that. "What was she like?"

"She was my twin. My heart." David's gaze adjusted upward, to the sun, and she realized angels could look directly at the blinding white orb. It turned his brown eyes the amber of hellfire. "I should have killed him the first time he laid a hand on her. But she protected me. She was better than me. Stronger. I didn't save her."

She'd meant his mother, but he'd just given her something she didn't expect. Anna had suggested he'd dealt with a great deal of his past in his first years in the Heavens, so Mina found it odd that this part of him was still so raw. As if he'd merely buried it in a shallow grave inside of him, the corpse of it festering, tormenting him.

"It sounds like she wouldn't let you save her." Touching his arm, she drew his eyes to her again. That fiery color, too close a cousin to red, bothered her. "What if I won't let you save me, David? What then? At what point do you deal with this, once and for all?"

"How do you deal with it, Mina? You tell me." He touched

the scars on her face, passed over her brow and withdrew before she could push him away. "How do you fight an enemy who takes the form of a memory? How do you ever accept the unacceptable?"

She of course had no answer to that. While she wasn't pleased that he'd pried into her past without her consent, she had to admit she'd rather him find out from a Memory Keeper than having to tell him herself. Some memories didn't need revisiting, because the life she'd led since then reminded her of it every day. He was right. That *was* the problem.

"How do *you* think it can be done?"

David studied her, then leaned in. Tightening the curve of his wing, he slid her forward on the rock, showing he had the strength to move her with the feathered appendage. When his face was close above hers, she could see the fires still simmering in his gaze, demons of his past mixed with the power he held now, an uncertain mix. "You can drown out the sound of it in a very . . . adult . . . way . . ." His attention dropped to her mouth, and her lips parted, despite herself, desire unexpectedly spreading a warm hand across her lower belly. "Or you can do it the child's way."

He was too quick for her. It only took a second to register the shift in his expression, the flash of mischief, but in the time she grabbed at him and the paper bag, which still held her two cookies, he was aloft, beyond her reach. So he thought.

The retrieval spell coiled around his wrist, jerked, and dropped the bag neatly back into her arms. But then she shrieked as he swooped in swiftly, made a grab. He twisted and she ended up in his arms, in the air, her body swinging over his. Losing her grip on the paper sack, she grabbed at his shoulders. In her worry about falling, she'd abandoned worry about her broken finger, but he hadn't. Before she could make the mistake of seizing at him with both hands, he'd completed the rotation, landing her on her feet, holding her with one arm around the waist, the bag dropping into his open hand on the other side of his body.

"No honor among thieves or angels," she snorted, though a little breathlessly.

David grinned down at her, handed back the bag. "You'd probably refuse to charm them anyway."

"I'd turn them into great big bugs to crawl around inside you. Make you squirm when talking to Jonah."

"He can make me squirm all on his own." David chuckled. "Sometimes he makes me feel like a kid caught smoking in the school bathroom. His daughter's not going to be able to get away with anything."

"He does do the intimidation thing well. Even better than Neptune." She dropped her voice several octaves. "*I will vanquish you, pathetic mortal.*"

David let out a startled snort. "That came from Anna."

Mina shrugged. "I may not have a sense of humor, but I can borrow from others."

"Speaking of acting like a kid . . ." He stopped her with a touch on her arm, cocked a hip, a thumb sliding into his belt as he looked down into her face. A bracing pose, as if the words were difficult for him. "I should have handled all that better, at the diner. I'm sure I scared you. You're supposed to be able to depend on me. I'm sorry."

She shook her head. "We can't fathom the purpose of evil when it strikes those we love. Anna said that once as well. I assume it applies to everyone, even creatures as enlightened as angels."

"That sounded like your usual sarcasm. I'm feeling better already. Is that your way of trying to coax me out of a dark mood?"

"I would never do something that compassionate."

"True." David pursed his lips. "You might do it so you don't have to listen to me whine and moan about my past anymore."

"Perhaps you're starting to understand me after all," she said lightly.

He'd effectively pushed them away from the subject, but if the

Schism had raised it, whether he liked it or not, they would be visiting it again. She'd let the magic take care of that. For now, she had other issues. As if a curtain had lifted from the landscape, the house lay before them, no more than several hundred yards ahead.

————————

THE light impression of a dirt road was beneath their feet, the house driveway intersecting it. As they walked up the driveway, she examined the wood-and-stone two-story house that had been crafted by the master carpenter and his wife. There was a wooden split rail fence around it, and she saw the protection runes carved there, even as she felt the first wave of its specific energy reach out and assess her threat.

It almost made her stop, step back. But this was the moment of truth, and she wasn't going to cower from it. Squaring her shoulders, she moved forward. One careful step, then another.

David stayed close and watchful. Knowing David, he'd leap to her defense even before she had the chance to do it herself. It didn't anger her as it would have done less than forty-eight hours ago. Now it just made her feel an exasperation with him, as well as a reassurance she couldn't deny.

The house was simple. Beautiful. Built with love and yet careful alignment with the energies of the land. She suspected "Sam the Shaman" had been part of the design phase. Its position and construction made sure that no approach would go unnoticed, sitting just inside the scope of that magical fault line that didn't tolerate Dark Ones.

She opened the latch on the gate, pushed it inward and walked onto the grounds.

Well, apparently, it only rejected full-blooded ones. Unless it had a different line for half-breeds, waiting to blast them farther in the perimeter. Power flooded into her body, enhancing her own as it hummed throughout her system. No good or evil to it, just pure energy that vibrated beneath her fingers.

"There are fresh flowers on the front porch," she noted, letting out the breath she hadn't realized she'd been holding. And

David noticed, his hand pressing briefly into the small of her back, a gesture that felt far too welcome. Like the house itself.

"Anna probably insisted Jonah flash her over and let her add some homey touches before we got here. Or made him do it. You know she's like that."

"Yes." Mina kept her fingers away from the flowers as she passed, knowing the dew-kissed roses would wilt beneath her touch faster than they would in the desert heat.

The solid, wide oak door had an archway over it with the carved words "Be at Rest Here." For some reason, the antithesis flashed through her mind. Dante's *Inferno*: "Abandon Hope, All Ye Who Enter Here." Dante didn't know that his imaginings of Hell had come straight from the Dark Ones, but she did. She'd recognized it the first time she'd read the book, many years after her first dream of the Dark Ones' world. If men knew how many of their nightmares were simply windows into the world of the Dark Ones, trying to grasp at them through their dreams . . .

David glanced at his witch. She had gone very quiet as she scrutinized everything about her closely. When he pushed the front door open, she stepped in and he followed, flanking her, trying to gauge her mood. What she might need.

Mina felt his regard, but she focused on the interior. The furnishings of the house were all hand carved. Open kitchen, living area, lots of windows to look out over the flat ranges of desert. The rock formations rose as a backdrop, the sun turning everything brilliant reds and oranges that she knew would likely shift to purple and violet as the day waned. A rainbow offered each day to whoever sat in here and watched the canvas paint and repaint itself, shadows from the clouds always adding something different to the landscape.

There was a tire swing out back, hooked up to a lone leafless tree with spreading branches. Surely a Schism oddity, for it looked like a naked oak, which she couldn't imagine would survive this far away from a water source, beneath a baking sun.

She also saw an intriguingly ordered area comprised of rocks and sand, with patterns in the sand that seemed etched by the rakes propped at the cornerstones, four very large stones with the tops smoothed for sitting and perusing the pattern.

"A Japanese rock garden," David supplied, at her curious glance toward him.

Nodding, she turned from the view and toward an open staircase curving up to the second level. As she followed it, she studied the framed photographs on the wall along it. Mostly desert scenes, but personal, intriguing. Probably picked out by Anna, since she'd always been fascinated by the human ability to capture a moment of time on film, the way Mina admitted being fascinated by the way a writer could capture the same thing on paper. Or perhaps they'd been left by the carpenter and his wife, a shared gift for the next occupants.

Upstairs, she found a large bed in an inviting master bedroom. A thick quilt for the nighttime desert chill, with numerous pillows stacked at the headboard. A scattering of flower petals over the coverlet. The bed was a sanctuary unto itself, so wide and long that Anna apparently had not been exaggerating when she said Matt, the carpenter, was as impressive in size as Jonah. Mina checked the other rooms on the second level and discovered that this was the only one of the upstairs bedrooms prepared for sleeping.

"She probably remembered angels don't necessarily have to sleep," David said casually. Mina shot him a narrow glance, detected amusement there that she did not share.

"I think the only one making assumptions is Anna," she retorted. "She doesn't understand. She never has."

"Or maybe"—David's hands came to rest on her tense shoulders, a thumb making a passing caress along the base of her throat as he stood behind her—"she does understand. She does these things as a way of telling you she'd change it for you, if she could."

Mina shrugged that off, moving away from him as well. "No sense in that. It is what it is. And why does she assume I'd *want* any changes to my life?" She shot him a glance. "I'm left alone, with the recent exception of my popularity with overprotective angels. I've dedicated my life to study, so that I've surpassed my ancestors with respect to magic and knowledge of the world around me. I intend to keep building on that."

"And do what with it?"

"Whatever I wish," she snapped.

"Okay." He continued as if the air wasn't crackling with tension around her. "There's an underground spring that runs beneath the house. A hot spring. Jonah said the cellar leads to it. It's a good place for a swim or bath. There's also a cistern. Electrical power is fueled by the Schism's energy, so he said it can be a little unpredictable, but the point is that the house is self-sufficient. There's a general store about ten miles down the road, and an old pickup truck in the garage. I can show you how to drive it. Way out here, I don't think you'll have to worry about a license."

She knew he'd been trying to read her face since she stepped into the perimeter of the property, and she'd purposefully remained dispassionate. Because with every step, the meshing of the energy with her own, the stretch of the world out on either side, the heat of the desert, the blue of the sky . . . It was perfect. It was everything she could want or need. And the idea of learning to drive a vehicle was astounding enough to almost make her forget herself and insist he show her now. But she kept her voice even, with enormous effort. The expression "too good to be true" had come into being for a reason, she reminded herself.

"You think I'm staying here that long?"

"It's not such a bad idea, is it? This place would be safer for you. Better for your health." His gaze swept over her, seeing too much. "It's dry and warm. And Jonah said Anna would set up an account for you at the store. Before I go, we'll make sure that's been done."

There was a fan rotating on the ceiling. Just as the world turned, but suddenly it felt like the blade was careening in her stomach.

Turning on her heel, she went down the steps and out onto the back porch. Stopping at the edge of it, she drew a deep breath, trying to still the turbulence within her. Winced as she forgot her injury and tried to curl both sets of fingers into tense balls. The quiet had a whisper to it, that faint energy hum. Heat reached up from the desert, soaked into her bones.

She didn't turn around as he came up behind her, but when his body brushed hers, a faint tremor ran through her.

"Mina?"

"You're right; it'll work. For the short term. And I didn't want your protection from the beginning. So this relieves you, Jonah and the rest of them of the personal obligation. And when he decides to throw me out of this house, I'll know he's decided I'm not your problem anymore, anyway."

"Obligation?" He swore softly and turned her, despite her resistance. When he tried to lift her face to him, she jerked it away with a glare. So he hauled her closer, making her slap a hand on his chest to balance herself.

"Let me go."

"I think we need to make something clear," he said instead. "This setup will give you safety. Independence. Maybe the ability to get a good night's sleep. But you're not free of me, witch. I won't be out of your life until you tell me to go, that you don't want me."

"I don't want you. Go away."

He merely raised his brows, drew her closer, until her feet were between his, his hand sliding down the small of her back, and then lower, to cup one buttock with a proprietary ease that had her hackles rising and her nerves sparking. With his other hand he cradled her face, tipped her rigid chin with a not-so-gentle thumb.

"I meant when you don't lie about it. I'm not leaving you, Mina. Are you listening?" He bent closer, until their eyes were no more than a couple inches apart. "I'm *not* leaving you."

"Why do you think I care? Leave or go; it's the same to me. Just come around when you want this." She pushed her hips against his groin, which was conveniently getting aroused, to prove her point. "The thrill of fucking a freak."

"That's enough of that."

David hadn't meant to respond so ferociously, though the snarled command would have made Jonah proud. It startled her, made her eyes widen in her pale face. Jesus, there were times he had the most overwhelming urge to yank up her skirt and slap her bare ass until it was red.

"Stop it," he repeated, easing his touch when he realized he was gripping her hard enough to bruise. "I'm usually hard around you, and for some perverse reason you provoke me even more when you start snapping at me. It makes me think of all the ways I could keep that viper tongue of yours occupied. But I want more from you, and you know that."

"No. I don't care. I'm not going to listen—"

"Mina, do you remember what I said I'd do if you ever threw another detonation spell at me?"

Her gaze snapped up to him, and he nodded, satisfied. "I will do it for much less physical offenses, as well. And enjoy the hell out of it. So keep talking and give me a reason. Or shut up and listen."

She pressed her lips together. Waiting a bated moment, he took a breath. "This is a place we can spend time together, without having to be on guard against Dark Ones. That has an appeal to me. Watching you study your books, concoct potions. Getting to be by your side while you explore your fascination with the human world, making it your world."

"I'm not human, so why—" At his look, she whitened, crossed her arms over her chest defensively. "You wouldn't dare."

"Once more," he warned. "And you'll find out. In that little town where the store is, there's an old junk shop Anna loves. I know you'll find so many things there you'll like, to make this place more of your own."

He softened then. "Mina, you're not totally human, not totally mermaid. You're you. But I'd have to be blind not to see how this place appeals to you, how a human life would fit better with who you are. I can give you privacy and the solitude you treasure.

I do have a duty to the platoon and the Legion. But those are the only reasons I would leave your side, *temporarily*, and always, always *only* if I'm assured of your safety.

"So get it through your stubborn head. If I leave here to give you time alone or to serve the Lady, it doesn't mean I'll be gone from your life. You got that?"

Mina held her defensive posture, staring at his chest. "And I'm expected to believe Jonah is just giving me his house forever, for nothing."

"No." He shook his head. "Of course not. He assumes if you're here, under our protection, you'll do us the courtesy of continuing your current efforts to keep the Dark One blood you carry away from the use of your power. As to whether you might consider using your power to help protect the Lady's interests on occasion, that's something you'll have to decide on your own. But you have time before it becomes an issue." He took a breath. "Mina, I'm *asking* you to look at me this time."

She ground her teeth, her jaw flexing, but in the end she raised her lashes. She didn't necessarily like this, having an argument with their faces so close, where she could see the reflection of her scarred face in his irises, so she shifted to stare at his cheekbone and tried to ignore it, even as she crossed her arms more tightly across herself.

"As long as Anna and I have any say about it, Mina," he said, "you'll be left in peace. You can be safe here. Have a life."

"It's too much. Too soon. I can't . . ." She shook her head, turned away to look around the porch, back into the house. This time he let her, probably because he did know her. Well enough to know when to get in her face and when not to, maybe better than she did.

Two days ago, she'd not thought beyond the daily routine of her life, the need to survive, to struggle through each day. This house, the energy here, the way it was embracing her in a manner that was devoid of threat . . . it resurrected a part of her she'd thought she'd long ago destroyed. The wishes of the child were still there. The child who'd been abandoned, tortured. Who'd grown up in the cold and darkness, never expecting or daring to hope for anything. Determined to survive, enough to fight for it every moment she'd breathed, never questioning why she was fighting, for the answer would have been so desolate she would have lost the battle. For the first time, she might have an answer she could bear to hear, and the gift of it, after so long, might crack her into a million pieces.

"Mina."

"Don't tell me things like this, David. I can't believe them, you understand?" She turned and stared up into his eyes, trying to convey what she herself wasn't even sure she knew how to say. "I can't afford to believe them. I can only take it moment by moment, okay? You tell me I have this place for the next few moments, that I can consider it mine for just this little bit of time, I can do that. Okay?"

"Okay." He nodded, even as she began to repeat herself, then bit her lip, cutting herself off. He ran his hands up the outside of her arms. "It's all right. Okay."

She closed her eyes, and they stood that way a long moment. He just held her lightly, not pushing. Just reminding her he was there. He was there. And he'd said he'd continue to be there. "I want to go sit in the tire thing," she said.

"Then let's go do that." He stepped back, but retained her hand so they walked down the back porch stairs hand in hand. While her own cooperation flummoxed her, she nevertheless went with him. She stopped at the bottom, though, realizing she'd left her shoes inside, wanting to feel the texture of the wood, the energies moving through it, through her soles. Before she could turn to retrieve them, he made a noise, positioned her a couple steps up and then guided her to take a little hop to ride on his back, her arms looped around his neck, her chest comfortably mashed against his half-spread wings, the tips of the secondary feathers tickling the skin on the insides of her thighs.

"Don't your feet hurt?" Then she glanced down and saw his feet weren't touching the ground, which was scattered with various prickly forms of vegetation and heated sand. "Oh."

There was a cobbled path that intersected from the side of the house, so he let her down when they reached that, and they walked the remaining few steps to the tire swing.

"You sit in it with your feet dangling, and hold the rope, like this." Lifting her by the waist, he directed her to grasp the rope and guided her feet in through the hole with that effortless strength that never failed to impress her, though she tried not to show it. "And then you hold on."

He pulled her back, until he was farther off the ground and so was she, but not so far. About fifteen feet, just enough to thrill her. Then he let her swing free and forward, the ground rushing up and by, the sky coming fast at her from the opposite direction.

It was a simple childlike pleasure, and David waited to see if it would trip off a negative reaction from her Dark One blood. Her eyes widened in amazement, that tight mouth easing as she got the feel of it. When she started anticipating each push he gave her, the blue eye had softened, the crimson one going to a dormant stillness. A small proof that his theory about a different way of balancing her darkness might be right. Quiet pleasure gripped him, held him in the moment with her, carrying his heart up into the sky with hers.

He'd told her she could find a sanctuary here. It was unexpected to glimpse the possibility of one for him as well.

As her slim fingers gripped the rope, keeping her body close to the tire, he thought how resilient and fragile she was at once. It made him understand how loving a female could tear a male to pieces and make no logical sense. There was nothing lovable about her, but there was nothing about her he didn't love. He sensed so much inside her, a complexity that could hold even an angel's attention for the length of his immortal life. One moment she was coming at him with the venom of a harpy, and the next she was riding a tire swing, figuring out that its entire and unfamiliar purpose was play. And as she warily accepted that, he got to see the click of a miracle when she gave it to herself as a gift.

Eventually, when he sensed her tiring, he let the swing wind down to a gentle sway, holding the rope above her head to keep the tire steady. They stayed that way, side by side, her on the swing, cheek laid against the tire, while he stood next to her, both watching the sunbeams play over the rocky hills. A hawk passed over with a piercing shriek that echoed, and she watched it until it moved out of sight.

"I know it's hard to contemplate," he said at last, keeping his voice a soothing murmur. "But what if you did live here? Could you do that? Would you like that?"

"I've been alone my whole life, David." She tilted her head, laying her cheek on the tire to study him. And surprised him when she reached out absently to play with the ends of his hair lying against his shoulder, her fingers stroking his skin. The way she did it, it was as if she wasn't even conscious of it, just following a nameless desire to touch something that was only passing through her personal space, something that wouldn't remain.

"And that doesn't just mean being without family. It also means no place in an ordered society. No friends. Being invulnerable and indifferent aren't quirky personality traits. They're survival tools. I've created things to talk to, like the cat you saw in the boat, so I'd remember how to communicate. I've depended only on myself to survive. I don't know what feeling safe or secure is, and as fearful as I've been at different times, nothing frightens me more than being offered a chance to live my life differently, because I might forget how to just survive when it's all taken away." She tilted her head toward him. "Not if. *When.*"

"You've taken me several steps away from just surviving over the course of a couple days. Those steps can be lost in a blink, and when you lose them, it knocks you back twice as far, makes you question why you even risked it to begin with. If you don't risk it, the question will never be there."

"If you don't risk it, there's nothing worth living for. Life is supposed to be about more than survival."

"Not for me. I've lost control twice. As the dragon, I could have killed you."

"But you didn't," he reminded her. "Every new skill takes time to learn, and it can be risky. You have courage, Mina. As much courage as anyone I've fought beside. You take the risk to reach for something better, I'll be here. At your back."

She swayed in the tire, holding his gaze, the two of them resting on that thought in silence until she broke eye contact, looked toward the sky again.

What *would* it be like to live here? Watching the sky, knowing that the storms that cloaked the skies, the forks of lightning, could be David in a battlefield above. She'd read a book about a wife who waited for her husband to return from battle. If you loved anyone that much, would you let them face a fight alone? What if she was with him in the sky, fighting the same battles? Watching his back as he watched hers?

Her thoughts, besides being irrational, were based on the assumption he was telling her the truth, that he wanted to be with her.

"If I was the type of being who allowed myself to need someone, and permitted myself to tell that someone they were needed"—Mina cocked her head—"then I'd tell you—maybe—that I need you."

His expression spread warmth across her skin and down into her chest, making it tight. He had his head tilted, the wings folded, strong body leaned against the tire, so close and touchable. His thigh brushed the side of hers, his arm muscles within brushing distance of her lips, where he grasped the rope.

"I need to lie down in the big bed with you," she continued, holding his eyes with her own. "Have you inside me. And not leave me until I'm asleep, so I don't have to say good-bye. Not ever. Every time you come and go, that's what I'd need. I wouldn't ever have to say good-bye."

The wind whispered across the plains, the sun slipping down another notch, turning the sky a new, more brilliant hue of violet. Letting go of the rope, David leaned down. "Put your arms around my neck. I think we should practice. A few test runs, where you wake up and I'm still here."

She complied, her courage expired, even under the guise of speaking hypotheticals. Lifting her, he cradled her in his arms, carrying her back to the house. His gaze went up and then they were aloft, landing on the upper verandah that had been built all along the second level of the house, the flight done before she could get apprehensive.

Still, she'd tightened her arms around his neck in reaction, which gave her the excuse to press her face into his throat, brush her lips on the pulse there. She saw the desert stretching behind his shoulder, those still rock formations. It was the ocean, the clouds forming the shadows that water could create, but no cold and darkness. Not until the sun set. And then there would be warmth in here.

He'd known that for her to feel comfortable on land, to consider something different from what she'd always known, she would need a protected place like this, that felt open and yet hidden at the same time. She'd just given him an insight into her life she'd never given anyone, but now she wondered, when it came to David, did she even need to expend that effort?

She'd never dared to consider anything permanent except her physical limitations. So wanting something to be permanent would be a fruitless pursuit. But for just a tiny second, with him carrying her, she imagined, in the deceptive safety of her own mind, what it would be like if this *were* permanent. The wind, how it whispered in a way that had the tranquility of silence in the ocean. The sun's brush, its different colors embedded in rock and earth formations, colored there over centuries, now reflected against a blue sky. His broad shoulders, the smell of his throat and hair against her lips, the movement of his body against hers.

What would it mean if it was real? Enduring. For more than a moment.

But she knew better than that. All the blessings of the angels couldn't disrupt the curse of fear and revulsion that had affected so many generations of her family. She let the image slip between her fingers in the same way she let his hair slip between her knuckles as he laid her down on the bed, leaving the pair of glass doors swung open onto the terrace so she could smell the wind and desert, hear the lonely cry of the hawk.

"I can change. Like at the saloon, so you don't see the scars."

His hands had closed on her shirt, obviously intending to remove it in the light of day, when things were slow and gentle between them, not volatile and violent like the first time, where there was no time to pause or feel apprehension. Or the second, where she had used fantasy and illusion to heighten the intensity.

She couldn't believe she'd said it, offered such a thing. But he was so beautiful. He deserved something beautiful. She'd closed her own hand over his, stopping him. Afraid, remembering the reflection of her face in his brown eyes, so close. Like now.

In answer, he bent to her clenched fist, parting his lips just enough to make her attention stutter, stumble, her breath a hard object in her chest as he caressed the tender areas between her fingers with his tongue.

He hadn't chosen her unmarked hand. His mouth followed the length of the three fingers, carefully around the splint and then over the rough amputated stumps where two fingers used to be. Mina shut her eyes, something powerful breaking inside her chest, robbing her of speech, almost of breath. This might be dying, because she certainly felt that everything she was and knew was ending.

"David . . ."

When he lifted his head and looked at her, it left no room for doubt, even in her uncertain mind, that everything in him was focused on this moment. On her.

"Why?" she whispered.

Instead of answering, he lifted the shirt over her head. Freed the string tie holding the skirt and worked it downward through methodical exploration, his hands moving with slow, easy movements. Sure, no hesitancy or indecision that would have spooked her. What flesh he found, he explored with a long-fingered, sensitive touch, a stroking that made her tremble even harder.

Her rib cage, a section of hip. The tender crevice of her armpit, the shoulder blade behind.

Then he'd pulled it all free, dropping the garments to the

floor, and he was curved over her, sheltering her with the spread of his wings, his eyes intent, mouth a sensuous line.

He touched her neck first, one hand on each side, the warmth of him spreading down her body, over her sternum, liquefying over her chest, tightening the nipple on one side and even the other, though there wasn't one there. It occurred to her, hazily, that when he touched her, it was like it was all still there. She was whole, with no illusion magic necessary.

When he let his hands drift down, fingers spread, thumbs overlapping as if he were pantomiming a bird, gliding down her flesh, she drifted up toward that touch before she even had a coherent thought of it. As his hand at last closed over her breast, the other stroking the uneven mound beside it, she sucked in a hard, aroused breath, her lower body clenching as if he'd touched her there. It was as much his expression as his hands that made her react, for in his eyes she saw proof she couldn't deny, at least at this vulnerable moment. She was the most wondrous discovery he'd ever made.

When Mina reached out, David paused to watch her while she touched his wing, followed the curve. She tugged on a handful of feathers. Though his desire was a simmering fire, he let himself be drawn to the side, back on his elbows, stretching both wings to half-mast, since the full six-foot stretch on either side would have knocked lamps off the night tables. He laced his fingers behind his head when she guided them there, squeezing his wrists once as an apparent request to keep them there so she could continue her play with him.

Or perhaps it wasn't a request. His witch could get somewhat imperious herself. Perhaps she didn't know that she and Jonah had that in common.

She'd sat up to give him room, and now his humor was swallowed by something more powerful as she leaned forward to run both her hands down the primary and two sections of secondary feathers again, as well as the inner wing layer. She did it slowly, repetitively, almost as if she were playing a harp, strumming down them, one hand following the other, down then across, tracing the arch.

He watched her eyes, the set of her mouth as she stretched out her arm to see how it lay against it, the comparative lengths. Then she turned her attention to his arm, following it from where the elbow bent, down to the crease of shoulder where arm joined to the upper torso. As her fingers lingered on the tautly bunched biceps, her tongue touched her lip, an entirely unconscious move that made more of his blood churn in a downward direction. Noticing his response, she let her hand drift that way as well.

But she paused on the now scarred-over burn mark on his chest, laying her palm over its mirror image in his flesh. That touch almost broke his control. He wanted to take her over, put her beneath him, but then she slid down. Pushing the half tunic out of the way, her thumb hooking on his belt to tease his stomach muscles, she curled her fingers around his heat.

"Mina, look at me." He put his hand up against her face, drew her gaze to him. "Come down here. Let me feel your body lying on mine."

She came to his mouth eagerly. While so little about her was innocent, her complete lack of self-consciousness because of her sexual inexperience was, and it made him crazy for her at the same time it stirred things in him which held him back, wanting to prolong the sweet torment of watching her discover what pleased her.

Mina knew what she wanted. As she slid over his body, straddled him, his cock was there, beneath her thigh, pressed against the outer lips of her sex. She rocked against him, physical coordination difficult during the kiss. God, she loved his mouth. She could admit it to herself. He made every part of her body sing, but his mouth . . . If she had to choose her eternity, it would be one filled with those long, drugged kisses that drove away everything in her mind.

He was taking his revenge, teasing her with his cock now, bringing her channel down snugly on it and sliding her wetness slowly up and down its length with a firm hand on her backside, his fingers parting the cleft between her buttocks in a way that had her squirming, taking over the movement herself, building her own response.

"Want you inside," she gasped.

"Beg, sweet witch. Ask."

"I can't . . ."

He nodded. And then, using that effortless strength again, he brought her up his body and sat her fully upon his mouth.

Gods, shouldn't she have taken this lesson to heart earlier? She cried out, would have gripped the headboard, but he had both her wrists, held them pinned against her hips as he suckled her into his mouth, did with his mouth what she so needed another part of him to do. She rocked, bucked, but his hold was immovable. And the higher she got, the further away any resolve got until she was gasping his name.

When he moved her back down, he held her fast on his cock, which had gotten harder, so that when he split her lips with it again, pressing the engorged head against her clit, she screamed.

His eyes flamed. "Ask."

She couldn't. His gaze darkened, his hands tightening on her again. This time he flipped her to her stomach, held her over his legs, his cock pressed into her belly, and captured her hips up high with the other hand. He began to stroke her with just his fingertips, as if he were playing a musical instrument. Her whole body began to shake, spasms with no release, his clever fingers knowing just what to do to hold that out of reach.

She wasn't even sure when she began to speak, but in her dazed mind she became aware that she was gasping it out.

"Please, David. Please . . ."

"Please what?" He stilled. "And don't be crude. Say what you want. Ask for it."

"I need you inside me. Please." Her fingers were gripping the edge of the bed and something else frightening was happening. Her throat was aching, her eyes filling with tears. Damn him for doing this to her. "Please."

It was then it clicked, an understanding of why he kept doing it this way. Inexperienced she was, but not unintelligent. Overwhelm her, give her pleasure as a method for teaching her submission, and she'd find the trust that came with it. She wanted to rail, wanted to deny it was something she wanted. Needed. All her life she'd stubbornly maintained she was answerable to no one, going the opposite direction the compass pointed.

But she wanted, needed to trust him. Needed to belong to him in a fierce way that was frightening, particularly when she thought, at these moments, he held the key to all of who she was in his single touch. It allowed her mind to be blissfully empty, responding only to his direction.

David lifted her so she sat astride him again, his cock on his belly just between the vee of her thighs when she looked down. While his expression was still quite implacable, there was something in his eyes, when he put his hands on either side of her face, that kept a powerful hold on her attention. It told her anything she wanted from him, she could have. His heart, his soul. He'd just tear them out and hand them to her.

All she had to do was ask.

His thumbs pressed at the corners of her eyes, and when she closed them, a hot tear fell, making her jump with its betrayal.

"Take me in your hands," he said with an unutterable tenderness. "Put me inside you, deep as you can take me. Torture us both now."

When she complied, more tears fell. The ache in her chest was going to incinerate her. She opened her eyes as she curled her hands around him, guided him in, the ridged head to her wet lips, both of them shuddering at that first explosive contact.

"Slow," he reminded her, unsteadily. She was salivating to taste his mouth, to tear and bite. She took him deeper, deeper, and the downward descent was like sinking down into the sweetest torment devised by Hell. Oh, gods, she wanted to ride him wildly, buck fast, hard, pump him in and out of her until she was dizzy with the spin, but she obeyed, going as slowly as she knew how, and watched him suffer, a mirror reflection of her own face, she was sure.

"So small and fine," he murmured, tracing her collarbone as she shuddered, holding still for him. She understood the rules now, embraced them, because they gave her something, a fixed point in her chaotic universe. She'd wait until he gave her leave to seek the pleasure waiting in a waterfall just beyond her vision, the fast, rushing descent, the scream of exhilaration. The immersion in the pounding water at the bottom, the salty foam.

"Why are you doing this to me?"

"You ask why a lot." His voice was strained, but there was humor there, too.

"You don't answer a lot."

The amusement died away as his eyes became more riveted upon her face. "Because if you truly belong to someone, you'll be less afraid." He echoed her very thoughts. "And because I want you to belong to me, more than I've ever wanted anything."

"I want to move," she whispered, a soft moan escaping her lips as he did nothing more than let his gaze pass over her breast, the taut nipple, cruise down to the joining point of their bodies. She contracted upon him, an involuntary reaction.

"Come without moving. Milk me inside, with your muscles. Let me watch your body shudder and quiver. I want the intensity of seeing you come, bound to stillness only by my word."

Oh, gods. How could he make her even more aroused with such words? She tightened, and that glorious contraction came again. When she did it, she saw the flare in his eyes. Noticed his cock wasn't the only rock-hard part of him. Arms, stomach, chest, thighs. All drawn tight, held just as still. She contracted again and again, until she couldn't help it. It felt so good, and oh, Goddess, she was coming.

"Keep doing it," he said between clenched teeth.

So she did, and the release, restrained as it was, was an avalanche that exploded through every nerve ending, one long, slow slide to the end of each one before leaping to the next. Somewhere in the middle of the exquisite torment, his cock convulsed inside her, and she felt the flood of seed. Hot, a geyser that seared the sensitive, spasming walls and tore a shriek out of her that was all female, no Dark One.

He'd put his hands over her wrists, but somewhere along the way, their fingers had become entwined, hers biting into his.

When they stopped together, shuddering, his touch eased. Hers didn't. She couldn't seem to let go, and her mind was overcome with the frightening need to hold on to him forever, knowing she'd never had such a desperate thought, which meant it was fraught with peril.

It was he who pried her loose, but only to ease her down to his chest, folding his arms over her. She pressed her cheek over his pounding heart.

"David," she said quietly after several moments.

"Hmmm?" His arms tightened on her back.

"I can't be happy. Because of the imbalance thing. But this is the closest to it I've ever been. No matter what else happens"—she hitched over the words just a bit—"thank you for that."

David turned his face to her hair, pressed his lips there. "I love you, sweet witch. Sleep. I'll be here when you wake."

She closed her eyes, heart tightening as his words tipped the scales a little further into that well of happiness. And because of that, as she descended into dreams, she braced herself to pay the price.

Twenty

SHE couldn't remember what she'd thought as a child, the first time she dreamed of the Dark One world. It had always been part of her sleep, as the ocean had been the world of her waking hours.

Crimson sky, like their eyes, so familiar. Shadows across the barren landscape, formed by shards of lightning. Constant roaring wind, jumping fires. Suffocating heat amid ash that seared the lungs and eyes of any creature. Rocks, naked trees, even the steam that rose from the ground, held poison if they made contact with the flesh of something that didn't belong there, raising festering boils.

Forged of clay and ash, human existence started in that Hell, but the Goddess had spirited them away to Earth. The Dark Ones would not rest until humans were brought back under their control. But the original parents of the human race were creations of pure feeling, driven by hate and violence. They could only destroy.

To Mina, though, with the Dark One blood within her, it was a world of chaos that made sense. An order that couldn't be explained, but she felt it in the deepest part of her Dark One soul. She also picked up early the symbiotic relationship between the humans and the Dark Ones, and knew the nightmares in the landscape were shared in the dreams of the humans and the reality of the Dark Ones.

You belong with us. You are ours. Ours.

You will destroy him. You would destroy it all. You can't escape your blood.

She woke thrashing, clawing. David's voice was distant, on the other side, and she had a sudden panic that it hadn't been a dream. She was there. And he was there with her. *No.*

"Mina? It's all right."

David, his arms firm and hard, closing around her, holding her as she gasped, shuddered.

The spasms went beyond her trembling body, just as they would if they were caused by the cracking of the Earth's crust or the thunder of the firmament. The dreams were an elemental force. They were always waiting. They knew. It hurt so badly, just as she knew it would. Take two steps forward, and you would be slapped back thousands of miles, into Hell. She couldn't rebuild it all again. Time to return to reality. To push him away before she destroyed him.

A flash of silver and gold. Screaming from deep inside a dark void. The Abyss. A stone wall, salt water rushing with blood. Not her blood. Blue. David's. Strong, dark eyes as a head drifted by in the water with chestnut hair. *Too late.*

"No. No!" She struggled back out of the dream again. David's hands were there still, his seeking eyes, the heat of his living body. *Living.*

"It's all right. I'm here."

"No. No, it's not all right. Something's happened. Somebody—"

David stiffened abruptly, his expression turning inward. "It's Jonah," he interrupted her. "He's calling all of us. The whole Legion. The Dark Ones took—"

"The Resurrection Trumpet," she finished his sentence. "I just saw it. Dreamed it. They used my portal to escape. Somehow they figured out how to go through the portal. That's how they escaped Jonah's angels. Yours . . ." She forced herself to say the words. "They've killed them. The three angels watching the cave."

His expression hardened, his eyes darkening, the whites swallowed in the time it took her to feel the blade of loss pierce her heart.

"I have to go report to Jonah."

"I'll go with you. I could help. I—"

"No." He said it sharply. "Stay here. I'll tell him and then, if there's time, I'll let you know what's going to happen."

And he was gone.

She stood on her knees on the mattress, swaying, staring at the now empty room. A chill ran up her bare back; the sheet fell away. Less than a minute, and everything that had been built in the past few hours was gone. The intensity of their joining, the promises that had been implied or made, her tentative belief. It mocked her in the silence of the house, the uneasy tendrils of Schism energy drifting like dust motes through the air. Particularly in the warmth of his body lingering on the bed but unable to penetrate the cold which had returned inside her.

As she'd drifted off, she'd even imagined what it would be like to wake up with him still around her, as he'd said. Lay there and talk about the next meal. Watch a sunrise. Share anything they wanted to talk about as they touched each other. A simple, astoundingly arrogant fantasy, thinking she'd ever deserve something like that, be given something like the tales those books spun. They were not her stories.

Nothing was "always" in her world. She'd had those few precious moments. That's all she'd asked, all she'd been given. That was that.

She left the bed and began to walk. From room to room, from the upper level to the lower, then onto the front porch, then the back. Looked at every corner of this marvelous house, felt the sense of belonging it pulled from her. Tearing her to shreds on the inside, the way her body looked on the outside. It wasn't for her. Not the welcoming warmth or the inviting sway of the empty tire swing.

Get over it. Numbing her mind, she went back inside and made a tidy bundle of her clothes and few belongings. Making sure the strap she used was long enough, she stepped out into the front yard again and forced herself not to look back. As she stripped off the splint and tucked that into the bag, she pushed away the memory of how capably his hands had moved over her finger, setting it, wrapping it in tape. The way his gaze had flickered up to her face to make sure he wasn't hurting her.

She thought of their time on the sandspit, and what he had said when he wrote *I love Mina* in the sand in that charming adolescent fashion. No, they'd never really had the chance for first love like that. But if there was any comfort she could grasp to help her breathe better over the pain in her chest, it was that she knew, for a brief moment in this house, they had both found it. She certainly never had expected such a gift. Or the agony of losing it.

As she began to shift into the dragon, she estimated she could be back to her caves in less than a couple of hours.

"THERE is no way they made it past us into a rift. We found no open ones. They've gone to ground here on Earth."

"But they can't stay here that long. We know this. And why can't we detect the Trumpet? It's an object of enormous energy. You think we're just overlooking it?"

David paused at the opening to the Citadel's Shamain keep. Jonah's gaze found him immediately, he was sure because of the thought he'd just shared with him.

I know where they are.

He stepped out as they all quieted. They'd accepted him, every one of them. Angels, while proud, were not egotistical. They believed in the greatest good, serving the Lady. But the Legion were also military-minded. He'd made a terrible mistake. The best way to deal with it was to figure out how to solve it. But that didn't abate his sense of shame as he faced the angel whom he'd let down the most.

"There's a portal to the Dark Ones' world in Mina's cave. It was created by her mother many years ago. Recently, I believed the Dark Ones might have discovered it, though I wasn't certain. I had three of my platoon guarding it. They're dead."

"And why didn't you didn't tell me about this earlier?"

I will vanquish you for breakfast. Yes, that was an understatement for the expression Jonah had on his face now. David squared his shoulders. "It was a calculated risk. I was trying to win her trust. My intention was to come to you about it when she felt she could trust me more. It was a mistake." He dropped to one knee. "My apology, Commander. If you wish to relieve me of my command—"

"Have you seen to your dead?"

"No." David shook his head, feeling the usual dull weight in his chest that such a loss created there. "I felt my duty was to report here first."

"See to them, then. If the Trumpet is in Dark One territory, there is little that can be done." Jonah spoke brusquely. "No angel can follow it there. But we must prepare for its return. Now that they have it, it's certain they will try to use it."

"We can't anticipate where they will emerge. All they have to do is have the time to blow it." This from Marcellus, who, David noted, had two glossy dark green wings again. "Though why didn't they do that when they grabbed it?"

Gabriel stepped forward to answer. The angel had pure white hair, features so graceful and refined that on first glance he could almost be mistaken for female. He spoke softly, but the resolve in his face, the tension in his body, belied any impression of mildness. "The magics associated with it are complex and must be unraveled. It will take time to figure them out, and even then, only a Full Submission angel or an extremely powerful magic user would be able to use it."

"Like the witch," Marcellus pointed out.

The angels shifted back toward David, Gabriel's gaze pinning him, bringing the weight of a Full Submission angel's attention on him. "And she was here the day Gabriel brought it for tuning," the captain continued. "She could have affected it in some way, made it easier for the Dark Ones to take it."

"Where is she?" Jonah asked, pinning David with his gaze.

"She is not a part of this."

"Was that the question I asked you, Lieutenant?"

He was not afraid of Jonah, but he was not the only angel that jumped as the commander thundered out the words, making the walls of the Citadel shake, the skies above cloud uneasily over the sun.

"No, sir." David steeled himself to meet that dark gaze, which was sparking with fire. "She was with me, at the Schism house. I asked her to stay there until I returned."

"You have a bloodlink with her. Is she there now?"

David focused, and felt fear clutch his vitals. *Mina, no. Of all the times not to obey me . . .* But then, he thought despairingly, when had she ever?

Jonah was waiting. For one desperate moment, David thought of lying, and knew if he did, he would be going down a road from which there would be no return. The road to Hell. A Hell of his own making.

There was no avenue to persuade Jonah in this, David knew. The Prime Legion Commander would brook nothing less than absolute obedience this time. While he knew he would have fought to the death to protect Mina that day, he was facing the angel he respected the most, the one who had in fact been the father for him his father had not been. The being he trusted, more than any other, even at this moment.

"She didn't feel comfortable staying there alone. She's gone back to the ocean."

"To that portal," Marcellus snapped.

"To her cave. Her home."

Gabriel glanced toward Jonah. "If she has the power you say, she could use the Trumpet."

"She has no desire to do that. She is not part of this plan," David repeated sharply.

"Because you don't want her to be? Because you lust after her? David, you're not the first angel or male of any species to be thrown off track by a sorceress's wiles. You're young and—"

"So is she," David shot back at Marcellus. "She's a twenty-nine-year-old mermaid who has been tortured and tormented since she was born. Been treated as an outcast by everyone, and the only thing that has saved her life is the power she has to protect herself. She has used that power for that purpose. She hasn't had the leisure time to hatch a plot to destroy the world. Her greatest desire is to be left alone, not rule the universe."

He turned his gaze back to a silent Jonah. "Commander, I made a mistake, but it was not a lie. I have not lied to you. I have been inside her head. Her heart. Her body." He swallowed. "I would wager the life of the Goddess *she is not a part of this*."

"You will take great care in how you speak of Her."

Lucifer. The dark-winged angel had landed on the upper turret and gone to a squat, his long fingers tented on the stonework, his scythe balanced in his other hand. The ebony lengths of his hair fell forward, covering his forearms and the carved shaft of the lethal-looking weapon. As the only born angel of the Seraphim with color in his eyes, red flame flickered among the coal depths.

David bowed. "My apologies, my lord. My choice of words is not idle, however. It is to prove how certain I am."

"It is best never to use such words. Whether you are certain of her intent or not, your witch is already a part of this."

Jonah met Lucifer's gaze, nodded and turned to Marcellus. "You and ten of your battalion will come with me. We go to that cave." He shifted his glance to David. "You go ahead of us. We will set our strategy for patrolling the rifts first. I'm giving you a half an hour to see what you can find out from her, because I know she will not speak in front of us without difficulty. And to see to your dead."

David knew he was being dismissed. It was not a shunning,

but it was clear that, beyond his knowledge and connection to Mina, Jonah felt he had nothing to offer to this strategy session. Not until the inevitable battle occurred and his platoon would be called upon—as would the whole Legion—to defend the world from the destruction that the Trumpet could bring upon it.

Eli. Mark. Vincent. Those were the three angels he'd left to defend the cave. He was certain they'd accounted themselves well, but as he flew swiftly toward his destination, he thought of them, felt their loss. He could not be grateful for what might be ahead, but he didn't know an angel in the Legion who didn't eagerly embrace anything, even battle, to avoid the sharp pain of losing one or more of their brethren. And the Legion lost them often.

Based on his assessment of his three men, he knew it would have taken a raiding party of at least ten Dark Ones to take them. When he posted the trio, he hadn't anticipated a group that large coming to the cave, because he hadn't thought of the Dark Ones having a higher purpose to their discovery of the relatively small portal than routine escape by small clusters. But of course his and Mina's battle had alerted them to the presence of angels, so they'd come back prepared. Rift openings left by Dark Ones were typically guarded by no less than a platoon until they were sealed. He might as well have thrown out a welcome mat.

I'm sorry. He knew he would find only the physical shell of them in the cave, so he offered his useless prayer to the winds and sky now, where their energy would be, rejoining the Lady. *I'm sorry, to all three of you.*

He felt a savage desire to howl, rage against nothing but the still air, the lap of water against the rocks far below as he cut across a shoreline. Things of the Earth that simply went on, indifferent to everything else that happened.

He'd been an idiot, and maybe for reasons more than he'd first thought. He'd been focused only on Mina herself, and how she was handling her powers. As he sped through the sky, Jonah's words rolled through his head, along with Mina's dreams, her life, the Dark Ones' interest in her . . .

They'd assumed all along the Dark Ones' intent was to take her, use her power. But they hadn't considered the fact they might be recruiting her for a specific, strategic purpose. How would she feel, knowing that all the years she'd spent studying, increasing the range of her abilities, was something they'd monitored so eagerly, for something like this?

David's head start was giving him time to think, regroup and be able to contribute something more to the recovery effort than he'd first thought. He'd like to think perhaps that was Jonah's purpose, but he wouldn't be surprised if the commander just wanted him out of his sight for a while.

It calls to me . . . All I have to do is turn it up, just a little, and I look more and more like your enemy. Until you won't hesitate to strike me down.

He increased his speed. *I'm not wrong about her. I'm not.* Even though everything Jonah and Marcellus said made perfect sense, that didn't matter. But he should have overridden her objections and closed the portal. Her safety was important, but Lucifer was right. The protection of the Lady and Her Earth from Dark Ones was the most important thing of all, the umbrella over everything else that would ultimately serve both objectives. He'd led with his heart instead of his head.

Not a crime in matters of love, but in matters of war, it was fatal.

That was likely another reason Jonah had given him the head start. To do what he should have done in the beginning, even if Mina hated him for it.

MINA couldn't reattach the angel's head, but she did align it with the neck as much as possible. She'd found the three dead angels still in her caves, ironically kept there by the wards on the cave's opening, protected from scavengers as they floated in a ghostlike, repetitive cycle through the five interconnected caverns. Fortunately only one of the angels had been decapitated.

While she'd seen things more horrible in her dreams than the sight of those three corpses drifting through her home, there was no denying it shook her, the way those wings moved with the currents, curving around the lifeless bodies as if forming a loving shroud for the pure spirit that had inhabited the flesh. She could have just disintegrated their matter, but she didn't know what death rituals angels performed. David would need to see them, perhaps care for them in that way. She didn't want to just destroy them, as if they'd been debris.

It mattered what he thought of her. That was something she now accepted. More surprising was the fact she realized she did care about more than that. She cared enough to run a scarf around the decapitation point, tuck it in to cover it and steady the skull, touch the auburn hair on the angel's head and wish he weren't dead.

The problem is you feel too much. He was going to be right about that, too, wasn't he? Damn him. Now that he hated her, she supposed it was a moot point. It didn't matter what you felt or didn't feel, if no one cared.

She'd dissipated and lowered the water level below the ledge in the section where she kept her books so she could bring the angels to that flat surface. She'd been able to float the first one to the ledge, but once the water level was below it, getting the other two on it had been difficult work, and she was covered in blue blood that seared her skin. She didn't care much about that. She just didn't want David to get here, as she knew he would when he found her gone from the desert house, and see his men the way she'd found them. She noted the wings had started to stiffen in their curves around the angels' bodies, so rigor mortis affected those, too. She tried not to think about how David's would feel, if it were his lifeless eyes staring at her.

"I told you to stay in the Schism."

She turned then. He emerged from the water, stepped onto the ledge, water sluicing down his body, his wings gleaming with the drops. His gaze was only on her for a curt acknowledgment before it shifted to his dead. The angels beneath her touch were older than him, she knew. One of them probably well over a hundred.

"I thought it best to come back here."

He squatted and looked down into their frozen features, the staring, dark eyes. "Move back," he said quietly.

As she withdrew, he passed his hand several feet above the bodies. Silver light gathered beneath his palm in a sphere, then unfurled like a blanket that drifted down upon them, sinking into their wet, cold flesh. Slowly, the light became a pale fire that took them away with a quiet beauty, removing death from their faces, illuminating the tips of their feathers, fingers, the lengths of their limbs. When it was done, only silver ash patterns were left on the damp rock. He sang a soft chant during the process, a prayer of peace and rest, but in the roughness of his voice she could tell how responsible he felt. That he would miss them. The words of the chant revealed they were being sent back to the life force of the Mother until such time as they would be born from that energy again, centuries in the future. It reminded her that angels didn't have a guarantee on individual rebirth, a separate resting place for their souls. So he didn't know what awareness he would have in his afterlife, either. Another yin and yang comparison between them.

He was quiet for a bit afterward, then he glanced toward her. "I'm closing that portal."

"No."

He straightened. Mina shifted in front of the entrance, though she already saw it in his face as if he'd pinioned her heart with one of his daggers. No matter what he had to do to her to make it happen, he was closing that portal.

"I wasn't asking."

"You can't close it. Not until I go through it and send back the Trumpet."

———

HE didn't want to discuss it, probably thinking she was stalling, but with dogged persistence, she persuaded him to let her explain.

"You remember how I was able to get Jonah's sword to him in the desert, all the way from where I found it in the ocean? It's not an easy magic, particularly at this distance, but the connection is strengthened if I have a blood link to someone here, like I have with you. Once I lay hands on it, say the proper spell and offer it some of my blood, then the Trumpet could transport. The key isn't that it has to jump from one realm to another, but that the magic and mind's reach have to be sufficiently powerful. I can do it," she added resolutely, hoping she was right.

"You've never been to their world. You wouldn't get a chance to find it before they discovered you there."

"I have been there."

"A dream, no matter how vivid, isn't firsthand knowledge."

She bit back impatience. It was easier to focus on this than the flat way he was speaking to her, as if she were just a member of his platoon making a report. No, that was wrong. He loved the men in his platoon. She was far less than that to him now.

"*Dream* is the wrong word. I connect to it. See it, observe it. In some ways, they're aware of my presence, because there have been times they've turned toward me in the dreams, tried to speak to me. But they can't hold me there. They can't read my thoughts."

"So if you saw the Trumpet in the Citadel, there's no way they knew its location through you."

"That's what Jonah and Marcellus think, don't they?" *It's what you think.*

When he didn't reply, she tightened her jaw. She should never have let him matter. Should have figured a way to neutralize that blood link so he could never find her. The Trumpet might have been taken regardless. She'd be in mortal danger like everyone else in the world, but without this terrible sense of loss in her chest. "I know the landscape of their world, David," she forced herself to repeat the words. "I have their blood, so I can walk through the portal and survive there. I *will* locate the Trumpet. It's an item of tremendous power, so I can pick up the energy signature. I suspect they didn't take it far. They'll want to use it, as soon as they can figure out how."

"According to Gabriel, it requires a Full Submission angel or a strong, exceptionally powerful magic user to unravel the spells over it," David responded. "Has it occurred to you that they might intend you to be the one who does that? You told me that every day is a struggle not to walk through that portal, that they've always been calling to you. That they offer you the sense of belonging you lack here."

"I also told you that I know that's a lie, David. I can't belong to them. I'm not fully one of them. I'm not fully a merperson. I can't belong to anyone." She swallowed as something flickered in his eyes. "I guess you know that now, too."

She turned away, because she didn't have the courage to look at him. But she would give him truth. The bodies before her, everything he'd given her so far, had earned him that right.

"Yes," she said. "I believe they're trying to get me into their world to play the Trumpet. If so, then under the same criteria, I might be the only one who can get close enough to take it away from them."

"Why would they trust you?"

"I've got to convince them to trust me. It will be difficult, but I don't think it will be impossible." She looked toward the dark hole leading to the portal chamber. "They'll wonder about my actions at the Canyon and will probably test me on that. But one thing they understand is the nature of Dark One blood. I'm hoping they'll believe no Dark Spawn is strong enough to resist it when immersed in the energies of their world."

"What if they're right? I've seen what happened at the Citadel, Mina. Based on what I felt in that portal, it seems the balance tilts in their favor, exponentially. There will be nothing to pull you back the other way."

"I can impose some shields they can't detect to filter it." She didn't like the thoughts moving behind his eyes. Angry he might be, grieving, but damn it, his mind never stopped working. She crossed her arms, managed to bump her injured finger and bit her lip against the pain. "I don't pretend to care about the battle for good against evil the way that you do, but I do care about what's done as a result of my actions. If I had let you seal the portal when you asked, this wouldn't have happened. I intend to do what I can to make this right."

"It was my decision to keep it open. I bear responsibility for it."

"We're both responsible, then."

"Then we should both go."

"No." She'd seen it coming, but the icy hand of fear still gripped her. "David, have you lost your mind? You can't go. You're an angel."

"You can cast an illusion spell over me so I appear like one of them. You changed my appearance in the saloon, as well as yours."

"That's not the problem. There are energies in that world . . . Remember how you felt, just stepping into the portal chamber? Also, Dark Ones raise that battle instinct in you. Imagine that magnified a thousand times, with an illusion spell in place where you have to react as a Dark One would to another Dark One. You can't do that."

"You know every spell there is. Dark magics as well as light ones." His gaze slid around the room, over her books, back toward the room of her stores. "There's a way around that. Isn't there?"

And when his gaze came back to her face, she knew he'd seen something in her eyes or body language. Gods, they needed to stop talking about this. He saw too much. And he was too noble, too damn self-sacrificing . . .

"No," she repeated stubbornly. "I won't do it. You can't make me."

"Mina, do you know what the Resurrection Trumpet does? Blow one note and that tone resonates, plunges deep into the crust of the Earth, waking layers upon layers of the dead. A second blast, and the earth shifts, folds back peacefully to uncover those bodies. On the third blast, the dead begin to walk, to live again. Their souls return to them and they are restored to life."

"That doesn't sound terrible," she said, though she knew he wasn't done.

"That's what happens if an agent of the Goddess blows it. If the one with the Trumpet is evil, those who rise are not given their souls, or free will. Mountains crumble, and the shifting of the earth becomes earthquakes. They're the walking dead only, obeying only hunger and impulse. In short, they will be an army for the Dark Ones, creating the chaos they need to turn this world into a reflection of their own."

She had an overwhelming urge to put her hands over her ears, tell him she didn't care, but even she wasn't that brave. *Noble* and *self-sacrificing* suggested gentle traits, but when he became determined like this, the intensity of his presence, his resolve, crashed against the cave walls like sound echoes, creating a din inside of her almost as hard to bear as when the skeletons had fallen into piles in the freighter. The power of an angel's will was nothing that a mortal could hope to resist, and the energy of it was pressing her up against the wall, making her want to escape, the Dark One blood roiling within her. He was losing patience with her. The thing he'd once thought he cared about, until she'd lost him his men.

"You know the connection between humans and Dark Ones." He persisted, ignoring her distress. "Humans fight the darkness in themselves as well. This will be the ultimate act of chaos, of evil, tipping that scale, so the Dark Ones could use it not just to tear open a rift, but the whole damn sky, claim Earth and the humans as their own at last. So if there's a way for me to go, I need to go."

"You'd be a liability to me," she insisted.

"If that happens, abandon me," he said brutally. "But it's possible I can help."

"For the ten seconds before they tear you to pieces."

"I can help," he retorted, an edge to his voice. He met her gaze. The knowledge there lanced through her. "Not only for balance. An offering to prove they can let you get close to the Trumpet."

"*No.*" She lifted her head. How had he known? "*Don't* use my mind like that. I haven't given you any right—"

"So you've already thought of it." He stepped forward, even as she slid along the wall, trying to get away from him. "In the dark shadows of that brilliant mind of yours."

"And discarded it." She hated him for knowing her as well as she knew herself, maybe better, because everything in the past two days was shattering, becoming a lie. He'd never look back on it fondly, for he knew the extent of the evil, how deeply it reached into her now.

"Tell me."

"No. No. *No.*" She said each word more vehemently than the last, and when he put his hands on her shoulders, she struck at him. Not with her considerable defensive abilities, but in despair, slapping at his face, his chest, trying to shove him away even as he brought her in to his body, wrapped himself around her, his wings, cocooning her. "Don't touch me when you . . ." *When you don't want me anymore. When everything has changed.* Had to change, not only because of those three angels, but because of what dark things he'd just picked from her mind.

"Stop it, Mina. Stop. Tell me."

"I hate you."

"You don't have to say it. Just say it to me in your mind. Let me see it."

She couldn't resist his compulsion, but he couldn't make her do what she wouldn't. "I'll let you see it, but we're not doing it. I won't. I will convince them alone."

He was silent as she relayed the idea to him, and she expected him to stiffen in shock, or move away from her. He did neither. Which meant, to her terror, he accepted it. Accepted such a terrible thing could come from her mind, such a horrible idea, and he'd still hold her like this.

She couldn't let herself go down that road again. Breaking free of him, she slid under his arm and backed away. "I will convince them alone," she repeated.

"Mina, we need to go in with our very best plan, because there's only one shot at something like this."

Had she thought she liked the term *we*? Now she despised it.

"You want me to go. You need me to go. You think I don't know what it will cost you to step into that portal? That you're using that indomitable will of yours to squelch the terror of what it will do to you?"

She couldn't bear the softening of his tone, what it did to her insides, making her believe everything hadn't been destroyed. Things she hadn't even known she wanted and now, suddenly, two sunrises and sunsets later, she felt like she couldn't do without. But since when was anything like that a choice for her?

He came to her again, stood before her. Round and round. They'd circled that silver ash so many times it could be a casting, a building of power. There was nowhere to retreat as she stood on the ledge where it met the water, could feel it lapping at her human heels, for she'd shifted to human to lay out the bodies. His broad chest was before her gaze, so capable and strong, and yet so fragile, as all life was fragile. Raising her lashes, she stared at him. "No," she said.

His hands closed on her upper arms as she quivered at the heat of his touch, the way his face tilted over hers. A lock of his damp hair had fallen loose from where he'd slicked it back. "You won't ask me to sacrifice myself, even if it takes the chance of success from zero to the slimmest of possibilities? Even if you'll be lost to eternal torment and damnation without my help?"

His gaze seemed to reach down inside her, pick up her heart, for it felt like it was beating in the inescapable grip of his eyes. "I told you that you would eventually say it back to me," he murmured. "You're saying it now."

Mina stared up at him. "I thought . . ." She swallowed it back, but he had the courage to say it.

"You thought I hated you." His hands were becoming more gentle. Gods, stroking her skin. "Mina, I hate that I lost three of my angels. That I didn't realize I needed to trust Jonah with the knowledge of the portal and have faith in my ability to figure out another way to keep your trust. I hate what the Dark Ones do to you. But hate you?" She saw a glimmer of white, the rich brown warmth of his irises for just a moment in the flickering lights of her cave. "You won't get rid of me so easily, sweet witch. You know, in the deepest part of your soul, that you need me in order to do this."

When he slid his fingers over her hand, somehow now resting on his chest, she closed her eyes. "I'm so afraid, David."

"I know that."

"I don't want to do it. Not if I'm going to lose you. I don't want to risk you."

"Get over it," he said. "It's the plan that makes the most sense. And even if it didn't, I'm not letting you go into that rift alone. I made an oath to serve the Lady, and to serve you. I'm going to do both. We're going to go together, and we'll figure it out."

As he cupped the side of her face, Mina let out a soft sob, despite herself, and his touch tightened, holding her closer, fingers digging into her hair. He'd left her in anger and violent urgency, come back with guilt and pain. Now, in figuring out what needed to be done to fix mistakes, protect her and serve his Lady, he showed her why he was an angel. Beneath the passion and humor, tenderness, affinity for Rolling Stones' songs and chocolate chip cookies, the uncertainty that could attend making mistakes and learning from them, there was an old soul who understood what things mattered, endured. It pervaded that soothing touch.

She looked up at him then, her heart in her throat. "I really didn't want to care about you at all."

Now he did smile. "I know that."

With a rueful look, David stepped back, though he held on to her hand. "Jonah's on his way. He can be your transport point. You need a strong mind to connect to, one with enough power for a great distance. He's the one to do it."

"No." Mina shook her head, new resolve on her face. "It has to be you. You have to stay here. I don't want him connected to my mind."

"Mina, that's been decided. I'm going."

"You decided. And you can decide all you want, but it's up to me."

Ignoring her, he continued, "Have faith in Jonah. He may see the evil you fight, but he'll see the good in you that keeps you fighting it. I should have trusted him about the portal. Let's not make the same mistake again."

"What will he think when he sees the visions I've had of cutting her throat, tasting her blood on my hands?" She pulled back from him.

David closed the space between them again. "Why are you about to face the greatest fear you have, of the Darkness taking you over, Mina? Why does it matter what Jonah thinks of you? Or even me?"

"Because I'm the only one who has the ability to get back the Trumpet," she snapped.

"That's not it."

Her lip curled back in a feral snarl, her crimson and blue eyes firing as she locked them on his intent face. "Because I'm going to walk in there, be surrounded by them, their energy, their persuasion, and take something from *them*, damn it. The way they took everything from my mother, so she could give me nothing of herself but my life before she gave up and died. I'm tired of being afraid of it. Tired of fighting who I am, when I don't really know who that is. It's time to find out. And maybe if I can do that, I can believe that I do deserve something else. That I can find out about happiness and laughter. And kiss you just once, without being afraid."

When her gaze lingered on his mouth, David had to suppress the sudden urge to offer it to her, offer everything. "But I didn't want Jonah to know those thoughts I had about Anna," she added, a note of despair in her voice now. "I don't want her to know that, remember that about me."

Giving her hands a squeeze so she wouldn't be startled, would know all was well, David nodded. "All right, then." Then he glanced to his left and Jonah moved out of the shadows.

Twenty-one

MARCELLUS was on his right and another captain, Bazak, on his left. From Jonah's expression, David knew he'd heard the very best thing he could have heard from the seawitch's lips. Her determination to decide her own destiny, which superseded the hold either light or dark had upon her. And her very personal need to maintain the connection with the one friend she'd had since birth.

He's only been here for a couple minutes, he said to her in his mind, as Jonah and the other two angels took a moment to pay their respects to the evidence of silver ash, the remains of his three men. He wanted to be sure his suspicious witch didn't retreat from him, thinking all of it had been a ruse. She glanced at him, looking like she could murder him where he stood. For Mina, that was practically an expression of affection, however, and told him they were okay. As okay as any of them could be in this moment.

"The witch's plan has reason to it," Jonah said in a measured voice at last. "Your participation leaves a few holes to be explained."

Holes Jonah wasn't going to like at all, David knew. He'd stick with the high-level explanation. "The balance between good and evil within her is very precise," he responded. "She'll be going into a world where she'll be overwhelmed by that Darkness. I can help, even if I'm cloaked. We know the Trumpet can only be used by one of exceptional power. Do we take the risk of waiting until they emerge, if we have better odds sending her in after it?"

You were right about her power. Let me be her balance. She knows I'm right about needing me there.

"It's rude to talk about people in your heads when they're standing right here." Mina glared at the two silent angels.

Marcellus eyed her. "*You* are going to give lectures on courtesy?"

"Been craving any fruit and insects lately? Hanging upside down when you sleep?"

"No, but squid may be on the menu soon." He aimed a pointed look at her legs.

"Enough," Jonah said, shooting a hard glance between them.

"Just one jolt," Marcellus suggested, unsheathing his blade. "Not enough to kill her. Just to get her to shut up for two seconds."

Mina ignored him and stepped around David to face Jonah. "There are things he's not telling you."

"Mina—"

"First off, for him to survive in the Dark One world, I have to turn him into one."

The two captains shifted, muttered, but Jonah kept his gaze pinned on Mina. "How?"

Gods, being under that look was like being compressed beneath rock, particularly since she sensed David's gaze boring into her shoulders as well. Nevertheless, she held Jonah's look without flinching. "I need to inject the blood of a Dark One into his veins. Your men killed one." She glanced back at David. "I took several vials of its blood before I incinerated it."

"Why would you have done that?" This from Marcellus.

"Dark One blood is useful for several potions and spells. It's part of my stores. I rarely get the opportunity to obtain it so fresh." She arched a brow at the captain. "One of the things it can do is incapacitate an angel long enough to kill him, if prepared in the right way and sprayed upon his wings."

When Marcellus stepped forward, Jonah put up a hand. "Seawitch," he said mildly, "I think we're all here for the same purpose. Don't taunt my captain. I may just let him dice you as he desires. So David drinks this blood—prepared in a way I assume *won't* incapacitate him, and that will make the Dark Ones accept him?"

She inclined her head. "I would cast an illusion spell on him, for a short time, until we reached our destination. As long as he didn't have too much interaction with them, he would pass among them unnoted. They are creatures of impulse, but they do communicate and have identities. But he has to manage the effect of the blood to function."

"We all meditate, practice focus. Is it doable for him?"

She pressed her lips together, wanting to say no, but she didn't think anyone could lie before that dark, piercing stare. David was right. Jonah's daughter would get away with nothing, other than the things an indulgent father would allow. And she knew about the angels' ability for concentration. "Yes."

"Would he have to live with it forever, when you return?"

She felt David's tension behind her, knew he really didn't want her to keep talking. So she did, though hearing the words aloud was almost as hard as telling him the strategy in her mind. "We'll be lucky to get the Trumpet out to you. When we do, we will be deep in Dark One territory, with thousands of them between us and our portal to return. We won't make it back out. Which is why you should forbid him to go."

"We've already covered this. I'm not letting you go alone," David said, his voice resolute. "You will not go without me."

"For the sake of argument, let's pretend I am the Prime Legion Commander, and you take orders from me," Jonah said curtly.

Jonah, it's as I said—

"I heard you clearly, Lieutenant," Jonah snapped out loud. "If

I am your blood link contact, Mina, will you be able to communicate with me?"

She shook her head. "My link with you is like tying a line to a rock to find my way back, only I'll be sending the Trumpet along it. You'll know I'm successful when it appears at your feet. The link would need to be here, in these caves. This is the easiest focus point for me. You'll want additional reinforcements, for Dark Ones will flock to this portal once I'm successful."

"We have ten outside."

"You'll need more. Maybe fifty."

Jonah nodded to the second captain, and he was gone with a clean ripple of water that ruffled the feathers of the angels that remained. "Back out the moment you have it and seal the portal," Mina continued. "Bring down the cave. That will block it off for certain. Many of the things stored here would be dangerous in the wrong hands anyway."

She allowed herself a glance at her books, the potions and tools she'd collected throughout her life. Briefly lingered on the chimes, the ones she'd created, the one her mother had made her, the one gift that might have been prompted by the love she wished she could have given her daughter, if Mina believed in such things. "There is nothing here I will need," she said shortly.

"Leave me here with a platoon, Jonah," Marcellus said. "It makes more sense for you and the other angels to spread out over the Earth's surface and prepare for an attack, if she's unsuccessful and Dark Ones come through with the Trumpet elsewhere. I can do the link with the witch."

"That's fine," Mina said, giving him an indifferent look. "Though I didn't expect you to be brave enough to take my blood."

"Nothing about you frightens me, witch. Except that hideous face of yours."

"Enough. The two of you give me a headache." Jonah stepped in front of Marcellus. "This task is mine. I can get to all of you in less than a blink, and I will stay here and destroy the gate. Bazak will back me up with his platoon."

"So I am going with her," David said.

Mina's gaze darted back to Jonah, alarmed.

"I have not decided that yet," the commander said flatly. He locked gazes with David, and his expression was forbidding. "You think I'm such a fool that I missed she said there were two parts of her plan? When it comes to your witch, I can't trust you, David." His attention flicked like the brief sting of a lash at the center of David's chest, where that brand rested.

David's countenance tightened. "He didn't deserve that," Mina said hotly, stepping forward to bump toes with the commander.

"Yes, he did. It does not mean I do not value him. Have a care." The brief warning was all she got before Jonah's short blade appeared just beneath her nose. He ran it across his arm, a swift movement, the blue blood welling up, pure and ethereal, causing the blood within her to recoil, making her light-headed.

"Here." David was already behind her, steadying her with his body.

When David saw her arm aligned with his commander's, he realized how truly small and fragile his witch was, her thin forearm in Jonah's powerful grasp. Even he seemed affected by it, for his long fingers closed on her arm with a gentler touch than David would have expected.

He drew his own dagger. "Let me."

Passing the blade over her flesh, he opened it, cradling her forearm himself while Jonah turned his arm to clasp her elbow, bringing the two wounds together. Mina's gaze met David's. As he'd hoped, he saw being marked by his blade had steadied her, though the storm clouds were still there. She could brew all she wanted. His jaw tightened. He was going to win this one.

You know I'm right. I need to go. This is about more than your feelings or mine.

As if that thought brought something else to the forefront of her mind, Mina's attention now shifted to Jonah. David watched her struggle with the unfamiliar act of making a request. "I would be grateful, if you never tell Anna what you see in my mind. It would hurt her to know. I wish it were different."

"I think Anna understands far more about you than you've ever realized. She is goodness, as pure as any angel ever dreamed of being." As the depth of his feeling for the mermaid crept into the commanding voice, Mina was surprised to see something in the Prime Legion Commander's gaze upon her that might have been kindness. "And yes, innocent in many ways. But she has your bravery and intelligence, and true love goes into the darkest corners without fear."

His eyes went to David and back to her again. "I think that may be an appropriate understanding for this moment. So tell me the rest, little witch."

"They will trust me if I bring an angel to their world, bound with Dark Blood and my magic so that he is not only enslaved to my will, but can survive in their world that way. Proof of my willingness to serve their cause."

Marcellus didn't bother to conceal his expression of shocked horror. Jonah's face became thunderous. "You would sacrifice him."

"It is only one way. I can figure out how to do it without him, if I have no other choice." *Please don't give me that choice, because I can't say no to him. You can.*

She'd forgotten that an angel could read a mind when it spoke directly to him. Jonah's gaze locked with hers, that anger in his expression not clearing, but she saw his mind evaluating. *Just like David's*, she thought with despair.

"This blood link works quickly. My sense of your emotions on this is quite clear. You don't want him to go, are terrified of it, in fact. But you are lying about your chances alone. You don't think you can succeed without him."

David's hand whispered over the back of her neck in a reassuring as well as admonishing touch. "Some things are harder to do alone. She doesn't like to admit that."

It was like speaking over those jagged oyster shells again, the sharp pain of them cutting into her tongue, only this time it was her thoughts that cut into her heart. *All I need is his faith in me, though I'll die without ever understanding it. Or being worthy of it. Because if he goes, yes. He's going to be the sacrifice that buys me time and credibility.*

"Now who's being rude?" David muttered, a hint of impatience at her ear as he apparently sensed the dialogue. She ignored him, kept her attention riveted on Jonah.

The commander said nothing. Bending, he picked up and replaced the silver wrist gauntlet he'd removed for the blood link. "You say you can track the Trumpet," he said at last. "How far from the portal do you think it will be?"

"Not far," she responded, wishing he would make the decision, wishing he would say something so that the pressure in her chest wouldn't cause her to implode. But he was still deciding, and while he was still deciding, there was hope. "There are four towers in the corners of the Dark One world, used to concentrate rift energy. All rifts are entered through those structures. One is close to the exit from this portal, because I've seen it in my dreams. It makes sense they'd take it to that tower and open a rift to use it from there, when they're ready. They can open multiple rift points from one tower, however, so that doesn't help pinpoint where they might come through," she added when she saw the idea flash across Jonah's face.

"Because it's an object of great magic, they need to keep it strongly warded so it's bearable for them to handle. It's not truly a light magic, but it's been in angels' hands. That will resonate, leave a trail. I can find it easily if I'm wrong about the tower."

Jonah turned away then and paced to the end of the ledge, which she saw put him in the line of sight of the next water-filled cavern, which could not mask some of her more questionable stores. The commander's impressive wings folded down into a tight, narrow heart along his broad back, the tips twining in the space between his braced legs. She saw the greaves on his calves had the same silver scrollwork as his wrist gauntlets. Protections, praises to his Lady. The right gauntlet had an etching of a mermaid. Knights going into battle had always carried a favor of their loved ones. As she looked at the blood still staining the edge of David's blade, the small trickle of it clotting on her arm, she wondered if this was hers. While Jonah had the option of carrying only the token, keeping the loved one safely out of the line of fire, Mina was on the verge of offering hers up to the enemy to be torn apart.

The lapping of the water ruffled the bottom of his tunic slightly, but other than that, there was no movement from Jonah for several long moments. Marcellus stayed silent, watchful.

At last, he turned. "David will go with you."

As the two males exchanged a look, Mina sensed a great deal passing between them, probably much of it without words, the soul-deep understanding of what serving the Lady ultimately meant to the angels of the Legion, who dedicated the entirety of their immortal lives to it. Jonah had been doing it for over a thousand years, David for less than two decades, but as David had said, it was just something the soul knew. She wanted to scream.

"You sacrifice him carelessly," she snapped. "You do not care for him at all."

In a blink, Jonah was back before her, and instinct had her starting back, where she ran into the solid wall of David, whose hands settled on her shoulders, which she thought he must find reassuring, and she hated, because it was.

"Think you so, witch?" Jonah spoke in a soft, deadly tone. "Think if I could spare him by throwing you into the torments of Hell all by yourself, or even myself for that matter, I wouldn't? If you'd offered a plan that only sacrificed you, I'd have embraced it."

Mina recovered from her fright. "I did," she snapped, stepping forward, her red eye vibrant enough to have Marcellus shifting restlessly again.

Fascinating as it was to see his diminutive seawitch and the Prime Legion Commander snarling at each other, David stepped to stand at her side. "*I* would not embrace it. And while I have the greatest of respect for you, Jonah, this is my choice. It is the Goddess's will that I stand at Mina's side, her back, wherever she needs me. You've taught me that an angel is never confused about whom he loves. Mina is mine. This is what was meant to be. Do not suffer on my account, no matter what happens."

A muscle twitched in Jonah's hard jaw. Mina wanted to rail against the decision, but disconsolately, she realized there was nothing left to say. When David rested a light hand on her shoulder, she found she couldn't draw away from his touch, despairing proof of his words.

"You will make his sacrifice worth something." Jonah's attention was on her again. "You will take care of him, as much as you can. Anna will not think well of me for this."

"You are the sun, the moon and stars to Anna," she said, because she could only speak raw truth now. Everything else was over. Her defenses, her shields, all the games she'd used to play out her life. This was the end of it, she knew. The truth lost her no ground anymore. "As you will be to the girl child she carries. Love them well, as long as Fate gives you the ability to do so. The greatest blessing I can offer them is my absence from their lives."

She expected Marcellus to make some nasty comment of agreement, and was surprised when he said nothing. He studied her, his expression inscrutable, but inclined his head, just slightly. Perhaps to David, standing behind her.

"Will you disguise yourself?" Jonah asked at length.

"For a short time. To help me blend as well, get a little closer to the tower before I reveal myself. Once there, circumstances will determine our strategy."

"Let's go ahead and do it," David said, touching her arm. "No sense in delaying." As she firmed her chin, he took her arm, pulled her several steps from Jonah, made her face him. "Mina, I know you can refuse to do the magic. I know the choice of that ultimately is yours. But some things are not a choice. We have to do this."

She bowed her head, and when he laid his fingers along her

cheek, she pressed her face into his palm, holding it there between her face and shoulder, closing her eyes.

"We have to save the world, okay?" The gentle humor had a break behind it, and she knew it only reflected what seemed to be cracking within herself.

"Marcellus likely thinks it's all a lie. That I'm going to turn you over to them and take my place among them."

"Well, Marcellus isn't a very trusting sort. Much like you. I'm surprised the two of you don't get along better."

She didn't hear anything behind her to indicate Marcellus's or Jonah's reaction to that, but then David bent his knees to reach her mouth and wouldn't let her escape. He laid his lips on hers, held them there, tasting her, kissing her, making despair become yearning.

Mina, we need to do this.

Mutely, she nodded. She pulled away from his touch, but felt his hand drift down her arm, grasp her fingers briefly before letting her go. Under the gaze of the three angels, she moved to the edge of the dry rock, stretched out her hand and called to her the item she needed. They shifted out of the way as the sealed pouch rolled over and over, like a jellyfish drifting through the waters of her storage cavern. Then it broke through the rippling wall of water into the airbell.

It was made of the skin of a Dark One to keep it viable, and sensing that, the angels drew away from it. When she untied the top, the bitter smell of Dark One blood filled the chamber quickly, causing them further uneasiness.

Turning, she found David had recovered enough to step to her side again. His warm brown eyes and sensual mouth were close, the heat and strength, the perfect beauty of his body. The magnificent wings. Her hand trembled. "I can't."

He closed his hands over hers on the pouch. "You can. How do I manage it when it's inside me? How will it feel?"

She forced her voice to be steady. "It will exacerbate the emotions you've felt at your most difficult moments. You'll feel unexpected waves of rage, fear, anxiety. Hatred will be easiest.

Bloodlust is particularly strong. Be careful if we must fight, for it will come to your aid, enhancing your strength and abilities, but it's hard to bring it back under control."

"That's what you've dealt with all these years?" A ghost of a smile crossed his face. "And still you've managed to fall in love with me."

"I'm good at multiple tasks," she said. "And I've never said I love you."

"Didn't we discuss that? You didn't have to. You never have to." Raising his hand from her face, he showed her the tears she'd spilled upon it.

She swallowed, pushed the emotions away, for she simply couldn't bear them right now. "Don't," she said, and focused on the more practical matters. "The illusion spell will make you appear as one of the lower-echelon ones. They don't speak much, except with body language, grunting. The blood will give them your scent and sound, so you can pass casual scrutiny."

She did hesitate over the next part. Jonah's words were in her mind. *You will take care of him.* Until she threw him to the Dark Ones.

"David, I need your worst memory." It was an effort to keep her voice steady. "The one you won't tell me." The one she knew had made him unable to forgive his mother's incarnated spirit. *Take care of him.*

His fingers tightened on the skin of the pouch. "Why?"

"Because that's what the blood will fixate on. As it spreads throughout your system, it will view your angel blood as an enemy. It's going to be very difficult for the two to mesh. I can force them to do so, but it won't be pleasant. The entire time it's in you, it will be like a wild dog circling, looking for vulnerable points, ways to take you over completely." Her fingers were next to his, and when his touched hers, she couldn't help the jerk that went through her hand. "You're still young enough, human enough, the Dark Ones could try to make you one of them in actuality. Death is not the worst thing that can happen to you there. If I know the memory, I can help you keep control." She swallowed. "And when the time comes, I'll use it against you. To make things believable."

She wasn't sure if the muttered oath behind her came from Jonah or Marcellus, but she held David's stare until he gave a slight nod. At a murmur of sound, she turned her head to see Marcellus had gone, apparently retreating to one of the caverns closer to the cave entrance, leaving just Jonah.

"For privacy," the commander said.

"You know," she realized.

Jonah inclined his head. "We all know, Mina. But it is hard for him."

Mina turned to face her angel and saw the struggle in his face. "David," she said softly. "There's nothing you can say that will be worse than what we're going to face." *Than what she was going to do to him. Gods.*

He shook his head. "It sounds idiotic, but I couldn't bear it if you thought of me differently."

The idea sent shock coursing through her. He was worried about what *she* thought of *him*? But she saw it was the truth. A fierce feeling rose up in her chest, something she didn't recognize, but which spurred her to reach up, catching on to his weapons harness to give her the extra inches she needed, and kiss him. Hard, long, thoroughly, until they were both gasping. Then she rocked back onto her heels and gave him her typical irritated look. "I don't think of you at all, angel. I've told you that a hundred times now."

He couldn't conjure a smile, but he did put his hand over her wrist, holding it against his chest. "I know we don't have a lot of time. My father . . . he forced my mother to . . . Jesus, this *is* hard." He blinked, swallowed.

Mina laid her other hand on his face again, tilted his head so they were looking at each other eye to eye. "Tell me," she whispered. "Trust me, just this one moment. Remember?"

He swallowed again, nodded, and his grip tightened, his expression becoming fierce, as if he were preparing for battle.

"He forced my mother to . . . have sex with me. It was when

she found out what he was doing to my sister. He'd hurt my sister for all those years, while she—my sister—made me promise not to tell, to protect my mother . . . to protect me. Our mother tried to take us out of the house. My father held us there with a gun, made her . . . do that with me, said it was to make her no better than him. He was just so . . . He was insane, out of his mind."

With or without the blood link, she could feel Jonah's pain on behalf of the young man he loved as a son. She felt it herself. She'd experienced horror like this, so hearing it was like reliving her own.

"After . . . he left the house. My mother got dressed, took my sister and me to a building, and we all three jumped. She said . . ." He stopped, the tears in his eyes reflecting the harsh anguish in his voice. If, after all these years, it was this difficult to say, how must he have been when he first came to the gates of Heaven? And she understood a little better the bond between Jonah and David.

"She said that we were going to learn to fly with the angels. In a voice that said it would all be okay. So we jumped with her. For a minute, we did fly. I remember that, remember thinking we were where he'd never touch us again. And then I found out it wouldn't be that easy. As it shouldn't be, for I did nothing to save either of them. I was the man of the house. It was my job. I had a debt to pay."

"That was why you couldn't touch a woman for so long."

Nodding, he looked at the container of blood she'd drawn from the dead Dark One. "So whatever darkness that will put in me, I've been there, Mina. When something like that happens, you know there's a dark side to this world that's so vile, it makes not only life but existence itself not worth a damn. You wish nothing had ever been created, that the universe had remained a void and you were never aware of yourself, never existed at all.

"Then, when you get past that, you realize you *have* to fight that darkness." The expression he raised to Jonah was glittering, fierce. His attention shifted back to Mina. "I know why you fight it. I always have, even when everyone around you wonders why you do. Because you fight, *that*'s why I know you're worth saving. Worth loving."

It was also why the two of them had fit, she realized. So many confusing things about the day at the diner now made sense. As if reading her mind, he said, "If it wasn't for seeing her . . . Diane . . . I don't think I could have told you, could have handled the darkness of it. So I guess the Schism knew what we would need for today. A good omen, right?" Now he did attempt a smile, though there was a track on his face where at least one tear had escaped. Now she put her thumb on it and he turned his face, kissed her palm as she feathered her fingers over his fine brow, the straight nose, high cheekbone.

"Aren't you afraid?" she whispered.

His eyes opened, looked down at her. "Scared shitless. But Mina"—now his hands were on her face, holding her, his fingers tunneling in her hair, his intense eyes so close that there was nothing else—"there's nothing, absolutely *nothing* worse you or any Dark One could do than deny me the right to do everything within my power to protect you. Stand by you. So for the love of the Goddess, don't do that to me. Don't leave me behind."

Mina closed her eyes. *And there was nothing worse he could do to her than make her agree to this.* "Okay," she said, when she could trust herself to talk. "So we do this."

SHE found a conch shell, poured the vile liquid into it. While Jonah watched, she helped David lift the shell to his lips, keeping her hands over his, for his thumbs had slipped over her fingers, holding her there while he drank, his eyes closing against the taste and odor. His body began to shake after the third swallow, sweat breaking out on his arms and across his bare chest.

As she started the chant that would build the magic she'd need for the blood integration, thoughts slid through her mind. She'd endured a lot of things. Fought for her own life, and control of her actions. Learned early what hatred and evil were. Maybe it was the buildup of all that which made this so hard, the final straw. But she thought she'd happily, joyously jump into the torments of Hell Jonah had described, rather than change David one bit.

As he made the last swallow with a groan of effort, she knocked the conch away and grabbed his face hard. When she kissed him this time, it was openmouthed, insistent. She poured her energy in on top of the blood, sending the molecules scattering, punching out of his intestines and into his bloodstream, making them spin through his system so rapidly, his angel immune system couldn't latch on to reject them before they were flying along the same arteries and veins, tangling together.

He was helping, giving her some of his energy to direct it, to quell the instinct of the angel's blood to reject the interloping fetid cells.

When she drew back at last, she looked into brown eyes glinting with red and felt the tremor in his body beneath her hands.

"Jesus." The word was scraped out of a raw throat. "I hope to the Goddess this isn't how you feel every day." He shook his head, backing up, dropped to one knee as if a lower point of gravity would help steady the roller coaster going on inside of him.

"I was born with it. It's different. I don't have angel blood to integrate with it. Human blood is far more accepting of the Dark One blood." She couldn't help hoping something would go terribly wrong and he'd have to stay here. While she couldn't fix what she'd just done, at least he'd have a life here, and certainly it would be much easier to have a normal life balancing angel and Dark One blood than what her circumstances had been.

"No." She snapped the warning as Jonah stepped toward him. David was bent over, breathing hard, his wings quivering with the violent tremors of his body. "You can't touch him now. They'd see your touch on his skin like a beacon. And he won't be able to bear it, not with what he's dealing with right now." She squatted next to David, placed a hand on his shoulder, didn't flinch as his head jerked up, his eyes wild.

"David. *David.*" When he shook himself out of wherever he was, she made her voice hard, sharp, drawing his attention.

"Everything you learned about focus and concentration, you're going to have to use it, harder than you've ever had to use it before. The smallest feelings, harmless in this world, a moment of jealousy or anger, will magnify and spike and easily take you over. If we get challenged, fighting is a last resort. Tell me you understand."

"Lieutenant." Jonah's tone made her sharpness sound like a mother's absent cooing. David's head jerked toward him. "Pay attention to her. Did you hear what she said?"

"Yes. Yes, Commander."

Mina stood, backing away. The strength she relied on in herself wavered as she turned her back on the wreck she'd just made of him and faced Jonah. "He can't do this. I can't do this to him."

"He can, and you already have." Jonah's tone was equally stern with her, though lower. "You knew this was necessary. So did he. Distance yourself. Think, and help him."

Never one to respond to authority, still she was grateful for the snap in that voice that had her back stiffening, her chin coming up. Turning, she dropped back down before David, seizing his hands to draw his attention to her.

"David, I need you to choose a *good* memory now, something that forms a picture in your mind. You'll use it to bring you back to yourself, every time the blood tries to take control. The thing that most reminds you of who you are."

It struck her in the gut when he didn't even hesitate. "You. The way you ate the orange." A trace of a strained curve of his lips, even as blood seeped from between them, where he'd bitten himself. The hair was damp at his temple as she ran her fingers along it. "Unless the . . . lust . . . is a problem. It was the way you took it from my fingers."

He closed his eyes, visibly struggling. A snarl burst from his lips, quickly cut off as his fingers clenched into the rock of the ledge, digging in. Then he opened them again, looked at her. "It was as if you might one day consider trusting me. I knew that was the most important thing I could ever do. Win your trust, so you'd let me love and protect you. That's who I am. Your champion."

Slowly, breathing deep, he straightened. There'd been a disconcerting hissing to his words, but when he faced Jonah, she saw the angel holding the reins over the blood. For the moment. "Commander. I'll fix what I screwed up, with Mina's help. With the Goddess's help, we won't let you down."

"You never have," Jonah said. Then he glanced at Mina. "You should have told me before you changed him. I would have liked to—" He stopped.

"It's okay." David coughed. "Better this way. No unmanly good-byes. Luc would approve."

"Lucifer will miss you as much as I will," Jonah said roughly.

David swallowed. "If she makes it back out, please give me your word you'll protect her. Help her."

"David—" she protested.

"You don't have a say in this," he said quietly. "Be still."

Jonah studied him. She suspected, in the arrogant way of overly protective men, they were saying something to each other without her being able to hear it. She quelled an urge to zap both of them.

David could tell it was irritating her. It was oddly reassuring, just like the glint of understanding humor in Jonah's eye, followed by a more serious look.

You have my word.

And you have my gratitude. As Marcellus returned, David acknowledged him with a nod of his own, then turned and extended a hand to his prickly witch. "Let's go."

She took it. As they turned toward the defile that would lead to the portal, the darkness that had so repelled him when he'd first touched the Dark One skin holding the blood now had an enticing moan to it. He surged forward.

"Fight it," Mina snapped. Her fingers dug into his arm, slowing him down. Mild irritation became a flash of anger shooting through him, and he'd clamped down on her hand before he thought. Emitted a low growl that startled him but she'd apparently expected, for she didn't back away or try to remove her hand from his grip.

"That's the direction we're going," he grated.

She nodded. "But make it your choice, not your desire. Your desires and intuition are no good to you now. Use only your mind. The decision you feel most strongly about in this state is likely the wrong one."

"South is north," he muttered. Slowly, he loosened his grip. As they passed into the narrow tunnel, her cavern disappearing behind him, he felt the portal's approach and forced himself to slow down, just as she'd advised. It was like digging in his heels against the force of a gale shoving behind him. Jonah and Marcellus seemed leagues away now, instead of just a few feet.

"I liked the house, in the Schism," she said abruptly.

Through the odd buzzing in his head, the waves of red heat that waxed and waned inside his system, he felt the incursion of a different kind of warmth that helped steady him. He looked toward her. Her profile was the unscarred side, and when she glanced at him, the blue eye was momentarily unguarded.

She would have learned to love him. He was sure of it.

He forced himself to extend a hand again, opening up his fingers, surprised how difficult that open-palmed gesture was. A simple act of affection, and it weighted down his arm, making it hard to lift. If nothing else, this blood was helping him understand more and more why Mina had put so many physical obstacles in her life. Anything that would give herself something to hold out against it. And he knew if she did ever decide she loved him, he wouldn't deserve her. No man could.

"So you would have liked staying there, with me," he said.

She sniffed. "I didn't say that. But I might have let you come around, now and again."

He fought for the smile, won it and knew it was worth the effort when her gaze riveted on his mouth, lifted to his face. "Mina, it wasn't . . . when we . . . it didn't feel like this with me, did it?" *Please Goddess, I hope every moment of pleasure wasn't stolen from a moment of darkness.*

"Yes and no." As she turned her head, her blue eye and crimson one met his fully. "Always a balance. A perfect one, I think."

Then she looked back at the portal where they now stood. She spoke in a language he didn't know, telling him the blood was interfering with his automatic translation abilities. His heart began to race as Dark One energy gathered and the door misted, became a vortex of black smoke that drifted out toward them with eager fingers.

Lacing her fingers with his, she looked up into his face once more. "The best moments of my life were spent with you," she said.

They stepped forward together.

Twenty-two

I T reminded David of the sci-fi movies he'd watched as a boy, the nauseating spinning and tumbling through a wormhole, where gravity and speed pulled cells apart like gum, leaving the body a distorted, stretched mess on the other side.

Which was why it was surprising, after what had seemed like an endless passage, to find himself standing next to Mina on a landscape that was the Hell of evangelical imaginings.

Far worse than that, really, for it wasn't Hell. Lucifer ruled over an ordered Hades, structured for justice and redemption, followed by eventual rebirth. This was a place without meaning or purpose. But the images of fire and ice, monstrous shadows wheeling in the sky, creatures dragging themselves through the mud with red staring eyes, were only a flash of impressions before pure chaos and disorder struck his mind, driving him to his knees.

As he fell, his hands hit the frozen ground, while his knees landed in what felt like a bed of embers. He rolled to his side, found himself in sucking mud. Images drilled into his brain. Horrifying vignettes, as if he'd fallen into a theater of endless stages, a parade through every nightmare that had inflicted itself on a dreaming mind.

Torture, murder, screams of pain that couldn't stop echoing

before another set began. Creatures in that sucking mud, trying to burrow into his skin. Falling, a sense of falling, the ground rushing up, the wind shrieking in maniacal triumph.

And of course, with all those millions of nightmares, he would fall right into his own. A man with his hands on a child's throat, raping, as a mother did the same to a son, the gun there. Always there.

I'll have you again. You'll never escape. This is where you'll always be.

David, find your memory. Me, eating the orange. The chocolates. Her voice was in his head, small hands on his crawling, shuddering flesh.

Mina. Taking the orange from his fingers. Giving him that wary glance that said there was a desire to trust, a challenge he wanted to win . . .

When he pried open his eyes and looked down, he scrabbled backward before he remembered the illusion spell she'd placed on him. His hands were skeletal. His teeth cut his lip where the fangs curved on the outside and under his chin. At least he had wings, though they were thin, leathery things with far less maneuverability, as if his shoulder muscles were tied in permanent taut knots.

A lower-echelon Dark One, he reminded himself, the kind he regularly destroyed in the sky as an angel. Here he was in their world, writhing on spiky, frozen, burning ground, while above, a sky of searing red flame reminded him of an ocean of fire. Like the aftermath of a wartime bomb raid.

Trees. How odd it was, that there were trees. Thousands of them, naked, black branches stark against the sky whose billowing flame created canopies, the tongues of fire flickering, giving the illusion of leaves.

The sucking mud, crawling with things that tried to burrow into his skin, had been real. As something slithered over his fingers, he let out an oath and used the wings awkwardly to tear himself free, find himself on land again.

But it wasn't stable. Nothing was. It was as if he were hanging on to the handle of a spinning top, uncertain what was up or down, or how to get it to stop. He staggered and went down again, and snarled as the nightmares surged up once more, trying to curtain his vision, his awareness of anything but them.

Focus. David, let the blood protect you. Work with the blood, use its purpose as your own, yet never let it lead, like a monster you have to trick into thinking he's doing what he wants, when you're really controlling him. Remember.

He couldn't. Everything he was, had made himself, was being torn away by that Dark Blood, and his angel self instinctively fought, even knowing it had already lost.

Damn it.

Of a sudden, she was pressed against him. He still bore his daggers, for she'd drawn one. Instinct had him gripping her wrist in defense, but then she changed her angle, turned the blade so it was against the bare flesh exposed by her cloak, above her breast. If he'd been in his right mind, he would have been furious with her, for in his current state, he might have driven the blade all the way through her.

Remember the way it felt. To take command of me, mark me as your own with such control. Give me pain now. Take control of me.

Pain and pleasure at once. The gritty edge of sex, so passionate it could straddle the line between love and violence, exist in Hell and Heaven at once, in both light and darkness.

Bearing down, he heard her catch her breath at the erratic cut, and when he bent to clamp his mouth over it, taste that blood and flesh, her fingers tangled in his hair, sending a rush of response to his cock at the willingness of her body to comply.

Control. Of her. Of himself. To protect her, first and foremost. To get her to the Trumpet.

She'd turned the tables on him. In his world, he'd used dominance to help teach her trust, give her an anchor. Here she was using that learned submission to teach him the same, steady him.

Orange and chocolates. The smile, that very first smile. Gods, he wanted the chance to spend time with her, get her to smile, over and over. Hear her first laugh.

It fought inside of him, that image, the mission, with the darkness of the blood that demanded he think of other things. Like the fragility of her throat, how easy it would be to snap it. What it would be like to turn her over, seize her hips, force himself into her while she screamed and struggled, exciting him more.

Like his father raping his sister, the sick pleasure in her struggles.

"No. *No.*" He released her as if his hands had been burned and backed away, shaking his head. "No. Jesus."

"David." She was trying to catch hold of him, following him, but he fended her off, tripping, falling against ice. He had his hands up to his face, digging. He'd rip his mind out of his fucking skull before he had another thought like that.

"No." He jerked away from her. "Don't touch me."

"David." She said it sharply enough, but it was the face punch that got his attention, her swing much stronger than he would have expected. The angel who might have understood such a steadying gesture was overwhelmed by the bloodlust that it provoked. When he glared, a hiss coming to his lips, she thrust herself even closer, dropping to her knees to grip him aggressively with knowledgeable fingers, closing over his shamefully hard length like a steel vise, her nails digging into his testicles.

"Bitch," he swore at the pain, but a movement only tightened her hold. Regardless, he caught her by the shoulders, lifted her off her feet and slammed her to the ground, pinning her beneath his body.

She had no fear, though, her wholly red gaze glittering at him. Her lip curled back, showing far sharper canines than typically possessed by human or merperson. "I want you."

And she opened her legs to him, surrendering, not fighting as the blood demanded, but that wasn't going to slow him down. When he drove into her tight channel, only the ready slickness kept him from tearing tender flesh. She groaned at his size, but kept her body open to him, to his demands and unnatural hungers. She was his. His in all ways, and he needed her to know that, in the deepest part of her mind, in every part of her. For every time she'd irritated him, drove him to distraction, tried to defy him or turn her back on him. When things couldn't be controlled, that's when they couldn't be protected. Not even from himself.

He stopped. She quivered beneath him, but he forced himself to clear the shadows and blood from his gaze and see his hands. They were braced on the ground on either side of her head. She had one arm up, her hand curled over the top of his fingers, her thumb stroking. Soothing. The witch who was never nurturing, never kind.

Oh, Goddess. What am I doing?

"No," she said. "Don't pull away. Take control of it. Don't let it control you, David. Don't let it make you doubt and hate yourself just because it had a scant second of victory."

He forced himself to concentrate. Gazed down at her where she lay, curiously docile. Her cloak had fallen off one bare shoulder, her smooth shoulder.

"You're not . . . disguised."

"Not to you. Come to me. Please."

Now he bent, laid his lips on her skin, felt the rush of blood beneath. He had the desire to set his teeth there, so he did that as well. She trembled beneath him, in desire.

Physical intimacy was capable of becoming magic, but now he knew why people in dire circumstances, deep in dungeons or prisons, could turn to this. They were surrounded by all the vestiges of evil and Hell. Nothing living, not in the manner he understood as an angel, with that moaning roar on the wind at all times, the occasional patter of raindrops and hail that fell like acid. Changing from oppressive heat to frigid cold with each step, so the body could never adjust or brace itself. Desolation and tedium, sick apprehension and dread weighing over the shoulders like Atlas's burden, in a cross carved for no purpose.

He'd asked his mother, when he was ten, when she was oblivious to the tragedy happening in their own home, "What if Jesus carried the cross for no purpose, no reason?"

If there is no good to seek in the world, then living and dying mean nothing. It is all nothing. Jonah had helped him find that answer, much, much later.

She lifted her hands, reaching for him. David settled back on her body, feeling the odd terrain of scars and curves beneath the skeletal illusion of Dark One, but mainly he felt her. As he slid back into her, her legs rose to clasp his hips, welcoming him. In pain or pleasure, she welcomed him into her.

Warmth, wetness. The softness of a woman's thighs. Her body rising to the stroking of his. The grasp of her fingers, desperate and savage, as he built her toward a climax. She reared up, wrapped her arms around his neck, held him close, and her fingers punctuated the illusion so he felt them bury in the feathers that lay beneath the enchantment and hold on. Her skin, her breast, were pressed against his upper body, her hips seeking, pumping higher, taking him deeper, stroking the length of his cock with sure muscles that had so quickly learned what could drag him to the edge. He had to fight his base urges not to give in, and his base urges clamored much more stridently in this place.

The connection he had with her was now more than just the initial blood link they shared. It was the link of the Dark One blood, that red tinting to his eyes that reflected in the pure crimson fire of hers. It was a terrible thing, but he didn't mind having one more bond with her. He wanted to bond with her in every way. As soon as he had the thought, he knew in a heartbeat that was where he needed to take this. His ultimate defiance against the hold of such a place.

"Mina." He said her name, held on to it through the pounding in his head, the agonizing beat of the blood rushing through his veins.

As she lifted a hand again, he held it by the wrist, letting her fingers brush against his face. Mina spread her other hand on his abdomen, drifted down to scrape the sensitive pubic region, then traveled around to ride the rhythmic clutch of his buttocks, digging her fingers in. Arching up at the burst of searing sweetness that rocketed through them both.

"This is true. No matter what." He said it with his mind linked with hers like their hands. "No regrets."

"It's all regret," she whispered.

"Just promise me not to regret what we've had. Not a moment."

She nodded, and then he pushed her over the edge, but Mina apparently didn't want to go alone. She held him inside her, stroking in a rhythm that had his hold going erratic. He exploded on a growl, the Dark One blood augmenting his ferocity as a male warrior as he surged into her hard, offered her seed. Offered himself in a way that he knew she wouldn't expect.

As they at last came down, David drew deep breaths. Steadying breaths. He could feel the Dark One blood, but he could feel his own as well, a tense stalemate that created an irritating, low-level hum throughout his senses, which oddly matched the outside roar of this world, as if a weaker frequency. But they'd done it. Mina had known what he needed to weather the worst initial moments. Clever, sweet witch.

He'd reclaimed what had been knocked out of his mental grasp upon entry into this place. The energy angels used, from grounding in meditation, or a woman's body, to find the still center of the soul, and hold it inviolate against anything. A balance. Similar to the type of balance Mina had practiced all her life.

He'd typically have cleansed his soul at this point to strengthen it, but he knew that center also had to have the fouling presence of the Dark One blood, so that he could maintain his focus in this wretched world. He would endure its roaring insistence, use it as she'd said, while refusing to give it what it wanted. He might not make it out of here, but if it was in his power, she would.

"WHAT have you done?" Mina struggled up on her elbows, and then to her feet. His gaze was reassuringly aware, despite the red flickers, and he helped her up with a powerful arm around her shoulders. Despite the harrowing first few moments when she was sure she'd made a terrible mistake, when she told Jonah that David could do this, she could tell that incredible focus angels possessed had taken the upper hand.

It didn't mean she wasn't going to skewer him with one of those blades in the next two seconds. She was a witch. She knew the feel of life and death. Releasing fertile seed was a choice for angels. A choice he'd just made in her body. "What did you do?" she repeated.

"Gave you something to live for, if you make it out of here."

She stared at him, sure he'd gone mad. "David, I can't have a baby. I can't. I'll kill it. I can't love it."

"No, you won't, and yes, you can." He reached out toward her hand and she batted it away. He returned, caught it anyway, squeezed in reproof. "There has to be a seawitch for the next daughter of Arianne. Your Fates are entwined, remember? If you're worried, Anna and Jonah will raise the child. But you'll take care of her, Mina. I know you will."

He let her go, checked the sheathing on his blades. "Which way do we go?" he asked, that startling hiss emitting from his normally velvet-toned voice.

"If I thought we'd live through this, I'd promise to kill you later. If we're caught, I'm going to tell them to torture you first."

"Understood." He nodded placidly. "So?"

She nodded toward the west, where a spear of irregular rock thrust into the sky. The tower she'd known would be there.

If his seed found a fertile egg, she knew she'd feel it. Could kill it with barely a thought of her mind. She wasn't feeling cruel enough to say that, though, which suggested that he'd mellowed her in two days far more than she'd anticipated. Another reason it was a good thing they weren't going to survive this.

But as remote as both their chances were of getting out of here alive, hers were better. And he'd known that, damn him. If she felt that connection happen in her body, then he knew she wouldn't give up, even if he was taken from her.

"Okay." He gestured toward the tower, though his eyes were on hers, as if reading her thoughts. Mina turned her back on him and began to move in that direction, picking her way over the ground.

"It's a little late to ask, but why didn't we attract any attention just now?" He asked it a few moments later as he circled another creature in the mud, choosing a patch of ice instead. The jellyfishlike animal was the size of a football, with teeth and legs. It paid them no attention except for a menacing hiss when the air of David's passage attracted it. "There were Dark Ones, flying through the sky when we arrived, weren't there? Or was that just all in my head?"

She sighed, relented. "They're here. Across that plain there, they landed in the trees. Lower echelon, like you. Keep moving. Look purposeful. And Dark Ones, though they are all male, do couple for physical release," she added. "They're not modest about their needs. Our actions out in the open were not unusual."

David winced. "Sorry I asked. Are there any humans here?"

Mina shook her head. "Much as the Dark Ones want to reclaim the humans, the spark of light the Goddess gave them when she stole them away made them unable to survive here. The humans have to embrace the Dark Blood in themselves first, before the Dark Ones can bring them home."

"*Home*. I've never heard that word used to describe our little paradise."

Mina spun. David flipped two blades into his hands as he whirled in the same motion. She went to a defensive crouch.

"Impressive."

What had been right behind them was gone, moved in the blink of an eye. A purposeful twitch drew her eye upward. The pleasant voice had apparently come from the creature now sitting in the crotch of the tree to their left.

To all appearances, he was a human male, in his thirties. Pale, but with a face almost as beautiful as an angel's. He had no wings as many of the Dark Ones did, but there was no mistaking his heritage, for both of his eyes were brilliant red with dark lashes and silken brows that blended with the tangle of dark hair that fell over his high forehead and bare shoulders in wild disarray. Human in form, but most definitely not. Somehow different. She studied him, her eyes narrowed.

His clothes did not match the handsomeness of his face. The ragged pair of trousers appeared to be pieced together from scraps to provide a rough and filthy covering. His upper body was lean muscle, though his bones were evident. Hungry. Curling his upper lip, he revealed a pair of sharp fangs, not as long as Mina's in her Dark One form. More refined.

"You're like me," he said, his gaze fastened on her. "Dark Spawn." David shifted to a more aggressive posture before the witch.

"Think you can move faster than me, lower Darkling?" the creature hissed.

"Yes," David said. "You won't get near him."

"Him?" The visitor's eyes glittered. "It may look that way, but all is not as it seems with you two. And Dante smells female. Welcome *home*, little sister."

David took a deliberate step forward. "You're about to bring trouble on yourself."

"This one serves you, but hard to manage, no? Good disguise, but unnecessary. Dante knows. They know you." He was still staring at Mina, paying David little attention. "You came for the shiny horn. They wait for you. No one will stop you from getting to the tower. I'm to tell you that."

Then he was gone. "Well, they're waiting for us," David commented. "Just as you expected."

"Yes." Mina felt a weight on her chest as if the scorched air had become too difficult to breathe. "I don't think they're sure about you, yet, however."

"So we keep going."

"They'll be coming out to meet us soon, I think. He was the warning. Let's just . . . take a minute." Putting her back against one of the inert trees, she sank to the ground on a cluster of its roots, staring at the tower rising above the macabre landscape.

David squatted at her side. Curved a lock of her hair around her ear in familiar affection as she let the Dark One illusion melt from herself, while keeping his in place. "What's the matter?" He asked it quietly. "Are you frightened?"

She gave a bitter, short laugh. "What if Jonah's right? What if the most dangerous weapon the Dark Ones have is me? Doesn't it make more sense to destroy me and then they have no one to play the Trumpet?"

"Someone else would eventually be able to do it. The way of objects of power is they want to be used. They must be guarded carefully for that reason." Straightening to step over her, he tugged her forward and settled behind her, putting her between his thighs with her head nestled under his jaw, his arms crossed over her front, holding her.

"What are you doing?" she murmured, not struggling, not wanting to do anything but stay here in his embrace, even if this was their view for all eternity, but vaguely curious at his timing.

"You implied we have a few moments before we have to face the fire. I didn't get to hold you after being inside you. I like that part."

"I've heard merwomen say most males don't care for that."

"Well, I have to think of your feelings. I wouldn't want to die with you thinking I'm insensitive."

Mina closed her eyes, her throat working. "I wish I'd never met you."

His lips pulled in a smile against her temple. "You're getting closer and closer to shouting out your love for me. I can feel it."

She stared at the hated tower. "They're going to hurt you to test me."

"I know. It's all right. The Trumpet's return is the first priority."

Putting her temple down against his shoulder, she breathed him in. "David," she said softly. Then again, once more, pressing her face harder against him, while his hand came up and cupped her head, held her forehead to his chest, his legs tightening on either side of her.

"Yes, sweet witch."

"I didn't ask anything."

"You did. You wanted to know if I love you. I heard it every time you said my name." He nuzzled her neck. "And I do. With everything I am."

"Will you sing to me?"

When he nodded, she settled back. He hummed the song at first, then eventually sang the words. This one was about a man who was missing the time during his life he'd spent sailing the ocean, watching whales and dolphins, thinking of them as his brothers. She could almost see it, her and David in a boat, lying in each other's arms, slowly gliding with the currents of wind and water, wherever they took them.

"That's another one of those human songs, isn't it?"

"*Mm-hmm*. And either my singing is really good or really bad, because I think the Dark One blood was threatening to spew out my ears to get away from it. It was performed by a group called the Little River Band. I'm sure the words were inspired by one of the music angels."

"I can't do this. I just can't."

"You can." He pressed a kiss to her temple. Held his lips there, hard, as he spoke against her skin. "It's time to talk about this. I expect they have their spies, like this Dante, who have noted my apparent physical devotion to you. If I'm under your enchantment as your slave, I'd only strike out or fight at your command. I might occasionally try to fight it, but on the whole, I'd have no ability to escape it. So can you actually do that? Bind an angel with that kind of spell?"

"With the Dark One's blood in you, yes. It's likely."

"Then do it."

It startled her, and she pulled back, looked at him. "I don't need to—"

"Yes, you do. It's got to be real. You understand? We can't take the chance that they'll doubt you."

She said nothing for a while, but she held tightly to the arm he had banded across her chest. David felt the tremor in her body, knew the nerves were there. But when he knew they could delay no longer and helped her to her feet, she shrugged him away irritably. "You know I don't think a Trumpet is worth your life. Not the whole damn world, the Goddess, or any other part of it."

"How about Anna and her baby?"

"Why do you think I care? You *always* think I care."

Taking her hands so she couldn't draw away, he stared down at her. "I know how this will rip you apart inside. I've known from the beginning you weren't evil. You're an incredible, powerful sorceress. An absolute hellion who will stand toe-to-toe with Heaven's toughest angels and dare them to strike her down. But you're also a woman who wants a quiet place to read her books and swing on a tire swing. A child who wants to be loved. Like all of us."

As frustrated tears gathered in her eyes, he pressed his thumbs there, let her rest her face in his hands. "Maybe you're not good, but you're the antithesis of evil. You are pure will, the strongest I've ever met. I love you, Mina. No matter what happens, you don't forget that. All right? Do what you have to do."

He stepped back. "Bind me with the spell. When we arrived, when you were helping me with the blood, that had the appearance of a struggle, and that probably helped. Remember what Dante said? 'This one serves you, though he is hard to manage, isn't he?'

"So, considering we're likely being watched . . ." He drew his dagger, turned as if surveying the area, and then when she didn't move, he turned, rushed her.

"*Rigor,*" she snapped, and the burst of energy focused in the single word brought him to a sliding halt on his knees before her, the dagger clutched in his hand still. While she'd reacted instinctively, she suspected he'd done it more to instigate the spell than to perform for those watching. He'd known it was going to be difficult for her to do it without provocation. David did know her too well, as she'd feared.

"Bound by power, held by blood, you are slave to my will, whether for ill or good." She spat out the words like poison, for they were. The power flow for her here was so easy, too easy. She had him wrapped in tendrils of it before she barely finished the chant. For good measure, she seized his hair and tugged it so he stared up at her, the pain goading the fury in his eyes, reddened by the Dark Blood. Whether he'd learned to use the rage to mask his real thoughts that quickly, or it had come to the forefront on its own, it was still believable. "You will stop these pointless attempts to resist me. Follow me to the tower, protect me against any attack, serving my will only."

He'd been wrong. Under the reality of the spell, David had no room to resist her at all. He could still reach out and touch her mind for reassurance, but he was physically unable to deviate from following her path or keep himself from scoping the area for threats to her.

He hadn't expected her hold to be unbreakable, since as an angel he would have been able to shatter almost anything she imposed upon him. The Dark Blood apparently gave her the markers she needed. Of course, in a flash of grim humor, he thought it was a wonder she hadn't tried this kind of spell on him earlier.

I will try to be worthy of your trust, David.

There were things he'd been unable to control in his life that were difficult to accept. But he'd never experienced having his will taken from him. He tried to focus on her voice in his head, that flat tone that always implied she expected herself to be a disappointment. Somehow, he found that reassuring. As was the reminder to himself that she'd left him with the most important desire intact. To protect her. It helped him control the fear.

"THEY will kill you if you try to take it, you know."

Dante was back, weaving his body through the branches behind them, eerie, serpentine movements.

"You're annoying," Mina said, with a bare glance of contempt. "Shoo."

As the creature snarled and sprang from the tree behind them, David moved. While he was too fast for Mina's eye to follow, David caught Dante in midair, a hand clamping around his throat, and flipped him to his back. Slamming him down to earth with a heavy thud, he trapped him with one foot pressed hard on his groin. One hand held the dagger to his chest while the other remained clamped on his throat.

It was an impressive maneuver, to say the least, one that stirred the violent blood in herself. The exacerbation of primal emotions in this environment forced her to shove down the urge to bite David. Lord, he'd just had her, moments ago it seemed. Of course they seemed to have an unending hunger for it in their own world, so why should this one be different? And she *was* a witch, trained and intuitive in natural inclinations. Life-threatening situations made the adult body hunger for carnal connection, and she couldn't think of many situations more perilous than going hunting in the Dark Ones' world.

Using that feeling, she slowly let the illusion melt away from David's shoulders, revealing his true species, the white and brown wings now marked with red, like a blood-drenched paintbrush slashed over his wingspan. It was a dramatic effect that went well with the battle maneuver. She almost felt the energies of the world come to a momentary, stunned halt before the roar of the wind picked up. And the shrieking in the tower began, sending a bolt of terror through her. For David.

"No, no." Dante struggled without success against David's immovable hold, hissing. "Angel? How an angel? Not vampire. Wanted you to be vampire."

Mina's brow furrowed and she came forward, circled him. "A Dark Spawn vampire," she said slowly. "How is that possible?"

"Like you. Rare. Rare as a natural death here." He choked on a laugh, but it died as David's intent expression upon him did not alter. "My mother was brought here. Took her long time to die. Long time. Quite mad. Had her in chains when I was born.

Suckled on her blood, her ankle, had to keep her chained so she wouldn't rip out my throat herself."

Dante giggled. "Nothing like a mother's love. Drained her. Died. Starved, then staked at last. I staked her." His gaze rose. "She begged. Been alone, long time now. Years and years. Eat from weaker Dark Ones. Their blood, but makes me sick. They bring me humans once in a while. Must eat fast, for they die as I eat." He nodded to himself. Looked up at David. "If she is Dark Spawn, she can feed me. Half human, right?"

"No," David said curtly. "You can't touch her, unless you're ready to die."

"Out. Can you get me out?"

"I think that was just what I threatened."

As David pressed a little harder, Mina's hand wrapped over his shoulder.

Easy.

"What can you do to help us?" she asked.

"Nothing. Can't. If Dark Ones know I helped . . ." Dante's gaze went a deeper shade of red as he focused it on David. "Death at his hands much better, no matter what kind of death."

"Why haven't you gone through a rift?"

"Can't fly. And won't let me. Have it so I can't leave. You have to say my real name to give me exit, the one my mother gave me. My mother tell me story and when I said I'd call myself Dante, she laughed. Not pretty sound," he reflected. "Gurgle, like death rattle." He frowned. "Maybe was."

Mina straightened. *Gods, if I could destroy this place, every vestige of everything within it, I would. This place was never meant to be.*

With the Dark Blood surging in his own veins, so that David felt the unnaturalness of it like a hammer pounding at him, he couldn't disagree. The very existence of such a place was the explanation of evil, random pockets of chaos, spawned by who knew what energy. Was it an emotional garbage dump for some world? A repository for human nightmares? A place to drain off excess aggression, and the Dark Ones had emerged from those pools like repulsive amphibian life-forms, shrieking their hatred and misery as their birth cry?

"Let him go." Mina's hand was on him again. "I'm tired of this."

But as they continued toward the tower, David noted Dante skulking, following after them through the thick branches of the tall, dark trees. He didn't like the vampire, the way he watched Mina, hunger and desperation muddled up with an elusive, malevolent undercurrent.

Brains were not Dante's strong suit, however, for in a few moments he bounded ahead and was waiting, though safely back in a tree, to address them again. "So you here to stay? Not to take Trumpet?"

She flicked him a dismissive glance without responding and continued on. David found the magical tether she had on him had changed to an exact five paces behind her, for when he fell one extra pace, trying to keep his eye on the elusive vampire, electrical energy surged through him, driving him to his knees with a gasp. Mina threw a glance at him. "Keep up, or it will get worse."

Weakness was viewed as opportunity in this world, so David wasn't surprised that Dante made another leap, this time at him. Despite the pain, David's hand was on his throat again, holding him at arm's length as Mina barely batted an eye.

"Can't kill me with your pet," Dante gasped.

"No. But he can crush your windpipe, and that would make you far less irritating to me." Mina stared him down. "But do stay close, Dante. I may have a use for you."

David released him once more, tossing him about twenty feet away. After rolling to an ignominious halt in a puddle of mud, Dante made a show of dusting himself off and stared defiantly at her down that oddly aquiline, aristocratic nose. "I may not wish to be used."

"You will if it suits your purpose. If I ask, it will."

She proceeded onward, regal as a queen. In the prison of his body, David had to marvel over it, the way she walked over the tiled, frozen and fiery earth with the demeanor of royalty, David as her enslaved angelic bodyguard. There was no hint of the careful, furtive way he'd seen her move across the ocean floor, or her hesitation with each new experience he'd presented to her.

But then, she'd told him, hadn't she? The voices had been in her head all her life, telling her this was where she belonged. She'd told him how to control the blood, use it as a weapon, because she knew how to do it herself.

Mina?

There was no answer. Pushing aside the uneasiness, he told himself her attention was likely on what lay ahead of them, drawing closer every moment.

The tower had no doors. Only openings all the way up, jagged ones. It reminded him of a dead tree, petrified into stone after woodpeckers had gnawed deep holes into its sides. As he watched, Dark Ones began to emerge from those holes, as she predicted, and wing their way across the sky toward them. Taking an attack formation.

David glanced back to see that Dante had disappeared. The Dark Ones' scavenger and spy, but only barely tolerated by them, he'd warrant. He might still prove useful. The traitorous bastard.

As David drew two of his daggers, Mina at last looked toward him. Even with the illusion gone from her, both her eyes were bloodred. "You should drop those."

"Your spell gives me the mandate of protecting you. They're not going to touch you, if I can prevent it. Protect yourself however you need to do it."

"All right," she said. And blasted him with a current so strong it somersaulted him backward.

David hit the ground hard, just as she lifted her arm and a sizzling green and purple dome of energy crackled around them, causing the Dark Ones to sheer upward, then turn, shrieking and snarling. She responded in the same language, shrieking and keening in that shrill voice.

After a few dizzying moments, he was able to sit up, shake himself and retrieve his daggers. She let him move back to her, close enough to protect. If she'd let him. In the meantime, she'd snarled, hissed and apparently threatened her way to a satisfying conclusion in their peculiar communication form. The Dark Ones now adjusted their flight formation, giving more of an impression of an advance guard preceding her toward the tower. But they were hovering, staring at him. Waiting.

As she turned and looked at him, the command exploded in his head, like shrapnel striking nerve centers, driving him to his knees.

Strip. All of it. Leave it all.

He fought her, fought himself, and yet couldn't stop his fingers from unbuckling the harness, letting it drop. Unbuckling the belt on the tunic, unwrapping it, dropping it so he was entirely naked. Weaponless. She had complete, ruthless control of him.

His father, with a gun. Ordering him to strip. Mina, doing the same. He fought to keep it separate in his mind.

I will use it against you . . .

But then on top of that, he couldn't rise, was kept on his hands and knees from the force of her spell. The Dark Ones shrieked in startled amazement, swooped in, but couldn't come inside that dome of energy. They grazed it, risking the crackle of electric energy along their eager talons, the singeing of their wings.

Some had landed, and while he'd been distracted by the ones in the air, there were Dark Ones on foot who'd also come out to meet them. Gathering around, closing in, their presence making his head pound, even with the Dark One blood.

Crawl, angel.

As she issued the mental command, she turned and began to walk toward the tower. David felt the fire searing his skin, the ice freezing it. The purple and green energy faded away, leaving him facing a nightmare come to life.

He hadn't permitted himself to feel fear, made himself view

everything up to this point as steps to prepare for battle. Now he would face it weaponless, to honor the Legion, the Lady and himself. And most importantly, to protect Mina. This was how he would serve her best.

The Dark Ones closed in on him, their shrieks filling his ears, rupturing them as talons and teeth began to tear at his wings.

Twenty-three

MINA didn't look back, just kept walking. A tile of ice, a tile of fire, the stench of sulfur, Dark One decay and waste. The wriggling, grotesque life-forms they fed upon.

This life was the part of her she couldn't deny. The part she likely understood better than the human, merperson or seawitch.

When she'd been locked in chains against the Abyss wall, there were times, at the very first, when the pain and horror of it had been so overwhelming that she'd broken and screamed. Screamed until she had no voice. Pulled against the chains, both the magical and physical, until her blood attracted even more predators. Then, after a while, there was no sense of the passage of time. There was just now. Getting through the next minute. No past, no future, just an existence to which her body kept clinging for whatever reason, when anything seemed better than this.

But knowing all that, remembering it, she knew this was worse. What was about to happen was too horrid to contemplate, to handle, so she simply shut down. She knew she was evil now, because even if it was the only way the Trumpet could be recovered, no one with a scrap of good inside their souls would have come up with this idea. There were some things that the universe *should* be sacrificed to preserve.

Perhaps it was a blessing they weren't going to survive. He might call it love now, but what would it be after this?

She didn't let her steps falter when they wrenched the first scream from him. Drawing on the Dark One blood within her fiercely, just as she'd told him to do, she immersed herself in it. She could go so deep her conscience would drown. She'd feel the same thrill as they did when he cried out. That deep, she might forget why they were here, but it was unbearably tempting. She couldn't do this if she felt his agony as well as heard it, knowing she was trading his torment and life for this.

I will love you no matter what.

No one should be loved no matter what. Nobody deserved that, particularly her. She'd never loved anyone. And not only had she never been loved, she'd never been loved unconditionally. He'd given her both without requiring anything from her. She wasn't strong enough for it.

At the base of the tower, she was lifted under the arms, almost respectfully, by two of the winged Dark Ones. Lifted up, higher and higher, headed toward the top. Her fear of heights didn't touch her. Being dropped and all her bones crushed by impact might be a welcome mercy, after all.

As they lowered her on the flat expanse of the keep, littered with rubble from the spires that surrounded it like rotting fingers pointing at the sky, she saw the Resurrection Trumpet.

The gleaming gold and silver instrument had a long and slender throat, a red silken cord and white sash of silk wrapped around the handle. They had placed it on a stone tablet, surrounded by a circle of thirty or so higher-echelon Dark Ones. Higher echelon because they were taller, with eyes that narrowed with a far greater intelligence. She identified the one standing directly behind the Trumpet as the most powerful, for energy pulsed from him, and the containment spell, buffering them from the emanations of the complex spells the angels had on the Trumpet already, bore his signature. He was likely the one responsible for figuring out how to circumvent her cave wards and enter the portal from the ocean side. She narrowed her focus to him. He was what she had to defeat.

All she had to do was touch the instrument with a bloodied hand, and it would be gone, in Jonah's hands. She would die. Perhaps after being tortured as long as they could make it last.

David would be destroyed as well, for the binding spell on him would destroy him if she were killed. But the Dark One she was staring at would figure that out before he killed either of them. He would keep her alive long enough to use David's Dark Blood to make him truly one of them and unravel her binding. Then Jonah would one day face his young lieutenant and be forced to strike him from the sky, incinerate his putrid, monstrous body.

No. There had to be another way. Gods, she'd spent her life in study of magical systems, historical conflicts and survival strategies among various species. She should be able to think of something different than this pointless martyrdom for a tin horn. But she knew all the other ways were too risky.

We only get one shot at this. We have to choose the best way.

Thirty pairs of red eyes followed her as she approached. David had been brought up as well, for the flock of bloodthirsty Dark Ones dropped him to the surface on the rough ground behind her. She could hear his panting breath, knew from a brief glimpse out of the corner of her eye he was on his side, struggling to lift himself on one arm. The other one appeared to be broken, useless, a wet gleam of white bone poking through his upper arm and at his wrist. Someone stepped on it as she watched and he screamed. A rock was shoved into his mouth, wrapped in a filthy cloth. It was too large and it was forced in, hard enough she heard the snap of his teeth.

An oyster shell, leaving wounds that took nearly two years to heal well enough for her to be able to comfortably eat . . .

She yanked her attention away.

"Who is he?" The tallest one's voice shrieked along her nerves, but she could not deny her sire's blood also responded to it, such that it perversely helped steady her.

"An experiment." She cocked her head. "You know they have been guarding me from you, thinking you intend me harm. He is young, and I was able to get him alone, tricked him into drinking our blood, and bound him to me with an enslavement charm. It is part of why I have come. The experiment was successful, but I could not stay there without invoking the wrath of the Legion."

"You stole an angel for us."

"I stole an angel for me," she corrected coldly. "I brought him to you so that the Legion could not take him away from me." She tilted her head, allowed a feral smile to stretch across her face, reveal her fangs. "But I might be coaxed to do it to other angels. Slaves that serve you all. And your children, the humans."

"How do we know if you lie? How do we know he is fully under your power?"

She arched a brow. "Look at him. He cannot fight them off. Though he continues to struggle, his powers are hampered. He can only strike out in my defense, not his own. You know angels cannot bear the stink of your kind. If he could kill all of you, he would."

There was muttering in the circle around the Trumpet, hissing, suspicious looks. She lifted a shoulder. "You've been hovering over me in my dreams since I was born, and you don't feel why I'm here? I am tired of being neither one thing nor the other, of running. Of being cold and wet. If I have a place here, then that ends."

"You helped them."

"Yes. In the past. Unlike your pathetic Dante, I choose my allegiances for my own reasons, but it allowed me to get close to them, to learn to do this." She jerked her head toward David. Still didn't look at him. "But you've never cared about that. You knew the blood was calling me. The dreams enticing me to come have increased, even as you pretended to seek me for revenge. It was never about revenge. You want me to unravel the magic bindings on the Trumpet and play it." She gave the tallest one a derisive look. "Can't figure it out yourself, or can't play it if you did?"

His crimson eyes went to malevolent slits. "You should not taunt us."

Shrugging, she flicked her fingers, sent a zap of electrical power toward a small Dark One that had been creeping up on her ankle, probably to bite her. It retreated with a yelp.

"Chaos on the blue green place will give us more of what we want," one beside the tallest said.

"So what does that give me?"

The red eyes narrowed. "We will use the humans to help us procreate, make more Dark Spawn. Stronger than humans. Replace them. It will become your world, instead of theirs. You are powerful, but we think you have not truly embraced your power. You reject it because of your mortal mother." His gaze shifted behind her, to the scuffling sounds going on, the groans and thuds. "But we are encouraged by this."

The *this* was drawn out, sibilant, but she noted he cut it off. Trying to appear civilized, articulate? It was laughable, considering their surroundings.

She considered it. "It can be done. It'll take some destruction, some reworking of the firmament and terrain after you use the Trumpet, but it can be done."

"You will help us?"

"Perhaps."

"You think you have a choice?"

"Of course I have a choice." She took a deliberate step forward, until the nearest Dark One around the table was only several feet away from her. Meeting his gaze just long enough to get him to shift his, she swept the faces of the ones around him with a disdainful look. "If you make it not a choice, you won't get anything from me. I care nothing for pain or death. I've experienced both, and I wasn't impressed. And there is no one I care about."

"Even the daughter of Arianne? What if we brought her here, cut her babe out of her womb while she screamed, let her bleed and die before you?"

Jonah would tie you in a ball with your own intestines and kick your bony ass back here before you got within a hundred miles of Anna. And you know it. Else you wouldn't want a girl to do your fighting for you.

"You already know I am cursed to protect the daughter of Arianne, no matter my own wishes." She laughed, an extremely unpleasant sound, rough to her own ears. "It never occurred to you *that* was why I was in the Canyon? I never did one thing to protect the angels. Only her."

There was shifting, muttering, a consultation of sorts. Mina waited, maintaining a dispassionate mien, walling out everything. The gag must have fallen out, for another terrible scream came from behind her. The kind of scream that ripped from one's throat when one had an appendage torn off. She remembered her fingers, a small barracuda biting them as she tried to fend it off. Then there'd been several other fish, and she'd lost the fight.

She felt the close regard of the Dark One Council. Sighing, she gazed boredly out over the landscape. *Gods, I will do this. Damn the whole world, but I will do it. I will get that Trumpet back, for David. Then I will annihilate all of you. All my life I've repressed my Dark Blood. It's time to use it.*

"You are right." The tall Dark One was looking at her with different eyes now. Not completely convinced, but far closer to it than a moment before. "It is something we had missed. The angels who have been following you around made us uncertain."

She lifted a shoulder. "Her mate feels that I did it out of regard for her. She is an innocent fool, a being of light. He thought I needed protection, and as I said, it gave me the opportunity to study the angels more closely. If you want to disembowel her, and can figure out a way to do it where the curse won't compel me to protect her, I would savor the watching."

"If all you have said is true, we will welcome you," the tall Dark One said. "I am Amal. The beginning for the Dark Ones." He looked down at the Trumpet. "Prove yourself to us. Unravel the spells on this so that we may use it. Can you do it?"

If she'd had any sense of impending victory, it would have

surged through her now, but all she had was simmering violence and a clamp on her emotions so strong she was certain she'd never feel anything again, even if the universe disintegrated around her. The rein on her control was so tight, it almost made her nauseated, but there was no time to steady her stomach. She stepped forward, and the Dark Ones parted, let her come forward, press her hip against the side of the stone tablet to still the distracting ache, the beginning of a cramp starting there. "Yes. I can do it."

"How long?"

Mina ran her hand over top of the instrument, not touching it. "A few minutes."

A hiss of surprise. "Our oracles tell us true about your power. If you are telling *us* the truth."

She tilted her head, gave him a sidelong glance. "Only one way to find out, right?"

Amal lifted a lip in a bloodcurdling expression that she supposed they might call a smile, if Dark Ones knew what a smile was. It was all right. She didn't really understand smiles, either. Any more than she would ever know what laughter was.

Amal spat out three words, and the universe disintegrated in truth.

Twenty-four

IT was as if the Dark Ones' world had been a paper backdrop and his words had punched a hole into it, the ends curling back, already on fire, disappearing. Stars, a swirling pinwheel of them. She remembered when David had shot up in the sky with her, that first time when she'd had little but fear of him. How she'd fought and he dropped her. There'd been this moment of suspension, very brief, when the mind registered that it was about to topple in a free fall. This was the same, only the heights were far, far greater, the terrain of the Earth far below, the moon off to the right, looking the size of the Abyss.

Before she could draw breath, she was snagged in the sharp talons of one of the winged Dark Ones. They were spiraling through the dark sky, past that moon and all those stars, down toward Earth, so fast it was like traveling with the angels.

At least it was over quickly. In a blink, they were past the ozone layer and standing on a high, frozen mountaintop, where it seemed the air was so thin she could barely draw breath, though she'd had no apparent problem in the reaches of space where there was no oxygen.

And David was still with her, a blessing and a curse. They dropped him in the snow twenty feet from her. A spray of blood spattered the ground, a momentary impression before his captors were covering him again, like piranha over a water buffalo. Being the lowest of the lower echelon, like the one that had tried to gnaw her ankle, they were simply hungry pets for the more evolved Dark Ones. David was being used as a bone to keep them occupied while the adults took care of business. She saw a flash of his other hand, trembling fingers, showing he was still alive, and then she forced her gaze away again.

She'd even taken away his ability to fight back.

"Do not get angry with them," Amal commented, now at her right side. "They will not kill him. They know he is yours. But we have suffered so much at their hands, and of course it is so irresistible to have one at our mercy."

He couldn't control the sibilance this time. She thought if she ever heard the word *irresistible* spoken again, she would be sick.

Then the Trumpet was lowered on its stone dais before her. The Dark Ones carrying it backed off, leaving only her and Amal, and that half circle of his cronies. "The angels will locate us quickly now that we are in their sphere," Amal said. "Do it. Prove yourself. We can feel the blood in you reaching for us. For this."

They pressed around her, those tall ones. Talons drifted across her nape, an unexpected intimacy they'd bestow on a child toward whom they had improper urges. She suppressed a shudder.

They had wasted little time once reasonably convinced of her willingness to help, which suggested they feared the angels coming up with possible alternative magics to render the Trumpet inert. They were afraid of losing their opportunity to at last realize their dreams of ultimate destruction. Like comic book villains. She had a couple of comics, favored fare of the sailors on the freighters. Now she found those graphic pictures far less fictional and overly dramatic than she'd first imagined.

Most of the sounds behind her now were the Dark Ones. She wondered if David had seen her looking and was now straining, using every bit of his energy toward silence so as not to distract her. He knew her indifference for the lie it was. He'd known she was a liar from the beginning.

Of course his attempt to remain silent would make them torment him further, see what could tear a scream from his throat, whether he willed it or not. Angels couldn't pass out from too much pain, after all.

As if summoned, a small handful of feathers drifted past her, clumped with blue and red blood, a trace of black. The Dark One closest to her pounced on it, jammed the wad in his mouth and swallowed, cackling. The heat in her rose, a red film starting to close over both eyes.

From the time Mina was cognizant, her mother had taught her the first priority. Control the Dark One blood within her. Repress its sadistic urges, lock away its potential for destruction. She'd lived her life on that knife edge, refined that balance to the point that every moment, every experience or thought, was a calculation. The only time she'd ever been swept away from it without consequence was when she was with David. He pushed her onto a knife edge as well, physically and emotionally, and had revealed what it was to be suffused by joy and heartbreak at once.

That was what love was. The best of both worlds, the dark and the light, the perfect balance.

But the rage building up in her for what they were doing to him, it called for something different. What if she used a lifetime of control to embrace her Dark One blood fully and unleash it? See where it took her. Take the risk of not being able to call it back to heel.

It was against everything she'd taught herself to do, but why the hell not? As she'd told David, she wasn't a warrior for the light or a denizen of evil. She cared nothing for either side. What did she have to lose? The world? What had the world ever done for her?

She laid her hands on the Trumpet, felt the energy sing up her fingertips, the angelic wards attempt to burn her, reject her touch. Gritting her teeth, ignoring that, she analyzed the complex magics around it. Difficult, dangerous. Almost impossible to defuse without harm to the defuser. Unless they knew exactly what they were doing.

It was like pulling a knotted string at the right end, knowing which side would result in the whole thing coming unraveled and which would just cause more knots to pick out.

There was blood on her shoulder, where the Dark Ones' talons had cut her, and that blood was making an inexorable track down her arm, almost to her elbow. It would be to her hand in a matter of seconds. All she had to do was say the chant, charge the necessary energy, activate it with her blood, and the Trumpet would be gone.

"When you blow it, the earth will begin to shift." Amal was speaking in that rasp, his red gaze focused on the land stretching out around the mountain. "The dead will rise, an army. The angels will come down in the sky and try to stop this, but it will already be started." He turned to the others gathered around the dais. "Call your legions forth now and be prepared to engage. The angels will be weakened as the energy of chaos builds. It will disrupt their power base and we will be able to decimate their numbers."

His red gaze shifted to her. "You do this, witch, you know you will have a place with us. You will belong with us."

"Until one of you decides to try and slit my throat." She picked up the Trumpet, watched the blue light start to coat her hands, her flesh start to singe. "Watch me do this, Amal, and remember." She met his gaze. "You will not give me anything. What I want, I will take for myself."

Mina felt the truth of it boiling through her veins, the blood of a Dark One, of a fifth-generation seawitch, more powerful than any of the previous ones. More powerful than anything standing near her now.

She spat out the unraveling spell, watched the blue light twist, contort and then whip around the Trumpet, retracting like snapped twine. It dissipated, destroying the Dark Ones' containment spell as an afterthought. Light flashed around the instrument, bright enough to drive the other Dark Ones back and envelop her, but she had no fear of it. She had enough darkness boiling through her now to swallow even the Lady's light.

She brought the Trumpet to her lips and blew a single clear note.

It was thunder and music together, the meaning of the word *herald*. The mountain on which they stood shook, and that shaking spread, rumbling out from the ground, faster, farther, until the vibration was in the sky, all throughout her body, her bones.

What was it they said? Power corrupts. A story told by mothers to frighten children. Told by her mother to frighten her. Now she called all of it to her. Dark Blood roared up inside her in triumph, overwhelming her senses, overwhelming everything.

The dead. As they stirred, she felt them throughout the earth, beneath her feet. As she embraced the flow of the power, it opened channels inside her that had no geographical limit. She sent a thousand tendrils and probes through those channels, all over the Earth so she not only felt the dead stirring in this mountain, but in the cemeteries in Sweden, the Mediterranean, Saigon, the California shore. The skeletal and partially decomposed, the newly dead. Even the beings fossilized in stone, dead long before there were burial grounds. Closing her eyes, she blew the second blast.

A roar this time, one that made the sound of a volcano blast dim in comparison. The terrain below her split, large, jagged cracks running out from the base of her mountain and away, moving as rapidly as light. Faster than white light. Fast as only the shadows could gather. The dead were clawing, clawing upward, and she was helping them get toward that light. Her body arched upward, trembling toward daylight and life. Mimicking them, pulling them.

Putting the Trumpet to her lips once more, she blew the final blast.

Silence was a sound more deafening than any other, and that was what the last blast was. No sound at all, but a vibration that rocketed through her nerve endings like electrical charges. The earth looked as if it had been slashed open all around them. As the vibration echoed away, a thunderous clamor rose. Mina raised her gaze to see the Dark Ones, almost blotting out the light in the daytime sky. Thousands of them, perhaps all the Dark Ones that inhabited their hellish world, streaking out of the rift hole from which she'd come. Assembled, ready, and now diving as figures began to climb out of the Earth's crust.

She looked beyond what her eyes could see to the extended vast reaches of her mind.

Human as well as animal, mythical and prehistoric. She stood on the mountain, holding the glowing Trumpet, surrounded by the blood light of the Dark Ones, and watched the skeletal form of some type of large dinosaur lumber out of the ground and thunder out a cry of hunger, staring this way and that with empty eye sockets, its teeth bared. As it moved forward, it grew skin, a muscle covering, but those eyes remained empty. No soul.

Chaos. She was seeing chaos unfold before her, a human world gone to chaos and terror.

"You are one of us at last." Amal's voice, whispering in her ear, fetid breath leaving a moist oil on her skin. "Use your powers fully. Delight in the screams of the living, savor the bloodlust of the dead and the Dark Ones. Your own bloodlust. You can lead us."

Amal's voice still, but more than his. Thousands upon thousands of Dark Ones, joining in, seeing in her power something they'd never had. The upper hand. No more would they run from angel attack. No more would they be limited to the pit of fire and brimstone that was their world. Their whispers filled her subconscious, which expanded like an ocean to contain them, gather them to her.

She swayed with the overpowering feel of it. As the dead rose at her channeling, and the Dark Ones spoke in her mind, she realized something that had always been there. Like the embrace of her power, it was something she'd missed because she was so fearful of grasping at this.

When she'd dreamed of the Dark Ones, they'd turn and try to speak to her. She'd told David that. Now, she reached out beyond the channeling of the dead and discovered the Dark Ones. Like the dead, she could *feel* inside each one, hold each heart in her hands, make the connection. As she reached out and did so, there was a frozen stillness in the sky, in their swarm down upon the Earth, as they registered her touch.

She could turn them to her will, just as she was controlling the dead, but only to dark purpose. They had no good in them, just evil, but it was an evil seeking cohesion, and with that cohesion, nothing would stop them. They would destroy, again and again, making each world they conquered just like the pit of despair they'd left behind, because it was a reflection of what they were inside. They hadn't been trapped there. They'd created it, and would continue to do so, as long as that was what they were.

But did she really care about that? About them? It was the power that would keep her warm. It was keeping her warm now, growing ever stronger. It was all the rage she had ever felt, every moment she'd been helpless, afraid, in pain, cold. It was the true place she belonged, inside its loving grasp. The universe was in her hand, to crush and destroy. She could play with the stars and moon like toys, roll them like marbles across the galaxy with a flick of her mind. Kick the earth viciously and watch it explode into fragments, leaving her floating over and over like a gurgling baby, in simple, self-satisfied solitude.

The beginning of a new universe, where she would be the all-powerful deity, who would never make the mistake of creating any world or any being that could hurt her, turn against her, remind her what loneliness was through rejection.

It is a tempting choice, young one. But still a choice.

A different warmth. Whereas what was in her now was searing fire, capable of disintegrating everything to ash, what had materialized at her back was the warmth of hearth fire. Comfort, reassurance, but more than that. A power great as her own. Perhaps greater. It had no fear of her. And that was a mistake.

She spun as Light exploded behind her, knocking away the Dark Ones, obliterating everything except the darkness Mina had collected around her. She no longer saw the mountain or the earth below it. Just a dark sky and a light one, split in a sharp line down the middle, she on one side, that power on the other. Flashes of lightning strobed through both, as if they were curtains hiding a battle in progress. The angels, fighting the Dark Ones all over the planet, in the skies, on the ground. The battle of Armageddon at last.

The Goddess. This was the Goddess. Strength and yet counterpurpose. Mina defiantly stared into Her face, felt that power peel her skin back and leave just the skeletal face of a Dark One, knew her eyes had both gone to flame already. She didn't care about her body. What did a body matter when the soul could cloak itself in this blast of pure, malevolent energy?

Where had this Goddess been when the creatures of the sea had torn at her flesh, when her mother had been raped? What did she owe Her? Nothing. She owed Her nothing.

What do you owe yourself?

Though the Goddess asked the question, Mina answered it, savagely. *This.* She could stand toe-to-toe, bring dark against light, swallow it whole, and the darkness would be all around her. A new order. And angels needed order, right? They could serve her, serve the Dark Ones, just as Amal wished.

Unlike the Goddess before her, Mina could bear the proximity of Dark Ones, felt no exhausting strain at their presence. Their very closeness sucked at the female deity, just like how the angels made Mina feel. Mirror images of each other, she and this Goddess. However, unlike the Goddess, who could deal with Her weakness only by holding Dark Ones' at arm's length, Mina now knew how to bring angels to heel.

She felt the angels pause outside the screen of that curtain, as the threat of her mind became manifest, all the darkness eagerly channeling toward her, ready to move forward, move over the Goddess like a wave and drown her as soon as Mina released it.

She knew what they saw. The world hanging on a cliff edge, as the two entities stood face-to-face. What the Goddess had attempted as an alliance would become a war that would tear the world apart. The battle decision lay right here.

Even knowing that, Mina sensed one dark-winged angel

changing his course, abandoning the head of his army to charge toward them, to split open that curtain, come to his Lady's aid. Lucifer. The Lady's champion. Mina had no fear of him now. It would be too late if she but spoke the word.

She got a hint of the Goddess's face, of unfathomable eyes, the color hard to discern behind the light. But she saw a soft mouth, a humanlike form, wings somewhat like the angels but far wider in their span, spreading out, white and gleaming.

It is the way of those who love you. They will do anything they must to save you, even when everyone else thinks it's too late. A delicate pause, a tendril of energy that touched Mina's face before she could avoid it. *Where is David? Have you forsaken him?*

Mina backed away from that touch and her heel hit something. Looking down, her feet were on the mountain and she saw David's limp hand, though all else beyond him remained black, cut off.

Just a flash, but she couldn't look away fast enough. For the moment, whether by the Goddess's will or some other effect, no Dark Ones were upon him. His wings were gone. Torn and broken, ripped away, so that all that was left were a few shards of bone glistening with blood. Skin had been taken from so much of his body, not just from the rotting poison of their touch and saliva but from a dozen sets of teeth as they'd tried to tear him to shreds. They'd have spit out his flesh, unable to stomach it, but they would have wanted the violence of taking it, of tasting his blood. His eyes . . . oh, gods, his eyes were gone as well, his nose broken, hair ripped from his scalp. Nothing left of his beautiful cock and testicles but blood and gore. He was a broken, hideous thing, and yet as she knelt, curved her hand over his limp one, that one thing was the same. The only part of him that seemed untouched. His other hand . . . Her eyes closed. All of the fingers were gone, chewed off.

David.

But she knew she'd get no response. There was a wet pool of blood on his chest, a gaping wound from his belly almost to his throat. The only way to kill an angel was to remove his heart and destroy it.

Oh, gods . . . Damn all of them to Hell. Her hand fluttered over it, but she couldn't bear to touch it. Instead she looked back toward his face. *Scared shitless . . .* How could anyone have walked into this world, completely turned himself over to the hands of another, known what would happen and been fearless? He hadn't been. He would have been afraid. But he'd been more afraid of failing her, failing himself. And that was the best definition she could think of for courage.

His beautiful eyes. What had he said that day, when he cupped her scarred face? *I see you. I always have.*

It didn't matter now. She was going to destroy it all. Everything that breathed would pay for this. She knew he'd been willing to make this sacrifice, accepted not only that he was going to die, but die after prolonged and terrible pain. He was a good man, a good angel, a good soul. But she wasn't good.

What do you owe yourself?

She'd never desired anything until him. Never dared to. If she had him, maybe there would have been other things she'd have wanted. Like a garden to go with that tire swing. And that junk shop he'd talked about . . . an array of things, like searching a shipwreck.

What odd thoughts to have here, on the edge of total destruction, power vibrating on her palms, rushing through her veins. She was invincible, a deadly force far more powerful than anything she'd ever feared. And yet all she could think about was an empty tire swing, drifting in a faint wind against a desert landscape.

The curtain of dark and light had grown translucent, so she could see the Goddess's army. Those not currently employed in direct combat on the Earth, an Earth that was now far below, hovered just beyond Her light. Apparently, She'd told them to hold, wait on this moment of decision.

They didn't understand. How could they know what it was to

be born to evil and make the choice, every day, not to embrace it? Not for any hope of anything better, just out of sheer hatred and defiance. Living on the edge of madness, so that when something like this was finally offered . . .

It's a lie. It's always been a lie.

She remembered telling David that. She'd always known what the lie was. Her despair had been in not knowing what the truth was. But here it lay, just before her.

In David's arms, it came together. The dark and the light were at peace with each other and there was no struggle. She could claw and bite, draw his blood, and yet be filled by him, kissed by him, held safe and warm. That was what this power couldn't give her. And maybe if she'd never had that, it wouldn't have mattered. But she had. For two ridiculously short days.

All her life, she'd studied, practiced, and she'd missed the significance of it. It was more than a way to keep the darkness in her under control. There was a wider purpose. Though she didn't know where she belonged, light or dark, the one thing she knew was that there had to be a balance. David had known that. As above, so below. Just as she'd always had to have the balance to exist, so, too, did the world.

Now she was one of the keys to that. She could tip that balance with just a whispered word that fluttered in her throat. But as her gaze drifted down to David, to the remnants of the wings they'd torn from him, the bruising on his face and upper body, the gashes and burns on his legs, she knew that was an imbalance she didn't want. She'd wanted him.

And whether she saved the world now because she had wanted him, had allowed herself that, or because it was for the higher good, didn't matter. To the world, it wouldn't matter.

It is all the same, young one. Believe me.

She'd always lived moment to moment, making no plans, the only certainty being the here and now. Wanting him was the constant. The Dark Ones had believed the Dark Blood would overwhelm any good in her. They'd thought she was theirs. But she wasn't. She'd been his. David's. All the subtleties of submission and surrender, that willingness to trust, it became the rock. The rock on which she could stand, could shelter her soul. Could depend upon.

He is the Rock, His works are perfect, and all His ways are just . . .

A Bible was the most common thing she found in wreckage, an irony, she'd thought. But when she'd read the book, it had become clear it was not a ward against misfortune, but a guiding light through it. And that phrase had apparently embedded itself in her mind.

She turned her back to the Goddess. Or rather, put the strength of that light at her back. She would deal with her grief, the deadness in her heart later. What mattered was that Anna would have her baby. Diane would have her twins. Life would go on, because that was what David would have wanted. What he'd died for.

Will you follow my lead, my Lady?
I am here behind you, young one.

Controlling the dead was probably one of the easier things Mina knew how to do. The Lady's energy was already aligning with hers in a smooth, miraculous way that she couldn't help but pause and marvel at a brief second, the wisdom and skill of an ancient providing her a challenge to improve her own skills. But then she shook it off, imagining David's amusement.

Can you save the world first, little witch?

A jagged ache was in her soul as she raised her own arms. The Lady's light spread, so that Mina's body became a silhouette before that outline, the winged figure taking the same posture, arms raised and stretched, so they were a reverse image. Instead of light throwing a larger shadow of darkness behind it, Mina was the darkness shadowed by the fiery power. As the powers aligned, the click of connection was simple, seamless, and filled Mina with a sense of power and belonging far more than anything she'd ever expected to feel. Dark and light combined, and the power of it shimmered out from them both, in every direction.

Chaos faltered, and Mina broke out of her amazement to

seize the power from its hands, yank it free, and add hers and the Goddess's. A tremendous sphere of energy, growing rapidly larger, like a child's balloon. Twining the two energies together, she imagined herself at a loom, the wheel spinning madly, her hands flashing over the threads until at last, concentration unmarred, she severed it, sending what they had created whirling out over the Earth.

It hit the stratosphere and engulfed the Earth, closing around it, the smaller blue green orb now inside a much larger one. A prison. As the thousands of Dark Ones swarming over the Earth realized the tide had shifted, they shot for the skies, and were repelled, slamming against that energy and finding no escape, nowhere to turn except into the swords and arrows of the angels charging among them, free to pass in and out of that energy blanket at will.

Then she turned her attention to the rift from which she'd come. She could be a force of salvation, or destruction. All she had to think of was David to know which face she would bring upon that hellish world.

Reaching out to the towers in the Dark Ones' world created specifically to call open rifts, it took only a touch, for she was Everything. All she had to do was press her lips together, blow a breath, and it became a tornado that split into four churning forces. They spun out to the corners of the Dark Ones' world. In her mind's eye, she saw the towers explode, a hailstorm of stone and debris, sparks of red power and tendrils of energy striking the surface like broken, whipping wires, melting into the fire, freezing into the ice, destroying the rift-opening magic. The few Dark Ones left on that world would have no way to leave it, ever again. Unless she willed it.

It was then she saw Dante, standing at the edge of the open rift. Entering his mind was as easy as touching her own consciousness, and his gaze whipped up and around him.

My Lady . . . His mental voice was a whisper. A plea.

You cannot leave, Dante, because you were never named.

Your mother never named you, and the Dark Ones saw no pur-
pose to it. You will stay in this deserted world, where only a
handful of Dark Ones and life remains. You will make some-
thing of it. Prove to me you deserve to be set free. And perhaps I
will come back and do just that.

She saw his face, furious and yet terrified, his fists clenched,
his body surging forward toward the rift, though she knew he
would strike against it uselessly. She sealed it before he had the
opportunity, creating a new star with a crimson tint.

BACK to the Earth again. The Goddess moved with her, a separate form of consciousness. Mina had an army at her disposal to
assist the angels, and she put it to use. Many of the Dark Ones,
their avenue of escape cut off, were headed to ground. She turned
the dead on them. The fossils of dinosaurs and dragons, centaurs
and hippogriffs. Masses of human bodies, from the dawn of time
to the present, fighting with nothing but teeth and blunt weapons
picked up in soulless, mindless hands, drove the Dark Ones back
into the sky, into the savage grasp of the angels again.

The Legion had sustained severe casualties in certain areas, so
as the Dark Ones took to the skies there, another splinter of her
power created the illusion of twenty angels in places there might
be one, herding them back to where the angels had actual greater
numbers and could cut the Dark Ones down more effectively.

Those angels that had backed the Goddess had been sent by
Her to join their brethren, so now the most powerful of the angelic
host lent themselves to the struggle. She had a glimpse of Jonah
and Michael, twin forces of destruction. Uriel, the angel of ven-
geance who worked as Lucifer's shadow. Azriel, the angel of death,
who would likely consider generations of his work being unearthed
an affront. Even Raphael, the angel of healing, throwing a spear
which appeared to have no limit to its range, or in its ability to return to him. His golden hair was gleaming, blood smeared on his
face.

But her army of the dead, and the Goddess's army of angels,

were not the only ones. While there were those who cowered in confusion, the eye of her mind, which gave her as much scope and detail of what was occurring on the Earth as she wished, also saw merpeople in the seas, Neptune at their head, his trident in one hand, a lethal sword in the other. The fairies and other magical beings who still lived in the shadowy corners of the world were taking up arms as well, working alongside the remains of their ancestors to repel the obvious threat. As were the humans.

She was able to catch glimpses of stunned amazement as humans came face-to-face with not only the shadows of their nightmares, but the light of their faith, seeing angels with their own eyes, fighting on their behalf.

The world was going to change. Perhaps for better, or for worse. Or maybe it would only change for a little while before going back to what it was. That didn't concern her. She was tiring.

It is time to start laying them back to rest, wouldn't you say, young one?

The Goddess's light had drawn closer, but not too close. She understood they could be integrated, but not meshed. Mina would have long, lonely years to reflect on the glimpse she'd had into the Deity's mind and study it in recall. Mina had never imagined that the purity of that light could work in concert with her own darkness so effortlessly.

Always something new to learn. The Goddess had that same gentle amusement that made her heart ache for David. Mina was beginning to think humor was a whole other type of magical system she needed to explore, for it certainly had wrested unexpected responses from her when David used it.

David . . .

Enough for one day. She pushed it aside. With the balancing of the Lady behind her, she reached out, began to lay the dead back to rest as the Lady restored Her Earth, the cracked mountains and ruptured plains, the flooding caused by the disrupted oceans, as if they'd never occurred.

Amongst all of that work, the angels continued their bloody

and fiery work, dispatching Dark Ones trying to escape them. The incineration of the bodies caused repetitive bursts of flame in the air, then a sweep of light below as the wind and weather angels stayed busy, carrying the ash away.

It took some time, the sense that the threat and challenge had passed, but even as she grew so weary it felt as if death were closing in on her, she kept on, for with each thing she didn't have left to do, the sense of loss she'd staved off was closing in as well.

Her spirit and body were exhausted. As the adrenaline drained away and she watched the angels finish their work, report in to the Goddess such that the Lady let her know she could dissipate that sphere of energy and open up the layers of the Earth's atmosphere again, a numbness began to settle over her. Even the Dark One blood, which usually was eager to goad at her despair, was silent. Maybe because it knew, for today at least, it had lost. Nothing could touch her today.

She was on the mountaintop again. Alone. Snow beneath her bare feet, a pale sun in the sky. All she had to do was turn, and she would see him. What remained of him. He was right next to her, for in the corner of her eye she could see the crumpled form. Loose feathers brushed her calves, brought there by a taunting wind, and she clutched them before they could get away, bringing them to her face, smelling him, feeling the softness.

Oh, gods, she couldn't bear it.

And then a familiar set of fingers curled around her ankle.

His heart was still in his chest.

She dropped to her knees by him, and where she'd been afraid to touch before, now she did, probably causing him discomfort, but she had to see. It was a wound. A knife wound, but they hadn't taken his heart. Amal had said they would not kill him, and they hadn't.

"David. I'm here. It's done. We did it."

His mouth moved, but it was torn, his teeth mostly gone, his tongue a swollen mass that seeped blood from the corner when he tried to talk.

"*Ssh . . .* " She laid her fingers lightly on his mouth, barely a brush, and still caused him pain.

You knew he was alive. She sent the accusation toward the presence she still felt hovering close. *You could have told me.*

The choice had to be yours. You needed to know to what lengths you would go to honor his love, to see how it changed you.

So you risked the Fate of your world, your angels, the humans, for that? Mina raised her head, stared out at that light, the shimmering shape of a woman in it.

What goes on inside each soul, young one, is far more important than epic battles. Inside each soul the Fate of the universe is decided, every day. And that will continue, even as gods and goddesses wax and wane. Who you became today saved us all.

WHEN Raphael and Jonah got to the mountain, the Lady's light had faded. Mina was weeping, her hand resting on David's face, over those sightless eyes. With her body bent forward, her forehead was pressed into the blood on his chest. The Trumpet lay on the ground near them both.

It was Jonah who gently extricated the witch, amazed by the slightness of her, after all they'd just seen her do. As he lifted her coiled body in his arms, her residual power was still so prominent it washed over his skin, briefly illuminated the script praises to the Goddess branded into his gauntlets. It also heated the frozen earth beneath his feet, turned snow into mud and sprouted several small fir saplings.

"Let Raphael heal him," he murmured, trying not to look at David's ruined body. "Let us take him back to the Citadel."

She nodded against his throat, her hands curled over her own face now, hiding the way the anguish distorted the scarred features. "Take me back to my cave."

"Don't you want to—"

"I can't stay at the Citadel. That hasn't changed. Nothing's changed. This is because of me."

Jonah caught her chin, forced it up, and was rewarded by a tiny flare deep in those still, red eyes, even though he realized he could be putting himself in grave peril. Ignoring that, he gestured around them. "You just annihilated the Dark One threat to this world. *That* is because of you."

"It doesn't matter. He was what mattered. Just take me back to where I belong."

Twenty-five

So she'd saved the world. Big whoop-de-do. She'd discovered that word in a crossword puzzle book she'd found floating in the water on one of her scant outings. Probably dropped over the side of a pleasure cruiser.

What the angels had been trying to accomplish in small skirmishes for thousands of years had been done in the course of several hours. The significant decimation of the Dark One numbers, the destruction of their rift mechanism. Jonah had been right. They would have a time of rest, at least against this foe. The humans would struggle with their darkness on a more favorably balanced playing field. Jonah could have time to enjoy his daughter.

She had no worries about the irritation of guardian angels anymore. The generally accepted theory was that very little was a threat to her now. Dark Ones certainly weren't going to be coming near her anytime soon. Listlessly, she kept tabs on Dante and the remaining ones through her dreams, for Jonah occasionally dropped into her mind to ask. Annoying blood link. She needed to devote some energy to figuring out how to neutralize or reverse that.

The ocean water was colder today, it seemed. So cold. She

kept the cave dry most of the time now, not venturing out for much. Her joints ached and muscles cramped as they always did, and as always she used them to balance the darkness in her against whatever the hell the other part of her was now.

She was lonely. Lonely for David, in a way that made the aching in her muscles and joints minor twinges in comparison. But he certainly didn't need her. She'd gotten him tortured, nearly killed. There was nothing she could do to help heal him. Hell, when it came to the two of them, it had always been her heart and soul more in need of rescue.

Rising, she moved to her bookshelves, found the yellow bound book, took out *The Littlest Angel* to retrieve the feather trapped there. One of his daggers lay on the shelf beside it. She'd returned to that mountaintop in her mind, scoured the snow and found his weapons, for she'd suspected the Dark Ones had brought them to the final battleground. Probably had used them on him. Gods. She'd sent the rest to Jonah, but this one she kept. Holding the grip now, she rested her forehead against the flat of the blade. Thought about how David drew it across her flesh, used pain to make the pain go away. And trembled.

She might not need protection from Dark Ones anymore, but she needed protection from her thoughts, which could bedevil her in her solitude until she went mad.

That's it. She stood up, slamming the book down on the shelf and jammed the dagger into the rock wall, squeezing the grip hard. She couldn't bear it anymore.

She still couldn't claim to understand what love was. She'd thought it was staying away from him. But it was becoming apparent she couldn't any longer. And maybe that was love, too.

Strange witch. You make love potions more often than any other, and yet you claim to know nothing of love.

She could almost hear his voice. Sighing, she focused on the Citadel, sifted through energies, and found the blood link with the Legion Commander.

Jonah. How is he? She asked it daily, though she knew what she would hear. Each time, it left her with a lingering uneasiness, as if it was *she* who had the answer to the question. Yet still, she'd done nothing. Kept stalling, an exercise in self-discipline. He *didn't* need her.

Same. A pause, but she waited, knowing Jonah wouldn't spare her. He'd done that at first, and she'd snapped at him. Informed him that, while he was used to dealing with a woman with much more easily bruised feelings—with feelings, period—Mina was not that woman. Though they both knew the insult was misplaced, for Anna had a core of steel underneath her sensitive nature.

The Dark Blood is inhibiting his healing. Maybe some other things. He paused again, and this time he surprised her with something new. *It is in my mind that he would do well to see you.*

She remained silent a few moments. *Oh, gods, that sealed it.* As long as she hadn't had an invitation, she could keep her resolve. Oh, hell, no, she couldn't. She was pretty sure she'd been about to break just now, go with or without any encouragement.

She needed David, in order to deal with this dreadful loneliness. "He said he loved me," she said aloud to her solitary cave walls. She frowned. "No, it wasn't that. He just needed to save someone."

No, that wasn't it, either. He'd needed to save someone whom he loved. And she had to trust him enough to let him do it. She'd rather face an army of Dark Ones again. Or worse, one of Anna's hugs.

May I come see him, then?

Would you come even if I said no?

Yes.

Then thank you for the illusion of courtesy. I'll tell the advance guard to expect your appearance.

Can you clear the roof platform?

Another pause, laden with curiosity. *It's clear.*

Mina closed her eyes. It was a long leap, and it was going to hurt, but what didn't?

The energy she had within and around her required constant

exercise, in small and large ways, and there was never enough to occupy it, something that was also interfering with her sleep. Like a pack of restless hounds, it milled inside of her, barely under control but manageable, as long as she had a focus.

She could turn her cave into a warm, dry palace if she wanted, a maze of never-ending rooms filled with all the things that intrigued her in the human world. She need only summon them to her fingertips. But always, there was the Darkness within her. Maybe she could control it and still have some of those comforts, but old habits and precautions died hard. David had thought there was another way, but that way involved him, and she wouldn't ask anything of him now. She had no right.

However, she had enough power to be dangerously close to chaos, could feel it boiling and bubbling in the back of her mind at all times. Only one person could steady it, help her work through what was happening to her. In the maelstrom of the battle, when a million voices of Dark Ones had called to her, it was believing in David's love that had held her fast, anchored her.

So again she faced the conflict. What was best for David, versus what she needed. And could she live with the guilt if she chose the latter?

———

Her apparitions tended to be accompanied by a defensive flash of fire, a percussion wave like an explosion that would knock back anything within twenty feet of her arrival. She was experimenting with toning that down, but she couldn't deny a certain satisfaction that she managed to misjudge her distance and blow out a section of the keep's border wall. She *had* tried for courtesy, however, since she did ask for a clear platform, despite a niggling desire to see a few angels somersaulting through the air like disgruntled bugs bouncing off a windshield.

No, she was never going to be truly good.

Jonah was sitting on the far wall, paging through a book, much as he'd been doing the day she came here as a dragon. He glanced up as the air around her settled, the fire dissipating. His gaze passed over the ruined brick, his hair still rippling over his shoulders from the blast. He seemed to be wearing it longer these days, making her wonder if Anna liked it that way. Did she like running her fingers through it as he lay over her, his powerful body pressing down on hers, the weight of his cock insistent between her legs?

A tiny tremor ran through her. Oh, yes, she missed David for other, fairly base reasons. That was for certain, even though she knew his condition made him incapable of such things. But it was more than the physical, unfortunately. It was everything the physical passion he'd shared with her had implied, the needs of her heart and soul he met when he held her, took her.

Raphael had come out to join Jonah, and she approached them now in human form. The white light of the Citadel pulsed around her, but another experiment she was testing was a different level of shielding that might allow her to expose herself to a place like this for longer periods. That in itself kept the wild dogs within her occupied, because there was of course a boatload of white light here.

She glanced at Raphael. "How is he? More specifically."

"He's not worsening, but he gets no better. The wounds will not close and begin to heal. His wings will not regenerate. Each time we try, the Dark One blood simply neutralizes the healing energy, or makes it worse, attacking a new area. I have stopped doing anything but seeing to his comfort." Raphael considered her. "You have said you are not skilled in healing. But just seeing you may help him. He has been asking about you. Constantly."

"Well, why didn't you—"

"He wouldn't let us," Jonah cut across her before she could unsheathe her claws.

Raphael nodded. "He would not allow us to summon you until you were willing to come on your own."

She'd needed time after that battle, she told herself. She'd known Raphael was most equipped to see to him. She'd never tried to heal severe injuries of the flesh or mind. And if he was dying, she was too much of a coward to watch it.

The problem was that she was a coward, period. She still visited the Dark One world in her dreams, but her nightmares were about David. About his screams and her doing nothing. About the way he'd looked when they were done with him. How could she heal what she had caused?

That had been her illogical reasoning. But the angel healers didn't have the skill to heal injuries related to Dark One blood. She'd known that, of course, when Raphael had only limited success in restoring her energy after the Canyon Battle. She'd hoped it wouldn't affect the healing of an angel. Who would have anticipated an angel with Dark One blood running through his veins?

In point of fact, there was only one angel she'd ever known with an aptitude for healing an injury involving Dark One blood. Her brow furrowed, the wheels of her mind turning. Raphael's attention sharpened. "You've thought of something."

"Maybe. I don't know. I have an idea, but I can't explain it. I just have to feel my way through it. Let me think." She shifted her attention to Jonah. "And so when you checked on me, under the pretense of asking about things in the Dark One world, what did you tell him?"

"It was not a pretense. It is a matter of importance. But if you must know, I told him that you were as charming as ever. That you were out saving orphans and planting flowers and had no time to see him."

At her stare, he let out a sigh. "I told him you were safe. That was his main concern, initially. He is a soldier, and you were his charge. I told him you were no longer in need of our physical protection. As to whether you are still a threat to us, that I could not address."

"Did he ask that?"

"No, I just did."

She pursed her lips, even while noting an impatient shift from Raphael. He was a healer. If she had an idea, nebulous or not, he wanted her to be pursuing it. Which told her David was worse than even their grim words portrayed.

"You know I'm still a threat," she said to Jonah. "But there isn't much to be done about it, is there?"

"What I need to know is if you are an ally or an enemy."

"I'm not your enemy. I don't know much about being an ally." She turned to Raphael. "Where is he?"

Raphael gestured to her to follow him, giving Jonah a glance.

"Mina."

She stopped, turned as Jonah straightened from the wall, laying down the book. "Thank you for your help retrieving the Trumpet."

"I caused every problem you had," she pointed out.

"Perhaps. But you fixed them, and in doing so, things have changed. Perhaps for the better."

"Or worse. And I didn't fix all of them. I don't know if I'm a threat," she said abruptly. "But know this. You can't stop me. You can't control me."

She noticed then that Marcellus sat on the wall around the curve of the bailey, which was now in her line of sight. He must have sustained some serious injuries, for as he rose he showed some stiffness, as well as a fairly noticeable scar line that ran from the base of his throat across his chest. A close call. Some Dark One had almost succeeded in ripping his heart from his chest.

With his face unreadable, it took a moment before she realized he'd risen from the wall as a sign of respect. *To her.*

"There are checks and balances in all things in nature," Jonah's sharp tone cut through her shock, drew her attention back to him. "Yours might not be evident, but they will be in time, if we had to stop you."

"But how many bodies would pile up before then?" She shook her head. "Whatever that 'check' is, find it soon. Just in case. I won't look for it myself. If I knew of it, I'd seek a way to counter it."

"You checked yourself, several weeks ago."

"Because of him. Because of his love." Mortified, she found she was having to blink back tears. "Find it, damn it."

Jonah studied her. "I believe you are one of the most extraordinary beings I've ever met." He inclined his head, and she knew she could take it as his promise to her. "We'll find it."

Turning on her heel, she followed Raphael deeper into the chambers of the Citadel.

The area they'd given David was a corner room, with a plethora of the large open windows that were scattered throughout the Citadel to let in the strong sunlight. He was on his side on a bed, the cover pulled just over a bare hip, revealing the multiple burns and gashes. She also noted new ones where, as Raphael had mentioned, the Dark One blood she'd given David had countered their attempts to heal him. All of the wounds seeped blood and infection, pervading the room with a sickly smell. The remains of his wings, those jagged ends of bones, rested in a listless pile behind him.

Because of the wounds, the bed was stained and damp. At her accusing glance, Raphael shook his head. "I could have suspended him in the air, and we do sometimes, though he prefers the bed. But he can't bear bandages. I cleanse the linens each time I enter the room, but we can't stop the running of the fluids. He will not die, but it is a horrible way to live."

All this in a low voice, so it wouldn't carry to the patient. She nodded, swallowing. Moving forward, she circled the bed. As she did, she laid one hand on his bare foot where it extended out from the loose sheet at the end.

His head shifted, and then she saw him turn his face down to the end of the bed toward her, as if he could see.

He was so pale, gaunt. Somehow seeing how horrible he looked now with the wounds cleaned was worse than when he'd been lying on the ground, torn and bloodied. For this was it. There was no chance it was better than she'd feared. Goddess. She put a hand to her mouth. She'd done this to him. *They'd* done this to him.

Somehow, she was back at the door, leaning against it, her fingers digging into the frame. Unnoticed, the Citadel trembled on its magical foundation, as the anger surged up on her. There were still some Dark Ones left in that world. She would go back through the portal, and she would turn it into a barren landscape, devoid of life for the next million years, until some bare cellular form of life would dare to evolve, instead of a form of life that never should have been.

And would she incinerate herself as well? This was *her* doing.

"My Lady." Raphael's soft voice, and though it was an unexpected title, Mina's head came up, her red eyes meeting his. "He spoke to you," he added carefully.

Mina turned back toward the bed. David had shifted, his hand seeking something on the table they'd put next to him. A cloth . . . a sash. As she watched, he fumbled, trying to put it over his empty eyes.

"No." She was back by the bed in an instant, her hands settling on his wrists. The feel of the abraded but warm flesh made her throat thick with tears. "No. It will hurt."

"It hurts you to look at me." His voice was rasping. The damage they'd done to his mouth and tongue, she knew.

"Yes, it does. It should. Leave it."

She shifted her grip to his hands, the one perfect, the one with no fingers, and she noted the irony that her perfect hand was her right, his the left, so they could interlace the fingers of those two hands when facing each other, while she simply curved her three fingers over the square, fingerless palm of the other.

"Where have you been?" he asked. No recrimination, though she'd essentially been in her cave, uselessly brooding, while he'd been here, suffering like this. Of course, he hadn't been alone. The fact Jonah and Raphael were both present said they'd been keeping close watch on the young angel. The fresh flowers resting in a vase said Anna had been here. Everyone but the one for whom he'd sacrificed himself.

No, I will never be good. And she felt no amusement at the thought this time.

She sat down on the edge of the bed at his hip when he pulled her down beside him. His fingers, so strong and capable, as clever with a woman's body as he was with a weapon, were bony, with a sickly tremor.

"We've talked about ending this," he said conversationally.

"What?"

He stroked her fingers. Gods, soothing *her.* "They can't fix it. And I'm no good to anyone like this. It might be what's best."

"No."

"So you'd miss me, then?" He attempted a smile with his damaged mouth, but then it died. "I can't live like this, Mina. I have to serve a purpose. I—"

She'd been looking at his face, remembering the patient brown eyes, seeing his mouth curved in a true smile, or a resolute line. Not a mouth drawn taut and hard against pain, the grooves of stress so much like old age that no angel had. The ache in her throat was becoming excruciating, and she followed the need of it, leaned forward and put her mouth on his.

Sickness made his taste fetid, but she didn't care. She put her hands against his nearly bare skull, resting as lightly as possible on the burns and bite marks there. As she kissed him, her arms slid around him, holding him as close to her as she could, while his hands slipped to her waist. He was weak, so she drifted down so she was lying next to him, her calf trapped between his ankles, her face tilted up to him.

She put everything into the kiss she couldn't put into words, wishing for him, wanting him.

"I can't." She pulled away abruptly, sitting up and drawing away. "Damn it, I want to, but I can't, all right?"

"Can't what?" Frown lines marked his forehead. "Mina, what . . . I'm repulsive to you."

"Oh, don't be an idiot," she snapped, and missed the easing of his features, the hint of an almost smile that registered with a startled Raphael. "I can't give you up. I know I should, know that's what's best. I don't know what love is. I can't love you back and you have all this love to give. All I can do is need you. I need you to make it worth it to keep the Dark Blood balanced in me, to teach me what a sense of humor is, because I think it would really help. I want your body, too." She glared at him. "And I'm glaring at you, by the way."

"I can hear it in your voice," he said cautiously. "But I don't know how—"

"I need you to heal my scars. My fingers. Right now."

David's brows, what was left of them, rose. "You lost me." He worked himself upright, his color draining such that Raphael moved forward to help. Jonah was there, too, apparently having appeared during her outburst. "You said you didn't want that."

"I didn't want a lot of things. I didn't want you disrupting my life with your hands and mouth and smile and making me feel like I could feel happiness and not be overwhelmed by darkness. But you did." She drew another deep breath, braced herself. "So now I need you to heal me, as we both know you can."

"Make him drain his energy so you can be pretty again? Is it worth the risk—" Raphael started, anger suffusing his expression.

"I don't *want* it," she snarled. "Do you know what beauty can do? How much power it can hold? Don't I have enough to handle as it is? Look at all of you, the way you affect anyone who sees you. Do I fucking look like I need more power to control?"

"*Sshh . . .* " David had caught her hand as she jumped up, and he somehow managed to give her enough of a yank to topple her back down beside him. "*Sssh.* Easy."

She stopped, her breath rasping in her throat. It was then she realized the misty tile floor had become crimson as her temper built, her panic. She let the power ease out of her fingers, let the warm, electrical furor of it seep from the room.

"It's like I'm standing under this tidal wave all the time, trying to figure out which direction to make the water go so it doesn't drown me or anyone else." She shook her head. "It doesn't . . . I'm not saying you have to take on that responsibility. That's your choice, whether this works or not. I just . . . I can't bear seeing you this way."

"Mina, slow down." His fingers pressed into hers. "What are you talking about?"

"As you heal me, I think I can help heal you at the same time. I'm not sure, but it's worth the risk." She reached out, ran a quick, unsteady hand down the side of his jaw. "I'll do anything to make you what you were when I first saw you. Whole, beautiful. Perfect."

"I'm afraid the 'whole' part only happened when you came along and let me love you."

"I never let you. I fought. You insisted."

David smiled then, let go of her hand to find her face, managing to cup her cheek in that tender way of his, not even seeming to notice when the residual crimson light from her roused emotions sparked down the scorched flesh of his forearm.

They'd hung his daggers and weapons harness on the bedpost. Probably Jonah's doing, to make David feel as if he'd not lost everything he was. She drew one now, brought it to his palm and closed his fingers over the grip. A sob came from her before she could bite it back. "David, heal me."

"He can't afford to lose any more blood. He's too weak as it is." Raphael stepped forward, but in the corner of her eye, Mina saw Jonah reach out, put a hand on the golden angel's arm.

David held the dagger, but tilted his head, as if he were considering her with his piercing gaze. "Are you planning something that could cause you harm?"

"No," she lied. "I'm just frightened of it. Of what will happen, of what it will mean." She stopped, stared for a long moment at the covers. Couldn't stop herself from leaning forward and running one knuckle over the curve of his bare hip, the upper part of his thigh that the sheet's shift now revealed. One small patch of untouched skin. Like the one patch on her face. Only they'd just overlooked it on him. He'd healed it on her.

"I've never trusted anyone, David. I've never believed in anyone, couldn't even trust myself." She took a deep breath. "I can't do this without you. I can't control it without knowing there's someone worth controlling it for. So before you heal me, I need you to know that. That the reason I'm doing this is mostly because I need you. I need you to be whole and well, and there at my back. There's a chance over time I'll learn to control it on my own. So if you change your mind down the road, realize that you don't love me, you could leave." She steadied her voice. "I just don't want you to think I'm doing this because I'm self-sacrificing or generous, or any of that."

His face had gotten sober. Reaching down now, he looked for her hand and found her arm, caressed a small portion of it with a knuckle. "Mina, I love you. I felt it the first time I saw you, like when you watch your child be born and know from that moment on, everything is going to be different. I love you now. Tomorrow, yesterday. Forever. And it will not change."

"Everything changes," she said desperately.

"You're right. Some things grow stronger, richer, more powerful over time. This will be one of them. Trust me for this moment, remember? Believe me. And promise me you won't go away from me like this again, where I can't go to you." His hand drifted to her neck and shoulders. "You've been sitting in that damp cave of yours, getting muscle cramps and joint aches. You're tired." His fingers passed over her eyes, under them, along the lines of her cheeks. "You're not sleeping, baby."

"David." The tears were coming back, and she sprang up and away. "I can't promise anything, you understand? I run away when I'm angry or hurt. I need solitude. But I need to know you'll be around, always. So it's completely one-sided. All I can say is if you're not there, I will give up. I'll just annihilate everything, because total destruction feels better than this loneliness I feel when you're not nearby. And *what* are you two looking at?" she snapped at Jonah and Raphael, who had been staring at her throughout her tirade.

"Mina."

David had managed to sit fully upright with his feet on the floor, the badly mangled wings doing their best to balance him.

He was swaying. Despite Raphael and Jonah's speed, she was there first. She gripped his arms, for he'd dropped the dagger on the bed next to him. She held him until he steadied.

"Mina," he repeated. "It's okay. I'm an angel. I take a lot of things on faith."

"But what if I'm not worth your faith?"

"Do you want to be?"

She remembered his question of long ago. *Do you want to belong to me?*

"Yes," she whispered.

"Then let's get you healed and see what happens. I have faith in you, seawitch. Though I know you're lying. You're risking something of your own well-being on this." His hand captured hers, tightening a moment. "But you will tell me true. Are you risking anyone else's?"

"No." She let her fingers turn. "It didn't . . . It apparently wasn't the right time. Or perhaps the magic . . . it didn't take." She'd been surprised to feel a loss, knowing that.

He seemed to weigh her words, the truth of them. Then he bent forward again, pressed his lips to her nose. "We'll try again sometime, if you want to. And next time, I'll ask first."

"You better," she managed.

"All right, then." He cleared his throat. "So we're going to do this. Because I know you love me. And I love you so much that my heart breaks when you're not near, when you hurt, when you won't let me help. Okay?"

She stared at him, then inclined her head, a slow nod.

The skin around his eyes crinkled. "It's rather pointless to nod around a blind man, isn't it?" He picked up the dagger when she guided his hand mutely back to it, then cocked his head. "Can one of you help hold me up while I do this? I don't want to break off in the middle."

It was of course Jonah who came and put himself at David's back, bracing him with his hands on his shoulders. His magnificent wings were half spread, while David's broken and wasted ones brushed his bare chest. Then David lifted his arm, drew the dagger unsteadily across flesh already raw and inflamed. He didn't even flinch, though. Just let the blood start to well forth.

When he bowed his head, Mina felt his concentration as he drew from scant reserves of energy to do what only he might be able to do, as he'd proved the first time he'd healed that small section of her face.

Mina met Jonah's gaze over his shoulder, knowing the commander's thoughts easily, for they were written on his stern face. *You better know what you're doing.*

Since she was going into fairly new territory, she was sure he wouldn't appreciate her answer to that. Anyhow, she had all she could do to control her terror. David was depleting his life force to heal her. That was going to be hard enough on him without her fighting him.

Blood drained down his arm, glittering blue with traces of red and black. As he let it run to his palm, she lifted her cloak over her head and sat bare before him. When he reached out, he found the mangled skin where her breast would have been, the most central point from which the magic could flow.

"Don't be afraid," he murmured, knowing her so well.

She pushed aside the fear, for she had a task of her own, and she wasn't going to be a coward this time. She'd done enough of that in the past several weeks. As his hand settled, wet with fresh blood, she closed her own eyes. Laying her palm over an open wound near his abdomen, she felt how sticky and hot it was, infection. The putrid sense of Dark One malevolence, lingering on the edges of the blood vessels. As terrible as the wounds were, how much more awful had it been for him to lie here, Dark One blood roiling in a body that was designed by its Maker to be repelled by it?

His power drifted into her. A weak flow at first, then he pushed himself, his body starting to shake. She sensed the wounds were oozing faster, perspiration building across his forehead. The evidence of a failing system, a body she loved for its strength and raw power. His heart could explode in his chest, accomplishing the same thing as a Dark One attack. Even knowing that, she forced herself to send the urgent words into his mind.

Keep going, David. Push yourself as hard as you can.

Raphael was likely getting alarmed, for David was sure to be turning the color of white light in truth. She kept her eyes closed, though, concentrating, gauging the fading, the rate at which he was getting weaker and weaker. The timing had to be perfect. She started to chant. It was a complicated healing charm, mixed with some Dark Magic that would likely char the pure walls of the Citadel. As she worked the spell up, she used her blood link to communicate with Jonah.

You must hold him steady. No matter what. Tell Raphael he must keep David's hand on my chest. The flow of energy mustn't be interrupted.

Raphael's wings brushed her as his hand pressed over David's wrist. Jonah shifted as his grip apparently tightened on David.

Most beings would resist dying. She knew she didn't have to worry about that. David's focus on her, his dedication, was absolute. He didn't care about death. He cared about her. When she felt him push past the automatic survival instinct, keeping his mind only on her, his heart pumping so hard she could hear the arteries gasping, she knew it was time.

Throughout his system, she visualized the Dark One blood, like so many tiny demonic creatures, despising their surroundings. But just as the angels instinctively fought Dark Ones, so these elements of Dark One blood were like terriers, unwilling to abandon their fight to destroy the angel blood, claim his body for their own. Unless they thought he was dying.

Pressing her hand harder over that wound, she summoned the Darkness to her. Their queen, who would not be denied. She used her power, half command, half coaxing. *Come to me. Look inside me, where there is a greater welcome for you. Here lies darkness. Your home.*

The blood waffled, undecided, for as much as like attracted like, destruction was its true purpose. Blocking out all else, sending a mental warning to the two angels, Mina changed from persuasion and took away the choice. She reached in with her mind, netted them and ripped them out of the arteries and vital organs, bringing them to her, clawing and screaming. His blood boiled in his veins, his heart rate increasing exponentially. That great organ strained, close to rupture.

As he cried out, it took her back to his screams beneath the teeth and talons of the Dark Ones. Her own body convulsed, so violently that she didn't feel Raphael grip her shoulder to augment his hold on David's wrist. She was in the throes of power, his and hers, what they were doing to each other.

She screamed as she forced the blood into herself, a rape of her circulatory system. The scream was part rage, part pain, part need, but as David had said, she had an indomitable will. She held on to that thought. She would not fail. She couldn't fail.

The remaining Dark One blood was rushing into her now, her threat of annihilation speeding its travels. But she would not relinquish her hold as she sent a command to Jonah.

Charge one of his daggers and drive it into his lower back. Now.

Her imperious command was obeyed, no room for doubt, thank Goddess, for if Jonah had hesitated, she would have lost the connection or the courage. David cried out again and the Dark Ones' blood within her screamed as well. The noise alone was going to overwhelm her.

Releasing their host, the last of them fled the blue fire rushing through his system, taking the portal she offered to escape sure destruction.

As she opened her eyes, she saw the room they were in had gone dark, perhaps a reflection of the sky outside, the ominous rumbling around the crown of the Citadel. Distantly, she sensed a gathering of angels, for Jonah had likely been unable to spare attention to let them know what was happening.

Then, before she had another coherent thought, fire was scalding her. Her face, her body on fire. It was as if the sea creatures were tearing at her flesh again, making her relive the terror of it, unable to move.

But she wasn't there, wasn't in the Abyss. She was here, in the Citadel, and David still needed her. She fought through it.

"Heal him," she rasped, fixing her burning eyes on Raphael, bent anxiously over David's body, slumped in Jonah's arms. "Blood. You. Heal him now, quickly. Or he's dead. Life force, will . . . slip away."

"He is dead."

"No. Not. Life spark there. *Do it*."

Her voice thundered through the structure like the shock wave from an explosive blast. Then she convulsed again, falling with a thud to the floor, an animal snarl coming from her lips.

"*Do it!*" She spat out once more before she began to seize, thrashing across the stone tile as if a Dark One had possessed her. Gods, her skin had to be on fire. Things were breaking down and building at once.

Raphael forced himself to turn away and laid his hands on David, charging his palms with power. Probing deeply, he was amazed to find she was right. A single spark, so tiny he was almost afraid to reach for it, coax it back to life.

Jonah, we will need many of us.

Jonah nodded. Reaching out to the seven levels of the Citadel, he called on the other angels. Marcellus consolidated the energy of his battalion, as did the acting lieutenant of David's platoon. Ezekial, Bazrak, all of the captains. Even the Thrones in Zebul, and Lucifer, down in Hades. The call went out to all, a flood of energy returning that ignited the room with white light, covering them.

Raphael, the witch. She can't—

She is taking care of herself. She is shielded. I will channel this away from her as well. Do not fear for her.

Satisfied, Jonah returned his concentration to the charge in his arms. As he helped steady the healer, Raphael took the white light and worked that energy into David. The wounds began to close, the hair to grow back along his skull, the fingers and other ruined and mangled parts to sculpt back into the body of a powerful and graceful young male angel. Jonah swallowed, moved by the act of re-Creation that, of all the healer angels, only Raphael could do.

David's ruined wings ignited, burning away in a wave of heat and wind. The ash drifted across the bed, mingling with the blood and infection, all of which was abruptly seared away as if it had never been. White light surged through the healing centers of David's body then, jerking him. His head fell back lifelessly on Jonah's shoulders. The commander held him close, steady. Raphael kept his hands on him, his lips firming with determination. As the white light intensified, Jonah, who could look at the sun, had to shut his eyes.

Come on, damn you. You can't go. I won't permit it. And she needs you. Don't give up.

———

MINA caught only glimpses of what was happening on the bed. In the fight for her own life, she could no longer offer anything to David, could only hope she'd done enough.

Her body was working fiercely to accommodate what David had been able to do for it before his energy ran out, as well as handling the new Dark One blood she'd just acquired. They warred for the same space, her Dark One blood leaping on the other and trying to destroy it. She wanted to retch, but she kept it down, helping her Dark One blood sear out of existence what she'd pulled from David.

The pain took her deeper, until she was nothing but the pain, her mind shutting into that simple survival mode she knew well. Just one moment to the next. Or no passage of time at all. It simply was. Fire on every part of her skin, a fierce aching in her bones as intense as a break. It got so excruciating it crossed her mind to just give up, let oblivion take her, but she hadn't earned that. And if there was a chance she'd succeeded and could see David's face once more . . .

Trust me for one moment. Just one more moment.

A long time later, voices came through that red haze. "I don't think we should touch her. Just wait. Watch over her. Watch over them both."

"I'll watch over her." A quiet voice, one that couldn't be Marcellus, for it had too much compassion, but it sounded like him.

"Clean bed," she rasped. "Make sure he has clean bed. Hates being dirty. Don't leave him like that."

Then later, maybe much later? Another voice. The voice she needed to hear to penetrate the fog of her own dull, mindless pain. "Give her to me."

She was lifted, the sense of feathers brushing her, and then she was on a soft bed. Clean. Smelling of clouds and sunshine. David's arms around her. Lying on David's chest. His heartbeat strong and steady.

It seemed the hardest thing she'd ever done, but she managed to tilt her head back the inch or two needed, crack her eyes enough to see his looking down at her. Brown, warm and steady.

A sigh slipped through her lips. She slept.

SUNSHINE. Her shields had held, amazingly, but too much time had passed, for they were thin. Thin enough that the presence of angels all about was enough to give her an oppressive, closed-in feel. But she opened her eyes and found she was in David's arms still, and that made it bearable for the time being. As she rose on one arm, she gazed down at him.

He had some faint scarring on his body, like Marcellus, that would fade in time. But he had all his fingers back, his rich mane of brown hair to his shoulders, though there was an interesting tawny streak now that she brushed with her fingertips. Then she couldn't help touching his mouth, the bridge of his nose. His throat, tracing the breadth of his shoulders. Her throat thickened as she saw one scar that had not altered. The handprint burned into his chest remained.

A polite cough, and she looked over to see Jonah on the window ledge. Watching over them again. David slept on, even though his arms stayed curled low on her hips, reluctant to release her even in sleep.

As she turned to look at him, Jonah straightened, staring at her. Raphael and Marcellus had entered as if he'd summoned them, now that she was awake. They stopped as well, just as they stepped over the threshold.

"Holy Goddess," Marcellus muttered.

She swallowed, trying not to panic, and turned her focus back to David. His wounds were gone, the health returned to his face, his body clean, yes. But he was wingless. Since he was half turned toward her, probably an old habit of not sleeping on his back, she peered over his shoulder to see a broad, unmarked expanse of skin and muscle. She ran her palm over it.

"We're not sure what happened." Raphael cleared his throat. When she glanced back at him, he kept his gaze fixed on David. "He appears to have all other elements of being an angel. Speed, quickness, strength. Immortality."

"You have a theory," she said. "You just don't want to tell me."

"It's possible the wings were too corrupted by the blood, and in the healing, the best thing to do was to just get rid of them."

Mina looked toward Jonah, her expression requesting the full truth. "There is a great deal of magical energy in the wings," the commander said quietly. "It's possible he drew on them at the last for you, drew too hard."

That would be just like him, she knew. She closed her eyes. "Please stop staring at me," she said to the walls. It was time for her to leave. Her shields were expiring. David was healed. He would come to her if he wished. If he didn't, well, he didn't.

"Thinking of taking off on me again, little witch?"

David's voice, quiet but groggy.

Relief swept her, so strong it almost drained her of strength. When she would have toppled into him, he caught her arms and stared at her face. She waited, wishing to be anywhere else as his gaze coursed down, slowly, then back up. He lifted her hand, the one that had three fingers. Now she had almost five. The smallest finger was still missing the top half of the digit.

"I'm sorry," he said with a tired smile. "I ran out about there." At her expression, he sobered and cupped her face, his thumb passing over where her cheek had been pitted but was now as silken as the other.

"Don't worry. I still see the scars," he whispered.

She closed her eyes and he drew her in to him, held her against his heart as her body began to shake. The whole Citadel began to shake in fact, for things were welling up in her, so hard and fast, she couldn't control them. But as he tightened his arms around her, murmured to her, he contained it, held her soul and heart against him such that at last she did feel as if she'd managed to crawl inside him. The first sobs burst out of her, and she was only vaguely aware of the startled angels withdrawing respectfully.

It was everything, all of it, everything she'd had to do and be to get to this point. And somehow he still loved her. She couldn't comprehend it, and it was going to tear her into pieces. But it was okay. He was holding her. He was always holding her.

"I was so frightened," she said into his chest at last. "I was so afraid I wasn't going to be strong enough. I hear your screams when I close my eyes. I can't bear to sleep."

David closed his eyes. That terrible trek from the Dark One tower to the mountain was nothing he was likely to ever forget, either. He laid his head on top of hers. "I'm here now. And it's over. You did it. You did what we needed you to do, what was right. Mina, when it comes to inner strength, I've never met anyone stronger. And I'm sure I never will."

"I was lucky."

"Someone once told me that luck is fickle, and she has no use for it."

"I'm afraid of not having the scars."

"You don't need them. You have me." Touching her mouth, he drew her tear-streaked gaze up to his face. "I told you, angels mate for life. You won't ever have to be lonely again. Only alone when you desire it, though I hope you don't desire it too often. I tend to need you far more than you need me."

She didn't think that was true, but of course she couldn't tell him that. But she did hold him more tightly, laying her head back under his jaw.

David smiled, feeling it, then looked toward Jonah at the doorway. Felt the angels gathered in the Citadel, the strength of their connection to him. The emotion of it, of having them as well as the woman in his arms, filled him. The loss of his wings was painful, the idea that he would no longer be able to fight with the Legion, but that was as it should be, he thought.

They may come back. This from Raphael.

David lifted a shoulder. *It doesn't matter. She bears a great burden. It's my task to help her with it.* He shifted his thoughts toward Jonah. *You've told me before it's not about what we want; it's about our destiny. Well, I got both. Mina is what I want* and *my destiny, for better or worse.*

Jonah inclined his head, his expression saying he understood completely.

––––––––

THE Prime Legion Commander drew Raphael and Marcellus outside the chamber with him. Raphael paused with Jonah as the two males looked back in, to see David had lifted himself into a sitting position so he could hold her in his lap, murmur and rock her as she cried.

"Have you ever . . ."

"It was like looking on the face of the Lady." Jonah wondered at it. "I felt her beauty, the power behind it, slam me all the way down to my toes."

"A mask for Darkness. A dangerous one." Raphael shook his head. "Now I understand what she was saying. I thought it was just gibberish, but everything she said . . . She knows how dangerous she is."

Jonah nodded. "That's why she didn't want him to heal it. But she was willing to risk her soul and our universe to heal him. She's not our enemy, Raphael. I'd bet my soul on it. The key to her is David, and it explains a great deal to me about why the Lady sent us a man who was barely more than a boy to be an angel."

"But is she an ally?"

"When the mood suits her." For the first time in several days, Jonah allowed himself a tight smile and got a soldier's grin from Marcellus. "But have faith, Raphael. After all, we are angels."

Epilogue

THEY went back to the house in the Schism. David didn't have to ask her. He knew that was what she wanted. He politely asked for a lift from the Citadel, which seemed to confuse her until she remembered and shifted to dragon form. He could tell she was worried about his reaction to the loss of his wings, so he made sure to show little concern about it.

Mina, on the other hand, knew how much it bothered him. Felt the guilt of it, but she also understood they were both fragile, both needing time to get used to the changes the past few weeks of monumental events had wrought. She left it at that. For now.

He spent his first few days acclimatizing himself to the house, making sure their surroundings were comfortable, going to the store to get a wide variety of foods that interested her. It required him to drive, something she remembered he'd promised to teach her. It was the first laughter she heard from him, when she insisted he change places with her in the driver's seat on the way back to show her how to handle the vehicle on the dusty and mostly deserted road.

She had many things to occupy her, but her favorite was watching him while she sat on the swing or porch. Seeing him rummage through the workshop in back, finding tools to make simple repairs that were needed, finding other chores she could do and showing her how to help, another way to occupy her energy while she learned to manage her power.

Then there was the music. When he'd picked them up some clothes—and she intensely liked the jeans and snug T-shirts he wore—he'd also picked up a secondhand guitar, drums, and a flute, accumulating a variety of instruments to keep his music magic skills sharp. On the porch swing at sunset, she listened while he sat on the top stair and strummed out the chords to "Beast of Burden," playing the music while humming the song he'd sung her on that magical flight together. Studying his intent profile, the soft strands of hair falling over his forehead, those fingers moving over the strings, she understood the lurch in chest and loins experienced by every girl who'd been a rock band groupie.

While he could still perform tasks as rapidly as an angel, there were times he seemed to like a mortal pace, talking to her while she sat on the porch steps, watching him hammer or paint. Until she couldn't bear watching him anymore and instead came up behind him, sliding seeking hands beneath the T-shirt to the muscled tension of his back. She'd follow that curve, damp with sweat, up to his shoulder blades and then let her hands slide around to the front to his chest even as he turned and tossed his tools aside to give her more direct attention.

Perhaps it was the overflow of magic, or just the lingering horror of the way she'd almost lost him. Or the fact that for the first time in her life she could reach out to another and seek pleasure, intimacy, but she really couldn't get enough of him. Fortunately, an angel's limitless well of carnality was completely unaffected by his injuries. If anything, like hers, it seemed to have increased as a result of them.

He might lift her in his arms, take her no farther than the hammock swinging on the side of the house before he'd slide the panties off her silken legs and put his mouth on her until she was writhing and clutching at him. He seemed to love putting his mouth on her there, and she'd no objections to his expertise. But in the end, what she most wanted was to strip him of the jeans and feel his body settle on hers, his hard cock pushing inside her, filling her, making her whole, balancing their universe.

Sometimes they'd take it even slower than a mortal pace. She'd wake in the middle of the night, find his face with her questing fingertips, and he'd hold her, no space between them as he kissed her, over and over, until she was pressed so tight against him, tears gathering in her eyes as he slowly, so slowly, slid inside her, keeping their bodies intimately twined together, coupled close in the darkness so she felt she could never get lost there, except in a way she wished would go on forever.

Sam the Shaman, as she caustically referred to him, didn't immediately visit, though he sent a greeting in the form of a flock of buzzards, which she found somewhat amusing. She was fine with that delay. For now, she was learning a new terrain in herself, and a good portion of her day was spent working with it, plumbing the depths of what it was inside her, all the new corners she had to explore, particularly with the reassurance of David now around. She'd brought her cave stores here, so she expanded her grimoires and potion lists, noted different spells and their effects, tested them benignly on her outside landscape, creating rainbows, storm clouds, summoning up tornadoes and dust storms and containing them. She made one tornado lift the pickup truck to ensure she could safely spin it through the spiral and bring it back down to the ground again. An experiment that David requested she not perform on the house, which led to an explanation about foundations, plumbing and electrical connections she found fascinating.

Every boundary she pushed just opened up another, or suggested another avenue she could pursue, though she knew there were places she had to be more cautious about exploring than others. Always that balance. Darkness could rise up in waves when she tried something that didn't work as she'd hoped. Like when her power got hopelessly knotted with Schism energies and she nearly caused a fatal rupture that could have swallowed fifty miles of land into a sinkhole. But Sam the Shaman made his first appearance on that day, guiding her, and David was at her back as always.

She experienced firsthand his skill with music magic when David used the wooden flute to help them realign the energies, creating a breathtaking symphony with her and Sam's magic and restoring the balance. She proceeded more cautiously after that, but with more confidence as well.

There were other days when they did things that had nothing to do with angels or great cosmic powers. Those were her favorite days. Like when David took her hiking, buying her the right kind of shoes, commenting on how small her feet were. And when he brushed her hair each night and she fell asleep to the lullabies he offered her. She took the songs with her into the dark landscape of her dreams and found she could travel without fear. Get some real rest.

Some days they walked along the rivers at the bottom of the Grand Canyon, over which the angels and Dark Ones had fought to save Jonah. Often the angels went to the more remote gorges to do their training exercises, and David particularly enjoyed watching them. His platoon was now being led by another, and this, too, didn't seem to bother him.

But it bothered her. And she wasn't stupid.

"WHAT do you want?" she asked.

David cut himself off mid yawn at the sharpness of her tone. She'd left the bed before dawn, apparently to wait for sunrise in one of the porch chairs, something she frequently enjoyed doing. Now, however, she seemed intent on other things.

Giving himself a moment to digest the question, he lifted his mug to his lips and thought how nice it was to enjoy a wake-up cup of coffee. His witch generously worked her magic on any food or liquids he liked tasting. He appreciated it, though it was a minuscule effort for her. Even now, the rocks in the backyard were forming animal shapes and small versions of people that looked like rock children doing comical somersaults.

Some of the things she could do were awe-inspiring, magnificent, more than a bit frightening. Then there was this side, where she could be . . . cute. Since he valued his life, he didn't make that observation, particularly since it appeared she'd awakened in a less than pleasant mood.

The swing was swinging without any visible form of propulsion, and this morning she'd added a mirage of the sea to the normal sunrise view, with dolphins cavorting in the waves. He could hear the soft, rhythmic rush of the surf. Because it was a mirage, it didn't harm any of the actual life in the arid landscape, but he knew she could create oceans. Probably could terraform an entire planet if she wanted.

Jonah, Sam and others were speculating on just what purpose she could have. They wondered if she eventually would be too powerful for this world, her energy expanded to the point she would need a larger area, an expanse of universe that would allow her to spin her magic safely.

That was all well and good, but not until she was ready. Each day she explored more of the bizarre connection within her between light and dark, she became bolder, though the Schism near disaster had set her back a little ways. *Take it slow, seawitch*, David had counseled her. *We don't want to irritate our neighbors by swallowing their homes*. He'd won a small cautious smile from that observation. So far, he'd gotten a total of five smiles out of her, each one a rare and unique experience he kept filed in his memory, a growing treasure chest whose sparkle would never fade as he revisited them there.

He had been telling the truth. While there was an ethereal, overwhelming beauty to her now that simply stole the tongues of anyone who looked at her, he did still see the scars. Hades knew, she'd retained her irascible temper and distrust of pretty much anyone. But it was his hope, as time went on, that he could heal the scars that had remained beneath the surface. Though she didn't fully believe it, he knew the key to her control of the darkness was in her own strength, and the more her scars and fears healed, the stronger she would grow. He was already seeing it.

"David."

"Coffee first," he suggested, then winced as she shot him a searing look that scattered one stack of rocks across the porch and bounced several off his ankle. As he sat down on the top step, considering her, he noted she wore the outfit he'd gotten her in the ghost town, the colors of the desert landscape in the print. Her dark silken hair spilled down her back, held back by a pewter dragon comb he'd bought her. The crimson and blue eye focused on him, both now embellished by those soot dark, thick lashes. Goddess, she was beautiful. And ornery as a snake. He smiled into his coffee as she sent another scattering of pebbles over the bare foot he had propped against the opposite side of the porch steps.

"If you're going to be mean, I'm not going to talk to you at all. Come here." He gave her a steady look over the coffee.

She rose, came and stood to the right of him. And four pebbles tumbled from the roof edge into his coffee. *Plop. Plop. Plop.* The fourth one he caught before it hit, never taking his gaze off of hers.

"Are you angling for a spanking this morning?"

She cocked her head. "What if I—"

He was so relaxed now, so leisurely in his approach to so many things, Mina often forgot his ability to move with an angel's speed. The coffee was tossed aside and he had her seized and facedown on his lap, where he administered several quick, stinging slaps to her bare bottom, for she'd not bothered with underwear this morning.

"Ow. Stop it." But then he set things to pulsing in her as he flipped her back over in his arms and got his hands under her shirt to close over her breasts.

"Spread your legs for me." The demand was there, quick, implacable, and she did for him what she did for no one else. She obeyed.

"Now, put your hand down there. I want to watch you."

"What are you going to be doing?"

"Get me my coffee back, and I'll tell you."

She studied him, her breathing erratic, but she didn't even have to gesture, barely had to think of it, before a second mug came out the door, settled into his outstretched hand. He kept the other around her back. "I'm going to sit here, drink my coffee, watch this beautiful sunrise and you. Just that."

The way he looked at her, as if the heat and intensity of his gaze alone could hold her, was almost enough to push her over. As it was, it was no time before her own fingers, and his insistent, demanding mouth had her rocking and pleading, begging to go over, for of course he never let her go until she begged. And that, too, was part of the balance. The checks and balances.

When he finally agreed, his cock was an iron bar beneath her wriggling bottom. She exploded on him, his mouth fastened on hers, swallowing her cries until she lay panting and replete in his arms.

"That's not going to make me forget the question," she managed at last, wanting to feel him release, but his arm remained tight over her, holding her in place.

"I thought this was my answer."

Reaching up, she touched his face, his mouth, wet from hers. "Please tell me."

"You. This. Everywhere we go, the two of us together." He straightened her so she was straddling him, worked her legs around him and snugged her there with a hand on her bottom. "I served the Goddess as a platoon leader. I serve her still, by serving you. Which means protecting you, loving you," he amended, with a glint in his eye. "No way I'm giving you the impression that I'm serving you, witch. I know how demanding you are."

"Stop it. You want nothing for yourself? There's nothing I can give you, in return for all you've given me?"

David stopped then, shock flitting across his expression at the pure frustration he heard in her voice. He lifted her hair in both hands, diving deep into the thick lengths of it. "Put me inside of you," he murmured, "and I'll tell you something."

She was always eager to feel his heated length in her hands, so she didn't mind opening his jeans and having the momentary discomfort of taking him into her channel where the tissues were still ultrasensitive from her climax. "*Ah* . . ." Her breath escaped her as she sank down on him. His fingers gripped her hips, his eyes dark on her face.

"In case you haven't noticed," he said in a husky tone, "taking care of you, watching over you, that's the job I chose, Mina. Being your protector and lover forever. If there comes a day when you're not so much work," he teased her, though there was a catch in his voice as he wrapped her hair around his fist, "I might do some world traveling. Go to Disneyland. Learn macramé. But right now, my slate is full."

He was moving her now, slow, slower, and she could tell how insane it was making him by the clogging of air in his throat. "But what about your wings?" She put her arms around his shoulders, cheek against his temple, and held on as he gathered her in closer. She wished she'd taken more time to enjoy the soft feel of his feathers, the strangely erotic resilience of the arch of wing, curve of bone. Gods, she missed them, too. It wasn't aesthetic. It was a part of him.

Being an angel just is.

"Raphael says they may come back one day, as I mature. But right now, it doesn't matter. This makes more sense, because I can go into places humans frequent without excessive notice."

"You obviously haven't noticed how women react to you in restaurants and stores."

"I said *excessive*." His smile was lost as his breath got more labored, and his hands tightened on her hips. "Jesus, it's never enough. You feel so fucking good. I want you to come with me again."

"I can put an illusion spell on you so you can go wherever you want, with or without wings. I've gotten really good at them so you—"

"Hush," he said. And he lifted her away from him and put his mouth on her breasts, suckling the nipples. He took his time, running his tongue up the cleft between, squeezing them together until the combination of stimulus had her writhing on him and unbelievably going up the edge of a climax again.

"Just you, Mina. I'm here for you. I love you. Believe it, and stop doubting. What is it that *you* want?"

"Oh, Goddess, please . . ."

"Come for me."

He released at the same moment, sending her over, their bodies moving together in sinuous rhythm. She put her mouth on his flesh, then her teeth into his shoulder, holding her grip there, drawing blood, until they slowly came to a stop.

"That's the real question, isn't it, Mina?" He spoke when he had breath again, but continued to hold her close, her head pressed down on his shoulder. He brushed his lips over her hair. "What is it you want?"

"I was thinking about Anna." She traced the area in between the shoulder blades where his wings used to be. "Her baby. Is it a symbol of hope or of sacrifice? I mean, she wanted to have the baby. So, if she does die because of the curse, Jonah will have a daughter to love, for however long he's given. But I think she's also having the baby in order to say to that curse, 'You have no hold on me. On what I want to do or be.'"

Raising her head, she looked at him. "You do take care of me, David. You always will, because you told me so. But you're also a soldier. You fight the Dark Ones in a different way."

She put her hand on his heart. "Give this back to yourself. You can be more than one thing. I'm not afraid of losing you that way, not anymore."

David stared at her, felt the energy gathering under her fingertips. His energy. She was summoning energy *from* him, calling it forth, twining it with her own. "Mina, how did you—"

But in the next moment it was gone, the words ripped away as he caught hold of her body with both hands to keep from toppling her. The wings surged forth from his back, the architecture of vertebrae and skeleton altering in a smooth transition that nevertheless rocked him forward as they stretched, spread out to dry their afterbirth in the sun. He looked at one, blanched, then looked at the other.

Until he was fifty, the wings would have been the wings of a fledgling, white with tips of brown. But apparently, his timetable had been accelerated, for he was looking at a solid black wing on his left, a solid white on his right, a wholly unique pattern he'd never seen before.

Mina reached over his shoulders, stroked through them with both hands with childlike delight. Coming away with one small feather of each color, she pinned them into the comb pulling her waist-length hair from her face. "I think they're holding afternoon drills if you want to go join them."

At his look of indecision, she cradled his face in her hands this time. "I'm right here. I'm yours. You can be at my side in moments. What I need is help to protect the world from me, and you help me do that, David. By loving me. But you need to keep being the warrior you are. We can't keep growing together if we aren't growing separately. The nature of all things is to change," she reminded him. "And so we will change. Always growing stronger."

"Okay," he said at last. "Okay." He kissed her fingertips, one by one, then pressed his forehead to her hands, the significance of what she'd just done sweeping over him. "Thank you."

"I knew you missed them. I missed them, too. I'd been working on it, and I'm glad it worked." She shot him an arch look. "Would have been terrible if I'd gotten mixed up and you ended up with bat wings. Marcellus would have been so jealous."

He snorted as she slid down next to him on the porch step. After he watched her rearrange her clothes, making her feel warm under his regard, he retrieved his coffee once more. He restored his own clothes as well, though Mina thought she might have liked it if he'd kept that top button carelessly undone, as he did sometimes when he first pulled the jeans on.

"I'll think about the drills," he said. "Don't nag. Let me just sit with you here for a while."

She accepted that, though plucked a feather for the nagging comment and earned a tug on her hair in return. They sat together for the next few minutes, looking out at the desert, one of his wings pulled around her so she could enjoy stroking her fingers through the feathers again. "I've been thinking about Dante," she said at last.

"Really."

She gave him a curious look. "What?"

"I didn't much care for how he looked at you."

"You were jealous?"

"You're a powerful, beautiful Dark Spawn. He's Dark Spawn. I suspect he would find you very intriguing, if you're the only other one he's met that's reached maturity."

She tilted her head. "I don't think you have to worry so much. He's a little psychotic for me."

"Oh, sure, that's what girls always say. Then they go for the bad boy. Look at me, I'm an angel. Harps and haloes, purity and goodness. What chance do I have?"

"Good point," she agreed. "You did have the Dark One blood in you, though. If you remember how, you could cultivate a sexy kind of broodiness. Jonah broods on occasion. Anna says she finds it very stimulating."

"On that note," he observed, amusing her by ignoring that topic, "your shielding has improved. And you said the Schism buffers you as well. We could test it out by spending time with Anna and Jonah, if you'd like to see Anna more. Maybe start by having them to dinner one night. We've been working on our cooking. She'd probably like to try some of the things you've made."

Have Anna and the Prime Legion Commander for dinner? "You are a frightening man," she responded, when she could make her tongue work. But as disconcerting as the domestic picture was, what was more disturbing was it had some appeal. Despite the glint in his eye which suggested he'd also brought it up to shock her. However, she also knew it was likely his continued attempt to prove that the more they strengthened the positive reasons she had to fight the Darkness, the easier the balance might become.

Easy had never been a word she'd applied to any part of her life. But only a couple of days ago, she'd dropped ice cubes down

David's shirt and he'd chased her around the yard and the swing. As she ran, she'd felt the absolute glory of it. Running without pain in her muscles or joints, such that she'd forgotten the teasing and just run. He'd picked up on her needs as always, so that he'd abandoned the game and simply matched her pace and let her run until she ran herself into exhaustion.

Mina.

Surprised to hear the object of their discussion in her head, Mina's head jerked up. At the same moment, apparently getting the same alert from Jonah, David surged to his feet. A second or two later, Jonah landed in the yard in a skidding dust cloud, carrying his pregnant wife in his arms. "She's gone into labor," Jonah said unnecessarily. "And she said she had to have the babe here, with Mina."

DESPITE the alarm that announcement caused, Mina managed to mask it. "Raphael's on his way," Jonah added, giving her a surge of relief.

As her attention shifted to Anna, Mina thought that, while David's healing had given her what could be considered beauty beyond what any woman would long to possess, Anna's beauty was simple goodness, and being pregnant had made her more radiant.

Those violet eyes could soften the heart of a demon. But her soft, loving nature was persistent and courageous, such that it was impossible to get her to back down from her intentions, whether it was to save a Prime Legion Commander from an army of Dark Ones, or refusing to consider a seawitch with the ability to destroy the world anything less than her best friend. Or deciding at the spur of the moment that she wanted her as a midwife.

Right now, she was in mermaid form, for of course during her pregnancy she could not shift. Purple and blue tattooing swirled in intricate patterns along her biceps. The gleaming purple and deep blue scales of her tail shimmered down to tinier pieces until reaching the delicate pink, pearlescent edges of her featherlike tail fin. She was still wet from the ocean, her golden brown hair dark and slicked back on her skull, and she smelled of the salt air.

While mermaid was only one of four forms Anna could take, Mina knew it was still the best choice, for a mermaid pregnancy and birth were much shorter and easier than a human experienced.

Now Anna's eyes fastened on her as she reached out, grabbing Mina's hand. "I'm so sorry. I should have told you," she blurted out. "But I was afraid you'd say no. Ah, heavens, here comes another." The rush of words expired on a gasp as her belly contracted before their gazes.

"Come inside," David said, looking a little pale.

Anna's hands had clutched Mina's fingers and Jonah's muscular shoulder, her face tightening, eyes turning inward to concentrate on what was happening inside of her body.

"We'll take her in the cellar, to the spring," Mina said, and instead of taking her hand away, she let it be held, moved inside as the commander carried his mate and David followed, guiding Mina's body so she wouldn't trip on the stairs.

The enchanted spring David had mentioned when he and Mina first came here had seen frequent use these past weeks. Mina loved the hot water, enjoyed swimming in it with him, the twining of their bare bodies together, her ability to shift to mermaid form if she wished, but not have the problems with the cold-water environment in which she'd used to live.

It was also the perfect environment for a mermaid mother's birth. But when Anna had to release her so they could move single file down the stairs to the cellar, she could see the worry in Jonah's face.

Mina knew as well as Anna that, as bad as the curse's trait of taking a daughter of Arianne's life at twenty-one seemed, the worst part of the curse was when the new daughter was born. Every generation was born with diabolically self-destructive magical abilities that cut the infant off from normal contact. In a way, it made dying at twenty-one a kindness, though Mina was sure only someone with Dark One blood might see it that way.

Fortunately, Mina's decision as a nine-year-old had saved Anna that one burden.

The mother would be worried for her child, while Mina knew Jonah's worry was for both. If Anna made it a few more months, to the age of twenty-two, they would know the events of the Canyon Battle had broken the curse, but the key to the death of the daughter of Arianne had always been that it came shortly after she had the next daughter.

Mina thought of a world without Anna in it and could understand the shadows around Jonah's eyes, the tautness of his mouth as he waded into the spring with her, held her an extra moment before he lowered her to the rock shelf. Anna's fingers lingered on the bracelet Jonah wore, the one made of her hair. Jonah's reminder of why he fought, of why he'd chosen life over death, good over evil. For her.

"Do you know how to do this?" David murmured in her ear, his body a reassuring brush against her back. He hadn't put his T-shirt back on, of course, and she was grateful for the distracting heat of his muscled flesh.

"My mother taught me, but no one ever came to me for it. Don't worry. Raphael's on his way. And I have extraordinary powers, right? What's the birth of one little baby?"

That angel better be here any minute, she added mentally.

"Mina?"

When Mina moved into the water toward Anna, she changed to her mermaid form to give her more stability against the current. The expectant mother had her hand outstretched again, and Mina found herself taking it once more.

"When I was born," Anna said steadily, holding her gaze, "it was you who saved me. I know this was horrible of me, because it could bring back such terrible memories for you. But then again, I thought it could be a new beginning. Or bring a close to it. Did I offend you?"

"No."

Anna nodded, relief easing her features. "Can you check anything now?"

Mina had to wait a moment for Jonah to shift to the other side of Anna. The commander wasn't letting go of her for long; that was certain. Mina laid her hand on Anna's distended stomach, noting the purple and blue scales closer to her distended belly were starting to turn a glistening pink, like those at her tail fin.

She closed her eyes. Probing, listening. A faint smile crossed her lips. When she opened her eyes, it was to Anna's amazed expression. "I've never seen you smile. Mina, you're beautiful."

"Yes, I am. I didn't have any choice."

David coughed over a chuckle and Anna's eyes sparkled. "Is it so bad?"

"No, but that's because David treats me the same. I like that. I need that." Mina glanced down significantly. "Except he can't really hide the fact that he's happier about . . ."

"Breasts." Anna rolled her eyes. "Males are so predictable."

David snorted. "I noticed she didn't tell Raphael not to expend the energy to restore certain of *my* parts."

"Well, I had to have some use for you."

The commander managed a half smile, but Mina saw that the worry in his expression didn't abate, though he managed a reassuring look when his mate's attention turned briefly to him. Then another contraction arrived. Anna gripped one of Mina's hands again, breathing through it.

"Heavens, this hurts a little bit," she managed to pant.

"You're going to be fine," Mina said. And she made herself change the arrangement of their hands so hers were around Anna's now. "I'm here. Jonah and David are here. We're all going to take care of you. And your baby."

"Okay," Anna said. As she kept her gaze on the seawitch, Mina didn't need any special powers to read what was there. Anna was a little scared, but she wasn't going to show it, not for the world. She wouldn't add any worry to her mate right now. "What did you feel, when you touched me and smiled?"

"I saw your baby," Mina said. "And she felt me, responded to my touch, so she has some ability already."

"What about the curse?"

"I don't feel anything." But before Anna's smile could blind them all, Mina added shortly, "I won't know for certain until she's outside the womb. But don't worry about that now. You just concentrate on getting her out."

Raphael arrived then, and when Mina would have moved back, Anna wanted her close, demanded it, so Mina moved to her head, where it lay against the curve of Jonah's muscular arm, the water lapping just under her breasts.

As Raphael examined her, Anna kept her attention on Mina's face, only about two feet between them. Reaching up abruptly, she touched Mina's earlobe. "You're wearing that dolphin earring I gave you."

"I've always worn it." It wasn't so hard to admit it now, the tiny bauble she'd kept hidden on her unscarred side, disguised beneath her hair. She reasoned it was a good test of her shields when Anna's smile nearly blinded her. Her soft sheen of tears would have sent an army galloping happily to their deaths if it would restore her happiness.

"We've beaten the odds, again and again, both of us," Anna said. "We'll do it again. I know I'm being a bit of a coward," she added, her voice lowering as if no one else were there. "But all I could think was you had to be here. And not just for that. You're my friend, Mina. My true friend."

Mina briefly met Jonah's gaze and then shifted back to Anna. "You know I don't know how to be a friend."

"You don't have to. You are." Anna's violet eyes held hers, steady. "You think that I don't know? You think I didn't pump David for information?"

When she reached up, Mina found her hand taken again. This time she found herself squeezing back, hard, and it wasn't because of the labor pain. It was a shared something Mina couldn't define, the thing that had always lain between the two of them. Not between the daughter of Arianne and the seawitch, but between Mina and Anna. Something she realized she valued.

A light smile played on Anna's lips now. "It's actually really easy to get David to talk. He's so in love with you. And you know, maybe we're not so different, the dark and light thing. I do think about murdering Jonah about once a week."

"You do not," Jonah objected.

"I do, too. You're overbearing and stubborn most of the time, but I love you anyway. And now you'll have someone else to be overprotective about."

"He'll have a whole battalion assigned to her all the time," David observed while Raphael hid a smile.

"Keep it up, and I'll make you the head of that detail." But then Jonah's gaze softened on his wife as she worked through another contraction. "All right?"

She nodded and lifted her chin, which he responded to by leaning forward and taking her lips in a long kiss, while she put her hand up to stroke through his hair. "It's going to be okay," she murmured against his lips, then broke the kiss to smile at a discomfited Mina.

"You can't make a joke out of the Dark Ones."

Anna sobered. "How can we do anything else, with the way our lives have been? I'm about to have a baby." A fierceness came into the expectant mother's face. "She is going to be happy and safe, because I just won't tolerate any other possibility. And you, you and David have each other now, you see? Someone loves you and is watching out for you."

"Putting up with her," David added. Mina shifted a narrow gaze to him.

"He's an idiot," she retorted.

"An idiot over you," Anna laughed.

"Shut up and have this kid already. I have things to do." Mina aimed her attention at Jonah. "You may not have noticed, but he has his wings back. So he's coming back to you. To the Legion."

Jonah blinked. Did a double take. "I'm thinking about it," David amended. "I've not decided on it yet."

"Your place will be there," Jonah said at last, giving an assessing, thoughtful glance to the bicolored wings.

"It's hard sometimes, worrying about them fighting. But it's what they do, isn't it?" Mina could tell Anna was trying not to look at Raphael's sober expression and worry. "And I suspect before long, you'll be helping them fight in some way. There are big plans in the universe for you, I think. Oh, here comes another."

Raphael took over the conversation then, thankfully, and Mina moved to Anna's opposite side as Jonah took a place on an underwater rock ledge, holding Anna in the cradle of his embrace to help her push, breathe and follow the healer's instruction.

As the birthing process happened, Mina let her gaze pass over them. Jonah, so absorbed in his wife, sharing every pain with her, every smile. Raphael, calm and capable but in his element, knowing just what to do, thank the Goddess for him.

And David. Just behind her in the water, his hand on the small of her back, a reassuring touch. It *was* an amazing moment, for her mind could not help but go back to the birth of Anna so long ago, the terrible chain of events it unleashed, but which somehow had led to this, a very different moment.

"Don't let your head get all big about that comment," David murmured, his hand on her hip. "I'm not a complete idiot about you. You can be a terrible pain in the ass. And I have thought about murdering you in your sleep."

She turned her face to his throat. "Anna defines that as love, I think."

"Loving Jonah, for sure," he said. He pressed a kiss to her temple, but then they shared a collective gasp as the merchild slid into the water in a burst of loosened scales that spun away like coins sparkling in the water.

Raphael caught her deftly, holding her beneath the water's surface. Mina knew a merinfant took additional moments to orient its gills and lungs, so they couldn't breathe above water for the first few moments. The healing angel made use of the time to clean off the afterbirth, clean out the nostrils and mouth. Since Jonah was still holding his wife, Raphael looked to Mina. "I think she wanted you to hold her first."

Mina nodded. Conscious of the anxious gaze of a mother and

the tension of a father, she slid her hands beneath the small body, still attached to her mother by the umbilical cord. Something soft and downy pressed into her palms, and she realized she was feeling tiny fledgling wings. *Gods. A merangel.* As she looked down, the baby's blue eyes opened, stared at her.

She couldn't help it. Not knowing the how or why, tears began spilling down her cheeks. David was holding her shoulders, steadying her, giving her the love that was so easy to him, so precious to her.

"All right, then. Let's take her up." Raphael, rather than taking her away, put his hands beneath Mina's and together they brought the baby up. Blinking through her tears, Mina focused, focused hard. She didn't find the trace of dark shadowing that had been the sigil of the self-destructive magic within every daughter of Arianne. It just . . . wasn't there. She shifted her glance to Anna's white face, shook her head.

"She'll be a shifter, like you, but whatever magical ability she'll have will be pure. And learned." She swallowed, wondering why her voice was trembling, why she was willing to offer hope, which she'd never believed in before. "It's a very good sign the curse is broken."

"Oh. Oh, thank the Goddess." Anna's face began streaming as Jonah's arms closed over her, his face pressed into her neck as she slid her fingers into his hair and tightened fiercely, the two of them taking the hope she offered and making it part of the love they already shared.

While they did that, Raphael guided Mina to lay the child on Anna's breast. Even the Prime Legion Commander looked somewhat choked up as they released each other to greet their daughter for the first time. He touched her tiny hand with one enormous finger.

Anna looked at Mina again. "If the curse is truly broken, then it would be broken for you as well. You no longer are bound to protect me."

Mina shrugged. "And a great deal of trouble you've been. I gladly turn you over to Jonah."

But when Anna smiled, lowering her attention to her daughter, Mina looked at the two of them, and knew Anna was wrong. "You looked after me, with no curse to compel you to do it," she said slowly. "You made sure Jonah sent David to me. You visited me, wouldn't let me be, even knowing all the time what I was." When Anna raised her gaze, Mina locked onto it with her own. "You assume that curse has ever been able to tell me what to do. I'll protect you if I want to, and you can't stop me."

The mermaid princess smiled again, the type of smile that made Mina look away, but not before she saw a look on Jonah's face that she was sure she misinterpreted, since it gave her the alarming sense he might reach over and embrace her in a flood of new father sentiment. She dropped back behind David, quickly, saving them both.

Thankfully, he shifted that look toward her angel. "Lieutenant, will you cut the cord?"

David started, then nodded. "I would be honored, my lord."

Out of habit, he always wore at least one of his daggers. When he drew it, Mina shifted so they were side by side. Anna lifted the baby and extended her again. "Hold her while he does it, Mina."

As Mina took the small body, and David bent over her, Anna spoke again. "We want you to be her godparents."

As one, David and Mina looked up.

"Jonah," David spoke, his voice thick with emotion. And Mina, wondering at more tears coming from her eyes, thought that between her and Anna, they'd be affecting the water level in the spring soon.

"And promise me, if something happens—" Anna continued.

"It won't." This came, adamantly, from three voices. Jonah, David and Mina at once, making Anna blink away renewed moisture, but she lifted her chin resolutely. "I want to believe it won't. But if it does, promise you'll step in, be her mother, Mina. I know you think you can't, but you can. You and David can, together. I know it. Promise."

Mina looked back down at the tiny infant with huge blue

eyes. Her mermaid tail had the coloring of Anna's. But she had a dark mop of hair already, her father's. As well as the little wings. Mermaid and angel.

There was nothing more pure than a child, so she remembered to up the strength of her shields as something filled her heart to bursting. Was this love? Perhaps it was. Stripping yourself bare, willing to take the chance that you would hurt someone by trying to take care of them, because the alternative, indifference, was worse.

Still holding that tiny, squirming creature, she watched David capably sever the cord between mother and child under Raphael's guidance. Those beautiful hands, that serious expression, the core tranquility in those warm brown eyes. As she looked into his face, she found she might have the courage to believe it was true and real. And say to him what she never had.

"I love you, too."

He raised his head, staring at her face with such raw emotion, she couldn't handle it. She looked back down at the baby, and when she did, the baby scrunched up her face and made her first attempt at a Jonah-intimidation stare. It was so like him, she couldn't help it. She laughed.

David couldn't breathe. So overwhelmed by the gift of her words, her joyous laugh made this moment everything he could ever want.

And because his seawitch was a young Goddess, as she laughed, the water in which they were resting started to sparkle, the blue of a Caribbean sea spreading across it. White water lilies appeared, scattering all around them, delighting the infant and her new parents.

"Yes," Mina said, encompassing them all in her mysterious, bicolored gaze. "We'd be honored to be her godparents."